sworn to the vampire prince

ainsley james

Book Two of The Vampire Prince Duology
A SANGUINEVERSE NOVEL

To the women who grew up too fast,
who learned to read moods to keep themselves safe,
and who bear scars no one else sees...

You are truly magickal.

Because you choose, again and again, to break cycles

CONTENT WARNING

Content warning: This novel contains dark themes, sexually explicit content, blood, violence, grief, death, body horror, forced transformation, possessiveness, and depictions of magical coercion. Language is occasionally strong. All intimacy between the central couple is consensual and enthusiastic.

Trigger warning: This story includes parental abuse (including maternal abuse), emotional and physical abuse, kidnapping, religious extremism and spiritual manipulation, public humiliation, loss of bodily autonomy, pregnancy themes, and self-sacrificial violence.

Reader discretion advised.

CHAPTER I
PROLOGUE

They call themselves the *Witches of the Darkness*. Well, I have a bone to pick with the title. It takes more than a wee drip of demonic energy to make you dark. You need an appetite for it. A hunger in the pit of your stomach. And, most importantly, the permission to eat.

At the heart of dark magick is the audacity to believe you're worthy of wanting. Not because you're evil. But because life is meant to be lived.

Most of these so-called "Witches of the Darkness" are playing with magick they don't fully understand. Treating demonic relics like scraps of power to nibble on. They have—oops. *You almost got me.* I nearly spoiled the surprise. Time to shut my trap.

Don't look sad, sweetheart. I know you like to be teased. You're not the kind of girl who wants it laid out all nice and neat. You want the ache of not knowing, followed by the sweet release of getting exactly what you want. (I'm the same way.)

Oh? Now you're trying to flirt the answer out of me? You

minx. You can bat your eyes and push your tits together all you like, I'm not going to say another word. You'll see soon enough.

Now, I'll let you rejoin the story. It picks up right where the last one left off. Bastien and Claire, alone together, at Château Rose.

Just remember what I said. Darkness isn't something you draw into yourself. It's something you have the audacity to become. And not everyone can stomach that much wanting.

CHAPTER 2
S'ÉVEILLER
CLAIRE

Ever since the graveyard, my body hadn't truly belonged to me. It felt occupied, as if something had taken up residence beneath my skin. My temper lived at the tip of my tongue. My body rode on the edge of desire. Yes, I had called flames from the dirt, but now it felt like the flames called to me. Demanding more.

The feeling stirred whenever I breathed too deeply or whenever I touched my demonic relic. It was imbued with demonic power and was the only way a Dark Witch could replenish her magick. Since receiving mine—a curved sheep's horn—I've wanted to keep it close by.

But now, alone in my bedchamber with my husband, I was craving more than power.

Bastien's feather-light touch slid beneath my silk robe, pulling it down my shoulder and exposing bare skin.

"Just look at you," he whispered. My head tipped back on a moan as his cool fingers traced the curve of a particularly nasty bruise. One Hera's vengeance had left behind. But instead of flinching with pain, I reveled in it. Between the power of the sheep's horn, which I was holding against my chest, and Bastien's touch, I felt alive.

He drew in a breath. "I will never forgive myself for what happened in the graveyard. Never. What she did to you..." His voice trailed off, and the weight of his remorse hung heavy between us. He cradled my face between his hands. A look of adoration and vengeance was swimming in the cool blue of his eyes. "I'll spend my life making it up to you. Protecting you with my body. My will. My army. All of me."

My white she-wolf, lying dutifully beside a large brown male, huffed in what sounded like annoyance. Both were familiars—creatures bound to a Dark Witch. After gaining my new magick, an entire pack had come to me, but only these two had survived.

Despite caring deeply for these creatures, I was preoccupied, caught somewhere between my husband's guilt and my own. He meant every word, every promise to keep me safe, no matter the cost. He would burn the world for me. But he didn't know everything. He *couldn't*. Not while I was still bound to Mama's curse on my lace choker. The one that demanded I learn every one of Bastien's secrets, including the location of as many demonic relics as possible. And because of that, I knew what I had to do. I had to become strong enough to break it, as only a true Prideaux witch could.

Bastien tilted my head to the side, opening my throat to him. Goosebumps rose over my skin as he studied me. His pupils stretched wide and dark, and he sank white teeth into his full lower lip. He was a predator, and I was his prey. His sanguine partner. But I was more than that. I was his mate. His wife. The only one who could satiate his every desire.

Haltingly, he lowered his mouth to my collarbone. One cold kiss came, followed by another. I shivered with delight, my breath hitching with every touch. In his careful way,

Bastien dragged his tongue over my collarbone, licking his way up, up, *up,* until his lips were on my neck. The thrill of anticipation narrowed my focus to one thing. *Him.* Always him. Only him.

"Never." *Kiss.* "Forgive." *Kiss.* "Myself." He repeated the words again and again until the edge of his teeth grazed my skin, drawing the smallest pinprick of pain. He'd taken a taste of me. A tease more than anything.

Sweat blossomed across my brow, and a slight twinge twisted in my stomach, but nothing more. While the mere mention of blood used to make me swoon, I was becoming more accustomed to it the longer I was with him. Likely because when he fed, it brought me unimaginable pleasure.

I wondered if he would do it now. Bite. Take. *Feed.* I knew he wanted to. I wanted it too. All of it. This endless, unsatisfied ache demanded it.

But still, he held back. Pulling away when I wanted him closer. And when he did, his guilt and shame passed through our connection—a bond that allowed us to share private words with each other as well as feelings—and broke through the wall he'd been trying to create. It sat as a sickening weight in my stomach. I'd seen Bastien in every light, and loved him, but this—this *guilt*—infuriated me.

"Bastien, look at me. Look at me!" I demanded.

He groaned my name, but kept his eyes averted. I said his name again, louder this time, until he glanced at me through thick lashes. "I don't blame you for what Hera and the other witches did. You had no way of knowing they would turn against you." I slid my free hand behind his neck and pulled his face to mine. But when I kissed him, he did not kiss me back. The temper that lived on the tip of my tongue flared. This insufferable man. "None of this is your fault," I reminded him sharply.

His reply was quick. "I disagree."

I held his gaze, neither of us giving an inch. He was determined to live in the past, to build monuments to his perceived failure, in the hopes of what? Never forgiving himself? I would not allow it. Not if it meant he wouldn't even kiss me.

However, I knew my husband to be a stubborn man. "Fine," I said. "Take the blame. You can have it." I brushed my nose playfully against his and let a smile spread. "But that means you owe me."

His look only darkened, *deepened.* And I was glad to see his hunger for me return. He cupped my breast, gently swirling the pad of his thumb over my nipple in a seductive rhythm that had my back arching. He continued in maddeningly slow circles, and the roughness of his skin over that sensitive little spot had me gasping. I rubbed the demonic relic over my other breast, enjoying the heady pleasure that came from his calloused touch and the smooth horn.

Lowering his mouth to the soft spot just below my ear, he whispered, "It seems I'm at your mercy." Another kiss. Another breath. "What penance will suffice, my lady? Ask anything of me, and it's yours."

The anticipation of what came next sent tingles across my skin that settled between my thighs. My need for him was like some great beast, restrained by knots that I wanted him to untie. Retie. And untie all over again.

My throat dry, my knees weak, I spoke two words. "Kiss me."

Holding my face, Bastien took my lips with his, kissing me so deeply that I nearly forgot how to breathe. Wanting only the feeling of his mouth against mine. Of his fingers stretching into my hair, holding me close. To be consumed by him. To drown in him until I was reborn as the woman I wanted to be.

His mouth wandered down my neck, and I turned,

catching our reflection in the vanity mirror. Bastien's pale blond hair had all but disappeared behind my curtain of copper red waves. A reminder of my new identity. If the want, the heat, and the pull of the relic weren't enough.

Bastien slid my other sleeve down my shoulder, revealing more skin. I smiled into the mirror, and my attention drifted to the demonic horn still clutched against my chest—the only thing separating me from him—as if to say it belonged here with us. Or perhaps that *I* belonged to it.

In one easy motion, my husband scooped me into his arms, holding me against his sturdy frame as he made for the bed. I buried my face into his shoulder, drawing in the heady scent of bergamot and pine that always seemed to cling to him. He carefully laid me down on black silk sheets with delicate gold embroidery. One of the small luxuries he indulged in.

Standing over me like a statue come to life, he drank in the curves of my body. Chest heaving. Hands clenched. I drew a line from his thigh to his stomach with my toes, trying to coax him into spreading my legs. He caught my ankle in his grip and slowly, carefully, lifted it to his mouth, placing a delicate kiss there. I waited for him to continue, anticipating what else he could do with those lips. Those teeth.

But still, he hesitated.

"You're hardly done with your penance," I said coyly.

His pale blue eyes left mine and settled on the horn, like it was a stranger in our bed. A flush of embarrassment tinted my cheeks. I hadn't realized I was still holding it. But... I didn't want to let it go. Not even now. I was protective of it. Having it in my hand made me feel powerful. It made me feel... *desirable.*

His attention returned to me, and he let out another low, throaty growl that did nothing to stop the demanding need under my skin. "I will spend my life in a state of penance. You have no idea what lengths I'll go to..."

His sentence fell apart when I undid the knot of my sash and parted the silk folds, revealing my body to him. He traced every line with his eyes, his gaze as tangible as his touch. I closed mine and relished the feeling. This was what I needed. Him and his undying pledge to love me no matter what I was or wasn't. But instead of gripping me under my knees and setting them on his shoulders, he lowered himself onto the mattress beside me and eased one of my legs over his hip. "My insatiable, beautiful wife. You need rest."

My blood ran cold. This was *not* the reaction I wanted. A wave of restless energy coursed up my arm and through my core, almost like I was pulling it from the horn. Magick tickled along my skin, dancing between my breasts. Suddenly, I was sweating along my hairline and overwhelmed with my need for him.

With the horn still in my hand, I shoved Bastien's shoulder against the mattress, pinning him there, and rolled on top of him. One spark, and I was ablaze with power. He stared up at me as if he was seeing me for the first time. As if the fire raging inside me had burned away all traces of the old Claire and replaced her with this new version.

"I want you. All of you. Just as you pledged. And no bruise or scratch or moment of guilt is going to stand between us."

"That cut on your head is *not* a scratch. It's barely stopped bleeding."

A flash of anger tore through me. I was fine. I'd show him. With my free hand, I reached between us and undid the laces on his trousers and pulled him free. The thick, hard piece of him that I wanted.

"Claire," he groaned.

"You said you were at my mercy. You said I could choose your penance." I paused, my emotions finally catching up with my want. "Bastien," I said, a heavy knot forming in my throat, "don't you desire me?" The question sliced against my insecurities, and I knew he could feel the intensity of it. My need for him and my need to be wanted mixing together.

With the speed and strength of a vampire prince, he grabbed my wrist and held me still. Then slowly, he rose into a seated position with me on his lap, putting us face-to-face, breath-to-breath. "Did my wife, *my mate*, just ask if I *desire* her?"

The anger burning inside me made me want to fight back. Wanted to throw a barb at him. Before he'd claimed me as his wife, he had spent many nights avoiding me. Even now, after he'd announced to his small council that I was the new Duchess of Roselyn, he'd sent me back to our room while he had private words with Tyson. Words he had not shared with me. But those angry sentiments fled like a terrified enemy in the face of his look. His darkened eyes. His clenched jaw. His uneven breath.

He wrapped my hand around his hard length, then covered it with his, holding me tight around him. Almost painfully tight. "This is what you do to me," he choked out as he began working our hands up and down. *Up and down.* Using the same rhythm he used the night I found him alone in that feeding tent. When he'd called out to me through our bond without meaning to. "I do not just desire you, Claire. You are an ache that *never* dulls."

I sucked in a breath that drew us closer, and wrapped my arm around his neck to hold myself upright, pressing our cheeks together.

He continued. Lips pressed against my ear. "One glance, one word, one breath of your delicious scent, and I'm ready to give you everything. To do *anything*." *Up, down. Up, down.* A bead of warmth dripped between my fingers, making them slick. "And that's how it will be until I draw my last breath. Do you understand?"

I tipped my head back, drawing in power from the horn. Sweat rolled between my breasts and down the sides of my face. And yet, it wasn't enough. Not hardly enough.

He let go of my hand and pressed a punishing kiss to my lips. One that did not leave me questioning how he felt. I scooted closer, closing the distance between us, wanting more.

"But you need rest," he said against my mouth. "I wasn't gentle when I claimed you. I didn't treat you like I should have. And neither did those witches." He pressed a kiss to the cut across my brow. When he pulled back, he licked dark red blood from his lips as if to prove a point. With a tiny, irritating smile, he added, "There is no rush. We can wait."

The power and heat that had been streaming from the horn dulled, and the absence of magick left me shivering. Panic tore through me while anxiety clawed at my throat, almost as tightly as the barbs of Mama's choker. The magick—I needed it back.

"You don't get to decide when I've had enough."

"That's true," he replied. "But I get to decide when *I've* had enough."

I let out a scoff. "I thought you said your want for me was endless."

"It is. Which is why I have to be the one to draw a line. Otherwise, the only thing we'd ever do is fuck and feed. Fuck and feed. You'd never sleep. You'd never eat. You'd only be mine. Over and over and over."

My lip quivered. I reached out through our connection to try to convince him another way, to let him see that I was fine, but I ran into a wall of stubbornness. He was afraid he would break me. That he'd gone too far, too fast. But I didn't want to be treated like glass. Not when power was collecting in my body. Not when I felt like *this* was the answer to my unstable magick.

I needed him *and* the demonic relic. Together, they would remake me. The two felt tangled, impossible to separate. I needed to become strong. For Sera. Always for Sera. And for him. And... for the thing we weren't saying out loud.

My throat tightened as I lifted my gaze back to my mate. Bastien had shown me a vision inside his council room. Of a baby. *Our baby.* The one he feared might kill me. The one I feared, he promised, Tyson would never be born.

When I closed my eyes, I saw his little face staring adoringly up at me. His cold fingers tangling in my hair. It was a vision so vivid I could feel my heart reshaping around it. It was the one image, the one thought, that felt like destiny. Opening my eyes, I saw Bastien's, which were the same shade of winter frost as our child's. I pledged to master my dark magick for them. To free myself from Mama's curse and be the woman strong enough to keep them safe.

I knew Bastien was absorbing the storm of my emotions through our shared connection. His jaw clenched and unclenched, as if he were waging a war between his desire for our family and his resistance to it. "I almost lost you twice. I will not risk your life again. No matter what."

"This has nothing to do with me needing rest. You're afraid of *him*. Our child."

He swallowed hard. "Of course I am."

For a moment, I had no words. I could only glare at him. "Since when has a baby scared the Duke of Roselyn?"

"Since I saw him *killing* you."

If I closed my eyes, I could see it too. The bites on my neck. The sickly pallor of my skin. The way my body failed while he thrived. I glanced at the horn, and something pushed back against that image. That wasn't how my story ended.

"You saw the girl I was," I told him. "Not the woman I am. Not the witch I will become."

"Claire…"

His pity stoked a flare of shame in my belly, burning hot up my throat. But I refused to buckle. Jaw high, shoulders squared, I gestured to the two wolves bonded to me. "Hera underestimated me. I'll ask you not to do the same."

He tried to reach for me, but I jerked away. He grimaced. "This has nothing to do with underestimating you. I've always seen the fire. I've always known you were made to burn as bright as the stars. But… there is much we don't understand about why you received this power and why it doesn't work properly."

"The answer is here! Between you and me. And in this horn," I insisted, holding it up for him. "I can feel my power charging when you touch me. If you would only *try*." He ran a hand over his face and gave the barest shake of his head, and with that one dismissive gesture, my temper came exploding out. "You and your stubbornness are what's keeping me from my magick!"

"My stubbornness is the only thing keeping you alive!"

And there it was. The truth he was clinging to. I pushed away from him, not wanting to hear the rest, but Bastien didn't relent. "You can't feed me and a baby, Claire," he continued as tears pricked in my eyes. "We would kill you. And the worst part is"—his voice broke—"you'd let yourself die trying to prove me wrong."

I crossed my arms and turned away from him. I had nothing more to say. Nothing at all. If he thought so little of me, if he put so much trust in some half-formed vision, then this conversation was over.

"Once we arrive at Chastity's Stronghold, she will know how to remove that necklace. I believe it's interfering with your magick. Once that's taken care of, we can discuss *everything else*."

I let out a disgusted huff. I didn't need the help of some witch I didn't know. I was ready to walk into the darkness, to embrace this power I grew up fearing, to become the woman no one needed to protect. And... to hold the baby I never thought I'd have.

"I want to charge my magick," I demanded in a voice that didn't altogether sound like mine. It was stronger. Fiercer. The voice of a woman who didn't quake. I lifted the curved sheep's horn Cora had gifted me. The one she'd claimed was her Gran's favorite relic. I was the new owner of her grandmother's magick, so it seemed fitting that I follow this instinct. "And when I do, I will take care of the necklace myself. Then I'll prove that I'm strong enough to bear our child."

The pressure of phantom barbs squeezed around my throat, a warning to bite my tongue about the necklace. I tried not to let the pain or the panic show on my face, but Bastien's attention was on the relic. He was looking at it with the coiled focus of someone spotting a shadow where there shouldn't be one. Something ancient passed across his expression, so faint most people would miss it. But our bond wouldn't allow it.

"What is it now?" I asked.

He slowly reached for the horn. I jerked my hand away, not wanting him to take it, but he grabbed my wrist and held me still. As soon as he touched me, the world inside him *detonated*. Our bond surged so violently that I gasped. Shockwaves of emotion slammed into me before he could shut it down. A dark, violent flash of *knowing* so old it tasted like iron.

He let go of my wrist, and the connection between us slammed shut like an armored gate. Breathless, he said, "I need to speak with Sir Gavin about the plans for Roselyn's security while we're away."

He was hiding something from me. I could sense it. But I didn't want to know what it was. Not if it was another half-formed vision. The anger that had been simmering under my skin boiled over. "Yes, by all means, go speak with Sir Gavin!"

"Do *not* do anything *reckless* while I'm gone."

I narrowed my eyes. "I wouldn't dream of it, *Your Grace*."

I tried to spin around, but he caught me by the wrist again. Holding my gaze with fire in his blue eyes. "You are my *everything*. Trust that I know what I'm doing."

He wanted to keep me safe. But safety wouldn't break the curse on my necklace. And neither could the Dark Witch he wanted me to see. Only a true-born Prideaux could. A fact he didn't know and *couldn't* so long as I was beholden to Mama's necklace. I needed to solve this problem myself. I had to harness my powers to break the curse.

Before something in me broke *us*.

CHAPTER 3
L'APPEL
CLAIRE

Once he was gone, the room fell painfully still. I stayed where I was, staring at the door. Tears burned in the back of my throat. The old ache of feeling stupid and small and cast aside for my uselessness crept in, but I refused to give in to the sadness. It would do nothing for me now.

Instead, I paced back and forth, arms crossed, silently replaying the entire fight, until my attention landed on the large windows that ran along the farthest wall of the bedchamber.

Earlier, I'd sent a raven to Seraphina, my little sister, carrying a note and coin, along with my wish that she leave Prideaux Hill and join me here at Château Rose. I hoped she would open her eyes and see that the hate Mama had raised us on was a lie. Or, at best, not the entire story.

Beyond the glass, the snowy mountains rose jagged and dark against the fading twilight. Cradling the demonic relic against my heart, I pressed one palm against the window and drew in a deep breath. Holding the horn made me feel like anything was possible. And when Bastien touched me *while* I was touching it, power coursed through me.

But my husband had decided he wouldn't risk anything that might result in an heir. I understood his fear, mirrored it with my own. Having a real family was a dream I'd never dared let myself hold. I was meant to grow old at Prideaux Hill, tending to the ravens and the graveyard ghosts. But now, I had a husband. I had magick. And I wanted my own family. I blew out a breath that fogged the glass. If only he'd stop treating me like a breakable girl and *listen* to me.

A warm breeze rustled through my hair, and I had the strange sense that I was being watched. But that was silly. I pushed it aside. Only... the feeling persisted. Someone or *something* was standing behind me. My heart racing, I turned, ready to confront my husband about his mulish behavior, but found the bedchamber just as empty as it had been moments ago. Save for my two wolves, who were by the fire.

"Bastien?" I whispered, but no answer came.

I turned back around with a huff, facing the windows once more, determined to come up with some way to remove this necklace on my own and make my magick work, when the sheep's horn began *vibrating* against my breastbone. I nearly dropped it in surprise, but an unseen force ensured it stayed in my hands. Pulses of demonic energy raced through my body. Inhaling deeply, I closed my eyes and basked in the heat it produced. In the magick it was giving me.

I begged the demonic relic to fill me up with power that couldn't be taken away. "Please, Damien," I whispered, not knowing how to pray to the God of the Underworld. "Make me *unbreakable.*"

I didn't get a response, not that I believed I would, but something in me softened. My limbs grew limp, and suddenly the horn felt too heavy to hold. My grip on it slackened, and it slid down my stomach, gliding through a line of fresh perspiration, halting just below my belly button.

My breath stuttered. Heat blossomed in my cheeks. My pulse pounded loud enough that it shook the bloodstone Bastien gifted me. It wasn't just magick that was building inside of me, but *pleasure*.

Once again, I had the sense that I was being watched. I spun around, pressing my back against the cold glass, ready to confront whoever was there, but no one was. Save for my wolves. The white one was asleep, or pretending to be, and the brown one was standing guard, watching me intently. I let out a nervous laugh. That was it. It was just the wolf. No one was here.

I told myself to put the horn away, but it continued to vibrate *insistently*, as if it knew exactly where it wanted to be. I moved it a little lower. Then lower. Feeling equal parts embarrassed and reckless as I let it brush against me. Just *there*. Right where I'd wanted Bastien to be. And when I did, intense pleasure whirled through me, like I was melting and breaking apart at the same time. Bastien's lips and tongue had been world-changing, but this was something else entirely.

I pulled it away, knowing what I was doing was wrong. This wasn't what demonic relics were used for. I had a husband. I had no business doing *this*. And yet, I was intrigued. Bastien had stoked a desire that had nowhere to go. Now the fire inside me had taken on a life of its own, demanding a conclusion. Demanding release. And the horn had an answer.

I told myself I was only curious. That this was nothing more than testing the relic, exploring how its energy moved through me. The lie was just enough to quiet my own judgments. I glanced around the doorframe to ensure I was still alone, then tentatively brought it back, allowing the vibrating horn to touch me again.

The pleasure came stronger this time, rippling through me until my knees threatened to buckle. The sheep's horn was smooth on one side and ridged on the other. I slid it back and forth, *back and forth*. The more I teased myself, the wetter I became, until the horn was damp and slipped easily through, parting me until its vibrating tip brushed against the soft spot Bastien taught me about.

I sank to the floor, my back flush against the glass. I didn't know what kind of power this was, but if it could do *this* to me, I was enthralled. My legs fell apart on a slow sigh, and I let myself explore the sensations. I worked it in a circle, twisting it so the ridged side slid against me, which felt even better. After only a few moments, I was ready to come apart.

I pulled it away, giving myself space to breathe, to savor the torment of being close without tipping over the edge.

Then, madness overtook me. A half-formed thought. With my eyes shut, I guided the tip toward my center, to the place Bastien had claimed. My hips shifted forward without permission, my body answering before my mind could object, and gently nudged it inside me.

Stars exploded behind my eyes. I sucked in a jagged breath. I should stop. I knew that, but it felt too good. It felt too right. I urged it deeper, letting it buzz against that warm spot inside me. I surrendered to the wrongness of it, to the way my body opened without hesitation, welcoming the magick building inside me. My free hand slid to my clit, fingers rubbing in tight little circles as everything else spun wildly out of control.

I thought of Bastien. Of the way his eyes blackened before he bit me. Of the way he slid into me. I wanted him right here. I wanted his hard thrusts. I wanted to watch his face as he unraveled with me. I wanted to feel him dripping out of me.

But... this *wasn't* Bastien. It was ribbed and warm and *by Diana...* I was going to come. I worked it in and out until I was sighing and squirming on the floor. All the while, magick tingled beneath my skin.

It was working. *It was working.*

When I couldn't take any more, I gave in. With a soft moan, my body released completely, the pleasure stretched and swelled until it spilled through me in a rush. Afterward, I sat there, chest rising and falling. The horn continued to hum in my grip, almost pleased with itself.

But the magick under my skin needed its own release. *Proof*, I thought hazily. I needed *proof* this wasn't just my body fooling me.

Magick had betrayed me too many times in the past. It hadn't worked when Hera held a knife to Bastien's throat. Nor when I was five, and I had stood trembling in the dark at Prideaux Hill, cradling my cheek after Mama struck me with the back of her hand, demanding I try the spell again. I swallowed hard, remembering how small I'd felt afterward. The disappointment. The certainty that I was broken.

I wasn't that girl anymore. That girl was gone.

Raising my hand, I focused on one of the unlit candles on the nightstand and willed it to light. "Come on," I urged the magick. A frustrated beat of silence passed. I clenched my jaw, breath hitching, sweat gathering at my hairline as the familiar panic crept back in. Then, a burst of energy surged through my body, and the wick *ignited*.

A laugh broke free. "I did it!" I pressed a hand over my mouth, half afraid the sound would ruin the moment, and watched the candle burn with amazement. The flame mirrored the warm light of hope flickering in my chest. Fragile and fierce all at once. It burned alongside a quiet pride I'd never felt before.

I was right. This horn *was* the answer. And for whatever reason, it worked best when I was right on the edge, when my body was open and lit from the inside. The flame stretched higher, licking the air, and my heart lifted with it. Until... it flickered.

"No!" I shouted, scrambling to my feet. Rushing over to it, I held out my hands like I could catch it before it disappeared. "You have to stay lit!"

I had no idea how badly I needed this to work until *it did*. But despite my pleas, the candle extinguished, along with the light inside my chest. My shoulders sagged in defeat. "Why?" I whispered. "What happened?"

I stumbled back and stepped on something sharp. "By Diana!" I yelped, hopping away. When I looked down, I found a small seashell shaped like a tusk inches away from my foot. It hadn't been there before. Had it?

A chill crept up my spine. Slowly, I lifted my gaze to where the horn rested on the floor. It was still vibrating. Warm and patient. Which didn't make sense. If the power had faded, it should have stopped. If *I* had done something wrong, the magick would've drained away.

But it hadn't. It was still humming under my skin.

Maybe the flame hadn't gone out because the power was gone, but because *I* needed to go further.

Grabbing the horn, I whispered, "One more time."

CHAPTER 4

CONTENIR

BASTIEN

Sir Gavin was in the middle of explaining the security plan for the city when a stab of pain sliced through my shoulder, landing like an arrow. I tried not to let the shock show on my face, but judging by Sir Gavin's reaction, I wasn't successful.

"Your Grace?"

I waved off his concern, the invisible arrow pressed deeper, seeking my heart. My heart was a dead, useless thing, so I took the pain as symbolic. And there was only one person who held my heart.

And that was Claire.

I touched the place where my bloodstone was concealed. A coin-sized gem attached to a thin gold chain around my neck, which I always kept hidden beneath my wool vest and the leather chest rig. Its throbbing red light beat with the heart of my mate, and signaled to everyone that I had found my person.

When the council of witches who created us drafted the Blood Treaty, they knew there had to be limits on the power they were giving us. They wanted peacekeepers, not blood-

21

thirsty tyrants. And so, the matebond was created. When we were consumed by it, for the sixty or so years our mate was alive, it tempered us. And reminded us of the humanity we left behind. For love is the most powerful of human emotions.

A vampire's mate was chosen by Diana and Damien, and said to be born and reborn, again and again. I thought I'd been the one forgotten soul. But then they sent me Claire.

When I'd met her that night at Château Corbin, I thought it had been the end of my well-curated life. But it was only the beginning. However, in an effort to protect my role as Marius's war commander, I shirked my responsibilities to Claire and took her as my sanguine partner instead.

Another broken law.

Though thoughts of my mate and her safety consumed me, I kept them hidden. My focus had to be on protecting these people and negotiating the peace I'd chased for centuries.

Beat. Beat. Beat. The bloodstone pulsed with the reassuring beat of her heart. I knew she was alive. Well. But the pain that had lodged itself in my heart persisted. I'd been stabbed and pierced with arrows and broken bones, but this pain was unlike any I'd ever experienced.

I shifted my weight onto the cane, bracing myself. But the pain stayed. Images of Claire wounded flooded my mind. I should never have left her alone. I'd been foolish to let my temper get the best of me and leave her alone.

"Sir Gavin, let's continue this later."

I turned before he could respond. If anything happened to Claire, I would not survive it. Not because of fate or duty or destiny, but because I knew exactly what I'd become without her, and the world did not deserve that monster. That vengeful demon. That unrestrained reaper.

The laws of the Blood Treaty stated I'd be consumed while my mate walked the earth, and free to rule when she was gone, but that wasn't how it would go for me. Yes, I was more distracted around her. But her love made me a better man. When she died, the last of my humanity would too.

Beat. Beat. Beat. Her pulse raced faster and faster. I continued through the castle, moving slow enough not to startle my staff, but it wasn't fast enough, not for the monster. He was awake now. Triggered by the pain in my heart and the ache in my soul. He grew stronger with every fearful thought.

And I had much to fear.

Losing my reputation, losing *her*, losing the man I built myself to be ever since... Everything inside me squeezed into a tight ball, bracing against a memory I'd buried so deep I hoped it would never crawl back up. But fear makes old ghosts hungry, and the one I'd starved for years was stirring.

I rounded the corner, ready to take the stairs two at a time to make it back to my private residences. That horn... what if? What if it belonged to *him*?

Clenching my teeth, I reminded myself that it wasn't possible. I'd thrown it into the Starfall River. It was gone, just like *he* was. I didn't have the time, the patience, or the interest in entertaining shadows from the past.

I stopped just outside our door and closed my eyes. There were enchantments placed on my bedchamber, old spells to keep whispers from reaching even vampiric hearing. I liked my privacy. But those spells couldn't prevent me from feeling her emotions. We were close enough that I could open the link between our minds. The connection that allowed me to feel what she was feeling.

I nudged it open, just a crack, and a thrill of pleasure rolled down my spine. My cock came to life, growing harder and harder. I knew she was alone; no unfamiliar scents lingered by the door. And I'd given orders to have the private residence wing cleared of all staff, including her consorts, due to our marriage. Which could only mean she was *pleasuring* herself.

Resisting the urge to burst through the door, I bit my lip and took a long, slow breath in. But breath work didn't stop the desire. The want to fuck and feed from my wife. To thrust in and out, over and over again, until I came inside her heat, filling her. It was more than just a primal urge. It was a need. A want. A desire to watch her belly grow, knowing we'd created something beautiful together.

I imagined her with her hand between her legs and my name on her lips. I'd left my new bride unsatisfied, and the fire inside her was burning hotter than ever.

I slipped out of our connection, breathing hard. And the intoxicating thrill of her pleasure faded. I battled with myself, caught between my desire to show Claire exactly how much I wanted her and my duty to keep her safe.

But it was more than just the baby. I was still the Duke of Roselyn. My duty wasn't just to her, but to our people. If she were with child, how could I ever stay focused?

It was time to walk away from my room and see to my other duties. Clearly, Claire was safe. That phantom pain had been nothing more than nerves. No harm could find her in my bedchamber, and I had pressing matters to attend to. Namely, ensuring my army was ready to march into the Lawless Lands, because I didn't think a simple negotiation was waiting for me. Not anymore. Not after receiving Hector's head and Shayla's warning.

Just as I was about to return to the armory and apologize to Sir Gavin, the monster's hands coiled around my throat, claws digging in, like he wanted to split me open and crawl out, ready to unleash a hunger I'd kept chained for centuries. A hunger that had run wild in that graveyard. I hadn't cared who stood in my way. I'd killed indiscriminately. Young and old.

Those with pleas on their lips and apologies in their eyes. Anyone who'd thought to hurt her had died. I took no prisoners. Offered no mercy. A vampire possessed by rage, too far gone to ask Hera why she'd wanted her mother's magick or to drag her to Marius for judgment. She'd hurt Claire, and all I'd seen was murder.

It urged me to open the door and see her face. To ensure I had nothing to worry about.

My grip tightened around my cane until my nails bit into my palm, the sting forcing me to focus. Forcing me to stay inside my own skin. To hold the line between who I *was* and who I became when she was threatened.

I knew, just as that twisted thing inside me knew, that while I could talk myself out of believing she was in danger from the demonic relic, I couldn't keep her safe from the cursed necklace. It was the one threat I couldn't drown in blood.

She insisted it couldn't be cut off nor could she tell me who'd fastened it around her neck, but I knew it was bound with a dark curse. Ready to take her life if she strayed from whatever path she'd been sent on.

"She is *alive*. And I will ensure she stays that way," I reminded it. Me. *Us.*

"The Kemps were just the start. The world is fracturing. The blood treaty is crumbling. More will come for her. Including the one who owns her life. We could do more if you'd only let me out."

I snarled. The monster inside me wanted to solve this problem. It was more than just my vampiric nature, but the part of me that I struggled to control even as a witch. The part that had been seduced by something else entirely.

I breathed in a long sip of air and held it. I needed to understand more about what was happening to Claire. More had changed than just her hair color. There were so many questions that needed answering. About who she really was. About why these wolf familiars bound themselves to her. About the fire she'd summoned from the earth.

I hadn't told her how strong these gifts were, even for Witches of the Darkness. It made me wonder why she was abandoned at the doorstep of a convent that worshipped Diana when she was destined for so much more.

The only answer I had was that she was a witch someone wanted to hide. *Or use.*

And now, the woman who had been abandoned by her own family wanted one for herself. The one gift I wanted to give her, but knew would kill her. I couldn't thread this needle between loving her and keeping her safe if I were this monster. I had to be *me*.

A new scent caught my attention. One of steel, expensive red wine, and the faintest trace of rosewater. I turned to find Lady Natalia stepping out of a shadowy archway, arms crossed over a fitted jacket and black vest trimmed in gold. Her waist-length brown hair was braided, as always, and draped over her shoulder.

"Your Grace," she said with an expression carved from flint.

Natalia was my niece. *Mon sang.* My blood. My most trusted advisor. My second in command. We frequently exchanged barbs, yet the lack of warmth between us was unfamiliar. I'd grown tired of her continued accusations against my wife, and she had grown tired of my ignoring them. But something had shifted, and as much as I wished for the words to mend the divide, I had none.

"What news?" I asked.

She simply stared at me.

"If you've come to lecture me about Claire—"

"This isn't about your wife," she interrupted tightly, speaking in Sanguisi. *"Not everything is."*

A lie. Everything was about Claire now. Everything I did, everything I feared, everything I planned.

"Then what news?" I asked again.

She was quiet for a moment. "We have reports from Roselyn of a *sighting*." A coded remark. There was too much on my mind to interpret it at the moment. I opened the channel between our minds, waiting for her to clarify, but all she said was, *"A werewolf."*

CHAPTER 5

OSER

CLAIRE

I lost count of how many times I tried—and failed—to keep the candle lit. Eventually, it became less about conjuring the flame and more about the fact that I actually had magick. I had powers that were just for me. The kind that called flames *and* drove my own pleasure.

After half an hour, I told myself I needed a break. I'd been at it so long that even my brown wolf was panting. But the horn kept vibrating, insistent that I test my limits. As it turned out, my power for self-pleasure was inexhaustible.

With its help, I was free to explore my body on my own terms. I found my body was capable of more than I ever believed. Then there was the little pile of seashells. They'd appeared one by one. Beautiful, tiny things swirled with color. I couldn't explain why, but they felt like gifts.

I smiled and reclined on the pillow, relaxing into the silk sheets, staring at my shells and the horn, which had finally gone still. Not so long ago, I believed dark magick was an abomination. But things like the horn and these shells were changing my mind.

I stroked the curve of it, grateful for what it had shown me, yet I knew in my heart that in order to break the curse on the necklace, I needed real power. It couldn't be just me and the horn. There was a missing piece to all this: *My husband.*

Soon, we would be leaving for the Lawless Lands. I had no idea what to expect on our journey, except perhaps cold nights in a tent with a man who refused to risk anything for fear of creating an heir. He would still crawl between my legs, feast on my blood, and still use that skilled tongue of his, but always with restraint. As if my body were something he had to manage.

That wasn't what I wanted for my marriage. And it wasn't what I wanted for myself. But who could I ask to help me unlock my latent power? One name came to mind: Devlinn. He was a Dark Witch, and more importantly, he was one of my trusted consorts. However, since I had chosen the three people I was supposed to take as lovers, they'd always just been friends. Even Alec. As handsome and charming as he was, and as eager as he'd been to please me, it was nothing compared to Bastien.

I swallowed hard. Yes. Devlinn would know what to do.

As soon as I made the decision to dress and find him, the stone wall across from where I stood *groaned.* Puffs of old mortar erupted into the air. I shielded my face with my hand, sputtering out a cough. The dust turned into golden sparkles of light, and behind it, as if drawn by an invisible hand, appeared two arched doorways. The doors swung open in perfect unison, revealing two staircases.

I could hardly believe what I was seeing. Magick, not wielded by a person, but cast from within the walls. It felt, absurdly, as if the castle had heard my vow and decided to answer it.

Cautiously, I drew closer to the open doors. The sound of

fur rustling and nails clicking told me I'd piqued the interest of my wolves. They might've ignored my cries of pleasure, but they couldn't ignore this kind of magick.

And neither could I.

I set my hand on the doorway of the ascending staircase and drew in a deep breath. The scent of parchment, tobacco smoke, and fresh citrus wafted toward me. It reminded me of the old family grimoires Mama kept. The ones seeped in light magick. Ones I'd longed to use as a girl. But I knew that would *never* happen.

I glanced down at the white wolf, who whined and nudged her snout into my knee. She was encouraging me up the spiraling wooden stairs. Meanwhile, the larger brown male was standing beside the staircase that plunged downward. I edged closer to it and drew in a breath of salty air and must. The sound of dripping water echoed from far below.

Taking a step back, I considered the doors. I thought of using my bloodstone to summon Bastien and ask him where these staircases led, but I already knew what he would do. He'd simply close both doors and say I needed rest. He'd reassure me that he had a plan to take care of everything and that I needed to trust him. Just like he refused to consider that maybe these powers came to me for a reason, and that I was meant to take the choker off myself.

My anger spiked viciously. Of course, I trusted him, but he wasn't returning the favor. He hadn't listened to me when I told him I could draw power from the horn. And I'd been right. The candles, the shells, these doors were all proof. If he'd just made love to me, I wouldn't be in this predicament.

I drew in a breath to calm myself. I was letting the fire consume me, and that couldn't happen. I was standing at a crossroads, and whichever direction I chose would change my life. Going up felt like seeking answers in a safe way. Going down felt like stepping into everything I'd said I was willing to become.

From the depths of the castle came a croaking voice. *"Come, Claire,"* it called softly. *"Come look into my waters."*

The fine hairs along my arms lifted, and my pulse thundered against my ribs. A voice rising from beneath the castle should have sent me running for Bastien. But I wanted to make new choices. To prove that I was the worthiest witch in that graveyard.

Answers, a quiet part of me whispered. Not safety. Not comfort. Answers.

My instincts were pulling me toward the voice. But if I was going to do this, it needed to be now. Bastien wouldn't be gone forever.

Gathering my courage, I slipped the seashells into the pocket of my robe, which I quickly tied, then held the horn out in front of me like a wand. *Or a shield.* My wolves fell in behind me as I began the descent.

After a few steps, the light from my bedchamber was lost, and I walked in near darkness. The temperature grew warmer with each step, as if the walls themselves were heated by a supernatural power.

Perhaps Tansy hadn't been joking, I thought dimly. *Perhaps a dragon truly did sleep beneath the castle.* However, when I rounded the next corner, I didn't see a scaly beast, but a cavern with sharp stones sticking from the ceiling like jagged teeth, looming over a large salt pond. Steam hung like a cloud over the water.

"Well, well, well," croaked the voice from somewhere behind the mist. "If it's not the Duchess herself. Prince Bastien's long-awaited *mate.*"

My heart pounded hard in my chest. Only those who had taken a blood vow knew about my marriage. This person knew things they shouldn't. My wolves growled, yet I did not turn and run. Not even when a skeletal figure emerged from the mist. Her long silver hair hung in dripping strands around a sunken face, and grayish skin clung to her bones. But it was her eyes that gave me pause. They glowed *emerald*.

Tansy had joked that a mermaid lived beneath the château, tending the dragon. This woman was no mermaid, but a witch. You could always see magick in a witch's eyes.

When Witches of the Light cast spells, they shone pale as moonstone. When Witches of the Darkness worked their power, their eyes burned like liquid rubies. But I had never seen anything like this. Emerald did not belong to either side. Perhaps she was a water demon, like Mama had warned me about when I was a child.

"Who are you?" I asked.

The woman's lips peeled back in something that might have been a smile, revealing a row of chipped teeth. "Is that what you wish to know? My name?" she croaked. "Or are you here to ask a different question?"

"What do you mean?"

"I only answer questions in exchange for payment. And you"—her gaze flicked downward—"only brought enough shells for one."

I reached into my pocket and drew out the small handful of shells. I realized these weren't gifts. They were currency. Payment for the old witch in the water.

The woman slipped beneath the surface of the lake and swam toward me, appearing again at my feet. I swallowed hard, fear tightening my throat, but I did not move.

She regarded the wolves sitting beside me, completely unafraid of them. "So many questions cloud your mind. Who am I? What should I do? What is my husband hiding?"

Unfurling her spidery hand, the woman waited expectantly for my shells. "Which will it be, *my lady?*"

The emerald of her eyes flashed greedily as she stared at them. She wanted these shells as much as I wanted answers, and I knew I needed to use that to my advantage. So I put them back in my pocket. When I did, the light dimmed from her eyes, and she crinkled her brow. "Come, girl, give me your shells and ask your question. The prince will be along soon. And something tells me you wouldn't want him to find you here."

"That's a bold thing to say," I replied evenly. "Especially from someone who refuses to tell me her name."

She narrowed her strange, shiny green eyes. "I am the last remnant of what existed *before*."

I didn't have time for cryptic answers. Frustration bubbled under my skin. The near-constant irritation that I couldn't seem to control. "Before *what*?"

A strange grin flashed across her face, like she had been waiting for me to ask this question. "You were born during a time when magick is either dark or light. Moon or demonic. From the great *mother*, Diana, or from the *father*, Damien. But it wasn't always that way."

She paused, seeming to watch the way the questions swam through my mind, then patted the lip of the salty lake. "If you want to know who I am, come sit by the water, and I'll tell you a story."

"I'm not giving you my shells to hear a story," I said. I came here for answers, not tales.

Her eyes lingered on the horn. She leaned closer, her joints creaking as she moved, bones shifting beneath parchment-thin flesh. "I'll tell you this one for free. But when the story ends, you *will* ask your question and give me your payment. Agreed?"

She held my gaze with those unsettling eyes of hers. I hesitated. The heat rolling off the lake had me sweating, making the horn slick in my hands. I didn't know who or what this woman was, and she was asking me to make a bargain with her. A bargain for the shells I'd created with my own magick.

Fear had kept me small before. I wasn't going to lose the chance to gain agency over my magick because of a creepy old woman. Besides, I had my wolves to protect me.

Lowering myself onto the damp stone, I winced as steam hissed against my skin, and the salty air stung my eyes. "Agreed."

Satisfied, the old witch settled herself onto a submerged boulder and crossed her skeletal arms. "You've never heard the story of Damien and Diana's daughters, have you?"

CHAPTER 6

RESSURGIR

BASTIEN

Claire was on my mind as I rode into the walled city that surrounded Château Rose with Natalia and Tyson. While I was loath to leave my wife alone, I had duties to attend to. And I wanted to hear about the werewolf firsthand.

The city of Roselyn looked peaceful beneath a blanket of snow. Chimneys breathed thin ribbons of smoke into the gathering night, and lanterns glowed. The homes of the wealthier citizens lived closest to the castle, their homes nestled within the inner ring wall—miners and merchants whose fortunes came from the mountains. Beyond the outer ring wall sheltered the smaller homes of tradesmen and military leaders, cooks and gardeners, seamstresses and shopkeepers, and soldiers with their families. Here, in the outer wall, beat the true heart and soul of the city.

This was a hardy town, its people as resilient as the mountains themselves. I guided us past the greenhouses, their windows slick with condensation. My thoughts returned to my wife, and how she looked with her hands in the soil, planting flowers, her laughter bright in the air. I longed to give her more days like that.

The rumble of my army grew the closer we came to the outer ring wall. They had been amassing in the valley, ready to march into the Lawless Lands at my command. As we trotted through the gate, we were greeted by raucous cheers.

I lifted my hand, and the warriors answered. Shouting louder, chanting, *"Duke, Duke, Duke!"*

Winter wind whipped through my hair, and pride swelled in my chest. This was one of the reasons why I had no desire to live in the capital. I was a warrior. A commander. I'd always been one of them, and I'd led generations into battle to protect the boundary between us and the witches who refused to set down their grudges and pursue peace under the Blood Treaty.

Over the centuries, their hatred of each other dwindled their numbers. The bodies of mothers, fathers, and children filled the great graveyard just beyond the mountain pass. I'd meet coven leaders throughout this time who had grown weary of fighting and wanted peace. We'd done things like build a tunnel for peaceful travelers. We'd set up independent villages for humans that were free from magick and that were protected from the war with spells.

These were small victories. But this new wave of leaders had given me hope. For those like Chastity and Hector, their mistrust of vampires was outweighed by the desire to see their children thrive. They wanted peace, and they saw the benefit of having an unbiased third party to ensure it held.

At least, that had been the sentiment before I received Hector's head in a box, and this new coven leader, Shayla, had learned to harness moon magick to create werewolves.

I hadn't wanted to believe it, but the proof was growing. "Where is this soldier? The one who saw a werewolf?" I asked.

Natalia motioned to the largest tent, and we cut a slow

path through rows and rows of men and women dressed in black-and-gold doublets.

"Is it strange that I'm hard right now?" Tyson quipped, running a hand through his jet-black hair. "Does that happen to you?" Both Natalia and I rolled our eyes. "What? I'm being serious. Surrounded by the army. All these people chanting. The bloodlust. It doesn't make your cock hard?"

"No," Natalia replied.

He leveled her with a look. "Come on! You have to feel *something*. Right in your cock. It's more thrilling than—than," he struggled for a word, then his dark eyes widened, "your first threesome."

Natalia burst out in a sudden fit of laughter. "You wouldn't know what to do with two lovers."

He gestured to his crotch. "I've yet to meet a lover who complained about my cock." Natalia only laughed harder. Tyson gaped at her. "What?"

"In my experience," Natalia was saying, flicking her long braid off her shoulder, "a man who advertises as loudly as you rarely has much to offer."

I leaned down to shake hands with a few warriors while my niece and nephew continued, and received well-wishes and warm words that, thankfully, had little to do with cocks. Tyson, who realized men wanted to shake his hand too, stopped talking.

Chuckling, Natalia muttered, "Do you think this is how they talk in the capital?"

We shared a smile, but hers quickly evaporated, and we both trained our attention forward. An unfamiliar awkwardness settling between us.

We tied our horses outside the command tent, where incense smoke mingled with the scent of roasting goat. The Captain of the Watch greeted me with a bow, his doublet emblazoned with the sigil of House Allard and the Unified Territories: a moon, a blade, and a coiled serpent encircled by twelve small stars.

I tucked my cane under my arm, and we shook hands like old friends. He did the same with Natalia. But stopped to leer at Tyson, who had stuck out his hand, waiting for the same warm welcome. As much as I liked watching him squirm, Tyson was my heir. So I cleared my throat and made introductions. "This is my nephew, Lord Tyson Allard, the newly minted Viscount of Aurenne. And my heir."

"Heir?" The Captain of the Watch grunted before shooting a sidelong glance at Lady Natalia. "Your brothers sure are busy in the capital, aren't they, Your Grace? Drinking wine and having parties and making babies while we do the hard work of the land."

I swallowed hard, trying not to think about *making babies*, as he put it.

"The viscount does love a good party," Natalia said with a laugh. She pointed the butt of her dagger at his chest. "By the way he's dressed, you'd think one was about to start."

Tyson glanced down at his double-breasted coat, confused. "This isn't what you'd wear to a party, cousin. It's distinctly military."

While he'd traded midnight blue for the black and gold of Roselyn, his attire was still much less practical than mine or Natalia's. Gold buttons. A black silk damask with gold filigree. The tassels. Not to mention the mink cloak hanging around his shoulders.

Tyson caught the way we were all looking at him, and the defensiveness melted into a crooked grin. "What can I say? I'm a rare breed. I like to fight and fuck and look good doing it."

Natalia scoffed, but the captain chuckled. "The maids do

love a pretty lad. Maybe I should get a fancy cloak. I'd probably have better luck."

I shot a warning look at my niece and nephew, hoping to inspire a little decorum. They both snapped to attention, and I returned to the matter at hand. "You have an urgent report to give?"

The humor drained from his face. "Yes, Your Grace."

The Captain's shift in mood was enough to cause concern. The three of us took seats around the large trestle table. A page brought out golden goblets of wine while a young, beefy man who looked no more than twenty entered. He knelt before us, a dented helmet tucked beneath his arm.

The Captain announced that the young soldier had been in my service for four years, and had been through the pass to the Lawless Lands once before. I thanked him for his service and bid him start from the beginning.

"I was walking the tree line, Your Grace," the soldier began. "Near the old watch stones. I stopped to warm me hands by the fire. It's been brutally cold, Your Grace. And that's when I heard a sound. Twigs snapping. Leaves rustling. I could tell by the sound that it was too big to be a squirrel. So I pulled out my bow and crept a little closer. I saw a flash of tan. At first, I thought it was a big doe, and I got real excited, I did. Venison would've made a nice meal." The smile on his face fell. "But then it stood. On *two legs*, Your Grace. And I realized it was no deer."

"What did you think it was?" Natalia asked.

The man swallowed hard. "A *were*."

I steepled my fingers under my chin, contemplating the man's story. He was young, but he wasn't a green boy.

Tyson leaned closer to me and whispered in Sanguisi. Once upon a time, most witches spoke Sanguisi, but the language had long since died out, replaced by the Common Tongue.

Now, vampires were the only ones who kept the old language alive. *"Look at the crescent moon brand on his right hand. He's a follower of Diana."*

Sure enough, there was a mottled pink brand on the back of his hand. Not all of my human fighters bore these marks, only those who kept the ways of one god or the other. It passed as a way to tell what kind of burial rites they'd prefer.

Tyson continued. *"He's probably heard the tales, maybe even seen pictures of weres in storybooks growing up. It makes his story more plausible."*

This assertion was surprising, coming from my nephew. I'd thrown him out of my tent when he'd laughed at Alec's story about being scratched by one. *"I thought you didn't believe such things were possible?"*

He raised his brows. *"People change, Uncle."*

I nodded, not agreeing with him, but rather impressed that he was demonstrating some growth. And that he'd caught the brand on the back of the soldier's hand. That kind of attention to detail was important.

Maybe he wasn't as useless as I feared.

Not to be outdone, Natalia chimed in. *"If Tyson had been visiting the army instead of spending time with his tailor, he'd know that rumors have been circulating around camp. The men know we're going to the Lawless Lands to fight werewolves. He could be projecting."*

She also made a good point. It wouldn't be the first time rumors like this flew around camp before we left for the Lawless Lands. If this had happened a year ago, I would've written it off as nothing more than fear. But things were different now. *"The scratch marks on Hector's severed head are reason enough to believe this man might've seen a werewolf."*

The more disturbing part of all this was how a were was on this side of the border. I exhaled through my nose and touched the place where my bloodstone was concealed. Reassured by the way it beat under my fingertips. I wasn't sure if werewolves could cross the boundary between lands. I'd need to assess the condition of the barrier when we crossed.

"Thank you for this information," I said. "You are dismissed." The soldier bowed once again and departed the tent. I turned to the captain. "Tighten the outer patrols. Double the watch. I don't want them walking alone."

The captain made a note. "It'll be tight. We're still waiting on Lord Aurélien's men to arrive from Carrion Hall. But I'll make it work, Your Grace."

"I can join the watch tonight," Tyson offered.

"*They won't be playing Dépouiller,*" Natalia hissed.

He shrugged. "*Maybe we will in celebration of my capture of the were.*"

"*You? Catch a werewolf? Don't make me laugh. We know nothing about these creatures beyond the old myths. Not even Uncle Bastien has seen one.*"

I held out my hands to stop their arguing before Tyson inevitably brought up his *cock* again. "Lord Tyson will stay with the army tonight. He will conduct rounds with the captain and look for a trail."

The Captain of the Guard grunted and made another note. "Freeze my balls off in the woods with the viscount. Sounds fun. Anything else, Your Grace?"

"No, that will be all." Tyson leaned back in his chair triumphantly. I shot him a warning look. "*You're not in the capital anymore. Nor the training yard. Don't make me regret this.*"

Flashing me a bright smile, Tyson replied, "*I wouldn't dream of it, Uncle.*"

His promise did little to reassure me. Which was why I wasn't going to leave him down here unattended. "Lady Natalia, you are in charge. Ensure the army is ready for the journey. I'm going back to the castle to ensure all preparations have been made for Roselyn's security. We leave tomorrow at nightfall."

She dipped her head. "I will see it done, Your Grace."

I exited the tent, but my niece followed after me. I untied Lucien's lashings, waiting for whatever she wanted to say.

"There's something I want to tell you before you go." I lifted my brows, waiting. *"I don't trust Claire's wolves."*

I shook my head. *"There is nothing to worry about."*

"What if they are werewolves?"

"Preposterous."

She stomped her foot. *"She's keeping things from you. You said it yourself!"*

I stabbed my cane into the hard-packed snow. *"It's not her fault. It's that choker. She can't tell me who did this to her without it killing her. But she wants to."*

"Doesn't that seem like the most suspicious part of all of this? That someone would risk her life to keep their secret?" She threw her hands into the air. *"Wake up, Uncle. She's a spy. A spy who grew up loving Witches of the Light, and that has two wolves that she conveniently got while you were away."*

"That's enough," I snarled. *"You don't know her as I do."*

She set her hand on her hip. *"Right. I can't possibly understand her, because I don't share her bed."*

I lifted my cane, holding it precariously between us. The fragile alliance that we had built on the ride over was disappearing. *"You are out of line."*

She said nothing, only glared at me.

I mounted Lucien, ready to leave.

"Fine. Maybe I am out of line," Natalia admitted. *"But that's why you made me your second in command. Because I see things other people don't. And right now, I'm seeing trouble."*

I'd grown weary of these arguments. I squeezed my calves

around Lucien's big body and clicked my tongue. He started back in the direction of the gate.

"If you don't listen to a thing I say," Natalia shouted after me, *"at least separate her from those wolves. And for goddess sake, don't let her keep them in your room."*

I pulled back on the reins. The disrespect. To shout at me like this. I swiftly dismounted, set on stripping her of command. But when I stared into her eyes, I saw the young girl who'd just told me her most closely guarded secret. I saw the fiercest fighter of her age, shunned by a father who wouldn't accept her words as truth. I'd sworn to her that I'd never be that person. That I'd never punish her for speaking her truth. And that I'd believe her.

Now, I was going back on my promise.

"And what do you suggest I do with them?"

Pleadingly, Natalia said, *"Give them to me! I'll tie it up for you!"*

"What kind of message would that send to my mate if I tied up her wolves?"

For the longest time, Natalia had been the most important woman in my life. I cherished her counsel. But now I had someone else. And I had to think of my wife first. I had to.

She let out a frustrated breath and shook her head. *"Fine. Don't listen to me. I'm probably just seeing threats in the woods. I just... "* Her voice trailed off. *"After what happened at Kemp Manor, I worry about you."*

I nodded. She disappeared back into the commander's tent, and I turned back to my horse. I rode back through the streets of Roselyn alone, contemplating all that was on my mind. But I wasn't alone with my thoughts for long. As I trotted by, mothers and children emerged from their homes with baskets of flowers. They threw long stems of baby's breath along the dirt road. A ritual offering to soldiers before they left over the pass.

I stopped for a little girl, who was no older than three, holding out a flower for me. She was dressed in rabbit fur that didn't look nearly warm enough for the weather. Her pretty golden blond hair was whipping around red cheeks.

Dismounting, I knelt beside her and took the flower she was offering.

Her mother, who was hovering an arm's length away, said, "Your curtsy, Annalise! Don't forget your curtsy!"

The little girl tried, but nearly fell over. I quickly steadied her with a hand. "Annalise is a very nice name. My name is Bastien."

Smiling, I removed the brooch holding my cloak around my shoulders, then draped it around her little shoulders.

"That's not necessary, Your Grace," her mother said.

"I don't need it," I told the little girl. "I'm a vampire. I don't even get cold."

She laughed, and so did I.

"Thank you, Your Grace," the woman said, collecting her little girl in her arms.

I glanced around the homes of the outer ring, and the bundles of baby's breath lining the muddy snow.

It reminded me of when I'd left my village for the last time, on the last night I was human. Even though my human memories were fuzzy, something thick formed in my throat.

This was the reason why I fought. I had a duty to protect them. All of them. The ones who came with me to fight and the ones I left behind. The people of Roselyn were a tough yet loving bunch who lived on the border between lands. They valued peace more than anyone else.

"We've begun laying the foundation for the youth home you asked us to build," her mother said, beaming. She gestured toward the furthest end of the city, where the outer ring wall brushed up against the tree line. "You should see it before you go. Maybe offer a blessing."

I nodded. "I will."

Starting this new facility couldn't fix what had happened to Claire, but it was my way of giving back. I didn't want anyone else to harm children who had lost parents the way she'd been harmed.

Getting back on my horse, I waved goodbye to the little girl, who was swaddled in my cloak, and urged Lucien in the direction of the youth home. I made my way down the less-trafficked streets that were covered in a soft layer of snow. The village lights thinned, lanterns giving way to shadows. The mountain air carried the scent of frost and iron.

Lucien snorted and flattened his ears. He refused to move any closer toward the wall. I followed his gaze and swore I saw the outline of a creature I hadn't seen since before the Choosing.

CHAPTER 7

SE PRÉSERVER

CLAIRE

The word *daughters* lodged somewhere deep in my chest. I kept trying to process what the old witch had said, but it wasn't making any sense.

"Damien and Diana do not have daughters," I insisted, my voice trembling. "That's *impossible*."

"Do you want to hear the story or not?" she croaked.

I considered her with a weary glance. My mother had always loved spinning stories, but not the kind that would help you fall asleep. She told the kind that made you want to avenge your bloodline. Dark Witches were evil. Vampires were complicit. And anything that didn't bow to the light deserved to be destroyed.

Mama's stories weren't meant to teach me the truth. They were meant to keep me afraid. To turn me into the perfect pawn for her revenge. I wouldn't put it past the old witch to try to scare me, too. Still, curiosity tugged at me. I was sent down here for a reason.

"As I said," the old witch began, "once upon a time, Damien and Diana had two daughters."

Steam rose over the lake, and I swore I could see images forming in the mist. Diana and her white hair slipping into the underworld to seek out the bed of a god. Then I saw pieces of the moon fragmenting like a daughter being born.

The steam sank back into the lake, and I found a pair of emerald eyes fixed on me. She continued. "The girls were lovely in their own right. Each talented. Each beautiful. Which was why they hated each other so much."

She paused, enjoying my reaction to her story. She was clearly excited that I was hooked. Desperate to hear more.

"The eldest daughter, Rosa, was smart, *very* logical, and ill-tempered. She believed everything should make sense. Maris was whimsical and saw beauty in every little thing. It's said that Maris was so precious to Diana that she gifted her with control of the oceans. Her sister, who was always starting fights, was sent to rule the wind. This angered Rosa. She wanted to be in charge of something more important than an unseeable force. Her anger whipped up the wind, causing great storms. She raged just to destroy the delicate balance of Maris's tides. So, Diana gave her favorite daughter the gift of foresight so she could warn the people who lived where the tide met the sand when one of her sister's storms was coming."

One sister, logical and ill-tempered. The other, whimsical and full of wonder. It should've been a beautiful story of balance. But instead, it spoke of fighting and jealousy.

Without trying, I thought of my own sister. Sera. We weren't like Rosa and Maris, but we were very different people. By the time she was born, I was seven years old and already an outcast. With my silver lilac hair and lack of magick. She was cherished by our coven from the start. Doted on by her father, who rarely spared me a glance.

Mama never let me hold Sera, but sometimes I'd watch her sleep in her bassinet. Tucked in quilts stitched with moons and stars. And I thought she was the most wonderful thing in the world.

Her father died when she was a year old. It happened during one of Mama's many missions to destroy demonic relics. As my little sister grew, Sera became a hurricane of a girl. Blowing raspberries at our aunties during her lessons and chasing crows through the cemetery. She was like my very own relic. My moon. My only source of joy in a home that felt like a cage.

"Favor," the woman said softly, "has a way of making *enemies*."

I bristled at that. I'd never been jealous of Sera, not really. Sera took no joy in being more talented than I. If anything, as she grew older, she became even more reckless—balking rules at every turn and daring punishment—just to take attention away from me.

It was one of the reasons I loved her. And one of the reasons I worried about her so much.

"What does any of this have to do with you?" I asked, emotion suddenly clawing at my throat.

"Everything!" she hissed. "Magick flows from the gods. *All* of the gods. Including their daughters." Steam settled around her like a veil, cloaking her in a robe like a priestess. "Maris's devotees became the first Witches of the Tide. And that is who I am. Imogen Thadashi. Witch of the Tide."

Her eyes flashed brilliant green, and the cavern was flooded with light. The lake churned, and hot water slapped against my knees, soaking through my robe. I didn't doubt that Imogen had the power to control the water, or that she possessed the gift of sight. But magick didn't make someone honest. There was a reason why she was telling me this story. I just didn't understand it yet.

"If this story is true, then where are your fellow witches?" I asked.

The green light that had filled the cavern dimmed, and Imogen's shoulders sagged. "There was a time when the little goddesses and their devotees, witches of their respective trades, lived in harmony. Maris's Witches of the Tide and Rosa's Witches of the Wind weren't fond of each other, but they knew each was as important to the balance of magick as the Witches of the Light and Darkness. But divisions began, as they so often do. And eventually, the little goddesses and their magick disappeared."

I raised a skeptical brow. "What happened to them?"

"What happened, indeed?" she repeated. "It's hard to say."

Now it was my turn to cross my arms. "I thought you were a seer."

The old witch gave me a doleful look. "Seers don't have all the answers. At least not when it comes to the gods. All I know is when the war between the goddesses was over and the dust settled, the only magick remaining came from either Damien or Diana. Without their daughters' magick, the world became duller. Less playful. Less kind. And so the Witches of the Light and Darkness blamed each other. Turning *sister* into *enemy*."

I might not trust this Imogen completely, but I understood this part. She was right. Our world wasn't playful or kind. And Mama had always needed someone to blame for the weak spells or my purple hair. If something went wrong, it was because dark magick was allowed to exist. It was the vampire's fault for always protecting them and living in castles while the wind whistled through our windows.

And I'd believed her. I'd blamed Bastien, too, in the beginning. Absently, I started rolling the horn between my palms. My thoughts wandering through all that I'd heard.

If Diana and Damien were so powerful, why couldn't they

make their daughters get along? Why allow their daughter's people to die in an endless war? Only to let it happen all over again between their own people? The questions twisted inside me, shame and anger rising, until I didn't know who deserved my rage more: my mother, these gods, or myself for believing any of it.

"If this is all true, and the daughter's magick died out, then how are you still here?"

She turned her attention to the rows and rows of seashells she had stacked along the rocks. Straightening them one by one. "By Maris's grace and the power of my people."

As she moved the shells around, the air grew thicker, making it difficult to draw in a full breath. Almost like the cavern had sucked all the air out. The white wolf growled. The brown one snapped his teeth, hackles lifting.

"I am the steward," she continued. "The very last water witch. Tasked with staring into these waters with the hope that ancient magick will return to the world."

Despite the sickly hot temperature of the cavern, a chill ran down my spine. The goddesses. The war. The intimacy between Diana and Damien, only for it to all burn. It all swirled inside me until my hands were shaking and I didn't know what to believe.

"I've spent many, *many* years waiting for a sign of Maris's return. For an inkling that the goddesses have reawakened and their magick is gathering. Because a witch is *nothing* without her coven." Her attention drifted to me. "But I don't have to tell you that, *do I?*

"What do you mean?" I asked, hands trembling.

Imogen just stared at me, the green light intensifying, until the brightness blotted out my vision and the cavern dissolved beneath the sudden roar of water. When I opened my eyes, I had been transported somewhere else. I stood on a rocky outcrop carved into the cliffside, where the sound of the water-fall nearly drowned out screaming. Where the scent of wet earth and brine almost masked the metallic tang of fresh blood. A single tear rolled down my cheek.

But as quickly as the vision came, it slipped away, dissolving like a dream. I blinked again, and I had returned to the near-dark of Imogen's cave.

"I think you know *exactly* what I mean." She gestured at my pocket. "But if I need to spell it out for you, that will cost you your shells."

The familiar anger that lived under my skin and on the edge of my tongue was back. She was trying to manipulate me, just like Mama had. The horn came to life, and a blood-red light shone from it, spilling over my hands and across my legs. My shells. That's all she wanted. That's why she lured me down here. It was all for her own gain.

I stood, framed by my growling wolves. "It's time for me to go."

All humor drained from the old woman's face. "We had an agreement," she asserted. "A story for a question." She unfurled her long, bony fingers. "You must pay up."

I turned, determined to leave. "I don't need to ask you anything."

"No?" she asked. "Not even how to remove your necklace?" The question slipped under my skin and found purchase there. When I turned back around a thin smile cut across her face. "Ah. How the tides have turned. There *is* an answer you seek, even if it is not the one you should be looking for."

The cavern seemed to be listening. Even the steam had stopped swirling.

"You know how to remove my necklace?" I asked, and hated the way hope had slipped in.

She nodded once.

I reached into the pocket of my robe. They were just shells. Useless things. Trinkets. If she could give me a way forward— *any* way—then the price was nothing. Besides, I knew how to make more.

I dropped the shells into her waiting hand. "Fine. Tell me how to remove this necklace."

The old witch licked her lips greedily, so pleased with herself, before letting her eyes meet mine once again. "Which necklace? The bloodstone? Or the cursed choker?"

I stared at her blankly. "The choker, of course."

Imogen dropped the shells into the bubbling water. The lake responded immediately, spiraling inward like a whirlpool. She dragged her hand through the water, urging it on. I couldn't look away, not even when she began chanting. Drips of water fell from pointed stalactites, raining down on me. Her eyes flooded the space with an emerald light so fierce it stained everything. The walls, the ceiling, my skin.

"In order to remove the cursed choker," she began. I was holding my breath. The lace collar strained against my skin as my muscles tensed. "You must *die*."

CHAPTER 8

LA TENTATION

CLAIRE

The sound of blood pounding in my ears drowned out everything else.

I'd come searching for answers, but what I got was a death sentence. The same one I'd had when I left my home. Except now, I knew it didn't matter if I discovered the location or relics or not. In the end, the choker would kill me.

Imogen sank below the water, disappearing for so long I thought she might've drowned. The whole time I stared impatiently at the murky water, hoping for a sign that this was all some joke. But no such sign came.

Eventually, the witch reappeared, her silver hair dripping down the side of her face. Her skeletal fingers clutched a handful of shells. I realized she'd been collecting the ones she'd thrown into the water. She beamed at them like they were her children, showing off yellow, chipped teeth. "At last," she hissed, speaking directly to the shells.

I had no idea why this old witch wanted these shells, but if she was so thrilled to have them, she owed me a better answer. "What did you mean, *I have to die?*"

She swam toward her collection of shells and placed the ones in her hand with the others. "I don't think that requires clarification."

"There has to be more to it," I insisted. "A spell. A potion. Something you can give me to break the curse." My voice climbed an octave despite my best efforts to remain calm.

Imogen's expression went blank. "Funny," she said, "your husband had the same reaction when I told him how to break your matebond."

The pounding in my ears doubled. "My... what?"

"Bastien came, just as you came, desperate for a spell to sever your bond."

My chest tightened painfully. Bastien—here? In this place? It was almost impossible to imagine.

"And I told him the same thing I'm telling you. There is no escaping fate. Not unless you want to involve the gods."

I tore off my robe and shoved it into my closet, searching for something to wear as I battled with my thoughts. Ripping gowns off the rack in a flurry of black and gold, barely considering each one before tossing it on the ground.

"None of it is true," I reassured myself. "Not the goddesses. Not her prediction. Not the fact that I have to die to remove the necklace." I paused, gripping a dress. Bastien would never have asked for a way to break our matebond.

A sob lodged itself in my throat, making it hard to breathe. Maybe he had thrown a handful of shells into her lake, begging for a way to rid himself of me. He'd been angry enough with me after what happened at his Sanguination Ball. If that were true, he'd been carrying around this knowledge the entire time.

I threw the dress on the ground. "It was all lies."

Strengthening my resolve to find real answers from someone I trusted, I chose a black lace dress draped over gold satin. It had a pretty square neckline and long, tapered sleeves, with a row of buttons running up the center. I dressed as quickly as I could, fumbling over the million buttons.

Before leaving to find Devlinn, I paused in front of my vanity. My long, unbound red hair hung in thick waves. I'd never been taught how to style my hair in the ways of a real lady, let alone a duchess, but something needed to be done about it.

Hesitantly, I twisted it into a bun at the nape of my neck and secured it with pins, adding a thick black headband to cover up as much of the red as I could. Once I was satisfied, I tucked the horn inside my dress pocket, called to my wolves who walked at my side like two guards, and made for the wing of the castle where my consorts resided.

While our bedchamber was warm, the corridors were chilly—not just in temperature, but in mood. No one spoke to me, save for a curtsey or bow acknowledging my title as Bastien's sanguine partner. Our marriage was a secret, but that didn't stop the judgment. I felt it in the lingering glances at my red hair and the wolves padding at my side.

Bastien demanded respect and acceptance of all that came to Château Rose, and I was sure they had no problem with me being a Dark Witch. However, I didn't look the same, and surely the sudden change in my appearance raised questions.

Lena, the kind older woman who handled all affairs relating to consorts, startled when I approached. "Miss Donadieu!" she exclaimed before taking a moment to school her features into a smile. "I hardly recognized you! Your hair!" Shame flushed in my cheeks. An old shame. Put there by Mama. "It's—"

"Beautiful."

I turned and found Tansy standing in the doorway. Devlinn behind her. And the parts of me that felt confused and alone were soothed.

The two were a portrait in opposites. While she had deeply tanned skin and moon-white hair, he was pale, with freckles speckling his nose and copper-red hair.

Her arms were crossed, but she was wearing a cheeky grin. "I'm going to miss the lilac, but this suits you."

It would suit me better once my magick was working properly. I slipped my hand into my pocket, drawing comfort from the relic. Devlinn's eyes followed, and I wondered if he sensed its power too.

Tansy caught Lena's hands, folding them between her own. "If Alec returns, will you send him to the tea room?"

The brightness slipped from Lena's face as though someone had drawn a curtain. "Of course, dear." Her eyes flicked to me, apology sharpening them. "Miss Donadieu, I'm terribly sorry for all this trouble. If you'd prefer to meet the other consorts—"

Tansy cut her off once again. "We'll speak with Miss Donadieu about what's happened. But you'll tell us if there's any word?"

Any word about what? Confusion pinched my brows together. I opened my mouth, questions already climbing up my throat, but Tansy pinned me with a look.

"Come. Let's have tea." She tucked my hand into the crook of her elbow and led me out of Lena's office, guiding me through winding halls to a tearoom I'd never seen before. It was all black lacquered walls, dark wood grain, and gold accents. While it was Bastien's colors, it didn't feel like a room he'd ever voluntarily use. And not just because tea wasn't his drink of choice.

As soon as the attendants were excused and the door was closed, Tansy wrapped her arms around me, holding me tight against her. I soaked in her warmth and positivity for as long as I could. "It's so good to see you, Claire."

"It's good to see you too." She rubbed my back and made soothing sounds as she held me, rocking us back and forth. I buried my face into her white hair, just like I'd done countless times with Seraphina. Little by little, the anger I was struggling to control melted, allowing me space to breathe.

So much had happened since I last saw Tansy, and the gravity of it all was finally sinking in. Including the echo of the old witch's voice.

"In order to remove the cursed choker, you must die."

I didn't want to think about that right now. It would be easier to call the whole trip down to Imogen's cavern a fever dream and be done with it. But there was something I couldn't ignore. The fact that my trio of friends was missing a member.

"What's happened to Alec?" I asked.

Tansy pulled back to study my face. Her dark eyes lingered on the cut on my brow, the one I'd earned when I'd fallen headlong into a gravestone. Along with the red hair and unstable magick. "I was about to ask you the same question."

Ask me? How would I know where he was? I'd only just returned home. "I haven't seen Alec since the last time we were all together in the ballroom."

Tansy cursed under her breath, then nibbled on the edge of her thumb.

"What's going on?" I asked. "What's happened to Alec?"

The legs of a chair scraped loudly across the floor, breaking the moment. Devlinn had pulled out a chair for me. "Perhaps we should sit."

Reluctantly, I sat. He pulled out the chair to my right for Tansy before taking the one to my left. My white wolf placed herself between Tansy and me.

She cast a wary glance at the animal. "A new pet of yours?"

"Something like that," I replied coolly. The brown male came to sit beside Devlinn, who pretended to ignore the wolf. "They won't hurt you," I reassured them. "Either of you. I swear."

"Good to know," he said with a thin chuckle. Devlinn poured each of us a steaming cup of dark red herbal tea that reminded me of the shade of Alec's eyes.

I wrapped my hands around the warm cup. Steam rose, reminding me of the lake I was trying hard to forget. "Tell me about Alec. What happened?"

"Last night, after you left with the Duke, Alec was beside himself," Devlinn explained while stirring sugar into his tea. "He was going on and on about how he needed to talk to you. He said there was something important he needed to warn you about."

"Warn me?" I muttered. "About what?"

Tansy let out an exasperated huff. "We don't know! He wouldn't tell us! We chased him down to the stables, trying to stop him. We told him this was *not* how things worked." She lifted her teacup, but didn't take a sip. "We explained that he couldn't just steal a horse and go riding after you while you were with the Duke. But he wouldn't listen!"

"That's right," Devlinn confirmed, biting into a cranberry scone. "He was completely mad. Tore off into the night. Lena sent riders after him, of course, but none have returned."

I sat back in my chair. What could've been so urgent that Alec would ride out alone after me, in a land unfamiliar to him?

He wasn't from the Unified Territories, nor was he a warrior like Bastien. If he'd gotten hurt, or worse, *killed...* A cold pang of guilt twisted in my gut.

"Maybe he wasn't mad," Tansy said, more quietly. My gaze shifted to hers, and I found her studying the gash above my eye. "Maybe he was right to try and warn you." She set her cup down and leaned forward. "Claire, what happened to you?"

For a moment, I found it difficult to breathe. I wasn't ready to explain what happened in the graveyard. It was easier to talk about with Bastien because he was there. But now that I was sitting in front of two people who had no idea what I'd been through, in this very formal tea room, with a vase of freshly cut moonflowers sitting in the center, my voice stuck in my throat.

This wasn't a story for tea.

"You wouldn't believe me."

The white wolf set her muzzle in my lap, pushing her cold snout against my hand, as if to say *she* understood. She'd lost members of her pack, too. I set my hand on her head, gently petting her soft fur. As soon as I did, a scene flashed before my eyes. A woman and a man abed, entwined together.

"Why wouldn't we believe you?" Tansy reassured me. "We're your friends. Besides, you're sitting with the king and queen of unbelievable stories. Who has crazier stories than two witches who don't charge their magick, and who come from different covens? If anyone is going to believe you, it's us."

She was right. Of course, she was. I tried to find the words to explain what had happened. "Last night, the Duke and I were attacked."

Devlinn's tea cup clattered onto the saucer.

"Someone attacked the Duke?" Tansy rushed to ask. "In his own territory?" I nodded, and she covered her mouth.

"It wasn't just *someone*," I said, then stopped, unable to get any more words out. I was in the tea room and the graveyard at the same time. I was shivering despite the warm tea. I could taste the coppery flavor of blood in my mouth, which made my head swim. I was living in two realities at once. Stuck in two timelines woven together, no matter how much I wanted to separate them.

I drew in a deep breath and told myself I was brave. That I was strong. That I'd survived. But it didn't stop the tears from falling past my lashes. I wiped them away, embarrassed for crying in front of them. But I'd nearly died. Bastien had nearly died. Had it not been for Cora, I wouldn't be here to tell this story. She saved us both.

"You must die." Imogen's words. Haunting me again.

I'd escaped death once, only to be told it was inevitable. I reminded myself they were all lies. She was trying to manipulate me. She knew telling me these things would unsettle me. About my death. About Bastien.

"You don't have to tell us if you don't want to," Devlinn said. "It's okay. We understand."

I slipped my hand back in my pocket and gave the sheep's horn a squeeze. When I did, the worst of the sadness and fear began to trickle out of me. "No, it's okay. I want to tell you." I drew in a full breath and tried again. "The Duke and I attended a funeral at Kemp Manor. Or what I thought was a funeral. There was a spell. Some ritual. It went wrong and—"

"In generationem et generationem," Devlinn said. When Tansy and I gave him curious looks, he elaborated. "That's the spell. Well, it's a funeral ritual. It transfers ancient magick from generation to generation. It's sacred in old families. Not every coven has that kind of power."

"So you've heard of this before?" I asked.

He raked a hand through his red hair, mussing it. "My coven didn't possess that kind of magick. Probably why my family was so twisted and bitter." He expelled a humorless laugh. "That kind of inherited magick is rare. It's said to have come from the time when Dark Witches and demons would, *you know...*"

He left the rest of his sentence hanging, his gaze dropping to the swirling tea in his cup.

"Fuck?" Tansy offered.

Devlinn laughed again and lifted his cup to Tansy in acknowledgment. "You always know how to take the words *right* out of my mouth, love." He smiled at her in a way that warmed my heart. "Yes, when demons and Dark Witches would *fuck.* Long before the Blood Treaty forbade summoning demons."

My mouth dropped. First, Damien and Diana. Now demons and Dark Witches? *Was everyone having sex?* I removed my hand from my pocket and wrapped it around my teacup, trying to find a steady breath. Slowly, the dots began to connect. This darkness inside me. The simmering anger. The endless want. It wasn't just dark magick. It was more than that.

It was... *demonic.*

But if this magick was passed down between generations, then I shouldn't have received it, even if I was the most decent witch in that graveyard. "I think they were trying to pass it down," I explained, "but the spell didn't work. Something went *wrong.*"

There was a charged silence.

"It went to you, didn't it?" Devlinn said.

Tansy covered her hand and gasped, "Oh, Claire."

I kept my gaze trained on my cup, trying to stay present. "It all happened so fast. And after it did, they all came for me. Accusing me of stealing the magick. Bas—" I slipped, catching myself a second too late. "*The Duke* defended me."

I didn't mention feeling occupied by the darkness. Nor did I mention what I'd done with the horn alone in my room. Or Imogen's prediction. It was all too much, and I was already stripping pieces of myself bare that were still raw.

"Well, of course, His Grace protected you. He's a decent man. Not to mention you're his sanguine partner," Tansy said, completely unsurprised.

I swallowed hard. It was more than that. Much more than that. But I couldn't tell her that either.

Devlinn regarded the wolf at his side, then said, "You're more than just his sanguine partner now. You're a powerful Dark Witch. One with the power to lead an entire coven."

"I couldn't lead a coven," I said dismissively. "I don't know the first thing about dark magick."

I saw the tears swimming in his eyes. Saw the bone-deep empathy. Neither Devlinn nor Tansy charged their magick anymore. They chose to live a magickless life. But he understood better than I did what it meant to have dark magick.

"Claire," he said, "if the stories are true, you are more than just a Dark Witch, but a *living* relic. A source of demonic power."

I held his gaze, a crease forming between my eyes. It felt like trying to push a puzzle piece into a space that didn't fit. How could I be a source of demonic power when it wouldn't even work for me?

"I need your help understanding what that means, because these so-called ancient powers *aren't* working for me."

He scrunched his nose. "What do you mean?"

A swell of terror rose up, threatening to drag me back to that graveyard, but I clutched the horn even harder, leaning on it for strength. If I wanted answers, real answers from people I trusted, *unlike Imogen*, then I had to be honest. "Right after the magick came to me, I had the power to call flames from the dirt. But then," my voice wavered, "they just *stopped*."

Thoughts of my *experiment* with the horn and the candle swam through my head. "I can't seem to make the magick last for longer than a few moments. Even with a relic."

I reached into my pocket and removed the sheep's horn and set it on the table. When I did, a thrum of power shook the cups on their saucers.

CHAPTER 9

ENTRE DEUX MONDES
CLAIRE

I immediately regretted putting the relic on the table. It didn't belong beside scones and bone china. The curves, the point, the ridges—they belonged *with me*. In *my* hand. My fingers twitched in my lap, aching to snatch it back, but something inside warned me it was too late. What was done was done; the moment had already shifted.

Devlinn moved aside a sugar bowl to take a closer look. "Where did you get this?"

I swallowed hard, strangling the folds of my dress to keep my hands still. "It was given to me. By one of the Kemps."

Had it not been for her... Had it not been for the kindness and bravery of one person... I straightened my back, unable to take my eyes off the horn. "She asked me to charge my magick and preserve her grandmother's powers."

Devlinn reached out to touch it. I shouted, "Don't!"

The word had leapt from my throat, not of my own volition.

Beads of sweat collected along Devlinn's brow, glistening in the spaces between his freckles. I glanced at Tansy, who had paused with her teacup halfway to her mouth, her fingers trembling just enough to make the porcelain rattle against the saucer.

"I'm sorry," I said, trying to regain a measure of composure. "I just don't think you should touch it. That's all."

He gave me a weak smile. "Of course."

I took a sip of my own tea, which had gone cold. "Do you have any theories as to why I can't access my magick?"

Tansy and Devlinn exchanged a glance across the table. I waited, forcing patience even as my nerves threatened to crawl out of my skin. The clock on the wall ticked incessantly, each second scraping at my composure. After visiting Imogen, I needed real answers. Finally, Devlinn tapped his fingers on the table, eyes brightening with sudden realization. "Hold on, you're not a Kemp, are you?"

I shook my head. "No."

"If you aren't a Kemp, then the magick won't recognize your blood."

"Dark magick is so much cooler than moon magick," Tansy said under her breath.

Devlinn turned his chair toward me, startling the brown wolf. "Easy, boy," he said, patting his head, before continuing. "This kind of magick is passed down from generation to generation, which makes it tied to a bloodline. Only someone from that bloodline, in this case, a Kemp, has the power to become a living relic. Right now, the magick is just sitting inside you with nowhere to go."

Finally, someone had words to explain what was happening to me. This insistence inside of me was equal parts rage and desire.

"Yes!" I exclaimed. "That's exactly what it's like." A rush of relief settled over me. Now that I'd identified the problem, there was only one thing left to do. "How do I fix it?"

Devlinn bit his lip and tapped his fingers on the table again. The gesture made my heart pound. The answer was close. So close I could feel it. "Oh! I've got it! You could open a channel between you and the demon from whom the power originated and ask it to reestablish the line of succession."

Tansy sucked in a breath. "You can't be serious. Claire can't summon a demon! It's not allowed in the Unified Territories. Not to mention it's *dangerous*."

It wasn't the advice I was expecting, if I *was* expecting anything. What if the demon said no? Would I be stuck like this? Holding power that I could hardly use? Or worse? My hand rose to my throat, touching the lace collar around my neck. Would the demon take the magick away and leave me empty? Now that I had magick, I couldn't go back to being useless again. I wouldn't.

A sense of calm and surety washed over me. Even from where it sat on the table, it was feeding me invisible waves of magick. The power calmed me and focused my thoughts at the same time. No one was going to take *anything* from me.

If I wanted my powers, all I had to do was ask for them. It would be easy.

"Claire?"

I inclined my head. A hazy smile on my lips. "Yes?"

Devlinn reached for my hand, slowly, giving me time to pull away if I wanted to. His fingers curled around mine, his touch gentle as he took my hand between his. A warmth spread from where he was touching me. It collected in my chest and cradled my heart. I drew in a full breath, then another, feeling more like myself.

"There's more to being a living relic than just making flames come from the ground. Are you sure you want these powers?"

Tansy set her hand on my shoulder, and another warm

pulse came. "There's a reason why we left ours behind. The gods give us these powers, but they don't seem to care what happens to us once we have them." Tears shone in her eyes. "Everyone uses magick to hurt each other. I don't want that life for you."

My friends were supporting me, and yet scared for me at the same time. It caused an ache to form in my throat. I didn't want to hurt anyone. I just wanted to live a good life with the man I loved. But the only way to make that happen was to fight. To live.

I couldn't tell them the truth. Not about Mama's curse. But I could give them another. "I want to use magick to help myself. T-to free myself."

A pinch. A squeeze around my throat. Warning enough that I was going too far.

"From His Grace?" Tansy asked.

I shook my head, more tears collecting in my eyes. "No. Not from His Grace."

Tansy and Devlinn wrapped me in a hug, their arms twining around me until I was cocooned in their love. It was a magick of its own, having friends like them. The moment stretched on and on, as they held me and I held them. Tears slid down my cheeks. I was sad, so deeply sad. And angry. And desperate to be the woman, a witch, who could never be hurt again. I didn't push the feelings away. I let them stay, knowing I was safe with them. At last, they released me and returned to their chairs.

Tansy pushed her teacup aside and leaned in. "We should leave."

"The tea room?" I asked, confused. Blotting my tears with a cloth napkin.

She shook her head. "No. I mean, leave the Unified Territories."

I was too stunned to speak. Tansy gestured to Devlinn. "Tell her."

"There are isles south of here where it's warm all the time, and no one practices magick. We've heard whispers that they all worship logic."

It felt like cold water had just been poured over my head. Imogen had used the word *'logic'* when she spoke about Rosa. Damien and Diana's daughter. One of the two lost goddesses.

Tansy beamed at me in a way I'd never seen before, almost like the sun was shining on her, even inside this tea room. She brushed her long white braids behind her shoulders. "There's an island where people are committed to doing things that make sense. No witches. No demons. No war. Just peace and the ocean and logic."

Logic *and* the ocean. Rosa *and* Maris.

"And the world's best rum," Devlinn added with a devilish grin. "They use it in fruity drinks that you sip out of a coconut. Because what makes more sense than that?"

I shook my head, dismissing this, because I needed to ensure I was hearing them correctly. "You said the people worship *logic*? And they live on an island in the middle of the sea?"

Tansy giggled, looking younger and happier than I'd seen before. "Yes. That's what I said. Why do you look so confused?" She gently ran her cool fingers along my brow, studying the cut there. I winced. "Claire, how hard did you hit your head? We should take you to the healer before we pack our trunks."

Imogen's croaking laugh echoed in my ears. As if I could hear her mocking me through the layers of rock. As if to say *I wasn't lying about any of it.* Not the story. Not my death. Not Bastien's inquiry about how to break our matebond. I began trembling all over in a way that not even the horn's power could calm.

"We should leave," she continued. "Together. You, me, Devlinn, and Alec if he shows back up. We could be each other's family."

I was speechless. They wanted to run away? *With me?* They wanted to be my family? No one besides Bastien had ever offered me that kind of unconditional love. No strings attached. No need to prove myself. Just acceptance.

Her attention narrowed on the cut on my brow, and she grimaced. "This is what magick does," she said. "It consumes everything in your life. *Everything*. And His Grace, he was *made* from magick. Reborn in it. He cannot escape it. But we can."

Leave? Bastien? The words didn't even make sense. "No. I can't leave. I'm His Grace's sanguine partner. I am under contract."

They huddled closer to me. "Claire," Tansy said in a soft voice, "we love His Grace as much as anyone in this castle. He has paid us well and treated us even better. But there is going to be a war that even his army can't stop. I can feel it."

"We found a ship that sails south," Devlinn added. "It's not far from here. We can board it and never look back. We can live in peace. Away from magick. Away from all this pain."

I stared back at her in disbelief. I hadn't come anticipating this.

"Doesn't that sound nice?" Tansy asked. "Seashells and sand?"

I closed my eyes and saw the little pile of seashells that had appeared to me earlier. The ones I'd conjured with the horn. *The ones that Imogen had greedily taken.* I thumbed over the bloodstone Bastien had given me, thinking of him. Feeling into the bond between us. It was endless. My love for him was endless.

My future, my everything, was tied to him. And not just

because he was my mate, but because he was the person I wanted.

"I have love for you both," I admitted. "And if you want to find this island and drink rum from coconuts, then I wish you well. But I have to stay here." I couldn't stand the sad looks on their faces, so I continued, trying to explain something that I couldn't. "I have *obligations*."

Tansy frowned. "What obligation could be more important than to yourself? To find a quiet place to settle in peace?"

An uncomfortable tightness formed in my throat. There was so much I wanted to say, but our marriage was kept secret because the situation with the High Prince was so precarious. And I certainly couldn't tell her about Mama. So I just shook my head.

"Then why stay?" she asked. "Claire, the Duke is kind. After what happened to you, I know he would let you leave. He would understand. He would want you to be happy."

He would. He would want me to be happy. But what she couldn't know was that no world existed where I was happy and not with him. And even though Bastien said and did things I didn't agree with, we did have one thing in common. We were both concerned about the safety of those we loved more than our own happiness. He had the people of Roselyn, and I had Sera.

"Happiness is hard to hold on to," I said quietly. "It's not a rabbit you can trap, or a place you can visit. It slips through your fingers. I've learned there are things more important than being happy all the time."

"Like what?" Devlinn asked.

"Duty. Honor." I paused, thinking of the little baby that I wanted to hold more than anything. "*Love.*"

Tansy drew in a surprised breath. "Is that it? Do you love the Duke?"

CHAPTER 10
INTERLUDE

Did you miss me? I bet you did. You've been thinking about me ever since the story started, wondering if I would return. Hoping I'd interrupt for a little one-on-one chat.

You see, I understand your desire better than most. Probably because I'm a demon, and demons are pure want. But not in the mortal sense. We don't sit around wondering *if* we'll get what we want. For us, it's only a question of *when*.

And oh, I've been patient. So, so patient.

What's that? You want to know exactly what I've been waiting for? If you say *please*, maybe you'll get your wish. Go on. Say it. Right into the pages. I can wait.

Mm. What a bad little girl you are, conspiring with a demon. When you bite your lip, it's hard to say no, but I think I'll let you squirm a little longer. You look good like that.

What I *will* divulge is my realm of specialty: sex and disease. You're giggling at that, are you? Pretending those things don't cross your mind? Or maybe you're intrigued.

Either way, it won't surprise you to learn that mortals are always begging for my help.

Want your good-for-nothing boss to itch and ooze for weeks? Bring me an offering. I love a good goat. Need revenge on a cheating husband? I'll turn his manhood into a rotting stump and make sure he lives long enough to understand exactly why I did it.

Look at you, giggling again. You're even thinking of a request. Someone you want to geld. Aren't you? Fuck, I love that. I bet if you're honest with yourself, you're already kinda into me and the work I do. Easy now. I'm not here to get you wet, so don't get your knickers in a twist.

I'm here for my own reasons. Reasons that I'll be keeping to myself.

I hate to run off and leave you unfinished with such a juicy story dangling, but don't worry, we'll meet again. And when we do, blow me a kiss to let me know you remembered our little chat.

Oh, there's one last thing before I go. It's a request. Just a little thing. Don't tell Bastien you heard from me. Okay? Let's keep that our little secret.

CHAPTER 11
ESPIONNER
BASTIEN

When I discovered that Claire was alone with her consorts inside this tea room, I decided to follow one of the rules we established. I'd give her three minutes before I interrupted.

However, my vampiric hearing meant I was an invisible guest at the table. Forced to listen while two people in my service plotted to rob me of my wife.

My hands shook with barely contained rage, and I shoved them inside my pockets for fear I was going to break through the door and rip their throats out. I could almost taste their blood as it splattered across my face.

The only reason I remained where I stood was that they were right. She'd be better off settling on some quaint island where the weather was warm, and she would never be cold again.

Where I couldn't hurt her. And I had hurt her. Not just earlier today. But when I led her into that graveyard.

Tansy had asked, "Do you love the Duke?"

I waited for her reply, wishing, not for the first time, that I could be the kind of man Claire deserved. A man with a beating heart. A man who didn't need blood to survive.

"Claire, do you love the Duke?" Tansy asked again.

Breathing was more a habit than a necessity for me, yet I found myself holding it all the same.

"I do. Love him. *Very much.*" Pride and happiness swelled inside me, almost like my heart was beating again. "As many in his service do," she added.

I rested my forehead against the door. I didn't think I could take much more of this.

"And because of that love," Claire continued, "I cannot abandon him to handle this burden on his own." There was a tense pause. "I'm not supposed to repeat this, but apparently the Witches of the Light have discovered a way to become *werewolves.*"

Werewolves who had learned how to sneak past the boundary between lands.

"No," Tansy was saying. "That can't be true. They wouldn't."

"They *have*," Claire asserted. "I saw proof myself."

Hector's head in that box. A memory I would never forget. A good man. A good witch. Someone who had welcomed me into his home. And it was that very friendship, and his desire for peace, that had gotten him killed.

"Do you think that's what Alec wanted to warn you about?" Devlinn asked. "That werewolves were coming? He said he'd been scratched by one."

I froze. A new thought worming into my mind. I'd assumed the magick to make werewolves had come *from* the Lawless Lands, but what if that wasn't true? When Alec was first brought to my tent for questioning, he claimed to have seen a werewolf and bore a scratch to prove it. And now, he was missing.

One of her wolves whined, and Claire hushed it with a few reassuring words. I put my hand on the doorknob, ready to break up this conversation, needing to see my wife, when the sound of Claire's voice stopped me.

"They are coming to cut off the source of dark magick because they don't want balance. They want power. And they want to destroy everyone and anything that threatens their twisted worldview."

Claire had come so far after being raised at the Nightfall Convent. That she could embrace another viewpoint after two decades of indoctrination spoke volumes about her. Many witches with the same upbringing refused to accept the truth she saw so plainly.

"If there are werewolves, we need to *run*," Tansy said. "They'll come for *everyone* with red hair. It won't matter if you charge your magick or not. Trust me, I grew up with witches who were waiting for something big like this to change the game."

Of course. It wasn't just the Prideaux. There were other witches who harbored old grudges. They didn't have the desire to strike out without a way to defeat us. But if there were creatures who matched vampires in strength, perhaps more would defect.

I wanted to believe the Blood Treaty still meant something. That the peace I died to protect was still possible. Otherwise, everything was for naught. And I wasn't ready to give up yet. The more people we convinced to join us, the stronger the treaty became. It was one of the reasons I wanted to see the covens of the Lawless Lands brought together.

But Claire didn't need to be caught in the middle of my vows. I shouldn't be allowing it.

A chair pushed back. Then came Claire's voice. "There might be an island where logic reigns, but how long will that last? When will they come for it, too?"

No one said anything.

"The Duke stands for tolerance and acceptance. He fights for it with every fiber in his being. And that's the kind of future I want. A place where people aren't turned into weapons or forced to run from their homes. And if that means I need to walk through shadows, then I'll trudge through the dark. If that means I need to spill blood, I will face my fear of it. If it means I need to learn the ways of demons, then I will walk all the way to the Underworld if I have to. Whatever needs to be done to end this. Because I'm done letting other people decide my future."

It was quiet for a long time. I battled with myself, fighting against my desire to open the door and take her into my arms. I wanted to protect her from her own bravery.

And where it would lead her.

"I hate that you're right," Tansy said courageously. "There's a reason why we all met. And I think it's because you're supposed to help her, Devlinn."

Help her with what?

"Just so we're all on the same page," Devlinn replied, "we're saying no to the drinks and the rum and the sun to hunt werewolves?"

Tansy let out a humorless chuckle. "Yes. That's what we're saying."

"Well, I'd follow you anywhere," he responded.

I might've called Devlinn's vow pathetic before I knew what it was to love Claire, but now I understood. When you loved someone, truly loved them, there was nothing you wouldn't do for them. *Nothing.*

I pressed my lips together and closed my eyes, fighting the guilt churning in my stomach.

"If we do this, it can't be tonight," Devlinn explained. I straightened. Clearly, I'd missed something important before arriving. "It must be under the new moon, when Diana's influence is the weakest, and the veil between the Underworld and ours is the thinnest. The next one is in two days."

"We'll already be in the Lawless Lands. The Duke intends to ride tomorrow," Claire said.

I wrenched open the door, startling the two consorts. "Your Grace!" Devlinn rushed to say. The two struggled to their feet, Devlinn tripping over a chair as he did, then fumbling into a bow. Claire pushed out of her chair slowly.

Without breaking eye contact with my wife, I said, "You are dismissed."

Each of them kissed Claire's cheek, said goodbye, and exited the tea room. When the door was closed and we were alone, Claire set her hands on her hips. "Why am I not surprised that you were listening?"

"I told you I'd give you three minutes with your consorts if I required your company. I was generous and gave you four."

Claire raised a brow. "And what do you require?"

It was hard to stand across from her and not go to her. Not touch her. Hold her. But she was still angry with me, and I had to stop being so selfish when it came to her.

My gaze settled on the cut across her brow. I loved her with every ounce of my heart, but I was bad for her. In every way. She should run. As far and as fast as she could.

"Your consorts wanted you to leave with them."

"So what of it?"

The image of that little baby flashed in my mind. Everything about me, even my child, threatened her.

I opened our connection. I needed her to feel my words, not

just hear them. *"The war wouldn't spread that far south, not in your lifetime,"* I admitted. *"And if you wished to leave with Tansy and Devlinn—"*

"No," Claire interrupted.

"I'd offer you money and an escort to take you all the way to the Isles of Markal. I'd sign a contract stating you're still under my service so as not to trigger the conditions of your necklace. You could get far away from me and all of this."

By the time I was done, I was breathing heavily. I wanted to tear the fangs from my mouth. Wishing I could be a different man. A better one. One who could board a boat and go with her. One that hadn't sacrificed my life and afterlife to preserving an ancient treaty that no one seemed to care about anymore, save for those of us who were there.

Claire approached me with tears blazing in her eyes. Her emotions poured through me as if they were my own. The hurt. The pain. The soul-deep ache to be desired and loved. And... the love she felt for me. I could feel it like it was alive and real. Solid and immovable.

"Why would you say such things?" Claire demanded. *"Is that what you want? To send me away?"*

I didn't want to hurt her, but this hurt paled in comparison to that which could befall her. This was her last chance to have a quiet life. Away from me. Away from that horn. Because I loved her so much, I owed her a choice.

"Of course it's not what I want," I admitted. *"But I won't lie to you, Claire. Staying with me is not the easy path. Or the safe one. Not when it takes us to the Lawless Lands."*

"It's not easy for you either," Claire said. Fresh tears were leaking down her pale cheeks. *"There are consequences—"*

I couldn't bear to see her cry. Not again. Not at my hand. So I hugged her to my chest, holding her against me as tightly as I dared. I drank in the sweet smell of her hair and ran my hand down her back in soothing strokes. *"You could have a good life."*

She gripped my shirt, holding me closer. *"I already have what I want. You stubborn mule. Why is that so hard for you to accept?"*

Did this woman know what she was saying? I was trying to protect her. *"I'm dangerous. I'm going to take you to a dangerous place. For Diana's sake, I drink your blood."*

I knew saying that word would trigger her, yet I said it anyway to make a point. We could use other phrases for what I did. I could dress it up. Make her more comfortable. Drink from her inner thigh instead. It would not change the truth—I was a monster who only took from her. Claire released her hold on me, and I did the same. Regret and relief coursed through my veins. Maybe she finally understood.

She backed up a pace and wiped the tears from her eyes. When she did, I noticed a shift in her. The deep well of emotion had closed, and what replaced it was *something else*. Something darker. Something I could smell in the air. Something... that made me stand a little straighter. She blinked, and her honey-brown eyes flashed *crimson*.

She was using dark magick. I didn't think she realized what she was doing, but she was casting a spell, working her influence. *On me.*

My attention drifted to the horn on the table. I studied the curve of it. The color of it. I imagined how it might fit in my hand. I tried to remember the night everything in my life changed, embracing the memory instead of avoiding it like I usually did, but my human memories were distant.

Claire dragged a finger across the curve of the horn, and all of my desires narrowed into a singular focus. *My wife.*

"You're bad for me, is that it?" she asked. Voice thick.

A terrible war waged inside me. Between the beast who

wanted to protect her from me and *him* and everything, and the pull of her. Of our bond. Of my deep love for her.

"Yes."

She hummed in the back of her throat. A wicked smile stretched across her face. The scent of her arousal filled the air. It was... distracting.

"I see," she said. Plucking one of the white flowers from the vase and tucking it behind her ear. *"You're bad, and I'm just your precious moonflower. A helpless damsel in need of protection."*

Helpless? No. Never helpless. Just mine to protect. Just... *mine.* Blood rushed to parts of my body, coaxing them awake.

"That's not it." I shook my head, watching as she began to unbutton the tiny buttons on the front of her gown. I grabbed her hand, stilling her progress. *"You're too good for me. Too good a girl. You deserve a beach and warmth and..."*

Our eyes met, and Diana forgive me, instead of buttoning her back up, I ripped the damn thing half open. My breath stuttered at the soft swell of her breasts. I wanted to touch her. Taste her. Give her everything. Anything.

"You deserve someone to fuck you rotten." I dropped my hand, curling my fingers into a fist. I couldn't do this. I was stronger than this. *"I should be hanged for the things I've said to you. That I've done to you,"* I said. *"I'm–"*

"What, Bastien?" she asked, setting her hand on my chest. *"Bad?"*

"Yes," I choked out. I was bad. Very bad. She should know this. The way my cock strained against my trousers was a clear indication. She didn't look convinced, though. If anything, it was turning her on. The scent of her arousal was growing stronger. *"I made you my wife when it was against the law."*

Claire grabbed a chair, set it in front of me, and then climbed onto it so we were eye to eye. Nose to nose. Chin to chin. Chest to chest.

"Do you wanna know a secret?" she asked. My throat bobbed up and down as I swallowed hard. *"You don't scare me, Bastien Allard."*

Everything inside me stilled. I'd heard that once before. When I'd held a knife to *his* throat and told him I had come to banish him to the Underworld. *He'd* said the very same thing. Except... he'd called me *Sebastien*.

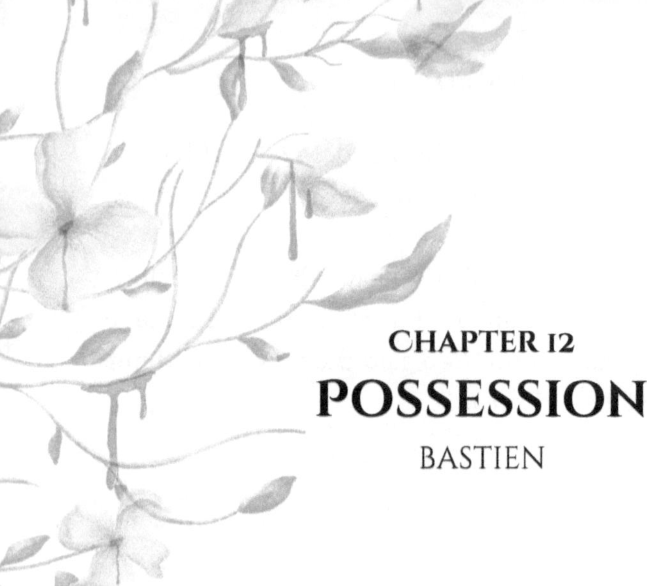

CHAPTER 12

POSSESSION

BASTIEN

I didn't want to believe the powers Claire had received during Temperance Kemp's death ritual were from the very demon I once banished. But it was hard to deny what was right in front of me. Just as I was starting to suspect that horn had not come from a sheep, but from *his* head.

In my youth, he was the first person I'd met who was like me. We both had tempers. We both didn't quite belong. And we were both attracted to men and women.

My coven wasn't a safe place for those like me, as my own mother often said. And the demon fed off my desire to explore my sexuality. I'd like to say he used me, but perhaps I used him, too. It was hard to remember now.

I took comfort in the fact that he was safely locked away in the Underworld. And the powers Claire had weren't *him*. They were only a piece of him. A piece that he must've seeded into the Kemp family. I also knew that his horn was just a source of power, not his mind. I'd told Claire Dark Witches weren't evil, and I'd be a hypocrite if I started treating her power as if it were.

This was about my past. Not her. I was the one seeing *him* where he wasn't. Claire was just trying to figure out how to live with her new magick. Something told me she was reaching for her magick because I was making her feel ashamed. And I didn't want to shame her in the way I'd been.

"I'm still waiting on your penance," Claire said. "How long are you going to keep me waiting, Bastien?"

I took her face between my hands and smashed our mouths together, mating our tongues in a wild dance. I grabbed fistfuls of her skirts, dragging them up until they were around her waist. Letting my fingers scrape over her garter belt as I did. I wound my finger around the strap and tugged at it, making her moan in my mouth. But I didn't stop there. No. I wanted more. I trailed the curve of her deliciously full ass and squeezed her hard. Reveling in the way her warm skin felt against my palm.

"I should terrify you," I said between kisses. *"Right now, I want nothing more than to tear your clothes off and drink my fill of you."* My fingers brushed against something lacy and soft, and I realized she was wearing some little scrap of fabric masquerading as undergarments. The knowledge sent fresh hot blood straight to my cock until it ached.

"Such a big, bad vampire," she teased.

Through our connection, her pleasure crashed into me, and suddenly, I was overcome with her emotions. With her deep feelings for me. And with... *her desire for more.* It was endless. She just wanted me inside her. Proving to her that I'd never try to send her away again. I could feel it as though she was shouting the words in my head.

Carefully, I bracketed her face with my hands. We could tease each other, but before this went any further, I wanted her to know the truth. *"You mean everything to me. Everything. More than the moon or the stars or this castle. You are my world. My whole world, Claire. And I just want to be good to you in the way you deserve."*

Candlelight reflected off her brown eyes, making them look molten gold. So delicate. So sweet.

She cupped my cock over my trousers and squeezed. I sank my teeth into my lower lip. Hard. Threatening to draw my own blood. *"The only thing I'm scared of,"* she said, *"is losing you."* She dragged in a slow breath. *"Tell me you'd never try to sever our bond."*

I threaded my fingers into her hair and drew a long, measured breath. This wasn't just about some carnal need for her. It was about feeling close. About knowing I wanted her close.

"Never," I murmured.

"You're sure?"

I pulled her closer, until my lips were nearly against hers. This time, I spoke my feelings aloud. "You are mine. I told you that the night I made you my wife. But if you need to hear me say it again, I will. Our love isn't about bonds. There is no cosmic tether holding you to me or me to you. Only the certainty that my life is yours. My breath is yours. We belong to each other. Even on the day Damien calls you to the Underworld, I will stand between him and you and demand he step aside."

The tension in her body melted like frost under the sun.

It was in that moment that her realization crystallized. She finally understood that nothing she could ever say or do would alter the depths of my feelings for her. Our bond was inextricably intertwined. My love unyielding. I was hers, and I would move heaven and earth to protect her.

Our lips met again in a maddeningly slow kiss. Open and wet and deep. It invaded my heart as much as it did my skin. Like I was trying to consume as much of her goodness as possible, and she was trying to swallow all of my darkness. The centuries of war and pain and loneliness. There was room for all of it inside her.

Like I was enough for her.

She moaned again, accepting my tongue as it slid inside her mouth. Claiming her. Tasting her. I broke off the kiss, both of us breathing hard. For a moment, I was lost in the lines of her face, standing atop that chair like my very own goddess.

Carefully, I removed the pins holding her hair up until her long hair flowed down her shoulders in shades of burnished copper. Another tear of blood dripped from her cut, and I couldn't stand it. So I reached for the last piece of my humanity that still pulsed with warmth. Though I lacked the power to heal her wounds completely, having sacrificed much of my power to become what I was now, I could at least close it.

I brushed my fingers over her skin and called to the very last of the magick that I had reserved for our treacherous journey through the mountains. It would be two weeks before I could recharge what little power remained to me.

Once it was done, she said, "How could you ever think you're bad?"

I lifted a brow. So, she wanted to see just how bad I could be? I backed up a few paces and turned the lock on the door, ensuring no one would interrupt us. Standing on that chair with a dress half-ripped, I admired my mate.

"Take off your dress."

The order was firm, and I enjoyed watching her eyes widen in surprise. "What if someone hears us?"

I smirked. "This is the consort wing. All these rooms have silencing enchantments on them."

Claire returned my smirk, then carefully stepped off the chair and undid the remaining buttons on the front of her gown, teasing me inch by inch. She slipped off one sleeve, then the other, and the dress easily fell to the ground. Showing me what was hiding beneath the heavy fabric.

My beautiful wife. With all her edges and curves.

"Claire," I gritted out. My jaw clenched. "Just look at you."

My hungry gaze raked over black nylons and up to the thin straps holding them to the belt around her waist. Then to the lace wrapped around her sex. My breath caught, but I didn't look away. Slowly roving up her stomach to the swell of her full breasts. Nipples taut and hard for me. The moonflower was still tucked behind her ear, making her look so innocent.

She smiled at me. Her smile. Not one of a demon. And it reassured me that I was right. Just because she had his power didn't mean he was influencing her. It was just magick. Magick, she didn't know how to control.

"Turn around," I said. "Let me see the rest of you." Claire spun in a slow circle, doing as I asked. "Did you put on that scrap of lace just to tease me?" I asked, throat dry.

The wry smile on her lips told me the truth. Without breaking eye contact, she lifted herself onto the edge of the table. Legs spread. Then beckoned me closer.

CHAPTER 13
FANTAISIE
BASTIEN

"What are you waiting for?" Claire asked.

Truthfully, I was savoring the view. With one foot propped up on the table and a hazy smile on her face, it was an image I never wanted to forget.

"Tell me what you want."

With a cheeky grin, she pulled the scrap of lace to the side, revealing all of herself to me. "I want you to watch me."

She slid her finger over herself, trailing down until it disappeared inside. A moan escaped her lips. One corner of my mouth curled up. Tomorrow, we'd ride into danger. The weight of responsibility pressed on me, but she was the reason I carried it.

She played with herself for as long as I could stand. But after a few minutes, I couldn't take it any longer. I shoved the back of the chair against the table and took the seat in front of her.

I gripped her ankles, guiding her feet onto my thighs. My lips trailed gentle kisses along her knees, then up the insides of her legs to my prize. I dragged her hips closer, mouth hovering above her heat. She gasped, but I held back.

"You have all my attention," I told her. Tilting my chin to look at her. Taking in the wild waves of red hair falling down her shoulders. The soft bow of her lips. Exquisite. Mine. "What does my wife want now?"

My fingers dug into the soft flesh of her ass, squeezing. She stammered out a few incoherent syllables. "J-Just you. I just want you."

"You already have me."

I bit softly into the soft flesh above her knee, teasing. A contented sigh escaped her lips, and by the gods, it was delicious. I didn't merely want her—*want* was too simple a word.

"Tell me what you want."

She tensed. "I'm nervous to say."

"If there's something you want," I told her, "I will give it to you."

"I don't want to start another argument."

My curiosity was piqued. But more than that, I wanted her to feel safe with me. "You won't. Just tell me."

She hesitated, then met my eyes. "I know you have your reasons for not wanting a baby, but just for right now... can you set that aside?"

"What do you mean?"

She let out a sigh and ran her fingers through her hair. "Bastien, I want to hear you say you *want* to come inside me. Just like you did that night I found you in the feeding tent. Something about it really turned me on."

It seemed we shared the same fantasy. I studied her face, waiting for her to continue.

"Can you pretend that you do want a baby with me? Can you pretend that you'd love nothing more than to get me pregnant?"

Standing, I pulled her against me and held her. It took a lot of bravery for her to bring this desire to me, especially considering our earlier argument, and I was proud of her. I kissed her cheek, then leaned back to look at her.

"Claire, I don't have to pretend that I want a child with you."

Her eyes widened. "You don't?"

"Of course I don't. I've always wanted a child." A knot formed in my throat, and I found this part was hard to say. "But I went unmated for centuries. And after watching my brothers marry and remarry their mates, and have more and more children, I put that dream aside, and committed myself to my job." I touched the side of her face. "I want to have a child with you. But if anything happened to you. If you were hurt because of me. Because of something *I did to you…*"

She placed a finger against my lips. "If you want it, and I want it, can we just pretend?"

"I already told you, I don't have to pretend. I think about the same thing." I pressed a kiss to her temple. "As long as you understand where my boundary is. Because as much as I might want to, I'm not going to risk it. Not right now."

"I understand."

"Good. And… one more thing before we get started." I remembered the way she rubbed the relic over her breast last time we were together, and even though I *knew* it wasn't *him*, I didn't want to see that right now. I needed more time to get used to it. "No horn. I just want this to be the two of us."

She hesitated, and I could tell she didn't like this condition. "I feel stronger when you touch me while I'm holding it. I can feel my power opening."

"If we're really going to try this, then I don't want magick involved. Let's pretend that we're just two humans who can do whatever we want. Who are leaving tonight to take a boat to that tropical island, free to live our lives for us."

For a moment, I wasn't sure if she was going to agree. I saw that dark flash in her eyes. The desire for power. The need to make herself stronger. But I wasn't going to give in. If we were going to do this, I would be taking on all the responsibility. It was on me not to slip, no matter how badly I wanted to, and I had no idea how her magick might influence me.

Finally, she relented. "I can agree to that."

She pushed the horn further away, and a sense of relief coursed through me, along with the desire to drop fully into this role as a man who not only desired his wife but wanted to give her a child.

Her fingers raked through my hair like she needed something to hold on to as I moved to her breast. Licking and sucking. Lavishing her with attention. I moved to her stomach and lingered there, pausing to look up at her. "I'm not holding anything back tonight," I whispered. "You're about to find out just how depraved I am. How I'd give *anything* to cum inside you."

"Bastien," she moaned.

I drank in the sound, as if it were my first sip of blood, letting it fill every corner of my being. My mouth returned to her skin, feathering kisses over her hips and along her legs. I was about to kiss her center when she tugged on my hair and pulled my face up to hers, smiling wide. Cheeks pink. I realized I was smiling, too.

"Before you take over, I want a turn." Her gaze dropped low, and I knew what she was asking for. I was loath to give up my turn between her thighs, but I wanted to encourage her to keep asking for what she wanted.

"You want me in your mouth, chérie?"

"Yes," she gasped.

With one more kiss to her inner thigh, I helped her off the table and gave her my seat. She looked up at me, eyes wide. She was so beautiful it was hard to breathe. Hard to believe someone like her had come into my life. I cupped the curve of her jaw, stroking a line across her cheek. "Then take what you want."

Claire unlaced my trousers, and I watched her with eager eyes. Her obedience was only a false sense of control. I was hers to command. And I always would be. My trousers fell to my ankles, revealing the hard length of my arousal, and Claire didn't look away.

I stepped out of my clothes and boots, fisting myself once before returning my hands to her face, gathering her silky hair in my hands. She sank her teeth into her lower lip, and I had to restrain the monster inside of me.

"Look at you," I rasped. "Are you ready for a taste?"

She nodded, and her pink tongue skated across her lips, wetting them for me. I stroked her cheek gently. "That's it, darling."

I readjusted my grip on her hair as she took the tip of my thick sex inside her mouth, her lips stretching around me. "That's good. That's so good. Take as much of me as you want."

Claire took me deeper, sucking me in and out, letting me fill her up with every piece of me. My body. My heart. My wretched soul. She moaned around me, and by the goddess, it felt too good.

I pulled myself out, and she looked up at me with lust in her eyes. Pupils blown wide. Unable to conceal her smile. "If you don't stop, I'm going to cum in that pretty mouth of yours." I brushed her wet lip with my thumb. "And we don't want that, do we?"

"No," she said eagerly.

"Get up and turn around for me." She stood slowly and spun around. Her long red hair flowed down her back. "Now bend over and grab the table."

Glancing over her shoulder, she gave me a wicked smile and did as I asked. Giving me the perfect view of her gorgeous ass. I hooked a finger around one of her garter straps and let it snap against her skin. She gasped. "When I'm done, you're going to be dripping wet. So full of my cum."

A wave of unadulterated pleasure spread from her and crashed into me, mixing with my own desire for her. For this. For the wish that our lives weren't complicated by magick and war.

I kissed my way down her back and over her curves, then shifted her damp panties aside, angling my hips to slip between her legs. I slid through her heat, massaging her sweet spot with my cock. With our connection open, I could taste the red-hot desire racing through her.

It took every ounce of self-control not to bury myself inside her.

"Please," she begged.

"Easy, my love," I said. "Not yet."

"Why?"

I ran my fingers over her, playing with her clit, soaking up each little moan, then dragged those same fingers across my tongue, sucking the taste of her off me.

"Because I said so." I walked around her and put one hand on the table. "And because I'm not done with you yet."

I shoved the dishes off the table, sending teacups and scones clattering to the ground. Porcelain shattered. I didn't care.

"Breaking things?" she said with a grin.

However, I was not smiling. "I'd break anything in your way."

Her smile melted into something darker. The space between us warmed. Lifting her up by the waist, I set her on the table and eased her back until she was lying down for me. Then I plucked the moonflower from her hair and slowly dragged the soft petals down her body, starting at her lips and gliding down her neck. Between her breasts. Over the smooth line of her stomach. Watching as goosebumps rose over her skin. I let the blossom follow the lines of her body. The soft V between her thighs. The curve of her hips.

"Bastien, please," she moaned. "I want it. I want you."

I set the flower down. "I like it when you beg for me." I dropped back down in the seat and set her legs over my shoulders. "Does my greedy wife want more?"

"Please."

I licked over her lace panties with slow strokes. She was warm and wet and oh-so-sweet. She squirmed. Her nails biting into my arms. "Hold still for me. Or I'll have to stop."

A soft whimper left her lips as she forced herself still. "Look how good you are for me." I slid the lace aside and found the place that made her melt. Each stroke of my tongue built the pull of desire in her. I could feel it. Inching her closer and closer to the edge.

She wanted more. Needed more. And I was going to give it to her.

I slid a finger inside her, curling it up and stroking the place that made her tremble. In and out. In and out. When she was *right there*, so close to falling over the edge that I could practically taste it, I let her teeter there. Giving her just enough to keep the pleasure alive but not quite enough to send her over the edge.

"I'm so close," Claire panted out. "Bastien, I can barely stand it."

I did not stop until she was twisting beneath me. Ready to take me the way I wanted to fuck her.

I dragged her undergarments down. Unfastening garters as I went. Leaving nothing behind but black nylons peeling down her legs and her leather boots. Claire propped herself up on her elbows to watch me as I wrapped the wet lace strap around the base of my cock. Eyes locked, I spread her legs wider and stepped between them. My dripping tip teased her sensitive entrance, gliding back and forth across her slickness. Letting the smooth lace tease both of us.

I thought I knew what it was to be painfully hard, but for her, I ached. I needed, wanted, craved her, And I wanted to make her come all over my cock.

"Sit all the way up for me, love," I told her. And when she did, I scooted her to the edge of the table until she was pressed up against me. Her hands bracing her weight. I took one of her legs and hiked it up on my hip. "You'll stay just like this for me. Won't you?"

She nodded.

"Good." I pressed a kiss against her neck, drawing in the scent of her deep into my lungs, wanting it to become a part of me. "Because I'm about to put a baby inside you."

As the words left my lips, I knew I was lost inside the fantasy.

"Bastien. Say that again."

I slid inside her warm pussy until there was nothing left. She gasped and moaned and clenched down around me. So tight. So sweet. All mine. I had to will myself not to lose control. "I'm about to put a baby inside you." I eased out of her, then thrust back in. "But you have to come for me first."

A string of incoherent words fell out of her mouth.

The table groaned beneath us. Threatening to break the way I wanted to break. I didn't stop until she bore down around me, clenching so tight. Through our connection, she screamed my name, and I roared with pleasure as she came around me. Lost to everything in the world but her. Another groan and crack came from the table, and I lifted her off it, still inside her. She clung to me, riding me, coaxing more waves of pleasure.

Every time the lace around my shaft rubbed against her, my eyes rolled back, and I had to clench my jaw to keep myself in control.

"Nothing feels better than you," she gasped. Her forehead pressed against mine. Sweat dripping down our bodies. "Nothing feels better than this."

"We'll see about that." I walked us to the wall and put her back against it. Letting her slide all the way down on me. Both of us were breathing heavily, foreheads pressed together.

Feeling her, all of her, cracked open our connection even wider. Each beat of her heart thrummed inside my chest like it was my own. The trust blossoming between us radiated around me. This was what it was like to truly be with someone. Trust them with your heart. It was a love like I'd never known before.

I dragged myself slowly out of her, only to thrust back in, harder this time. Claire moaned with pleasure, and I kept going. Thrusting deeper and faster.

"Bastien!"

The way she screamed my name, out loud, broke something loose inside me. "This is the only thing I want to do for the rest of my life."

Claire cried out my name again as her release built for a second time. I pumped in and out of her like I'd been born to do this. Made to make her come.

A feral noise tore from her throat.

"I'm all yours," I said, pumping in and out. In and out. "And you know it."

She was back on the edge, just where I wanted her. But I kept my pace, leaving her wanting because I had more to say.

"I'm not going to stop until I'm dripping out of you. And then I'm going to do it again, just to make sure it takes. Do you understand me?"

"Yes," she panted. Her nails bit into my skin as she ground down on me. Her tightness quivering around me. I bucked my hips into hers, giving her the friction I knew she needed. Unable to tear my gaze away from her face.

Our bloodstones snapped together like two magnets, and every feeling intensified until I was worried I might not last, which wasn't going to happen.

I pulled out of her for a second, just to carry her to a small conversation couch and set her down. I had never been harder in my life. Never wanted anything more. I caught the back of her knees and slid back inside her. From this angle, I could let loose. Fucking like a man possessed. My tight sack and the wet lace slapping against her with each hard thrust until I felt her pleasure cresting again.

"Oh, Bastien, I'm coming!" she screamed.

I picked up speed, hard and fast, making her clench around me, so tight and wet, until I couldn't take it.

"I'll come with you," I told her.

I wanted this fantasy to be real. I wanted to give her every single drop of my seed just to watch it leak out of her, but I couldn't let myself get that lost. At the very last second, I pulled out, fisting my thick length. Letting my cum find her stomach. Her tits. Her thighs. Working it free until there was nothing left.

I collapsed on the floor beside the couch, breathing heavily, my hand finding hers.

"Bastien?" Claire said tentatively.

I raised my brows. "Yes?"

"I—I've never felt this close to you."

I kissed the back of her hand. "Me either."

She touched the side of my face, staring into my soul with her molten brown eyes, when a line formed between her brows. "Never try to send me away again. Okay?"

I regarded her with such love in my heart, remembering when I thought our bond was cosmic punishment by the gods, only to realize it was so much more than that. Her love could never be a punishment.

I just had to be strong enough to keep her safe.

I kissed the top of her head. "I promise."

CHAPTER 14
FRANCHIR
CLAIRE

We left at twilight the following day. The mountain pass between the Unified Territories and the Lawless Lands was too treacherous for a coach, so I rode with Bastien.

It was hard to share a horse and pretend he was nothing more to me than an employer. Especially when his free hand was splayed over my stomach, holding me protectively against his chest.

"We're approaching the edge of the Blood Treaty's protection," he explained against my ear.

I nodded, but tried not to think about it.

After we'd left the tea room, he'd taken me back to our bedchamber and laid with me in our bed. Continuing the fantasy, Bastien kissed my stomach and whispered "I love you" in a way that brought tears to my eyes. I knew it cost him something to pretend like this with me when we had differing opinions. It only deepened my feelings for him.

Afterward, we lay beside each other and shared our dreams for the future. He told me about the youth home being built in the city where he intended to care for war orphans, and promised to take me there when we returned.

I shared my hope that my sister would come to visit us, and he told me she could stay as long as she liked. And when I fell asleep in his arms, I knew this was the future I was fighting for. It made breaking the curse on Mama's choker even more urgent.

In a day, when the moon was invisible, Devlinn would help me communicate with the demon whose magick lived inside me and ask it to reestablish the bloodline of inheritance.

As we navigated the knife-edge road down the mountain, I tried not to think about the fact that we were one strong wind from being thrown off, and I wouldn't have to worry about demons or curses. Instead, I tilted my head into the crook of Bastien's shoulder, looking up at the riot of stars. They were beautiful this far north, like a blanket I could curl up in. I searched for pictures in the sky, recalling the time I had stared up at it with Sera.

We spent many warm summer nights outside, making up stories about the stars. Our favorite was about the brave witch in the sky. In our tales, she was blessed by Diana with unimaginable power, and her spells filled the sky with stars so her people could see, even when there was a new moon. Now those stories felt hollow, tainted after meeting Imogen. I wanted to ask Bastien about the goddesses, but I couldn't bring myself to do it. Not because I didn't trust him, but because I didn't want anything the old witch had said to be true.

Bastien raised his fist to signal our host to halt. My wolves stopped beside us. "This is it," he declared. "The barrier between lands."

There was no line that marked the boundary, but I could feel the magick all around me. I tried to be brave, like the witch in our stories, but we were so far from the safety of Château Rose.

"Are you ready to cross?" Bastien asked in a low voice.

I hesitated only for a second. "Yes."

Bastien dropped his hand and urged Lucien forward. As soon as we were through the barrier, my hands began trembling, and perspiration broke out across my brow. Not wanting to appear weak, I kept my gaze fixed on the horizon, but the stars looked more like streaks in the sky, their colors exploding with light as if the brave witch in the sky had cast another spell.

A jolt of energy ripped through me, as if I had swallowed a bolt of lightning, and it was burning through every vein.

"Are you alright?" Bastien asked.

"I... I think so," I stammered, struggling to gather my racing thoughts. "It feels like...."

I opened our connection and let him feel everything going on inside me. He immediately halted Lucien. "Do you need to stop?"

His devastatingly beautiful face was illuminated by the faint glow of the stars and the remaining moonlight. "No. I think it's just my magick." I reached for the horn that I'd stuffed inside my fur-lined pocket, and the shivering stopped.

Bastien noticed the way I sought it out and frowned. After last night, when he'd asked me to set the horn aside, I knew there was something he didn't like about it.

Natalia rode up beside us on her white mare with an expression that would've made milk curdle. "Your Grace? Is there something wrong with the barrier?"

My white wolf answered, lifting her head and howling. The brown one joined her. Their voices echoing through the mountains.

"Shut those beasts up!" Natalia snapped. "Or everyone in the Lawless Lands will know we're coming!"

The anger that lived at the tip of my tongue came exploding out. "They're not beasts. They're familiars. And they sense things you can't."

She turned to her uncle. "You're going to allow an unruly pack of wolves to announce our position?"

"Fall back, Lady Natalia," Bastien said with a forced calm. "Your leadership is needed elsewhere."

His niece sneered at me but did as he commanded, falling back behind us. One by one, the army marched down the narrow mountain pass. As we pressed deeper, I continued to feel the same restless energy, the same shivers that had nothing to do with the cold. In fact, I wasn't even cold anymore. Sweat was soaking through my undergarments.

I wanted to ask Devlinn what this all meant, but he was too far back. So I sat with my anxieties and my magick as we continued to ride on through the night, not knowing what to do except hold the horn and pray for my powers to settle.

But I heard no response from the God of the Underworld, only Imogen's warning. *"In order to remove the cursed choker, you must die."*

Lies. They were all lies. I repeated it to myself over and over again, trying to quell the fear that was rising. But if they'd all been lies, then why had Tansy and Devlinn brought up that island?

I tried to be brave as the hours passed. The closer we came to the bottom, grass began peeking through the frost. Every once in a while, Bastien and I would talk in hushed whispers, but mostly he was silent, listening for trouble, and I was left to my own thoughts.

When we finally reached the base of the mountain, it was near dawn, and the muted light revealed an eerie graveyard that stretched for miles. Fog clung to the trees and grass, obscuring headstones jutting from the ground like jagged teeth. Many of which had iron cages over each plot.

Bastien slowed Lucien to a halt beside one such grave.

"Where are we?" I asked.

"This is the resting place of those who have fallen in battle."

The wind threaded through the iron bars, making them groan. "What's with the cages?"

"The witches place cages over the bodies to keep them from being used for ill will." When I gasped, he held me tighter against his chest. "Don't worry. We won't be going through the graveyard." He pointed to what appeared to be a stone mausoleum nearly hidden by snow-speckled moss. "That is the entrance to the graveyard tunnels that were created to allow those who carry peace banners to pass." My throat tightened. "They will lead us directly to the secret entrance of Chastity's underground stronghold."

He dismounted first, then grabbed me around the waist and helped me off Lucien's back. Once I was safely on the ground, his hands lingered on my waist, and the heat inside of me grew. With his hair whipping in the wind and his frost-colored eyes, he truly looked like a prince.

Bastien leaned down an inch, bringing our mouths a fraction closer. "I need you to tell me to back away," he breathed. "I'm feeling far too protective of you. And I need to do my job."

Even though I ached to feel his lips on mine. To hear his whispered promises. To let him linger a little while longer, we couldn't. Our marriage was still a closely guarded secret. It was against the laws of vampires to take their mates as sanguine partners. It was also against the law to command an army while mated. By all rights, we should be at the capital.

However, my husband was a stubborn man, and I believed in what he was doing.

"Back away," I whispered. "Do your job."

With my permission, he stepped back, but held my eyes for a long moment. Finally, he stalked toward the mausoleum. I followed after him, keeping my distance as he approached the arched doorway, and stopped a few paces behind him. Lifting his hand to the door, he knocked three times and said, "We seek safe passage under peace banners."

I held my breath and waited for something to happen. But nothing did. Bastien tried again, repeating the gesture, when the overwhelming scent of dark magick filled the air. Sweet and fragrant. There was a spell keeping the door closed. I could feel it. Natalia, Tyson, and Lady Okeri appeared beside me.

"What's wrong?" Natalia asked.

Bastien slammed his fist against the door. "The arch is sealed. Some kind of dark spell."

I didn't know why, but I felt suddenly guilty. "Why would they do that?"

"Werewolves," Natalia replied coolly. "Tracks are all over the place."

"And the stench of them is horrible," Tyson added.

A cold wind whipped through the graveyard, carrying the howl of a wolf with it. I pulled up my hood to keep the chill out, hoping I'd only imagined the sound. My wolves drew nearer, as if they heard it too.

"What are our choices?" I asked.

Bastien's eyes found mine. "Either we break the spell on the arch, or we take the long way around."

I stuffed my hand back into my pocket and found the horn waiting for me. Eager to help.

"There's only one problem," Natalia deadpanned. "We don't have an experienced Dark Witch to break the spell."

Bastien lifted his chin and scanned the ranks of soldiers gathering around us. "Send for Devlinn."

"I can do it." The words came out before I'd fully decided to say them.

Every eye landed on me. Natalia looked me up and down. "You don't count as *experienced*."

"Natalia..." Bastien growled.

"What?" she shot back. "She *isn't*."

Tansy and Devlinn approached. Her arm linked with his. Another wave of guilt and shame hit me. They were here, in this frozen graveyard, instead of on a boat, heading toward paradise.

"Your Grace?" Devlinn said, bowing low. I could tell he was leery of my husband after he barged in during our tea.

"Can you tell what kind of spell is on this door?"

Devlinn stepped forward and removed his fur-lined gloves. Carefully, he closed his eyes and pressed his hand to the stone. "It's a closing spell, Your Grace."

"I could've told you that," Tyson quipped.

"Shut it, Ty," Lady Okeri said, playfully elbowing him in the ribs. "Bad timing."

Devlinn placed his other hand on the door. "If I'm reading this right, the spell was placed on here by a demon. A powerful one. To counteract it with an opening spell would require an offering under the new moon."

Devlinn shot a look at me over his shoulder. I knew he was trying to walk a dangerous line between opening the door and helping me secure my magick through the ritual we'd discussed.

"So we're just supposed to wait until tomorrow?" Lady Natalia snapped.

While they continued to argue over which path to take, my energy kept building. I needed to do something. I had to protect my friends who willingly came along on this journey. If anything happened to them, it would be my fault.

"*Let me try,*" I told Bastien through our connection. It was only when everyone's attention settled on me that I realized I'd taken the horn out of my pocket and was holding it up.

In the distance, a crow shrieked. Another gust of cold wind sent strands of hair around my face.

Bastien studied me, uncertainty flickering in his eyes. "*I don't know—*"

"I can do this," I insisted, cutting him off. Speaking with words instead of through our connection. "Devlinn and Tansy can help me." Bastien's gaze hardened. He was going to say no. "*You've seen the fire. You know what I can do.*"

My husband pressed his lips together in a hard line, then relented. "Set up a perimeter and post guards. We're making camp."

He turned to Natalia and clapped on her shoulder, muttering something in Sanguisi. She gave a curt nod, then disappeared in the thick press of bodies.

CHAPTER 15
L'HÉRITIER
BASTIEN

I paced near the campfire where my nephew and his sanguine partner sat, reassuring myself that Claire was safe—tucked away with Devlinn and Tansy, working together on the spell that would open the arch. Knowing she was protected gave me the chance to speak to Tyson alone.

The cold gnawed at me, but it was nothing compared to the hollow ache in my chest. Steeling myself, I stepped closer to the fire. Okeri noticed me first, her smile slipping into something more reserved as she rose to her feet. "Your Grace," she greeted, curtsying. Her attention flicked to Tyson before returning to me. "Shall I leave you two alone?"

If only Tyson were half as observant as the women surrounding him. It would make my life so much easier. I nodded once. "If you don't mind. I need a word with my nephew."

Her lips twitched as though she might say more, but instead, she turned to the viscount. Whatever passed between them seemed to sober him slightly. *If anything did.* She slipped past me with a whispered, "Goodnight."

Regardless of how I felt about my nephew, I could respect his sanguine partner.

"If you're here to scold me, Uncle, you might as well get it over with."

I must've done something in a past life to upset Diana, because the humility required for this was nearly unbearable. Sighing, I gripped the bridge of my nose.

"Do me a favor and don't get yourself killed while we're out here."

"I didn't know you cared that much," Tyson said. "In fact, I'm fairly certain you told me you didn't."

"I don't," I snapped, though my voice sounded more tired than biting. Then I caught myself and forced myself to think of Claire and what I wanted to do for her. For us. For this family I couldn't get out of my head. "Marius has named you my heir, which means I have a vested interest in you staying alive."

His brows lifted. "What are you saying?"

"I'm saying, there will come a time when I'll need someone to take over for me."

Tyson cracked a smile. "You're not trying to make an heir, are you, Uncle?"

My answering growl cut through the cold air. Could he be serious for one minute? Or would I be forced to kill him before I told him what my intentions were? "Don't test me."

He raised his hands, palms out, but he was still smirking in a way that made me want to turn around and walk away. "My apologies."

I shoved my hands into my pockets to keep from strangling him. "As I was saying, there will come a time when Claire and I will need to leave. And when that day comes, you'll rule Château Rose. With Natalia's guidance."

The smirk faded from his face, replaced by something more serious. It was a look I hadn't seen on him before. He sat up straighter, brushing the snow from his gloves. An unexpected note of concern tugged his brows together. "If you return to the capital, you'll have to face Uncle Marius. You'll have to admit the truth."

"I know," I shot back. As if I hadn't considered the consequences. What did he take me for? A bigger imbecile than he was? I expelled a breath, my shoulders slumping as I took a seat beside him on the frozen log. I tapped the end of my cane into the slush between my feet. "I'm not counting on his mercy."

Marius had been a Witch of the Light once, just like me. And even though we gave up our allegiances when we made the blood oath to become guardians, I hoped goodwill still flowed between us. If not, and he decided I should die for my lies, then he'd have to fight me to the death. As much as I loved my brother, Claire was my mate, and I'd go to any length to protect her.

After last night, when we'd given in to that fantasy, I'd been considering what it would be like to have a child with Claire. Watching her stomach swell. Listening to our baby's heartbeat. I'd never thought fatherhood was something I'd get to experience. And while I had my reservations about what the baby would do to her physically, I told myself I would never let harm come to her.

For a blissful moment, Tyson remained silent, and together, we watched the flames dance over the wood. From the flames, I saw Claire pale and lifeless, her strength stolen by the very life she fought to create. The image burned behind my eyes. I didn't know if it was a premonition or a projection of my own fears.

I'd asked her to be brave, and it was time for me to do the same.

"Is the pull of the matebond really that strong?" Tyson asked.

"Yes. It is." I clapped a hand on his shoulder and shook him once. "One day, you'll experience it. And when you do, gods help you, you'll understand what I mean."

A smile crept across his lips. "I think I prefer the bachelor life. Maybe I'll be like you and stay unmated for five hundred years."

I let out a hollow laugh as I released his shoulder. "If you could be more like me in any way, it would be a blessing from the moon goddess herself."

His laughter echoed mine, but it didn't reach his eyes. He was uneasy, and I could feel it. I scooted closer, extending my hand. He hesitated, then clasped it. I pulled him forward. "I'm trusting you, Tyson."

"I know."

Perhaps he could see what this was costing me. But I couldn't trust him to intuit a thing. He had to be told. Explicitly.

"No, you don't know." My voice dropped to a rasp. "You could never know what it's costing me to hand my castle over to you. I never wanted to leave Château Rose. But for Claire, for the life we want to live, I will endure it."

His eyes widened, but I pressed on. "But hear me now. If you can't control your stupidity, or you make a decision that hurts the people of Roselyn, I will come for you. And when I do, there will be no law that can protect you. I will make you suffer in ways you can't imagine. In ways that will have you begging for the mercy of a death that will never come. You will be mine to torture until the end of time. Do I make myself clear?"

His bronze skin went slightly pale. "Yes, of course. I wouldn't dream of doing anything stupid."

"I hardly believe that." I released his hand. "But I'm trusting you anyway."

"I'll make you proud, Uncle. I swear it. No drinking. No games. No courtly attire. I'll keep with your traditions. I'll follow your example. Just maybe not with such a surly look on my face."

"Good." The word left my mouth automatically. I studied him for a moment. For the first time, I saw not just the boy he'd been but the man he was becoming. "When you stop trying so hard to act like you know everything, you almost look like someone who could lead."

His head jerked up. "Almost?"

I couldn't help the small smirk that tugged at my lips. "You've got a long way to go, but I see... potential."

The fire crackled, and he grinned. "High praise coming from you, Uncle. I'll try not to let it go to my head."

I snorted, shaking my head. "Try harder."

His answering laughter was genuine, and as it echoed through the cold night, I felt the faintest stirrings of something I hadn't expected: hope. I pushed myself off the log. "Don't forget to feed tonight. You need your strength."

Tyson nodded but otherwise remained thankfully silent. I stalked back to my tent, desperate to see my wife.

CHAPTER 16
L'INVOCATION
CLAIRE

The following night came too quickly.

I never thought I'd be on my knees—in the snow, no less—preparing to ask a demon for power. Yet here I was, preparing the ritual circle under lantern light. Every sound seemed amplified: the crunch of snow under my knees, the howl of wind slicing through the trees, the hiss of my own breath. Nerves and anticipation had my hands shaking, barely able to grasp the thin wand Devlinn had fashioned for me. The winter chill had stolen the feeling from my fingers, but I wasn't cold. Heat was burning beneath my skin like I was lit from within.

My vampire mate had insisted on attending the spell and wouldn't hear otherwise, no matter how many times I insisted his duty was with the army. He was hovering just beyond the circle, beside Tansy, like an inkblot in the snowy clearing. The only observers besides my wolves, my friends, and my husband were the guards stationed nearby.

Bastien still didn't know that I intended to open a channel to a demon. I hoped his ignorance of dark magick rituals would make it easy to explain this away. Perhaps I should've just told him the truth about my intentions, but he was on edge already. And I feared that if I told him what we planned, we'd already be making the long, cold march through the graveyard.

"Are you wearing anything that conducts magick?" Devlinn asked through chattering teeth from just outside the circle. I shook my head. "What about an amulet?"

I stilled, my gaze finding Bastien's. I wasn't wearing an amulet, but I was wearing something else of great importance. My bloodstone.

"Yes."

"Then it has to come off," Devlinn insisted. "It could interfere with the spell."

I didn't want to take it off, but I'd already come too far. Carefully, I set down the wand and went to pull my hair back.

"Stop."

It was Bastien.

And while he didn't agree with any of this, he came to stand behind me with the rigidity of a man performing a task he wished belonged to someone else. Someone who didn't know the taste of my mouth or the sound I made when he touched the back of my knees. Someone who hadn't whispered *I love you* against my belly in the dark quiet of our bed. Or who hadn't vowed to spend his life keeping me safe.

When he brushed my hair to the side, cold air kissed the back of my neck. A soft, involuntary shudder swept over me. The wind was so cold, even his fingers felt warm as they found the clasp on the chain. I had to fight the urge to lean back into him, and I had the sense he was fighting the urge to pull me into his arms and carry me back to our tent.

But we both resisted temptation. Carefully, he removed the chain he'd given me. As soon as it was off, an emptiness settled in my heart.

"Shall I keep this secured for you?" he asked. His words held a dozen meanings only I could hear. *Tell me when I can give this back. Tell me when I can breathe again.*

I nodded once, and he coiled the gold chain into his fist. I went to touch the empty place where the bloodstone had sat against my chest, but I stopped myself when I saw the way Devlinn and Tansy were watching us.

I told myself it would all be worth it when the spell worked.

"Kindly take a step back from the circle, Your Grace," Devlinn requested.

Bastien glared murderously at the red-haired witch.

"Please," I said through our bond. He drew in a long breath, then took a measured step back. Still close enough that he could lean forward and grab me if needed.

"You know what to do now," Devlinn reassured me.

We'd rehearsed the spell dozens of times. It was now or never.

Tansy gave me an encouraging smile. "You've got this."

I blew out a nervous breath, then lifted the horn into the air. "This circle is open. Let none disturb it." Then I slammed the horn against the frozen earth, embracing the very darkness I had once prayed would die out of the world.

A wave of energy reverberated through the air. And the wind began to pick up speed, circling around me, lifting my hair.

If I were to be a living relic, then I had to meet the darkness unafraid. "I ask for protection to be given during this spell. Lift my voice so it can be heard even in the belly of the Underworld!"

I didn't spare Bastien a glance even though I could feel his worry penetrating through the circle. I couldn't afford to let his fear stop me.

I called to the power beneath the earth, invoking the current of demonic magick that Devlinn insisted I'd be able to access. Sure enough, I felt it stir behind my palms. Felt it rise. Up my spine. Twisting in my gut. Clawing around my throat. The wind picked up, creating a wall of energy around the circle. "I call to the demon whose power resides in my veins, and ask him to join me in the circle!"

Bastien was gesturing wildly outside the circle, but I couldn't hear him over the sound of the wind and the blood thundering in my ears.

I waited for a shadowy figure to appear, but nothing happened. So I tried the words again. "I call to the demon whose power resides in my veins, and ask him to join me in the circle!"

My stomach lurched. I doubled over, coughing up a stream of black fluid into the snow. When it was done, my body shook with shivers. The black stain smoked where it hit the ground.

Bastien lunged forward, threatening to break through, but I raised a hand to stop him. "Don't!" I shouted. "I can do this!"

None of them understood how much I needed this to work. I wiped the liquid from my mouth, smearing it across my cheek, and set my teeth. The memory of flames burned in my mind—the wild, terrifying fire I had called from the earth. I closed my eyes and imagined speaking directly to the demon whose powers I possessed.

"I call upon your power, as your chosen vessel, your servant..."

Inside my head, a disembodied voice cut me off. *"You are no servant of mine."*

My eyes snapped open. That was not Bastien's voice. It was something else. Someone else. I looked at Bastien and knew, by the look of terror on his face, that he had heard it too.

My stomach lurched again, and more black liquid poured

out of my mouth. It was horrible. Disgusting. When it finally stopped, I was gasping for air, trying to find my breath again. The wind died down, and the clearing went still again.

"Why is she reacting like this?" Bastien demanded. Grabbing a fistful of Devlinn's fur cloak. "I thought this was an opening spell."

"She can't use her magick until the demonic bloodline is reestablished, Your Grace. The spell will be easy once she has full access to her magick."

He shoved Devlinn to the ground, and Tansy screamed. "Then why is she reacting this way?"

"I-I can only guess, Your Grace," Devlinn stammered while another stream of black vomit spewed from me.

I dug my fingers into the ground as my stomach churned. My throat burned. When the sickness finally stopped, and I could blink the tears out of my eyes, I realized my cloak and the horn were now covered in a thick, oily puddle. The smell alone made me want to be sick again.

"Then guess!" Bastien was shouting.

Tansy helped Devlinn to his feet. "It's like she isn't reaching her demon," he said. "It's almost like they're not in the Underworld."

Bastien went still. "That's impossible. He's there."

Through the sickness and the haze, I searched my husband's face. "You know whose power I have?"

He dipped his head. "Yes. His name is... *Gorrath*."

The name tasted familiar on my tongue.

"You're telling me Claire has Gorrath's powers?" Devlinn shouted. Sounding half-amazed, half-concerned. "*The Gorrath?*"

"Who is Gorrath?" Tansy asked.

"Who is Gorrath?" Devlinn said with a laugh. "Only the demon of sex and disease."

I stared at the black rot that had come from my mouth. Disease. And the desire I couldn't seem to shake, the near-constant ache. Sex. An anger that didn't feel altogether like my own tore through my body.

"I was the one who banished Gorrath to the Underworld," Bastien explained. "So I know he's there."

"This is the Lawless Lands, Your Grace," Devlinn offered. "They still summon demons. For all we know, Gorrath could be here. It would explain her symptoms."

Bastien flashed his teeth, and blackness consumed the blue of his eyes. "That's impossible!" he raged. "I sealed him there permanently."

I let out a snarl that sounded more animal than human. Bastien had banished my demon permanently? Things started to make more sense. His fear. His hesitance. It was cowardly.

"Tell me what to do!" I demanded of Devlinn, interrupting their useless bickering. "We need this power to unlock the door."

"Claire, you are done."

"You don't say when I'm done!" There was menace in my words, but I couldn't stop myself. I needed this to work. I wasn't going to let him stop it.

Bastien slammed his cane into the snow, then pointed it at Devlinn's chest. "Devlinn, get in there and charge your magick. You can unlock the door."

Tansy gasped.

"I won't do it, Your Grace," Devlinn said defiantly.

Bastien towered over him. "And what if I ordered you to?"

Without breaking eye contact with Tansy, Devlinn replied, "Then you'll have to kill me, Your Grace."

Bastien growled again, and I did not want him to do something he'd regret. "Enough!" I shouted at my mate. Then turned to my mentor, *my friend*. He was my only hope now. The only way I could free whatever was inside me. "Devlinn, tell me what to do."

He split a look between Bastien and me, as if waiting for permission to continue. When Bastien didn't immediately shove him to the ground, he got down on his hands and knees and faced me, just outside of the circle. Lantern light flickered across his features. "Claire, everything is going to be alright. Okay? I need you to know that first."

I sucked in my bottom lip to stop myself from crying. I was so angry, and tired, and burning from the inside out.

"Now," he continued, speaking slowly, "if you're not connecting with Gorrath, and he *is* in the Underworld, then you need more magick inside the circle."

A sob threatening break past my lips, but I wouldn't let it. Everything inside of me was trembling. "How do I do that?"

Devlinn spared Bastien another look. My husband looked like he was ready to draw steel any moment, but knew a sword wasn't going to help me. "There was one way my granny always swore by, and it-it's to make love in the circle. Release always pulls in dark magick."

The circle fell silent. Sex. The answer was sex. Somehow... I'd known. I'd known it was Bastien and the horn that would fix whatever was happening inside of me.

"You can't be serious," Bastien snapped.

Devlinn sat back on his heels and chuckled. "After watching your granny ride your papa in a chanting circle, you start to believe a thing or two about power."

I tried very hard not to allow that image to form in my mind. But it did anyway. And some of the anger flooded out of me. I remembered why I wanted this magick. And it wasn't just to open a door or to be powerful. It was to pursue the future that I wanted. Where I was free of this choker, and I could have a family with Bastien.

"Your Grace, I've seen it work," Tansy was saying. "Before we quit charging our magick, it was my favorite way to help Devlinn charge his."

I looked pleadingly at Bastien. He stared at me like he was facing a line of invaders. As if to say there was *no way* he was going to make love to me inside a magick circle so I could summon Gorrath.

"We're running out of time," I told him.

"It's too dangerous!"

I squeezed my fists together. *"This is who I am now."*

"I can help Claire, Your Grace," Devlinn offered, interrupting the silent argument. "If she wanted me to."

Panic clawed at my chest. "That is a kind offer," I said, trying not to look at Bastien. "But what about Tansy? I could never..."

"Claire, we became consorts for a reason," Tansy asserted. "We've never been intimidated by sharing each other. I know where his heart lies."

Their love was so strong, so pure, so endless that it was inspiring. To be so sure of one another. To know nothing, or no one, could tear you apart. I met Bastien's worried gaze and saw the passion and love there. I longed to touch him, to go to him. To make him see my perspective.

"It would be important that we release at the same time," Devlinn explained. "It's crucial to the flow of power."

A murderous rage flared in Bastien's ice blue eyes. Devlinn had no idea how close he was to being decapitated by my vampire mate. He would never allow another man to touch me, not even for this. But there seemed to be no other way. If he shut this down, I'd have to wait another month to perform the spell. And who knew what would happen in that time?

Devlinn stood and started removing his cloak, as if preparing to enter the circle, but before he took a step closer,

Bastien swung out his cane. "Close the circle. This ritual is over."

The anger was back. The heat was back. "No!" I shouted, my voice echoing through the clearing. Then something came bubbling up, a thought that drove me from angry to enraged. *"You were willing to help Hera secure her grandmother's magick, but you're not willing to help me get mine?"*

Bastien's eyes blazed.

"This magick is sitting inside of me with no outlet. If you think it's dangerous to call on him, it's more dangerous for me to keep this magick caged." Tears formed in my eyes. *"I need to speak with Gorrath and get him to reestablish the line of inheritance. So I can be balanced."*

He didn't move. He couldn't. And I realized this was one of those times that he needed me to give the order.

"Leave us," I told my friends. "Take the guards with you back to camp."

"Claire," Tansy breathed. "You can't be alone out here."

"My wolves will protect us. And the Duke is not without his talents."

Devlinn hesitated. "Your Grace?"

There was a long pause. My arms shook with barely contained magick that was begging for a way to be unleashed. The horn began vibrating insistently, and a sudden pulse of heat throbbed between my thighs. An ache. A need. A feeling so strong I had to grit my teeth and dig my bare fingers into the dirty snow.

My body knew what it needed. Him. And this horn. Together. And it was screaming for him to just listen to me.

"You heard her," Bastien said at last. "Go."

CHAPTER 17
INTERLUDE
GORRATH

Boy, does it feel good to hear Bastien finally say my name—something he's avoided for over five hundred years.

That's right, sweetheart. I am Gorrath. Demon of the Underworld. A member of Damien's High Court.

You're probably wondering how a demon like me and a moon witch like Bastien got tangled up in the middle of a war. Well, let's just say it was a lapse in judgment. The war had been raging for so long, none of us knew what peace looked like. Until one night, an armistice was called. Peace talks had begun. Drinks were flowing.

I saw him staring at me from across the fire with those baby blue eyes. I didn't stand a chance. Not after I got him alone and had a taste. What can I say? I'm a sucker for a man with blue eyes and a big cock. I'm sure you understand.

He was terrified we'd be caught that night and disowned by his family. I told him being yourself was always worth the risk of losing the people who claimed to love you.

Then he sawed off my horn and banished me back to the

Underworld. Sealing me there. Something he promised he wouldn't do.

Granted, it was less of a promise and more of a moan in my ear one night when we were alone. I don't have to tell you how convincing his pledges of fealty are. Do I? No. He's got you wrapped around his little finger.

I don't blame you. However, I do blame him.

CHAPTER 18
LA CONFESSION
CLAIRE

Once Tansy and Devlinn were gone and it was just the two of us, Bastien set his cane in the snow and removed his heavy fur cloak. He undressed quickly, removing piece by piece until he was down to a thin cotton undershirt and trousers.

"Do I have permission to enter your circle?"

I wiped what was left of the black liquid from my mouth. I couldn't believe he was agreeing to this.

"Words, Claire. I need your permission."

"Yes. Enter," I forced myself to say.

He lowered to his knees in front of me and undid the laces of his trousers, leaving them open. We stared at each other for a long moment, both of us breathing hard. Both of us stripped bare. Both of us willing to sacrifice our comfort, our morality, *everything* for each other.

I went to tell him how much this meant to me, but Bastien held up a hand. "There's something I need to say first." I waited, bracing for what was to come. But he simply said, "I'm sorry."

I wasn't expecting "*I'm sorry.*"

He ran a hand through his tousled hair. "I'm sorry for what happened that night."

"I already told you that you don't need to apologize."

He ignored me, barreling on. "I'm sorry I let things go too far, that I was blind to the intentions of the people around me. I'm sorry that *you* were the one who had to suffer."

The apology landed hard in my stomach. But I had a strange sense that he wasn't talking about that night in the graveyard. He was talking about something else. "What aren't you telling me?"

Pain flickered across his face. "I've been keeping a secret from you, because..." His voice broke. "Because I'm ashamed." Bastien dipped his head, and I saw tears were brimming in his eyes. "I didn't stumble on the idea of acceptance and tolerance. It wasn't something that just came to me one day. It happened," he drew in a shuddering breath, "because I-I befriended a demon."

My mouth fell open.

"Yes. Long ago. Before the Choosing. When I was still a Witch of the Light. When I was just Sebastien Bassett of Amara."

Amara. I softened more. I knew there was a reason why he'd been chosen for me. He was born in Amara, beside the banks of the Starfall River, the place I'd loved the most in the world, where the sound of rushing water always made me feel at peace.

"The demon—Gorrath—he and I became close. *Very* close." Our eyes met. "Do you understand what I mean?"

A flash of realization tore through my body like a bolt of lightning, making my heart race faster. "You two would... kiss? And...?"

He nodded. "Yes. We would see each other in secret."

Suddenly, everything began to make sense. It wasn't just my own want. It wasn't just my own attraction. The demon wanted him, and there was a time when he'd wanted the demon too. It was all caged inside me.

"It was a very long time ago. Before I was a vampire. Before I knew you existed," he said quickly.

"Of course," I said. Strangely, I wasn't jealous of the demon. Instead, I felt like I knew Bastien more.

"The more I got to know him, the more I realized he couldn't be trusted. Banishing him became my only choice. Especially after... my family..." he said, trailing off, but he didn't have to finish for me to fully understand what he meant. I knew the price people were willing to pay to be accepted.

His attention settled on the horn covered in black liquid. "I didn't recognize it at first. Or perhaps I didn't want to see the truth. But now I know that is one of *his* horns. The one I cut from his head."

I thought of the night I pleasured myself with it. Of the candles I'd lit. Of the shells that appeared. Of the passageways that opened. Of the feeling like something had inhabited my body. I stared at the horn now.

I'd put a demon's horn *inside* me. The same demon Bastien had once taken to his bed.

"*And you liked it.*" A deep, gruff voice sounded inside my head.

I knew it belonged to the demon.

Now I understood why I was having such strong feelings— the anger, the want, the restlessness—they were coming from a demon who could influence sex and disease.

"Why did you banish him?" I asked, needing to know more about this strange connection between the three of us.

"He was gathering sacrifices, planning to do something that would've changed the world. He had to be stopped."

"You're going to love this story. Ask him what I was planning," the demon urged.

Because I was curious, I indulged. "What was he planning?"

Bastien shook his head and let his gaze settle somewhere off into the distance. "There's an old story about Damien and Diana's daughters."

That was as far as Bastien got before I turned away, facing the woods, my hand wrapping around my throat. *Imogen.* Her story about the goddesses, her prediction about me... dying. Was it all true?

"Every word of it."

"You have to know that I have only ever loved you," Bastien said, mistaking my horror for jealousy.

"I know. It's not that."

Twigs snapped in the distance. Bastien's attention returned to the treeline, his vampire eyes seeing things that I couldn't.

My wolves, who had been pacing around the circle, growled in warning. And when they did, I knew they were out there. The werewolves. The ones Mama would've given anything to create. Even... her daughter.

My hand slipped from the choker and curled into a fist.

The power. I needed access to my power.

Bastien shifted to sit beside me, offering his quiet strength even though I sensed his fear—for me, for us, for whatever was coming. Instead of voicing those anxieties, we simply watched the trees and shadows. He reached for my hand, fingers entwining with mine. He believed he could protect me—with his army, with his life—but in the end, none of it would matter. My death felt inevitable.

Tears welled in my eyes. I was going to die. Mama's spell *would* claim my life. I wanted to tell him everything. All of it.

But if he knew that I was going to die, he would become something unrecognizable. Because as much as I had a piece of this demon inside me, so did he.

"If you perform the ritual and give me the sacrifices I want," the demon taunted, *"I'll reestablish the bloodline. And you can save yourself."*

I didn't like that this demon had grown comfortable inside my head. He sounded completely untrustworthy. I couldn't decide if he was trying to manipulate me for his own gain or if what he was saying was true. But if I did nothing, if I took no chances, I was going to die anyway. Whether as punishment for Bastien's past or to secure whatever future Mama envisioned for herself.

I, however, had the agency to make the choice. Just like I had when those two staircases presented themselves to me. I could stick with what felt safe, or I could descend. I could wait for death to claim me, or try to do something to stop it. And I already knew what my choice was.

"Claire," Bastien said gently, "let's go back to camp. I sent Natalia to Chastity's Stronghold. They will open the archway from the inside. We just need to defend ourselves until then." He set my hand on his chest, right over his silent heart. "You don't have to become something you're not just to save everyone. I'm sorry that this demon is trying to take out his revenge on me through you."

Stay safe. Take the upward staircase. Let me protect you.

I understood what he was saying, but the more pressing question was who I needed to become to save myself. Or Sera? Or Alec, who disappeared into the woods trying to warn me. Or my friends who had selflessly followed me to fight for something bigger than my comfort. And I knew my husband understood that.

"You gave up your life to become a vampire. To be someone

strong enough to save everyone," I told him. "Let me be strong too."

"Claire," he said, covering my hand with his. "He is dangerous."

"All demons are dangerous," I answered quickly. Words I'd grown up believing. But another truth also lived inside of me. "But a Dark Witch's power isn't inherently dangerous, no matter who she got it from. Magick only responds to the witch's intentions. And you've spent a long time teaching me that I am not bad." I touched the side of his face. "Please. Trust me."

My wolves howled again.

Bastien looked at me for a long moment. "If this is what you really want, then I'll all in."

CHAPTER 19
L'OFFRANDE
CLAIRE

I normally wouldn't hesitate to give my body to him, but every rustle of leaves had me on edge. I told myself it was only the trees shifting. Still, my skin prickled as if we were being watched.

"Are you having second thoughts?" my husband asked.

Absently, I wiped my mouth on my sleeve, imagining how horrifying I must look. No wonder he was worried. My nerves were a tangled knot, buzzing just beneath my skin. I tried to find something—anything—to break the tension, to keep myself from unraveling.

"No," I said grimly. "I was just wishing Devlinn and Tansy were here." He gave me a quizzical look, and a humorless laugh escaped my lips. "So we can ask them how to do it."

For a moment, the absurdity of the situation hung between us. I almost wanted to laugh for real if it weren't for the fear pressing against my ribs. Did he think I was losing my nerve? Or just losing my mind? Maybe both.

He smiled. "Not all magick needs to be taught. Follow your intuition."

He was right. I needed to trust myself. I closed my eyes and regained my composure, renewing my efforts to connect with the demon. As soon as I did, one word came into my mind: *Sacrifices*. He wanted sacrifices to reestablish the bloodline.

"You were close, weren't you?" I said. "What would Gorrath want as a sacrifice?"

He didn't hesitate. "Blood. Always blood."

My head swam. Of course it was. Everything came back to blood with us. Bloodlines. Blood oaths. Blood drinking. But it wasn't just blood that Gorrath wanted. He'd wanted desire. I picked up the horn, my mouth suddenly dry and my throat burning with the answer. By Diana, this was going to be awkward.

"Then I think you need to bite me," I said, forcing the words out before I could overthink them. He went very still. "While..." I gathered myself. "While..."

I couldn't force the rest out. I waited for him to follow the logic to its natural conclusion, but he wasn't getting there fast enough. The horn began vibrating, and his focus narrowed on it.

"While I use *this*. On myself."

The color in his face drained. "You're sure?"

I nodded shakily.

I thought he would forbid it and rip the horn from my hand. Maybe even throw it into the woods. His throat worked up and down, and he blew out a long breath. "Alright," he said. "If you're sure."

I couldn't believe the trust he was offering me. He'd fully committed to this. To me. To helping me become strong. "Give me your waterskin."

He unclasped it from his belt, and I rinsed the horn, cleaning the black liquid from it, then did the same with my hands. Bastien offered me his discarded cravat to finish the job. Once it was clean, we stared at each other for a long moment.

"Are you ready?" he asked.

I shoved the hair that was stuck to my face back. "Yes. I'm ready."

Very deliberately, he parted my knees and positioned himself between them. My skirt rode up to my thighs. "Go on. I'm watching."

Now it was on me to finish the ritual and do what needed to be done. With my eyes locked on his, I slid the horn underneath my skirt. The cold wind bit deeper than Bastien ever had as I moved it to the place that had been begging for relief. The first brush of the horn against my skin sent a jolt through my body—a gasp escaped me, back arching involuntarily.

"Does that feel good?" Bastien asked.

I felt slightly ashamed that something that belonged to Gorrath could do this to me, but I didn't lie. "Yes."

Bastien groaned in satisfaction. "Show me how good."

Red light spilled out from beneath my skirts as the horn switched on, vibrating harder than it had before. I gasped in shock before fully giving in to the feeling.

Bastien's hand traced up the front of my dress until it closed around my throat. He applied enough pressure to steal my breath, then released me.

Combined with the vibrations and the way he was looking at me, I was on the brink faster than I could've imagined. I tipped my head back, arching into the exhilaration, when a shift in the air made my skin crawl. The phantom press of a body materialized behind me—arms, not quite solid, wrapping around my middle. A hot, shuddering breath brushed my neck, making my entire body tense, straddling the line between terror and submission.

"Good girl," the demon praised. He was inside my head. And somehow, whispering in my ear.

Magick pulsed through me in powerful waves that mirrored the vibrations of the horn, growing stronger and stronger until I thought I might actually rip in half. Fire crackled under my skin. Burning hot. *Hotter.*

"I think he's here," I said around a gasp. "Gorrath."

Bastien looked up, and I didn't know what he saw behind me. It might've been a ghost. "Do you want to stop?"

"Do you?" I asked.

Neither one of us answered.

An invisible hand peeled my fingers off the horn, taking control of it. Sliding it over me. Teasing me. "Bastien," I gasped, too far gone to stop it. Too close to fight it. Too turned on by the thought of my husband watching it all unfold. If he didn't want this, he needed to say something.

I leaned back, surrendering my weight into that invisible chest, a shiver running the length of my spine. The magick inside me surged and writhed, threatening to spill over. My hands fell away, trembling. Bastien hiked up my skirt, his breath ragged, eyes wide as he watched the horn work. "Claire, if you want this to stop, just say the word."

"No," I said, tears pricking in my eyes. The horn twisted so the ridged edge worked against me. My eyes rolled back. "I'm going to come," I told Bastien. The horn moved to my entrance, threatening to slip inside me.

"No," Bastien gritted out. He grabbed the horn and pulled it away. The two of us breathing heavily. My limbs shaking. I felt like I was about to combust into flames.

"Too far?" I asked. Panting. Sweating. Barely able to focus. "Is it too much?"

He shook his head. "No. It's just that we haven't paid the blood price yet. I want this to work."

Horn in hand, he sank his teeth into my thigh. I had to bite down on my lip to keep from screaming in ecstasy.

After taking a long pull, he spat blood onto the horn. I'd never been more glad for the dark. Then he lifted his own wrist to his mouth and bit down once again, coming away with wet lips as he licked the tip of the horn.

I shook with unexpressed magick. Fire burning in my chest. My hands. My lips. Everywhere.

"Now you can come."

He pressed the horn back against my heat, holding it against me while his fingers curled inside me. The vibrations and his fingers brought tears to my eyes, and I screamed out into the night, unable to hold back any longer.

"Gorrath," Bastien said, the name a plea between heavy breaths. "Damn you. Give it to her!"

Invisible hands squeezed around my breasts, and whatever magick that had been contained within me *escaped*. I shook. I whimpered. I screamed. I saw fire and stars behind my eyes. Saw a boy with blond hair and bright blue eyes rising from the ashes. My son. My blood.

And as free as I felt, I knew it was fleeting. Like the candles I'd lit. There was more that Gorrath wanted. I could almost hear him whispering it to me from behind.

"He'll *never*," I whispered in response to the request.

"What?" Bastien asked, reading my face.

I sucked in a shuddering breath, my whole body aching with the absence of what had just been unleashed. The magick that had poured out of me began to retreat like steam drawn back into a kettle.

"He needs an heir." The words burst out of my mouth. "To reestablish the bloodline. It's his final demand."

"An heir?" His gaze dropped to my belly, widening. Then more firmly, he repeated himself. "An heir."

Tears leaked down my cheeks. "I won't beg. I know how you feel."

Bastien took my face between his bloody hands. "This is what you want?"

I studied his face. His beautiful face. And nodded. "Yes."

Bastien didn't offer excuses about my well-being like I thought he would. He simply handed me the horn, and I knew it was over.

When he reached inside his trousers, I froze. "What are you doing?"

The horn glowed red, illuminating his hard length, which was already dripping for me, and he slid me onto his lap. "Giving you what you want." Everything inside me melted. The heat reignited. Then, more tenderly, he said, "Claire, let me put a baby in you."

"Bastien?"

He wrapped my arms around his neck. And as I sank down onto him, he stared adoringly up at me. Something hot and intense jolted through me when he was all the way in. Bastien's mouth was a ruin of red, but I didn't care. I lowered mine to his, tasting the flavor.

He gripped my backside as I rode him deeper. Deeper. The friction and pressure of the position had taken over for the horn. It wasn't the demon who would make me come, *but him.*

"Tell me you're close," Bastien said.

"I'm close," I moaned.

"What do you need? Because I'm right there."

I squeezed my eyes shut. "Tell me you want this baby. Tell me it isn't just about the magick."

His reply scraped against me. "I want this baby."

Bastien moaned, and warmth spread through me. As soon as I felt it, the heat consumed me. I was lost. Gone to the flames. Gone to him. Just... gone.

CHAPTER 20
BASCULER
CLAIRE

I awoke with a start. Bastien was shouting for Devlinn as he held me in his arms.

"I'm right here, Your Grace!" Devlinn took one look at the blood on our faces and said, "I take it that you found a way to make the ritual work?"

Tansy rushed to my side, smoothing back my hair. "Of course they did. Look at her eyes, they're *red*."

They were? Had it worked? Had we done it? I couldn't seem to remember anything after that flash of heat.

"Are you alright to stand?" my mate asked.

I nodded. "Yes, I think so."

He carefully set me on my feet, then opened the waterskin he kept on his belt and offered it to me. "Drink."

I took a big sip and used it to rinse the blood and black rot out of my mouth before swallowing.

"Give her the spell to open the door," Bastien directed Devlinn.

He drew his sword, and I gave him a bewildered look. "The werewolves are coming. They've caught our scent."

With his weapon in hand and pale blond hair catching in the wind, I longed to be back in his arms. He'd done the thing he'd sworn he'd never do. And he did it to help me get my magick. I couldn't explain what it meant to me to know this man would do anything, *anything* for me.

"I take it *Miss Donadieu* can use her magick now?" Tyson asked, being pointedly discreet. He was standing behind Tansy, along with Lady Okeri. Both wore matching looks of amusement.

Embarrassment heated my cheeks. Tyson was a vampire after all, and his preternatural hearing meant he likely heard *everything*. Although I think I was loud enough that the whole army might know.

"You will protect her. With your life," Bastien commanded his nephew. "Swear it on your honor as an Allard and as my heir."

The word heir caused me to touch my stomach. The warmth of his seed was already leaking between my thighs.

"I swear it," Tyson said.

"Where are you going?" I asked, already knowing but not wanting to believe it.

Bastien continued speaking to Tyson as if he hadn't heard me. "As soon as the door is open, get everyone inside as fast as you can. I'm trusting you."

Only then did his eyes find mine. I knew he didn't want to leave his nephew in charge. He wanted to stay by my side and protect me. And even though I wanted him near while I tried to work this spell, and for a million other reasons, he was the general.

"Go. We'll get the door open."

His pained look nearly broke my heart in two. "I know you will."

"*I love you,*" I told him through our bond.

"I love you with everything inside me."

He was gone in the snap of a black cloak, disappearing into the press of bodies. Shouts and the scream of steel rent through the air.

"The spell, Devlinn! Give her the spell!" Tansy shouted, shoving him forward.

He quickly explained what I needed to say. I practiced the words a few times, still feeling weak. He handed me my wand back and gave me an encouraging smile. "You are powerful. You can do this." Taking another deep breath, I reached toward the stone archway, channeling every bit of magick I could muster. This was my chance to prove myself, to show everyone that I could be strong.

I focused on pushing the magick through the wand, inch by inch. But it felt foreign. Like the wood didn't want to answer my call.

Come on, demon.

"Don't think of the wand as something separate from you," Devlinn reminded me. "Think of it as part of you."

I kept at it, repeating the spell again. As I let the magick flow, something inside me *clicked*, like a key fitting into an ancient lock, and the power surged through me, into the wand.

When it did, the sound of a rusty chain paying out came from somewhere behind the arch. The metallic sound sped up, tipping the stone door *backward*. A sharp blast of musty air escaped from the gap as it continued to lower in fits and starts, inch by inch, until it revealed a narrow passageway wide enough for only one person to squeeze through at a time, leading down into darkness.

My white wolf pushed her head into my hand and whined. I swallowed hard.

"You did it!" Tansy cheered as she threw her arms around

my neck. I wanted to celebrate with her, but there was something about the darkness I didn't like.

"Of course she did!" Devlinn was saying. "She had an excellent mentor. If I do say so myself."

"As much as I love a good celebration, it's time to go. Uncle's orders."

"I should help them hold the line while the rest of the army retreats underground," Okeri said.

"You don't get to kill werewolves while I babysit the witches."

I crossed my arms. "We can hear you, you know?"

Okeri gave Tyson a stern look that made his grin falter. She pointed to the opening with her sword. "It's going to take ages to get everyone through this passageway in single file."

Tyson shrugged. "I don't care how long it takes. I need you. You know that. *And we agreed to stay together.*"

He said the last line under his breath, and it reminded me of how young he was. Eighteen. And had never left the capital before. The two of them were like me and Sera leaving Prideaux Hill for the first time.

The fight left Okeri, and she dropped her sword. "Right. Together."

Something warm and cold twisted in my chest, causing tears to prick in the corners of my eyes. I went to grab my bloodstone to let Bastien know that we'd done it, when I realized he hadn't put it back on me after the spell. It was still in his pocket.

Panic landed in my chest, and something in me wanted to run back to him. Even if he was fighting werewolves. I had magick now. I could help.

Tyson grabbed me by the shoulder and turned me back toward the arch. "My uncle gave me a very clear order. To get you into the tunnels."

I thought to argue, but there was no time. The longer we lingered, the longer the army would need to fight.

A soldier handed Tyson a lit torch. "Stay between Lady Okeri and me, and everything will be fine." A grin split across his face. "Until we meet my cousin in the tunnels and she realizes not only have we managed to get through the spell on the door without her, but that our uncle entrusted me with leading the mission."

Tansy set her hands on my shoulders, right behind me, and together, with my wolves, we followed after Tyson. I tried not to worry about my husband. I knew he was a fearless warrior, and his fighters would protect him. But still, doubt buried in me as we continued to descend into the endless dark.

The path leading down into the graveyard tunnels reminded me of the one that led down into Imogen's cave. Except that instead of stairs, it was damp earth. Every so often, my boot would get stuck in the soft dirt, and my ankle would twist.

"Stay alert," Tyson whispered. "I sense heartbeats."

"Heartbeats? As in… there are people down here?" I asked.

I set my hand on my belly. Wondering if there'd be a heartbeat inside of me soon.

"Well, this is a place of peace," Tansy offered. "That's what His Grace said. So it would make sense for people to be down here. Especially with the wolves running around."

"Exactly," Tyson said.

I gave Tansy an encouraging smile, but it was hard to trust Tyson when he'd never been in these tunnels before, and his bravado overruled his sense of right and wrong. But I had no choice but to keep my wand aloft and my ears open. I couldn't hear anything over the shuffle of feet and murmur of voices behind us.

I kept waiting to hear Bastien's voice or feel him beside me, but after a long while, he still hadn't appeared.

We continued descending deeper and *deeper* into the twisting passage. Tyson stopped and lifted his torch, illuminating a word that had been painted onto the crumbling bricks:

PEACE.

It was comforting to see that the people of the Lawless Lands valued peace. They had created these tunnels. They were open to negotiations with Bastien. Then, Tyson moved the torch, and three more words jumped to life: IS A LIE.

"It's probably just kids who wrote it," Tansy said with a laugh. But she leaned a little closer to me just the same. After what felt like an eternity, the tunnel opened up into a cavernous chamber with the kind of cathedral ceilings that belonged inside Château Rose, not a mile below a graveyard.

"Well, would you look at that," Tyson said, holding up his torch so the light extended further.

My chest tightened around a half-drawn breath. "It's a river," I said. But instead of water, it was filled with a silvery substance that looked like mercury. The water, or whatever it was, moved, rushing toward an arch in the wall that was large enough for a small canoe to pass under.

"By Diana," I breathed.

"Please don't invoke the goddess right now," Tansy said, half-teasing, half-serious.

I bit my lip. Saying and thinking her name was second nature. But down here, out of sight from the moon, I didn't think she could hear me. However, Diana must leave her place in the sky every once in a while if she visits the Underworld to have children with Damien. Everything I'd ever been told, every story, was a lie. Tansy was right. I needed to stop invoking the goddess.

Cautiously, we walked closer to the river, where there were small wooden boats tied up along the edge, bobbing and colliding into one another in the current. I didn't say it out loud, but something about the river felt *alive*.

Tyson abruptly turned, shining his light deeper into the cavern. "What in the...?"

<h1 style="text-align:center">CHAPTER 21
DÉRAPER</h1>

CLAIRE

I froze, heart racing, as I turned toward the orange halo of light. In the far corner of the chamber was a cluster of shapes huddled together. Our group took a step forward, extending the light until it illuminated *children*. Little knees were tucked to chests. Their red hair tangled. Their clothes hung off small frames.

They were watching us like we were monsters.

My heart broke for them. They were alone in this dark place. The oldest girl appeared to be no more than sixteen. Tansy's fingers slipped into mine, and she squeezed hard. Her hand was ice-cold. I squeezed back harder.

"Stay with Miss Donadieu," Tyson told Okeri. She positioned herself in front of Tansy and me with her sword drawn.

I waved off his concern. "I don't need to be protected from children. They're scared. That's all."

"My uncle would disagree," he shot back. Tyson sheathed his sword and crouched beside the children.

Devlinn followed after him, already unstrapping the water-

141

skin from his belt. "Here," he said softly. "Drink. You must be thirsty."

The children flinched, and none reached for the water. Their eyes kept darting past him. Past Tyson. Like they were watching the dark for signs of life. Perhaps their parents or whoever was caring for them.

The oldest girl stood, a wand in one hand. It wasn't the wand that scared me. *But her eyes.* There was something in them that didn't belong to a child. Like someone had reached inside her and scooped her childhood clean out.

I knew that look, and the realization hit so hard it almost knocked the breath out of me.

It was the look formed by long nights alone, staring at the ceiling and wondering if the gods heard your prayers or if your voice just disappeared somewhere between your mouth and the sky. The kind of nights where you whispered *please*. Then *why*. Then nothing at all. Because eventually you stopped asking for things to be different and started assuming you must deserve it.

It was the look you wore after being hit so many times they didn't even have to raise their hand anymore to make you flinch. Your body just knew what to expect. It was the look that drew my least favorite question, *"What's the matter with you?"* Like they had no responsibility for your inability to smile.

And worst of all, it was the look you wore when you started wondering if the world might be better off without you. When you caught yourself imagining how quiet everything would be if you just... *weren't here.* If no one had to trip over you anymore. If no one had to sigh when you walked into a room. But you were too scared to do anything about it. Or maybe— on the better days—too hopeful. Too stubbornly, stupidly hopeful that something might change.

My throat tightened until swallowing hurt. I didn't see

this girl as a threat. I saw a girl who had been raised on hate, the way other children were raised on bread and milk. Fed it every day until it was all she knew. Hate for herself. Hate for anyone who was different. Hate for the people who made her mother so angry. You blamed them for every beating you took. You hated so deeply that it became your armor. Your air.

And at the bottom of all her hate, I saw myself.

Her fingers were wrapped so tight around her wand that her knuckles had gone white, the tendons in her wrist standing out like cords pulled too thin.

She wasn't pointing it because she wanted to hurt us. She was pointing it because she didn't believe she had another choice. This must've been what I looked like to Shreesa the day she came to help me, and I threatened her with a fire poker. But Shreesa hadn't attacked me. She'd tried to help me see the truth.

And Bastien. Had this been how he'd seen me? Was this the look I'd given him when he'd shoved me against that bathhouse and I told him I blamed him for my awful, miserable life?

Had I looked like this? Ready to burn down the one person trying to help me?

"Get away!" she shouted.

I didn't hear a threat. I heard a cry for help.

Tansy and I pushed past Okeri. She tried to block us with one arm, muttering something under her breath, but it was half-hearted. Even she knew two armed men looming over terrified children wasn't going to help anything.

Tyson stayed crouched, hands open, voice gentle. "Easy now. I'm not going to hurt you." He gestured to the smaller children. "Something tells me you're not playing hide-and-seek down here. Are you?"

Despite being a vampire, Tyson wasn't much older than

the girl. But his easy smile did nothing to charm her. Nor the other children.

"It's alright. We're like you," I reassured her, removing the hood of my cloak so that my red hair spilled over my shoulder. I wanted them to see that we weren't soldiers or hunters.

They looked at me. Then at Tansy. And her moon-white braids and dark skin, and recoiled. I took Tansy's hand as a show of goodwill. "We're from the Unified Territories. Witches get along there." A lie. But it wasn't all-out warfare. "Just tell us what you're hiding from, and we can protect you."

I could tell by the way she held her ground when the others cowered that she was fierce. "We're hidin' from her kind! The wolves."

Her kind. The words were spat like a curse, and I saw Tansy flinch as if struck, her shoulders curling in on themselves as she quickly turned away. A hot surge of anger and helplessness twisted in my chest. Devlinn rushed over and put his arm around her shoulders.

"They just keep doing horrible things," Tansy muttered. "And when I think they can't do anything worse, they find a shovel and keep digging. Now they're attacking children. *Children.*"

"Look at me. Look at me," Devlinn said, taking her face between his hands. "This is why we decided to stay. Because we don't agree with this, and we're not just going to let them speak for everybody. Are we? We're not going to let them keep doing this."

I burned with the need to say something, anything that would lessen her pain, but the words stuck behind my teeth.

I set my hand on Tansy's shoulder, feeling her pain more deeply than I could explain.

Tyson gave the girl one of his winning smiles. "We're here to take care of those mean old wolves so you won't have to hide from them anymore. So how about you put your wand down and let us help you?"

The girl just shook her head. "They said the same thing. That we would be safe if we just listened. But it was all *lies*."

The word came out as a hiss. I knew her fear was fracturing into something more dangerous, but I didn't want to believe she was too far gone. "We can help find your parents," I said, trying to keep a hopeful note in my voice. "Are they down here too?"

Her wand drifted toward Tansy. "The moon witches took 'em." Red light flashed in her eyes. "They're all tricksters!"

She swished her wand to cast the spell. "No!" Devlinn shouted, pushing Tansy behind him, protecting her with his body.

I grabbed her wrist and lifted her wand toward the ceiling. The spell shot from the tip and ricocheted off the ceiling, nearly missing Devlinn by an inch.

Tyson went to grab her, but magick flared under my skin, making my hand glow with light, and I shoved him back ten feet in the air like he was nothing more than a feather.

People started shouting, but I stayed locked on the girl.

Her lip was trembling. Tears were filling her eyes. She didn't want to hurt anyone, but she was afraid. It was a fear I knew all too well. One that had been put there by stories of evil Dark Witches and merciless vampires. One that had been solidified by the blank eyes of dead relatives.

"I know you're afraid," I said in as calm a voice as I could muster. "But we are here to help you. I swear it."

She drew in a shaky breath, and a single tear rolled down her cheek. "They killed my Ma. In cold blood. Right after they," her voice broke off. She didn't need to say the rest. I understood.

I wanted to reach out to her. To hold her. To rock her in my arms. But she wasn't ready for that kind of love. It was foreign. So instead, I validated her pain. "I'm so sorry. That should never have happened. Your Ma didn't deserve that, and neither did you."

Someone shouted at me, but I didn't move. I had to make her see. If I could understand, she could too.

"Please, Mellie," said the little girl crouched beside her. She couldn't have been more than eight. "I want to go home."

"We can't go home!" she shouted back. "There is no home."

When she looked back at me, the hurt had disappeared, and all that was left was anger. Tears formed in my own eyes. It was like looking into a mirror. There was nothing Shreesa could've said to change my mind when I was hiding under that chair. There was nothing Bastien could've said to convince me that he wasn't evil.

It was in his actions. And Tansy's. And Devlinn's. Day by day. It was seeing kindness from people I'd been told were evil.

There was only one thing I could do to show her that we weren't bad. And that was to ignore everyone who was trying to tell me to move and show her that I wasn't afraid.

She pointed her wand at the center of my chest, and the pressure dropped again.

A warm, radiant light sparked in my chest that felt different from the insistent scratching of dark magick. It expanded until it touched the girl. Her eyes widened, as if she were being reminded of all the beautiful hopes and dreams she held. I pushed that light harder, expanding it out, knowing I could change her. I could make her see if she'd only reconnect with hope instead of despair, just like I'd done.

But the harder I pushed, the more she pushed back, until the light rebounded and I stumbled backward. All the hope and light disappeared, leaving me with the empty sense that nothing I could do would save her. At least, not until she was ready.

The moment before she fired the spell stretched on and on and on. I braced for death in the same way I waited for the back of Mama's hand, wondering if everything would become quiet.

CHAPTER 22
LE CRI
CLAIRE

My name was shouted, echoing off the walls of the cavern. Then suddenly I was tackled to the ground, and the wind was knocked out of me.

When I finally caught my breath and processed what was going on, I realized I was in Bastien's arms. My face hidden in the hollow of his throat. He opened our bond, and the all-consuming nature of being inside of it allowed me to take my first full breath since he left my side.

"Stop torturing me," he whispered through it. *"I almost lost you again."*

I buried my head in his shoulder. Wanting to cry but unable to make myself do it. My thoughts turned to that warm field of light and the way I could see the girl's hopes and dreams. I didn't have words for what it was, only emotions. They leaked from me, straight through our bond, until I was sure Bastien could see what I had seen. That he had felt what I had felt.

From outside our bond, I heard someone screaming, and it tugged my attention back to the world around us.

"What's happening?" I asked, trying to move, but he just kept me caged in his arms. I asked again, louder this time. "What's happening?"

"You don't want to know."

Then I heard Tansy sobbing uncontrollably, and I demanded to be let go. He released me, and I clambered to my feet. Breathless. Only to find Tansy clutching Devlinn's body as black smoke smoldered from a wound in his chest. The spell had burned through his thick fur cloak, finding flesh and bone. He was struggling to breathe.

I remembered the graveyard. I remembered the wolf who took the curse for me. The one who had saved my life. He'd died so that I could live. And now, now, it was happening all over again. Except it wasn't just a wolf, it was a man. One that I'd called a friend. One who had sacrificed his dreams of sitting on an island, sipping cocktails with the love of his life, to be here helping me fight for a belief.

My white wolf pushed her snout against my leg and whimpered. The brown wolf howled. Something in me broke open. I tipped my head back and screamed with a grief so sudden and complete that it tore from my chest and ripped through my throat.

When I was done, I realized I wasn't giving up on him. Not without a fight. I crossed the chamber toward the girl, who shook in Tyson's grip like a trapped bird. "Tell me the counter-curse!"

She shook her head, red hair clinging to her wet cheeks. "That spell rots men from the inside out," she whispered. "There is no counter-curse."

I whirled around. "There's about to be." I turned to Bastien, blood darkening his sleeve where a claw had torn him. Without asking, I dragged the horn across his wound and offered the demon what it wanted.

I could almost feel the horn purring with delight.

"What are you doing?" he asked.

"Fixing this."

I raced over to where Devlinn lay on the ground and fell to my knees beside Tansy, whose hands were coated in a putrid black rot. It looked exactly like the oily liquid that came out of my mouth when I tried to commune with the demon whose power I had received.

With shaking hands, I pressed the horn into the center of the wound. Devlinn sucked in a choked breath.

"Claire! Stop!" Tansy gasped. "You're hurting him!"

"If I don't do something, he's going to die!"

Weakly, she nodded. I called to the demonic power that lived inside me, and willed the horn to take the sickness from him, to drink it down and leave him whole. To obey me as it had with the spell on the door to these tunnels.

I was a powerful Dark Witch, and I'd fed him what it wanted. My pleasure. Bastien's blood. I'd given it more than enough tonight.

With my eyes closed, I reached for the disease crawling through his veins and tried to draw it out. I remembered the first time I met him at my prospective consort presentation. And when he'd *disrobed* beside Tansy. I'd been so embarrassed and angry at Bastien for sending me someone like him. But... Tansy had spoken up for him, and her love for this man, a Dark Witch that I would've otherwise written off as evil, had opened my heart to him.

And I was the better for it. This man, who was as funny as he was kind, came to the Lawless Lands for me. The magick flared in my chest, and I leaned into it. Drawing on the need to fix this. To save him.

"Keep going!" Tansy urged me on. "It's working!"

I opened my eyes and saw the black rot retreating inward toward the horn, like spilled black ink being sucked back into the pot. Reversing time. Devlinn locked eyes with Tansy and reached for her cheek with a quivering hand. A smile formed on his lips. "You are beautiful," he said weakly.

"And you've never been more handsome," Tansy told him, holding his hand tight against her cheek. He choked out a sound that might've been a laugh.

Tears pricked in my eyes, and I didn't stop them from coming as I refocused on what I was doing. Pulling the disease from him. But just like the candles that I'd tried to light, I felt the power slipping from inside of me. And when it did, the rot spread with terrifying speed, blooming across his chest, down his ribs, into places I could no longer reach.

"No! No! No!" Tansy sobbed.

Bastien crouched beside me and placed his hands on the horn too, offering whatever support he could. Whatever power he had. But it wasn't enough. It slowed the rot just long enough for Devlinn to say one last thing.

"Find peace, my love."

A line of black liquid trailed from between his pale lips, and I knew it was over. I stared at him, shaking, unable to believe this was real.

"You did everything you could," Bastien said gently, setting a hand on my shoulder.

I did everything I knew how to do, and yet, it still wasn't enough. This was all my fault. If I had just let Tyson grab the girl instead of trying to change her mind, Devlinn would be alive.

This horn, this magick, had failed me.

I ripped it from Devlinn's chest and hurled it across the cavern with everything I had. It struck the stone wall with a sharp, ringing crack, the sound echoing again and again like a broken bell, but it bounced off the wall and skidded back to me, inches from my hand, as if to say I wasn't getting rid of it that easily.

CHAPTER 23
LA BÊTE
BASTIEN

I had no idea what game Gorrath was playing. Did he truly believe that if he collected enough blood from me —enough pain, enough offerings—that he could free himself from his prison in the Underworld? But there was no time to consider what this all meant or to mourn the death of a good man. Because from the depths of the cavern, I heard sounds. Footsteps fast approaching. Heavy breaths. And the low rumble of a growl.

Claws tapped lazily against the inside of my ribs. *"Your wife. Your child. They need protection. They don't need you. They need me."*

The ruthless, angry thing inside me. The one that had torn through witches in that graveyard and felt nothing but relief afterward. He wanted out. I had an army to command, and that *thing* didn't lead. I swallowed it like poison.

"Lord Tyson," I said, already drawing steel. My voice came out in the tone of a commander who did not have time to grieve the dead. "Give the prisoner to a guard. I need you with me."

Orders were easier than feelings. And if I stayed cold and detached, I could keep that thing inside me at bay. I'd fought in the Lawless Lands countless times. This was no different.

Claire gave me a murderous look from where she sat on the ground beside Tansy, who was crying uncontrollably. "She's just a scared girl. She didn't want to do it." She turned to Tansy. "I know she didn't mean to do this."

"But she did," Tansy sobbed. "She did."

Devlinn's body lay between them, and I forced myself not to look.

Irons were clamped around the girl's wrists with a clank and a snap. Her wand was taken, tossed aside like a broken toy. She didn't fight. Just stared through us with hollow eyes.

"Get Tansy up," I told my wife. Neither of them moved. "Trouble's coming. We need to move."

"What? We can't just leave him here," Tansy choked out. "We have to take him with us." She was clutching Devlinn's cloak as if she held tight enough he might wake up. "Your Grace, please!"

The footsteps were close. The growls, too. "Fall back!" My wife, however, wasn't listening. She had her arms beneath Devlinn's shoulders, trying to help Tansy lift him. Something in my chest seized so violently I almost barked at her to stop. I'd carried plenty of friends to the pyres once battles were done. Plenty. But his death hadn't happened because of war. It had been so senseless.

His head lolled to the side as they lifted him, and I was forced to look him in the face. He was so pale and lifeless. So unlike him. Black rot oozed from his mouth. The same oily blackness that Claire had thrown up.

The rot. The disease. Gorrath couldn't be on the mortal plane. I'd ensured that. But somehow his influence was seeping into the world again. I glanced around the cavern like I might find him standing among my warriors.

But it was no use searching for ghosts.

"Soldiers," I snapped, already moving. Already pointing. "Help them."

Two men rushed forward, taking Devlinn's weight from Claire and Tansy before they could protest. The relief that flickered across my wife's face only made the guilt worse.

I should've been the one carrying him. He'd died because I hadn't done my job properly.

Natalia burst through the dark with the warriors I'd sent to Chastity's Stronghold. I was so relieved to see her face. To know she was alright. "Reform your lines! Weres!" she shouted. "Three of them!"

I tucked the grief back inside my chest and told myself I had to lead these soldiers. I had to be their commander now in order to protect my wife.

"You heard Lady Natalia! Reform your lines!" I commanded. My vision darkened at the edges as the change happened. The world stripped down to the things that mattered—heat signatures, heartbeats, the wet rush of blood through veins.

And somewhere ahead, three new pulses moved through the dark.

I planted myself in front of Claire. "Fall back with the others," I told her. "Go with Sir Gavin."

"No! I have magick too. I can fight."

I gritted my teeth. If anyone else had spoken to me like that before a battle, I'd have barked them into place.

But this was my wife.

Yes, she finally had control of her power, and I'd seen what she could do with it. But she knew no spells, only raw power.

And once the wolves knew she was the biggest threat, they'd come right for her. I couldn't let that happen.

I turned just enough to look at her. Her chin was lifted. Grief and fury burned in her eyes. Blood and smeared black rot on her face and hands.

Natalia slid into position at my right, sword read. She didn't spare Claire a glance. "That is not your place."

"My place is with His Grace."

I hated how much I loved hearing that. Her place *was* with me. But we had new responsibilities now.

"If you stand and fight against orders," Natalia said with forced calm, "then you risk all our lives. Because His Grace's attention will be divided. By standing down, you are doing your part."

Tyson took my left. "I hate to agree with my cousin, but Natalia is right."

Claire's heart pounded out a too-fast rhythm, and I could feel her fury building behind me. She wasn't going to move. Every instinct screamed to pick her up and carry her back myself, but it was too late now. The stench of the wolves was everywhere.

Wet fur and blood and that same stinking rot. Three men stepped into the circle of torchlight, and I realized they weren't *exactly* men. They had snouts where faces should've been, and fur split through torn skin. The only weapon they had was their claws, which were long and hooked. They weren't fully transformed werewolves.

But there was something else wrong with them. Their bodies were speckled with black pock marks, and thick, inky saliva dripped from their jaws. A bit dribbled onto an opalescent necklace.

I snarled, and they stopped when they saw the number of good swords behind me.

"They're living in the tunnels," Natalia explained. *"Which is why Chastity sealed them."*

"Ah, that would've been good to know before we opened the door," Tyson added unhelpfully.

"We don't want no trouble, Lord Vampire," one of them said in a thick, guttural voice. His long tongue licked over his sharp canines. "We only want those naughty little children, and we'll be on our way."

"We need to capture one of them," Natalia whispered in Sanguisi.

Tyson chuckled. *"You recruiting new consorts, cousin?"*

"For questioning!" she bit back. Natalia was always three steps ahead of everyone else. *"There's something about those necklaces I don't like."*

"They aren't yours to take!" Claire shouted.

Every head turned in her direction. The wolves'. My soldiers'. *Mine.* Frustration clawed up my throat. This was a standoff. Predators assessing one another. My objective, always, was to reduce casualties. And if that meant using my influence as a commander and the threat of violence to get these creatures to back off, then that was my duty.

The biggest wolf, who appeared to have taken on the role of the pack alpha, scented the air. I didn't need heightened senses to know what he smelled. *Me.* All over *her.* My bite. My blood. My claim. My seed. One breath and he knew she was my heart beating outside my body.

His attention drifted back to me, and he dragged a long, wolfish tongue over his jowls like he'd just found something interesting to tear apart. "Your mate speaks for you, Lord Vampire?"

With one sentence, he'd exposed the secret of our relationship to my entire army. Claire was my vulnerability. And now everyone knew it.

"Uncle," Natalia breathed beside me. *"Say something."* The fear in her voice was unmistakable. And even though something had broken between us, I knew she still bore love for me. The same love I had for her.

Before I could pull the attention back where it belonged, Claire shoved her wand through the narrow gap between Tyson and me and fired. The spell cracked through the air and struck one of them square in the shoulder, bursting into a spray of black blood.

The wolf staggered back with a snarl, more surprised than wounded. "You'll pay for that, witch!"

Natalia and Tyson closed the space between us, creating a shield between Claire and us. The monster inside me that wanted out banged against my ribs. But I still hoped for diplomacy. Fighting was always the last resort. Always. "Look around you," I told the wolves. "You are outnumbered."

One of the little girls started crying, and the young witch who had killed Devlinn grunted against her bonds. "There's a village of them down here!"

The big wolf snapped his jaws. "Shut your mouth."

Listening, I sensed more footfalls. More snarls. More grunts. Others were coming. "And you, you're their leader?" I asked, trying to keep him talking.

"We're Shayla's chosen." He slapped his furry hand against the opalescent gem. "She knows who is loyal."

"Where is Chastity?" I asked Natalia, keeping my features schooled in neutrality. *"Tell me her witches are on the way."*

Natalia shook her head. *"She let us through her wards, but didn't follow."*

More wolves appeared out of the dark. Creatures caught somewhere between man and beast. But none of the others wore the same stones that these three did.

I had a feeling this wasn't going to end with negotiations.

"Go stand with Sir Gavin," I told Claire, not taking my eyes off the dark. *"Do not make me repeat myself."*

"No. I can fight."

"If you're carrying my child, then your job is to protect him. Mine is to protect you."

It would take a week for her pheromones to change, and weeks longer before I'd be able to sense a heartbeat inside her. Which meant from this moment forward, I wasn't allowed to fail. If something happened to her, to them, this fragile hope that we were building brick by brick on very unstable ground and without a plan, I wouldn't just become the reaper. I'd break this whole world.

I'd agreed to create a baby, and now I was responsible.

Finally, she conceded, taking one step, then another, watching me until she reached Sir Gavin's line. Even when she was behind ten of the best swords, it didn't feel like enough.

The alpha whispered something to the beta beside him. I caught the words with my vampiric hearing.

"Whatever you do, keep the girl alive. I want her."

A switch flipped inside my head. The negotiations were over. I lunged. Natalia and Tyson moved with me. My ability to slide into their minds assisted the fight. *"Right. Back. On your left."*

But my gifts had other uses too. I could worm my way into the enemy's mind, saying things that I would never repeat aloud. It was one of the things that made me such a deadly commander. I could control what everyone else was thinking, except my own.

My mind was divided between Claire and the battle. I kept stealing glances at her, ensuring she was still safely behind good swords that I trusted. Since she couldn't join the fight, she sent her wolves, who turned out to be just as fierce. They worked in tandem against the weres. The brown one bit legs and groins while the white one tore out throats.

I glanced back at Claire, watching her tend to one of the small children, and the big beta barreled past me. I chased after it. Before I caught it, the were broke through Sir Gavin's sword line and shoved her backward against the wall so hard that her head snapped against the stone. As soon as I caught the scent of her blood, I lost all control.

I grabbed it around the neck, threw it to the ground, and shoved a sword in its neck. Snarling and growling into its face.

The whoosh of flames filled the cavern with light, and one of the werewolves caught fire. The scent of burning fur, thick in the air. I cursed under my breath. Claire. Another wolf charged at her, and I lunged in front of it and put my sword through its belly. More flames came from the tip of her wand. More wolves, recognizing the threat, approached.

"Stop!" I shouted. "You're drawing them right to you!"

My sword flashed as I cut through more bodies, each strike fueled by my rage and feral need to protect her. My vision tunneled; every detail sharpened—the wet snap of bone, the copper tang of blood, the desperate gasps of my soldiers. Blinded with battle rage, I became my weapon. *Slice. Cut. Slice. Cut.* When I took a hit, I felt nothing. I just kept swinging.

Flames illuminated the carnage in bursts. Smoke filled the space until men were coughing. Then the flames suddenly stopped, and mid-swing, I turned to find my wife limp in Sir Gavin's arms. Tansy at her side. The wound on her head. The spells. The fire. She'd overextended herself.

Because of my distraction, I took a claw to the jaw, then another to the ribs. The were's foul breath in my face. The pain was inconsequential. I slashed back. Again and again. Leaving a trail of black blood in my wake. The stench of death was everywhere. Children were crying. Charred bodies smoldered.

Until at last, there was only one wolf left—the alpha.

I spun my sword in my hand. Blood dripped down my face from one of many wounds that I did not feel. *This one is mine,* I told my fellow vampires.

The beast's lips quirked at the challenge.

"Hostage, remember!" Natalia shouted. *"He's more valuable alive."*

I tried to pull the bloodthirsty thing inside me back, but he was too far gone. I charged, sword raised high. We met claw and sword. Blow by blow. The thick gray fur covering his arms and legs was like armor, and my blade bounced off it. This was no normal beast.

But neither was I.

"When you're dead," the were told me, "I'm coming for your girl."

I roared, baring my fangs. "Never!"

The beast slammed into me, his arms wrapping around my waist as he tackled me to the ground. Claws dug into my chest, and a feral growl escaped my throat. That, I felt. I pushed against the cold ground, fighting for breath as the alpha bared its teeth.

"Should've sat this one out and let your mate fight for you, Lord Vampire," the beast said. "Guess I'll have to keep her company now."

A line of slobber dripped from the beast's jowls. I reached for the dagger that had skittered out of my chest rig when I fell, my fingertips inching closer.

When the growl of a vampire broke through the chaos. In a flash, Tyson was there, even though I told him to stand down, dagger raised high. He twirled his blade with an exaggerated flourish. "Bad puppy."

Tyson drove his weapon into the alpha's side. The sickening sound of steel on bone was followed by a strangled cry. I blinked in astonishment. My whelp of a nephew, whom I often doubted, had just saved my life.

I heard the wolf's heart beating, and I knew he hadn't delivered a death blow. But I would fix that quickly enough. He had threatened Claire.

I rolled him over, snatched up my dagger, and pinned him as he'd pinned me. A low growl left my throat as its eyes flashed.

"You can kill me, but it won't change a thing. Shayla will come for you."

"Uncle!" Natalia shouted. *"We need answers!"*

But I was already seeing red. I plunged my dagger into the alpha's heart.

CHAPTER 24
VEILLE
CLAIRE

I tried to sit up, but my body refused to obey. Even opening my eyes was impossible; my lids were heavy and limp as lead. With nothing else left, I strained to listen to the muffled voices around me, but it was like my head was submerged underwater.

I groaned, my head throbbing.

"I know you're a girl," a familiar gruff voice said, *"but you've got some balls on you. Don't ya?"*

Even half-conscious, I knew that voice. Gorrath.

I couldn't see him, but I sensed him the way you feel someone standing too close behind you—the prickling at your neck, the weight of their breath. It was the same uneasy feeling I'd had that night alone in our room, the night I discovered what the horn could do. *And again in the circle.* I squeezed my eyes tighter, mortified. The horn. Bastien's hands. The way the demon had—

"If you keep disobeying Bastien's orders and firing spells at werewolves twice your size, I'm going to start liking you. And that was not part of the plan."

163

Despite everything, despite my throbbing head and the fact that I couldn't lift my own hands, I huffed out, *"Sorry to ruin your plans."*

The demon laughed. *"I can see why he likes you. You've got spunk."*

I ignored him. Around me, the real world grew a little more real. Hands slid under my back, and my body tilted like someone was carrying me. The slow, swaying sensation of being carried made my stomach roll. I tried to force my eyes open and say Bastien's name.

"Easy," Gorrath urged. *"Stop fighting it."*

"Have to—" My tongue felt too big for my mouth. *"Bastien—"*

The demon laughed, loud and crass. *"Hate to break it to you, love. But you're not waking up for a while."*

I frowned. Even thinking hurt. *"Am I unconscious? Is that what's happened?"*

"Yes and no."

Sighing inwardly, I asked, *"Are you going to tell me more? Or are you sticking with vague responses?"*

A pause. *"I don't know. Can you stop blushing every time you think about my horn?"*

A fresh wave of embarrassment washed over me. *"Never mind. Just let me be unconscious in peace."*

"You have nothing to be ashamed of," he went on. *"When my magick chose you in that graveyard, a piece of me bonded with your soul. After what we did in that circle, you can't get rid of me. I'm part of you now. So playing with my horn is basically playing with yourself."*

"That is not how that works," I muttered. *"You're not just inside me. You have your own body."*

"Stop disagreeing with me," he shot back, clearly amused. *"I'm starting to like it."*

I tried to roll away from him out of pure spite and remembered I couldn't even feel my own legs. Nor could I escape a creature who was literally inside my head.

Scoffing, I asked, *"How did Bastien stand you? You're disgusting."*

"It's part of my charm."

I said nothing, wondering if five hundred years ago he was less annoying. Thankfully, Gorrath fell quiet, and in the silence, warmth began to spread through my chest. A gentle heat that made me relax into whoever was carrying me. Bastien, I hoped.

The demon, unable to stand a little peace and quiet, started talking again. *"As your new demon, it's my job to teach you the rules of being a living relic. The most important one, which you have learned the hard way, is that you can only hold so much of my power at one time."*

"Why?" I asked.

"Because if you had endless power, you wouldn't be a witch. You'd be a demon. And trust me, you don't want the paperwork that comes with that."

Despite myself, I smiled. *"So I used all of it?"*

"You burned through every drop like a drunk sailor with a purse full of coin."

"And now?"

"You recharge."

Embers of heat spread from my chest, down my legs, and into my toes. It tickled like pins and needles after you've slept on your hand too long. It was my magick, coming back to me.

"Is that you?" I asked quietly. *"Are you doing that?"*

He chuckled. *"Look at you. Smart and reckless. I'm liking you more by the second."*

Quiet settled over us again as he worked. I was grateful his horn wasn't needed for this. Or his hands. He seemed to be able to send me power through our connection.

In the space that the quiet provided, I thought of all that had happened. Of Mellie, the girl with the hollow eyes that reminded me of myself, and the man that she'd killed.

Tears pricked in my eyes. *"Why couldn't I save Devlinn?"* I asked the demon.

He didn't say anything right away, and I wondered if that meant he'd gone. But I could still sense his presence. Finally, he replied, *"There are some spells that even my magick can't fix. Like death spells."*

My throat tightened, and I went to reach for the lace choker around my neck even though I knew I couldn't make my hand move. *"It can't stop death spells?"*

"No," he continued. *"Including the spell on your choker."*

I said nothing, accustomed to keeping my mouth shut about Mama's curse. *"I live inside you, Claire. Of course, I know about your curse."*

I'd wanted these powers so that I could save myself. To stop Imogen's prophecy from coming true. But he was telling me I couldn't do it. A sob caught in my throat. And even though warmth was pushing into every corner of my body, I started involuntarily shivering.

"Sleep," Gorrath said. *"I'll take care of the rest."*

I awoke before my body was fully mine again, floating in that strange in-between place, aware but useless. So I didn't fight it, as the demon advised. I just waited. Listening to the sounds in the background as they became louder and louder.

But truthfully, the only person I was listening for was Bastien. Instinct told me he was close by, but that wasn't enough. I needed to see his face, hear his voice, touch him.

Time stretched on, whether it was minutes or hours; I wasn't sure. Until finally, after trying to move my hand for what felt like forever, my fingers twitched.

It was the smallest victory in the world. I was coming back to myself. Recharged and ready. But my body was still catching up.

Slowly, clumsily, I dragged my hand across scratchy wool blankets. The effort was exhausting and made my head swim, but I didn't stop trying to reach him. My fingertips brushed smooth cotton, then the cool curve of a button.

Bastien.

I followed it upward, mapping by touch alone. Button. Seam. The edge of a collar. Then cold fingers found mine, threading carefully through them. Twining us together. I tried to say his name, but found my voice blocked by the warm press of tears. I was so unbelievably happy and relieved to feel him again.

After everything that happened in the tunnel. And in that circle. I just needed him.

Bastien lifted the inside of my wrist to his lips, and my heart stuttered. "Chérie," he whispered against my skin. "Have you come back to me? Or is this another dream?"

The sound of strain in his voice—the pain in his whisper—broke something open inside my chest. "You don't dream," I managed, trying not to cry. "You're a vampire. Remember?"

He tried to chuckle, but it dissolved into a cough that shook his shoulders. "You're right." He pressed my wrist to his mouth again, kissing it once more. "But I've been in a nightmare ever since you lost consciousness."

"Where are we?" I asked.

"Chastity's Stronghold."

I forced my eyes open and blinked until the blur cleared.

And when I finally saw him, tears flooded my vision so fast it hurt.

Bastien was propped up beside me on a narrow bed. There was dried blood everywhere. Even in his hair. The pale strands a mix of sticky red and black. Deep tears in his shirt revealed angry claw marks over his skin. My head swam with dizziness, but I fought through it, forcing myself to catalog each of his injuries. Including his swollen and bruised jaw.

I went to touch it, but stopped short when he flinched away. "Why hasn't anyone helped you?" I asked.

"I'm not a very good patient."

I saw the sword resting on his lap, and I realized it was because he hadn't let them. He'd been guarding my body while I slept. Standing vigil instead of doing something to help himself.

I tried to push myself up, but the room tilted violently. I fought through the sickness once again. "Drink," I demanded of him. "Now."

"I'm fine," he muttered.

A blatant lie. Firelight from the nearby hearth revealed his ashen skin and sunken eyes. "Don't be ridiculous," I whispered. "Just feed. Please. I can't stand seeing you like this."

He attempted a smile. "I'm not taking anything from you while you can barely sit up."

This stubborn, impossible man.

Bastien smoothed the hair from my face, gently tucking it behind my ear. His knuckles brushed my collarbone on the way down. "I have something for you." He opened his palm and noticed he was holding my bloodstone. The one he'd removed during the ritual. "May I?"

I hadn't realized how naked I'd felt without it until now. "Please."

He draped it around my neck and fastened the clasp. I touched the gem, feeling whole again.

"There. Much better," he observed, admiring it. Then eased back against the pillow and closed his eyes.

"I didn't think you slept," I said.

He raised his brows, but kept his eyes closed. "I don't. But sometimes, I rest."

I kissed his cheek. "Rest, then."

His hand found mine, fingers curling around my wrist like even unconscious, he needed to know I was still there. Only then did the tension leave his shoulders.

Slowly, reluctantly, Bastien found the stillness vampires called rest.

I stayed propped beside him, watching. Love swelled in my chest until it ached. I moved our hands to my stomach and tried to rest, but every time I closed my eyes, devastation waited for me. The bodies. The wreckage. After everything—my husband's wounds, Devlinn's death—I still had no answer for how to remove Mama's choker.

I glanced at Bastien again, and tears fell down my cheeks. I cried. And cried. Until I didn't think I had any more tears inside of me. Grief as I'd never known before sat on my chest and refused to get up.

A whine sounded beside the bed, and I found my wolves waiting eagerly for me. Their bodies bumping against the mattress like oversized children desperate for approval. Their eyes were bright, proud, practically vibrating with it.

I couldn't help the small, tired laugh that slipped out of me.

"You two look very pleased with yourselves," I murmured, brushing away tears before reaching down to scratch the white wolf behind her ear. "You were brave. In the caverns." I patted the brown male on his head. "Yes, you too."

Even as I stroked their soft fur and looked into their eyes, my heart sank. They'd been brave. But so had Devlinn. And now... he was gone.

The white wolf's tail thumped hard against the bed frame. "I need to give you two names," I said, tears filling my eyes. "Or do you already have names?"

I wasn't sure how the bond with familiars worked. More questions I'd never get to ask Devlinn. The white one picked something up off the ground and dropped it onto my lap.

It was an opalescent stone attached to a length of cord. I picked it up, turning it between my fingers.

"What's this?"

CHAPTER 25

LA DÉLÉGATION

TYSON

Tyson swirled his cup, wishing it were Markalish whiskey instead of whatever poor excuse for wine had been poured for him. He didn't like this place, and not just because he'd been raised to appreciate the finer things in life. He didn't mind a little dirt on the floor.

Everything about Chastity's Stronghold screamed *death*.

The ceilings were too low. Everything carried a musty scent. Including the wine. Not to mention it was underground. And while Tyson was a vampire lord, born into a life where old age wasn't something he needed to worry about, he had a secret fear of death, a fear his mother had instilled in him long ago.

Another pesky thought flashed across his mind, and he plugged his nose and took a sip of wine. It was easier to act as if nothing bothered him when all the voices in his head were being drowned in alcohol. But the sour wine was the worst thing he'd ever put in his mouth, and he promptly spit it out.

For the first time, he told himself the buzz wasn't worth it.

Natalia, who was sitting across from him at the rough-hewn table, let out a disgusted snort. "Do you mind?"

"How does anyone drink that?" he wondered aloud.

"It's the house specialty," Natalia answered, returning to the journal she always kept with her, scribbling down whatever she thought was important.

He set the tin cup down on the table and pushed it away. "More like the house tragedy."

She lifted her eyes to his. "It's a mix of wine and herbs that's supposed to keep one *virile*."

Tyson sputtered out a laugh. "If that's what I had to rely on for virility, I'd let one of those werewolves throttle me. Gods."

Natalia studied him for a long moment. She'd already washed the blood from her face and hands, and re-braided her long brown hair. It draped over her clean white shirt and black vest.

"Be careful what you wish for," Natalia said, reverting to her writing.

Tyson swallowed hard, the taste of the sour wine lingering on his tongue. He'd met his cousin only once before coming to Château Rose. The only thing he'd known about her was the rumors that circled around court.

But Tyson had always thought the world of his Uncle Bastien. The unmarried uncle who refused to obey court politics and scared the piss out of everyone he met. He'd grown up hearing Uncle Marius tell stories of Bastien's great victories, including his first one. The one that earned a wayward second son from a small coven more votes than any other witch at The Choosing.

Natalia snapped her journal shut and tucked it back inside her vest. "They're coming."

Tyson sat up a little straighter in his chair and reluctantly moved his wine cup closer to him.

"Remember what I told you," Natalia warned. She pointed a finger at his chest. "You might be heir, but I am second in command. I speak for Uncle Bastien when he is away. You will keep your mouth shut."

The door to the small receiving room burst open, revealing a copper-haired witch in a tightly laced corset and a long, gauzy black skirt. Her lips were painted red, and her nails were painted black. Dark tattoos that resembled snake scales crept up both her arms.

Natalia stood, and Tyson did too.

"My Uncle thanks you for your hospitality," Natalia said.

The Dark Witch smiled in a way that made Tyson think she found Natalia's formalities funny. He grinned right back at her.

She gave him a long, unimpressed look, then promptly addressed Natalia. "Bastien thanks me with your mouth? How unlike your uncle."

Tyson couldn't help himself. "He would thank you with his own mouth, but it's swollen shut at the moment."

Natalia glowered at him. Then quickly forced a smile, addressing Chastity. "He was gravely injured in the battle to liberate the tunnels. And is resting as we speak."

"Bastien? Resting?" she replied, studying her long black nails. "Didn't he bring a blood bag with him?"

Tyson hid his laugh behind a cough. He thought the joke was funny, but his uncle wouldn't.

"She was also injured," Natalia forced herself to say. "My uncle is nothing if not chivalrous. He waits for her to be well enough to feed. Which is why we've come to treat with you in his place."

Chastity sighed and frowned. "Well, if he is unavailable."

She snatched the chair at the head of the table and spun it around. With a flourish of her skirts, she widened her stance and lowered herself onto it slowly, revealing stocking-clad legs and knee-high leather boots. She crossed her arms, leaned forward, and arched her brows, letting a slow, knowing smile hang in the air. "Well, go on. Treat then."

Tyson fell in love. Well, not actually *in love*. He didn't think it was possible for him to love anyone. Because no one ever saw past his perfectly crafted façade. And no one ever would. But his cock was another matter. He fell in love with many exquisite creatures over and over again.

And the fact that she was ignoring him was the cherry on top. He needed to turn his game up a notch. Because being charming and wooing lovers was just as good a distraction as liquor.

Natalia removed her journal from her vest and set it down on the table, then flipped open to a page. "On behalf of my uncle, the Duke of Roselyn, Prince of the Unified Territories—"

"Get to the point, Natalia," Chastity cut in. "I don't have all day to dally."

"You should make the time," Tyson said. The witch glanced his way. Her lovely gray eyes widening slightly. "To dally. That is."

Natalia groaned, but Tyson took it as a good sign that Chastity seemed intrigued. Negotiations didn't have to be boring.

"What's your name again?" Chastity asked.

"I'm Tyson. Bastien's heir."

A faint crease appeared between her brows. "I didn't think he had a son."

"He doesn't. I'm a court-appointed heir. The best of the best."

"My, my." She ran a tongue over her teeth, studying him in a way that made his cravat feel too tight. "And how old are you? I can never quite tell with vampires."

"Old enough," he replied automatically.

She made a small, noncommittal noise in the back of her throat. "One day," Chastity said, "when you've reached an appropriate age, however old that is for your kind, you'll learn how to get your day's worth of dallying done in an hour. You see, at forty, I don't have time to let a man dally around. He needs to know how to get in and get out."

"Please excuse my cousin," Natalia said. "He talks twice as much as warranted."

"That's alright. I like a man who can make me laugh. *At him*." Chastity picked up Tyson's cup of wine and drained it. "Now, I think you had some treating to do?"

Tyson let the comment roll off him like it didn't matter and forced a lazy grin. However, it didn't fit quite right on his face.

Natalia was back in her books. Trying to look official. "We request modest accommodations for our host. Two days should be plenty. Bastien would also like to acquire two relics, if you have any for purchase. And, of course, whatever information you have on the weres that were locked in the tunnel."

Natalia's pen hovered over the page of her journal, ready to record exactly what Chastity would say. Tyson glanced down at his empty cup of shit wine and his lack of preparation for this meeting, and another crack formed in his carefully curated mask.

"And what will I get for all of this?"

"We are prepared to negotiate your integration into the Unified Territories, protecting your land and people, as previously agreed upon."

"Stop right there." Chastity held up a hand. Tyson knew it was more than a gesture, but a roadblock. "I agreed to join the Unified Territories when Hector was at the negotiating table. Now we've got Shayla. And she's hellbent on renewing the war."

"What do you mean?" Natalia asked, scribbling.

Chastity's lips peeled back over her crooked teeth. "You saw those abominations down in the tunnels." Her fist hit the table, stilling Natalia's pen. "Those are just the ones we trapped."

Tyson finally understood what Uncle Bastien meant about the negotiations in the Lawless Lands. One witch dies, and it destabilizes everything.

"We understand things have changed," Natalia replied without missing a beat. "Hector's death is regrettable. But we believe we can offer you protection even without Shayla's cooperation."

"Your belief," Chastity said slowly, "is not good enough. Not with werewolves crawling through my tunnels."

Tyson understood the sentiment. He was currently nursing a werewolf scratch or two that hadn't healed because he hadn't fed yet. They were ruthless creatures.

The red-haired witch continued. "I've got it on good authority that your Blood Treaty is failing. That covens are breaking with it. And some are even trying to join us on this side."

"Have you had any visitors?" his cousin asked. "Witches who want to join you?"

Chastity shrugged.

Tyson didn't need vampiric senses to know his cousin was getting irritated. He saw it in the tightness around her mouth. Natalia struggled to keep a lid on her temper on a good day. This negotiation could go south fast.

"*Well*," Natalia said tersely, "I can assure you there is no cause for concern. My family has maintained five centuries of unbroken peace."

Chastity stood from her chair, walked around to where Natalia sat, and hopped up onto the table. One boot planted on the table top. "Well," she said, mocking Natalia. She reached down and closed her journal with two fingers. "I've already secured my own *protection*."

Normally, seeing someone as beautiful and dangerous as Chastity talk down to his rather snarky cousin would've brought him joy. But this was about more than just a power play. This was about the future he would soon inherit. A peaceful border was far easier to manage than one at war. And he didn't like the way Chastity said *protection*.

Natalia sat back in her seat and folded her arms across her chest. All decorum gone. "What kind of *protection*?"

"You saw the werewolves down in the tunnels. Did they look a little... *sick?*"

The black saliva. The lesions. The horrible stench.

"I suppose," Natalia conceded. "They had pock marks. But they were living in squalor."

"No," Chastity replied, tapping one of her long black nails against the top of Natalia's journal. "That wasn't *squalor*." Her gray eyes flicked between them, savoring the reveal. "That was a *demonic* plague."

Natalia rose from her chair so fast that it tumbled to the floor. "You made a deal with a demon?"

Uncle Bastien really wasn't going to like this.

"No, little Natalia. I summoned one."

CHAPTER 26
L'INVITÉ
CLAIRE

Knock. Knock. Knock.

The sharp rap of knuckles against wood. The sound made my head throb and nausea coil in my gut. Beside me, Bastien continued to silently rest.

My wolves growled, and I petted the top of their heads, scratching behind their ears. "Who is it?" I forced myself to ask.

"An ol' friend," came a gruff voice.

I froze. Heart fluttering in my chest. That voice. *That voice.* It was only ever *inside* my head. Not *out* of it.

The instant the doorknob turned, I seized Bastien's sword. It was heavier than I thought it would be, and I was too weak to hold it up. "Identify yourself!"

My wolves rushed to the door, barking and growling, when they suddenly backed off and ran under the bed, whimpering.

The door creaked open, and a man melted into the shadows of the dark room. Even though I couldn't fully see him, I could *feel* him. My body recognized him.

Gorrath.

"You don't need a sword," he said with a chortle.

I scooted closer to Bastien, unable to believe my eyes. He'd said the demon was locked away in the Underworld.

"Wake up. Bastien, wake up!" I breathed. But he didn't move. He was a living corpse. No heartbeat. No breath. The only certainty that I had that he wasn't completely dead was the pull of our matebond.

The demon stepped out of the shadows, and I struggled to pull in a full breath. He was tall and lean, with sculpted shoulders and wide hands. His skin was golden brown, and soft black curls fell into even blacker eyes. But the thing that unnerved me the most was the single curled horn framing the left side of his face.

"You can't be here," I said. "Bastien banished you. He sealed you in the Underworld."

"Aye. That he did," Gorrath replied. "But he forgot that he is dead. And magick dies when the caster does."

"When he became a vampire..." I said, my voice trailing off.

"His spell weakened. Chastity was able to break it."

My mind raced with the implications. But either way, Gorrath was here now. In the flesh.

He wore no shirt under his closely fitted jacket. Just bare skin inked with rose thorns. This close, his power seemed to call to the magick inside me. Stirring it until restless energy moved beneath my skin. A flush settled into my cheeks, and sweat rolled down my neck.

He'd been there in that circle. Holding me. Touching me. Invisible, yes, but there. He'd been inside my head. He'd messed with my emotions.

Gorrath pressed his hands to the footboard of the bed and leaned in until we were eye level. "Drop the scared little dove act. You're not fooling me."

"I'm not scared," I bit back.

He laughed under his breath and leaned an inch closer, invading what little space I had left. The aroma of frankincense wafted toward me. "Where's the girl who called me disgusting? I'd like to talk to her, please."

I held his gaze. Saying nothing felt like the only weapon I had. It seemed to disappoint him, which I took as a win. I didn't need to play right into his hand. He was here for a reason.

The demon turned his attention to my husband. "He looks like hell."

"He refuses to eat."

"Of course he does," the demon drawled. His gaze flicked back to me. "You're carrying our heir."

"Our?" The word tore from me. I crawled forward on the mattress, the fire igniting in my eyes. The power rising to meet my fury. "There is no *our*," I spat. "There is no world in which you get to use that word with me. If I am with child, it is *not* yours."

The candles along the walls flared to life. The bed frame groaned as I rose onto my knees. One finger pointed dangerously at his tattooed chest.

Gorrath unbuttoned his jacket and opened it, baring himself to me. He was chiseled and hard, and the thorns stretched down below the waistband of his trousers.

He pressed his lips together as though trying—and failing—to hide his satisfaction. "Hit me with your best shot, witch."

If he wanted a fight, I would give him one. "Do not speak about my baby again. Or I'll..."

"What?" Gorrath teased. "You'll curse me?" He smirked. "There she is. There's the fighter."

I wanted to fight him. The magick was right there. Sparking against my skin. But something stopped me.

Gorrath slowly buttoned his jacket back up, covering

himself once again. "Your baby will inherit *my* power," Gorrath continued. "I might not be the father, but I'll have a vampire princeling with a demonic bloodline." He folded his arms across his broad chest, looking entirely too pleased with himself. "Uncle Gorrath has a nice ring to it, don't you think?"

Rage exploded through me, so hot my vision swam. "You are *not* coming anywhere near my baby!" I shouted so hard my vision swam, and my head throbbed in protest. I sat back on my heels, struggling through a sudden wave of dizziness. "If you just came to irritate me, then leave. He's trying to rest."

The teasing curl at the corner of his mouth faltered. "Let me see that knock on your head."

"Do not *touch* me."

His gaze flicked briefly to Bastien, then back to me. And for a heartbeat, he almost looked ashamed. But if he could feel anything close to shame, he buried it.

"Relax, Mama. I came to give you an early push present."

I had no clue what kind of present the demon of sex and disease could possibly give me. I glanced at the horn that sat on my bedside table, afraid it was going to start moving all on its own as it had in that circle, and the demon roared with laughter. "Use it after I leave. Preferably before Bastien wakes up." He winked. "Don't worry, it will be our little secret."

I thought about throwing the relic at his stupid head, but I knew that's what he wanted. To provoke me. "Get out."

"But I haven't given you your present yet."

I leaned back against the pillows, trying to stop the room from spinning. "Hurry up then."

He fished inside his pocket and removed a small seashell, holding it up for me to inspect. "I heard there were some covens who could use a few relics. And since you already gave away my other shells, I figured I'd give you another."

Those had been relics? The shells I'd gifted Imogen? Was

that why she wanted them so badly? I pushed thoughts of her aside, but there was a coven that could use a relic. Shreesa's family desperately needed one. Bastien had told me they'd lost the ability to bind familiars to them.

I hesitated. "What is this gift going to cost me?"

He just smirked. "Haven't you ever gotten a gift before?"

I rolled my eyes, but held out my hand. He dropped the shell into my palm. When it landed, dark magick buzzed against my skin.

"I know just who to give this to," I told him, trying not to seem too grateful.

While I was tucking the shell inside my pocket, he picked up the two opaline stones that were sitting on the bed. "One more thing. You wanted to know if your wolves had names. Didn't you?"

Had he been listening to me? Outside the door, or in my head, it didn't matter. It was violating.

He whistled to the wolves, then clapped. They didn't come out from under the bed. "Leave them alone."

Gorrath flashed a too-wide smile, then tossed the two necklaces into my lap. "Put these moonstones on them, and they'll be able to tell you exactly who they are."

"What do you mean?"

"A moonstone is the only thing that allows a werewolf to control their transformation. You'll see what I mean."

I wanted to argue with him, but I was suddenly too dizzy to talk. The back of my head was throbbing in pain. When I touched it, my hand came away red.

Gorrath backed up a pace, then another, inching toward the door. "I'll come back for another visit when they've healed that knock on your head, and he's looking more alive." He cast a long look at Bastien, the grin slipping from his face. "We've got a lot to catch up on."

Then he was out of the room, gone like a shadow. I leaned against Bastien and clutched his bicep just to hold something solid and real. He'd been so confident that Gorrath couldn't escape the Underworld. Just as I'd been so confident that the wolves under our bed were familiars.

CHAPTER 27
MALCHANCE
TYSON

One of Chastity's healers scurried past him, and Tyson closed the door to his Uncle's room as gently as he could. "They're both asleep," he told his cousin.

Natalia rounded on Sir Gavin. "Why hasn't anyone been guarding His Grace's door? This is a gross oversight."

"My apologies, my lady. It will not happen again."

"If His Grace wakes up, I am to be notified immediately. And do not let anyone in. Witch or demon or goddess herself. Do you understand?"

The guards nodded, then stationed themselves outside the door.

Natalia strode down the narrow stone corridor, hips swaying, hands clenched into fists. Tyson raced to catch up with her. "Where are you going?"

"To fetch my sanguine partner. If our uncle refuses to eat, then I'm going to force-feed him."

"He'll be livid."

"I don't care."

She didn't care? Had she met our uncle? "When Uncle Bastien gets angry at you, you'd better say I had no part in this."

Natalia grabbed the front of Tyson's shirt and bared her fangs. "This is why you shouldn't be Bastien's heir. You're not willing to make the hard choices necessary for command." She shoved him against the wall. "It doesn't matter if someone is angry at you. That's a child's worry. What matters is that you did what was best for your people."

She released him, and Tyson tried to put his mask back on. Willing the pieces of his cracked façade to snap back into place. However, when he tried to smirk and brush off Natalia's words, the jagged pieces didn't fit as well as they had before.

"Do you want my help?" he called after her.

She offered him a one-fingered gesture as she continued down the corridor.

Tyson leaned the back of his head against the wall and tried to silence the voices in his head that were screaming at him. Shouting at him with his uncle's disapproving sneer. His father's wrath. His mother's insistence that he was something he was not.

He wanted to drink. To fight. To fuck. Anything to drown out the sound of his own ineptitude.

He exhaled slowly through his nose and dragged a hand down his face. He supposed he should do something selfless instead, like check on the wounded, or perhaps go and comfort Tansy, who wouldn't stop crying over Devlinn's rotted body.

That's what a commander would do. Wasn't it?

The only problem was that Chastity's Stronghold was just as big a labyrinth as the underground tunnels, and he had no *fucking* clue where he was. He looked left, right, then stopped, stilled by the sound of shouting.

Tyson drew his sword and edged closer to a bend in the corridor, back pressed to the wall.

"This way!" a female voice said.

"No, this way!" answered a male voice.

Tyson pushed off the wall just as two figures came tearing around the corner and collided with him full force.

The impact drove the breath from his lungs and sent all three of them stumbling. His shoulder struck stone. Someone's elbow caught his ribs. For a tangled second, there was nothing but fabric and limbs. Normally, Tyson would welcome this kind of situation, with a lot more wine and a lot less clothing. But unfortunately for him, he was trying to act more lordly.

He pushed to his feet and realized the two runners were unarmed. One was a man he recognized from Château Rose. He was almost positive he was one of Claire's consorts, although he couldn't remember the man coming with them into the Lawless Lands. In fact, he'd heard he'd gone missing.

He dropped to one knee, head bowed.

"My lord—"

Tyson froze, staring down at him. He didn't just recognize him. It felt like he knew him. Every inch of him. From his dark hair to his smooth skin.

"You don't need to bow," Tyson said strangely, because bowing was exactly what he was supposed to do. "Please, rise."

Tyson held out his hand, and the man glanced up at him with red-brown eyes. They were the most unusual shade he'd ever seen in his life. So captivating.

He shook off the reaction as he helped him to his feet. He'd just said he wasn't going to be fighting or fucking anymore. It was time to change if he wanted to be Bastien's heir, but he didn't know how to face himself or his fears without the distractions.

He offered his hand to the woman who was still on the

floor. She glowered at him instead of accepting his help. With tangled white hair and a face covered in dirt, she looked like she'd walked through the Underworld and had been spat out. But what bothered Tyson the most was that her dress was ripped and her bodice was loose. She lifted the dagger toward his throat without hesitation. He didn't try to stop her. He was transfixed.

"Move," she said, breathless. "Or I swear to Diana I'll cut you down where you stand, vampire."

Tyson stared at her. Her eyes were brown, just like the man's, except hers were flecked with gold. She was feral and entirely unimpressed with him. He cut a look between them, and something inside him gave way. Like a rope being cut.

It wasn't attraction, not exactly. Nothing like the way he felt when he saw Chastity's stocking-clad legs. This was a pull in his ribs, like a hook had caught him behind the breastbone. His body recognized both of them in a way his mind didn't understand.

Mine.

The thought flashed through him so suddenly that it made him dizzy.

And suddenly, a thumping started in his chest. *Beat. Beat. Beat.* His bloodstone. Tyson stilled. No. *Not that.* Anything but that. Two near strangers covered in dirt. One actively threatening to stab him. The other was a man who had almost been decapitated by his uncle when he caught him naked with his mate.

If his bloodstone was right, he'd just found his own mate. But which one was it? Which one had the stone recognized?

More footsteps thundered down the corridor, followed by the crackle of magick. Witches rounded the bend in a flurry of dark skirts and wands. Chastity's coven witches.

"There!" one of them called. "With the moonstones!"

Moonstones?

Tyson's gaze dropped to the woman's throat. An opaline stone hung there. One was also draped around the man's neck.

"Werewolves use those gems to control their shifting!" another witch shouted. "Shayla's magick!"

These two were wolves? But...

"Thank you for catching them," one of the witches said, lifting her wand higher. "These disgusting creatures will suffer our justice for breaching our defenses."

The woman angled her blade forward. The man beside her shifted as if preparing to lunge.

He should hand them over and rid himself of the problem they presented. If one of them was his mate and died here, they would be reborn decades—perhaps centuries—from now, and he could still inherit Roselyn unencumbered.

That hook that had landed in Tyson's chest gave a rough tug. And despite every logical protest, his body stepped between them and the witches.

Traitor.

"These two aren't werewolves," he explained to the witches. "They're consorts from Château Rose. When we killed the wolves in the tunnels, I gave them these necklaces as gifts."

The corridor fell silent.

"If Chastity has a problem with it," he continued lightly, "she can take it up with my uncle. Until then," he slung his arms around both their shoulders, "they're under my protection."

He internally cringed, wondering what he had gotten himself into.

"We will take this up with Chastity," one of the witches said. Then they backed slowly away. When they were gone, the woman neither lowered her knife nor thanked him. She simply studied him like he was a puzzle she hadn't decided whether to solve or stab.

He had sworn he would never let a matebond drag him back to the capital like a leashed dog. He wanted to be just like his Uncle Bastien.

He'd meant it.

"I think we all need to have a little chat," Tyson said, guiding the two of them in the direction of his room. Or where he thought his room likely was.

CHAPTER 28

LA DÉVORATION

CLAIRE

A choking sound cut through the dark, followed by the warm spray of something wet against my arms. I jolted awake.

Natalia was standing over Bastien. Her knee was pressed into the mattress beside his hip. Her fist was twisted in his hair, wrenching his head back. If that weren't strange enough, a man I vaguely recognized as her sanguine partner was hovering at her side while she wrestled a silver cup to Bastien's mouth.

"What's going on?" I screeched.

Blood spilled over Bastien's lips, down his chin, into the hollow of his throat, soaking into his tattered shirt. The coppery smell and the sight of someone else's blood in my husband's mouth made me more than sick.

I snatched my wand off the bedside table, then knocked the cup out of her hand. It clattered across the stone floor, spilling the rest of the blood. "Get away from my husband," I snarled.

"There's my fighter," said the gruff voice in my head. I ignored him.

"He hasn't fed," Natalia said flatly. "And I'm done waiting for you to do your job."

Heat and magick flared under my skin, and I realized the back of my head wasn't hurting anymore. Someone must've healed me while I was asleep.

Gorrath's doing.

Natalia's eyes widened when she saw the flash of red in my eyes. "He wants to rest," I said. "He deserves to rest."

His niece had never been my ally, and for good reason. I had been deceiving her uncle. But nothing in me wished to harm him. Not anymore. I wasn't the scared girl who had first met Bastien at his Sanguination Ball.

She flashed her fangs at me. "This is your plot, isn't it? To play sick. To starve my uncle. To weaken his command with every breath you take."

"No. You're wrong."

"Am I?" she spat back. "Because the evidence keeps stacking up." She began counting them off on her fingers, as if listing crimes. "His sudden, inexplicable matebond after centuries of nothing. Your necklace. The way you shattered his alliance with one of the oldest covens in his land. Your new, *conveniently* broken magick that required you to summon one of the most dangerous demons. Your wolves. Your sudden desire to bear his child." Her gaze sharpened. "And let's not forget disobeying Bastien's order to stand down in the cavern. Now our entire army knows you are his mate, which puts his life in danger because this very union goes against our laws!" She growled. "You are a *traitor*."

Even though I could understand how her long list made me seem traitorous, I lifted my wand to her chest. Natalia's gaze dropped to the tip of it, then slowly climbed back to my face.

"Touch him again," I said, "and I will set this entire room on fire. Starting with you."

The fire in the hearth popped and hissed as if on cue.

"As if I needed any further confirmation of your treachery. He might allow you to prance around unchecked. But I will not allow you to kill him."

"If I were trying to kill him," I shot back, my wand trembling in my grip, "I could have done it a hundred times by now." My throat tightened, but I forced the words through anyway. "We are on the same side." My voice broke. "I love him, Natalia. I love him. I don't know what else to say or do to convince you."

She pulled a dagger from her chest rig and handed it to me. "Feed him."

I swallowed hard, remembering the way she demanded I bleed into a cup and take a blood vow. I had gotten out of cutting my hand that time, but I didn't think I could escape it now. "If I do this, will you finally trust me?"

"No. But," she said, hedging, "I will consider it."

"Fine."

What was left of my blood phobia made itself known as I held the dagger in my right hand. I didn't just want to do this to prove Natalia wrong. I wanted to do it for Bastien. She was right. He did need to eat.

I dragged the blade across my palm and watched the skin part beneath it, watched red bead and swell and then spill in slow, trembling lines down the curve of my wrist. The sight of it still made my stomach twist. I forced myself to breathe through it. One breath. Then another. And I found I could bear it.

Slowly, carefully, I lifted my hand to Bastien's mouth. His lips were cold when they touched my skin.

"Bastien, it's me. I'm feeling better now, and I want you to feel better too." The sound of my voice stirred him. Groggily, his fingers closed around my wrist. "That's it. Take what you need."

Blackness bled into his eyes, and his fangs lengthened. I'd never watched him change so intently before. As soon as my bleeding hand met his mouth, he sank his teeth in.

I gasped as the pressure and momentary pain transformed into pleasure. But then he bit down harder, stealing my breath. Before I could react, he pushed me down against the mattress, his body covering mine, pinning me to the bed.

Then his mouth moved from my hand to my neck.

Teeth sank in, and pain flashed white behind my eyes. He drank mouthfuls like a drowning man. The bond between us opened, and I could feel the desperation clawing through him. He was starving. It terrified me how easily I would have let him take everything.

I heard Natalia curse under her breath before she grabbed Bastien by the collar and ripped him off me. Blood streaked his mouth and chin. It dripped onto my skin, onto the sheets. But his wounds were healing before my eyes. His broken jaw and the deep scratches over his chest.

"Uncle?" Natalia said.

Gripping him by the shoulders and shaking him. Her hard exterior crumbled when his eyes returned to their usual shade of blue. For a second, she was a little girl, standing before the uncle she so admired.

"Uncle, I failed you." Her eyes filled with tears. "Chastity doesn't want our protection. She's summoned a demon." She bowed her head. "Please forgive me."

Bastien put his hand under her chin and lifted it. "There is nothing to forgive." He smiled at her. "I am the one who is sorry."

They hugged each other, and I was glad to know they were

back on good terms. My husband turned his attention to me. "Claire," he said, hoarse and wrecked, "I owe you an apology too."

I shook my head. Repeating his words. "There is nothing to forgive."

He held out his hand for me, and I took it. "While I was asleep, I dreamt that Gorrath visited our room. Tell me it was just a dream."

CHAPTER 29
INTERLUDE
GORRATH

I was more than willing to come visit him in bed, but look at that, he found me first. Sword in one hand. That ridiculous cane in the other. Wearing a black riding jacket and gold cravat, as if he hadn't been languishing in bed an hour ago.

Noble Bastien. Hiding behind the Allard crest.

It's a bold move, considering the dirty vampire has broken more of his own laws than I ever did when I was a Witch of the Darkness, and yet somehow he still manages to look offended by *me*.

What? I didn't tell you that I was born a witch? Must've slipped my mind. I look better with horns, truthfully. Well, I did. Until he cut the other one off, leaving me with a thick pink scar where it used to be.

My deal with Damien is the very thing that caused Bastien to lock me in the Underworld, though history has a way of sanding down inconvenient details until only the villain remains. I wanted to bring back the lost goddesses. The covens didn't. Blah, blah, blah. I'm not here to reminisce. I'm far more interested in the near future.

The one where Bastien agrees to help me get what I want.

Just look at him. Strutting toward me in his vampire state. All black eyes and bad intentions. Come stand next to me, love. I don't want you to miss a thing. Because if I get everything I want, you're going to want a front row seat.

"I'd introduce you, but I hear you're well acquainted," Chastity says, crossing her legs and unnecessarily fixing her skirts.

I scratch my chin and smother a laugh. I love this woman. Chastity is a master of the subtle difference between power and performance.

She likes Bastien. She just doesn't trust him to keep her people safe. Not since she was forced to retreat to her underground lair because of Shayla's werewolves. Which is why she paid a pretty price to summon ol' Gorrath.

Bastien stops just shy of where I stand beside Chastity's chair and points his sword at me. "*He* was not part of our bargain," Bastien says to Chastity.

She scoffs. "Neither was my hospitality. But here I am, extending it to you and your army."

"You're also giving *him* your hospitality. And I'd wager he took more from you than just room and board." She holds his gaze, not giving an inch. But Bastien is still monologuing. He's angry. "Release him from whatever bargain you made. Join me, just as you intended. You'll retain autonomy over your lands—"

Chastity presses her hands against the arms of the chair and slowly rises from her seat. "Under the watchful eye of a vampire, who would be building a castle for himself and his court *on my land.*"

I rub my hands together, knowing I'm about to get a show.

Claire, on the other hand, has no idea this is all working out in her favor.

"I already told your niece and nephew, I don't have time to dally about. And I'm a much wiser woman than the girl you met years ago who had assumed control of her coven."

The black bleeds out of Bastien's eyes, and his fangs retract, leaving nothing behind but the colder, sharper features of the man I once knew. The version he's obsessed with maintaining because he doesn't want anyone to call him reckless ever again.

Not after his Mama caught us that night.

"I don't want to speak for Chastity," I say, sauntering a few steps closer, enjoying the way his grip tightens on his weapons. I glance back at her, just to be polite. She gives me the barest nod. Permission granted. I wink. She flushes.

Don't get jealous, love. There's plenty of me to go around.

"But no one wants to be a part of the Blood Treaty," I continue. "I know it doesn't feel good to be irrelevant, but it's time to let it go." I gesture to Claire. "You've got more important things to worry about besides who signs a useless scrap of paper. Like, who is going to come to your baby shower?" Bastien's lip curls. I grin. "Before you bake a cake and knit booties, your wife needs a spell to free herself from that collar."

I let the words sit there, making everyone deliciously uncomfortable.

"Admit it. That's why you really came here. Not to protect Chastity or preserve the balance of power." I tilt my head, studying him. Gods, he hates being seen. "But because you're selfish."

"Shut up," Bastien seethes.

"You want a spell, Bastien! Because you can't do magick anymore. At least, not like you used to. You've traded your power for blood and eternity and a superiority complex."

I wait while the truth lands. Soaking in the moment.

Now he's ready to fight back. "You have broken free from the Underworld. You sought revenge on me through my wife. You have collected more sacrifices from me than I was ever willing to give you. I'm a tolerant man, but now, it is time for you to go back to where you came from. And this time, when I take your other horn, I'll make sure you can't come back."

What a lovely speech. Very impassioned. Let's clap for him. You can tell he's been rehearsing it in his head since the moment he realized Claire had my power.

"Threatening me with magick you don't have?"

"You—"

I'm laughing before he can finish. The way he looks like he's getting ready to hit me with that cane until I yield is too funny.

I wipe an imaginary tear from my eye and smile. "Go on," I say. "If it will make you feel better, hit me."

Bastien is still clinging to the idea that this ends with a sword.

It won't.

Claire—bless her reckless little heart—knows this already. She doesn't have the language for it yet, but she feels it in her blood. She wants like I do. It's what makes her such a powerful Witch of the Darkness. And it's what's going to save her life. Because a want like hers and mine doesn't disappear just because you banish it. No. It goes underground. It waits. And when it comes back, it's hungrier than before.

"I'm not here for revenge," I admit. "If I were, you'd already be screaming." One side of my mouth lifts in an impish grin. I let that sit before continuing. "I'm here because of an age-old understanding."

"Which is?" he demands.

"The enemy of my enemy is my friend."

Bastien laughs. Claire doesn't. After all our chats, I think she's coming around to me.

"You are not my friend."

"I'm more of a friend than you realize." I run a tongue along my teeth. "You want Shayla dead. So do I."

Bastien shakes his head. "I never said I wanted her dead. I said I wanted to negotiate peace with her."

I ignore his little show, because he knows there's no making peace with someone who created an army of weres. "I made a bargain with Chastity to get rid of Shayla. And now I want to make a deal with both of you."

"I would never—"

"We should hear him out," Claire cuts in, finally finding that rebellious voice of hers. I do love it when she puts him in his place, so I don't have to.

"See, she gets it. She knows, just like you do, that this war doesn't end without me," I continue. "And if you're clever—if you're *very* clever—you'll stop pretending I'm the worst thing that can happen and start asking what I want in return."

I step closer, just enough for Bastien to feel the echo of the past crawl up his spine, just enough for Claire to feel the pull in her blood.

"You will not lay a hand on my wife."

"Relax," I reassure him. "I'm not here to take what's yours. I'm here to save it."

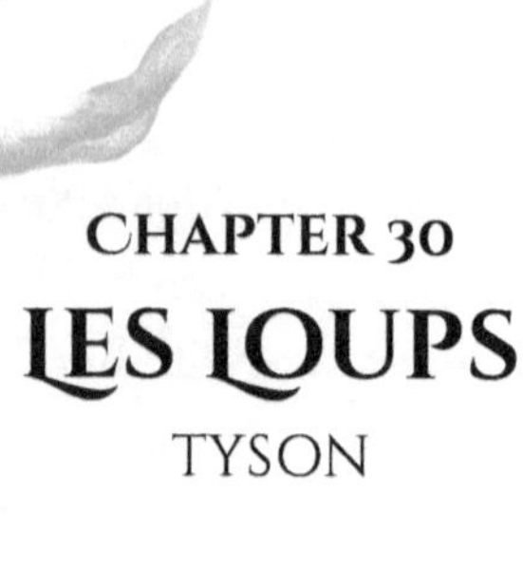

CHAPTER 30

LES LOUPS

TYSON

Tyson shut the door and bolted it, then promptly turned around and stared at his two companions.

How had he ended up in this situation?

A woman who refused to give him her name stood in front of him. It hadn't escaped his notice that she was still holding a dagger. His other guest was Alec, who looked like a man who had just realized he'd allowed himself to be locked in a room with a vampire.

Tyson studied them both in silence.

Beat. Beat. Beat.

The longer he was in their company, the more he longed to know them. He didn't just want to know how they liked to be fucked or whether they preferred white or red. He wanted to know how they had ended up here. The whole story. But getting to know someone required both parties to share. And no one truly knew who he was. Hell, he didn't even know who he was.

A discomfort he always tried to avoid threatened to crack his mask again, and he almost asked if either of them wanted a

200

drink, but caught himself before the words slipped out. He was not hosting a party.

He was in the Lawless Lands, concealing two near-strangers, while his Uncle lay unconscious, and negotiations with Chastity fell apart. And most inconvenient of all was that his bloodstone had decided that one of these two people belonged with him.

Just when Uncle Bastien had started to trust him.

The woman grunted. "Don't get any ideas, vampire. You are outnumbered."

"Are you going to stab me?" Tyson asked the woman. "Or can we put that away for the duration of this conversation? I promise not to bite unless asked nicely."

He laughed at his own joke. They just stared at him, probably wondering why he was such an idiot. "Or keep it. Whatever makes you happy."

"Let's get one thing straight. I don't trust you," the woman said.

"Well," Tyson replied, "you've made that perfectly clear."

He dropped into the lone chair, feeling like this couldn't get any worse. "Start talking. Names. Why witches were chasing you. Why you're wearing moonstones. And, ideally, why the gods decided to make you my problem."

They exchanged a look, and it seemed to Tyson that a whole silent conversation passed between them.

"Of course, Your Grace," Alec began. "We don't want any trouble. She won't give you her name. Not until she's ready." He pushed back thick black hair from his brow, but it fell right back in his eyes. Those red-brown eyes. "As for me, perhaps you remember me from Château Rose?"

The question dissolved through Tyson's frustrations with the situation. "Of course, I remember you," Tyson said. "You're one of Claire's consorts. Alec. Right?" The man nodded. Tyson bit his lip, eyeing him. "You drank her under the table, right before my uncle nearly murdered you." He chuckled. "And me."

Alec smiled, revealing a single dimple, and Tyson forgot how to breathe. He'd seen beautiful mouths before. He had tasted them. Laughed against them. And then conveniently forgot them by morning. But he'd never been so captivated by the curve of a mouth before.

At least, not one that wasn't already around his cock.

"I thought you wanted *me* to answer the questions, m'lord," Alec said.

Tyson could barely tolerate the cheek in his voice. He had to bite his lip again to keep from saying anything else. *This was going horribly.* Pinching his temples between his fingers, he gestured for Alec to continue. "Of course. Sorry. Keep talking. I'll be quiet."

Why was he being so awkward? He was *never* awkward. He could flirt in three languages. He'd charmed members of the human aristocracy. And yet here he was, tripping over himself in front of a man who worked as one of Claire's consorts. A man who he'd openly laughed at when he told his werewolf story.

The irony was not lost on Tyson.

"We need to speak with Miss Claire. Right away," Alec insisted. "It's very important."

It was hard to hear him say 'please' and then deny him anything. Perhaps he was his mate. A truly unorthodox pairing in vampire society, but not unheard of. It would absolve him of needing to create an heir right away. But the problem remained. He didn't want to be mated right now. He couldn't. Tyson leaned back in the chair and crossed one ankle over his knee, trying to act aloof and unaffected.

"What could be so important that you need to speak with Claire right now?"

The two shared another look, which might've been an entire conversation. Tyson, uncomfortable with how little control he had over his emotions, returned to humor. "If you don't tell me, I could hand you back to Chastity," he teased. "She seems very enthusiastic about jailing you."

Her nostrils flared before she kicked over the small wooden table between them. Tyson didn't move to pick it up, and neither did she. They simply watched each other.

He'd grown up around the women of his Uncle Marius's court who performed for him. Who fluttered their lashes in the hopes of earning his favor. Okeri had never been that girl. She'd been one to fight and laugh and drink with him. It was how they became such good friends. But this girl was different. She had an air about her that made his spine straighten.

"I am not afraid of Chastity," she said evenly, though the jumping pulse in her throat betrayed the lie. "And I'm not afraid of you."

When a woman put him in his place, he normally felt inadequate. Like the way he felt when his cousin did it. But when *she* did it, it made him want to be the man he thought he could be. If Alec's mouth had entranced him, then her anger unmade him.

Was it her? Could she be his mate?

Alec set his hand on her shoulder and gave her an earnest look. The familiarity between them twisted something unpleasant inside Tyson. "We should tell him."

"Absolutely not," she shot back.

More firmly, Alec said, "Yes."

Tell him what? Tyson couldn't take it. What did they know that he didn't? Which one of them was his mate? *Beat. Beat. Beat.* One of their hearts was alive in his stone.

The woman rolled her eyes and crossed her arms. "Fine. Tell him."

Alec gave her an affectionate look before turning his attention back to Tyson. "This is going to sound crazy, I know, m'lord. But we are Claire's wolves."

Tyson's brows lifted. Well. That was... *surprising*. "You mean the brown and white ones that fought with us in the tunnels?"

Alec nodded. "She *thought* we were familiars. But we aren't," he admitted. "We're both werewolves who didn't have the power to shift back into human form until we put on these moonstones."

Tyson opened his mouth. Closed it. Then opened it again. "What?"

The woman with the dagger growled. "We don't have time to explain every detail. The bottom line is that werewolves can sense things. And when we put on these moonstones, it was like we were plugged into Shayla's network."

Tyson stood from his seat. "Are you saying you know what she's planning?"

The woman shook her head. "No, it's not like that. It's not like I can read her mind. But I can feel them coming."

"We both can," Alec said.

"Coming where?" Tyson asked.

The woman made an impatient sound. "Coming *here*!"

Tyson studied their faces carefully, searching for exaggeration. He'd always been skeptical of tall tales, but for whatever reason, he believed theirs. "You're sure that Shayla is coming here?"

They both nodded. Tyson dragged a hand down the front of his jacket as if smoothing nonexistent wrinkles. "One question before we go find my uncle." He pointed at them both. "Do either one of you *feel* anything toward me? Anything you want to get off your chest?"

The woman narrowed her eyes. "I don't want to talk to you

or your uncle. I only want to speak with Claire. What I have to say is for her alone."

"Okay," he said quickly. "So you clearly hate me. That's very helpful. And you?"

Alec dipped his head. "I really just want to get back to Claire, m'lord. That's all."

Tyson stared at them both for a long moment. They didn't seem the least bit interested in him. Maybe his bloodstone was defective. Or maybe it was just him.

"Well, let's find my uncle. Hopefully, he isn't in too foul a mood after being force-fed. Although something tells me he will be."

Tyson opened the door and found he wasn't alone. Witches. Dozens of them. The corridor was packed so tightly he thought his eyes were playing tricks on him. Every wand was raised. *At him.*

"Hello, handsome," one said.

The spell left her wand without warning.

Tyson did not have time to draw steel, or step back, or do anything to protect the two people behind him. The force of the spell struck him square in the chest and drove him backward. His spine hit stone hard enough to steal the air from his lungs. The taste of blood filled his mouth.

CHAPTER 31

ÀNU

CLAIRE

Gorrath was right about one thing. I'd known for a long time that he was an important part of my becoming. His magick and his horn had changed my life. However, he explained that his power had limits, and breaking the curse on my choker was one of them.

"I thought you said you couldn't break—" I began to say, but the pain stole the rest of the sentence from my mouth. I lifted my fingers to my throat.

"Are you alright?" Bastien asked.

"Yes," I lied, swallowing around the tightness of the choker.

Gorrath studied my neck, and I had the strangest sense that he could feel it too. "I can't break death magick. Unfortunately, it's not one of my many talents." He fixed us both with a penetrating look. "But *we* can. The three of us."

Chastity let out a bubbling laugh. "The power of three will set you free." She licked her lips. "Please do let me know if you need a fourth." The two of them, seated side by side, looked like they could be lovers. And maybe they were. Gorrath, with his rose thorn tattoos peeking out from beneath his black jacket. And Chastity, with her snakeskin tattoos running up her arms. Both were dressed in black. Both exuding the kind of energy that made men and women melt.

Her eyes met mine, and they were laced with more than just curiosity. A flicker of interest stirred low in my belly. She was beautiful. With full breasts caged behind a black corset and a long neck. My attention drifted momentarily to Gorrath, who was leering at Bastien with the same intensity.

Even though the choker had relaxed, my throat still felt tight. He was the demon of sex and disease. I knew that the power of his horn fed my desires until they were difficult to ignore. While Gorrath and I didn't share the same kind of bond that Bastien and I did, I didn't need one to understand what he was proposing.

"Don't you worry, Chas. There's enough of ol' Gorrath to go around." He touched her cheek and gave her a fond look. It was hard to tell whether he was truly fond of her or just manipulative.

But when you were pure want, maybe you couldn't tell the difference. Maybe it was all the same thing. If your want was strong enough, there was nothing you wouldn't do to get it. That thought scared me, because I related to it a little too much.

I'd wanted things too. I'd wanted my mother's love so badly I was willing to die for it. I wanted magick so badly, I prayed to the goddess every night. And then, of course, there was Bastien. And our child. My want for him and our family was endless.

As much as I wanted to judge Gorrath for being so single-minded, I couldn't. I understood him. I was him. A part of him was already inside me.

My attention drifted to the place where his horn had been

sliced off. A horn that was in my skirt pocket. A horn that I'd used to make myself come over and over again until I was sweating and writhing on the floor.

"Can you give us a bit of privacy?" Gorrath asked Chastity. "Ensure we won't be bothered. Would you, love?"

The smile that had been building on her face fell. Her eyes went cold. "Of course. I have other matters that require my attention." She smoothed her skirts, taking her time as she retreated. "Bigger and better matters." Before she closed the door, she glanced back at the three of us, eyes narrowing on Gorrath. "Don't forget our deal, demon."

He winked. "It's at the top of my mind."

"Ensure that it stays there. I know how slippery your mind can be." The dark witch smiled, then disappeared, the heavy door closing shut behind her.

Once she was gone, Gorrath's dark eyes twinkled with mischief. "Who's ready to strike an accord?"

Bastien and I exchanged looks. Tension was thrumming in the room now that the three of us were alone. Gorrath wanted to make a deal, and truthfully, there was very little I wouldn't agree to at this point. Not because I wanted the demon in any sort of way. But because there were *other* things I wanted.

I wanted to be free of this collar. I wanted to protect the flicker of life that might be stirring inside me. I wanted to live. I wanted that quiet life with Bastien. And because of the strength of my wants, I knew I needed to step back from these negotiations. I didn't want to manipulate my husband into making a deal he was uncomfortable with. If we agreed to whatever Gorrath wanted, Bastien needed to want it too.

"What are the terms?" Bastien inquired, unnecessarily straightening his cravat.

Dust and bits of stone rained down as if the ceiling had coughed. Debris landed in my hair and fell down the front of my dress. I brushed it away, trying to remove the gritty texture from my skin. When I glanced up, both the demon and Bastien were watching me.

I stilled.

"We use the power inside us to break the spell on Claire's necklace," Gorrath explained. His voice had lost some of the gruffness. "I can't break death magick, but Bastien," he said, turning toward my husband, "*you* are the living dead."

Gorrath slunk forward like a feral tomcat until he was standing directly in front of Bastien. One hand was tucked between the buttons of his jacket. A careless black curl falling into his eyes.

"You are the power for the spell, as someone who has already survived death." The two men held very still. Gorrath was an arm's length away from him, but it might as well have been a breath. I knew my husband had done things with Gorrath, things that, if I were being totally honest, I was interested in seeing. "I am the amplifier," Gorrath continued. "And Claire is the conduit."

He slapped his hands together, making both Bastien and me jump. "Together, we give her what she needs to break the curse."

The words hung between us. Neither Bastien nor I had tried to open the connection between us. A deliberate action. On both our parts.

"I've never heard of such a spell," Bastien said. "What does it entail?"

"It's a union. Your power and mine. Together." Gorrath cupped Bastien's cheek. "Put into her."

I'd known Gorrath was going to suggest something like this, but it didn't prepare me for the way it sounded out loud. My body suddenly felt too hot. The air too thick. He was suggesting that the three of us come together. Just like when he'd opened my power and reestablished the bloodline. But this time, he wouldn't be an invisible presence. He'd be real. It would be the two of them *and me*. I tried to imagine what it would be like. The two of them touching me, our bodies moving as one. And as soon as I did, I knew it couldn't happen.

Bastien shoved the demon's hand away and raised his blade. "Absolutely not."

"Once the spell is complete," Gorrath continued, undeterred, "Claire will be liberated not just from the spell on her choker, but from death itself. She'd be like you. *Immortal.*"

Immortal. The word pulled at my weary heart. I remembered the first prayer I'd offered to the God of the Underworld, standing alone in my bedchamber, clutching Gorrath's horn, moments before it started vibrating. "Please, Damien. Make me *unbreakable.*"

Was this his answer to my prayer?

If I were immortal, then the vision Bastien had about me growing ill from the baby would never happen. I'd be like him, strong and immortal. It was the only thing that would push me toward saying yes. But I had to resist influencing my husband, who still had good steel drawn and pointed directly at Gorrath's tattooed roses.

"Wouldn't there be a risk of putting too much power into her body? What about the baby?"

Gorrath smirked. "She's stronger than you think."

I tried to ignore how that made me feel, because Gorrath was manipulative.

"How can we trust you?" Bastien asked.

If we agreed to this deal, we'd be performing an act that would be more than just a spell. It would be a life-changing event.

Gorrath had an answer ready for that, too. "You heard Chastity. She'll have my balls if I don't protect her from Shayla.

If I help Claire break the curse on her choker, you two will bring down Shayla for me."

Bastien ran a frustrated hand through his blond hair, mussing it more than it already was. Then he took my hand, twining his cold fingers with mine. I struggled to make eye contact with him, afraid of revealing my true feelings. I could barely draw in a full breath.

Gorrath leaned closer to us, his black eyes creasing at the corners. "Let me make one thing very clear. I'm not interested in forcing myself on either of you. This deal is either consensual or it doesn't happen. I can find another way to get rid of Shayla."

Bastien withdrew his hand from mine and gripped the bridge of his nose like he was physically in pain. "I need a moment with my wife. Alone."

The demon didn't argue or make a snarky comment. He simply clasped his hands behind his back and strode from the room. When the door was shut, the space felt too small to hold everything that was unsaid.

Bastien gestured to a rough-hewn table with benches, and we took a seat beside each other. My back was pressed into the raw edge of the table. Hands folded in my lap. Bastien set his sword and cane on the floor beside his feet before propping his elbows on his knees and resting his face in his hands.

"Are we honestly considering this?" he asked, speaking to the floor.

The guilt of it all was ready to split me in two. I was doing this to him. It was my past. My family. My choker. My curse. It was hurting him.

"Tell me what you're feeling," I said. "Don't hold anything back."

He took a breath that sounded like it hurt. "Where do I even start? The idea of him touching you—it makes me want to *kill* him." He turned to me, head resting in one hand. His blue eyes glassy. "It reminds me of when I caught you with Alec. Drunk and topless. His hands..." His voice broke off. "I'd been so close to killing *everyone* in that room."

Tears flooded my vision as well. That was the night everything changed. He'd given me the bloodstone that I was wearing right now and told me I was his mate. Then he'd dug out plants in his greenhouse, not just to make room for me in his garden, but in his heart. He'd put his life on the line, over and over again, just to keep me at his side. He even agreed to create an heir, when it was the one thing he was afraid of, just to help me unlock my powers.

He'd done it all without a second thought. But this, *this* felt like a step too far. And I didn't want to cause him this kind of pain. Nor did I want to lose his love or trust. "If this is how you feel, then it's not worth it," I said. "We'll find another way."

He dragged a hand through his hair. "I need to know something. And I need you to be honest with me."

"Always."

"Do you *want* him?" he asked. "I know how magnetic he can be."

"No, of course not," I answered immediately. Truthfully. "I don't want anything with him. Having his power is *more* than enough."

The tension in his shoulders eased slightly. "But doesn't the idea of him touching me disgust you?"

I scooted closer to him on the bench so that our thighs were touching. I ran my hand through his hair, carefully pushing it behind his ear. He watched me. "No. It doesn't."

"How?" he asked, sitting up.

"He is nothing. Not to either of us. Not in the way that we are to each other. He said it himself. He is just an amplifier. Of our bond. Our love. Unless," I hesitated, "does he still mean something to you?"

"No," he said flatly. Then, after a beat, "Whatever we were before—whatever mistakes I made—that was a *very* long time ago. So long that I can't even remember wanting him. My human memories are hazy, like a story I heard from someone else. But I haven't wished for him back in my life. Not one bit."

He exhaled, then added, "But I do want this power for you. Selfishly, I do want to be with you forever."

The tears that had been threatening to spill over my lashes broke free. Two fat tears rolled down my cheeks. "Me too." I dragged in my next breath. "But I won't trade your trust for it. If this would destroy our relationship, then eternity means nothing."

He leaned in and kissed my tears, catching the salty trails with his lips. His cool breath felt good on my flushed cheeks. With my face between his palms, he lifted my chin until we were eye to eye. "I would give you my immortality if I could."

The demonic horn that was hiding in my skirt pocket began to vibrate. Bastien and I both glanced down at it. Slowly, he let go of my face to fish it out of my pocket. Once it was free, he held the vibrating horn between us.

The ceiling rumbled again. More dust rained down.

Neither of us moved, but something dark and dangerous flashed in his eyes. He slid off the bench and dropped to his knees in front of me.

"If I'm going to consider this, I need to know if I can handle it or not."

I nodded. "Of course."

I wasn't sure what he had in mind until he began pulling my skirt up my legs, running the vibrating horn along the inside of my thighs. I momentarily forgot how to breathe when he spread my knees apart.

"Tell me what you want him to do to us."

My eyes widened. I hadn't been expecting this.

A long blink of his lashes. "Play along with me, cherie."

I understood immediately that he needed this. I nodded once again, and the horn slid against my center. Vibrating. *Vibrating.* My breath came unsteady and thin. The desire that always lived just below my skin switching on.

"Do you want to watch him choke on my cock?"

I moaned. My back involuntarily arched.

"You could sit on my face while he did it."

Another broken sound left my lips. The horn clattered to the ground, and his mouth was there. Licking and licking and licking. My fingers twisted into his hair, holding him closer against me, the heels of my boots digging into his back.

The tension that had been thick in the air ripped through me in waves as I imagined the scene coming to life. Two fingers slid inside me, thrusting in and out, and I whimpered. Heat and power and the ecstasy of being devoured by the man I loved came crashing together.

Bastien looked up at me, lips wet and pupils wide. "The only way I'd let him touch you is with a dagger against his throat. I'd tell him how to touch you. And if he strayed, I'd open his throat."

"Bastien," I choked out.

Everything inside me clenched. I was close. So close. He brought the horn back, holding its vibrating ridges against me. His fingers inside me. "Could you take us both? Could you stand that much inside you?"

A feral cry tore from my throat. Gorrath, with his rose thorns, Bastien with his scars. Gorrath meant nothing to me. Nothing. He was nothing. But imagining it? My husband and him? Feeding me enough power to turn me into an immortal?

"I can take it," I rasped.

Bastien set my hand on the horn, encouraging me to keep going, then stood over me. Trousers unlaced. His hard length in his hand. He watched me with lust in his eyes as I teetered right on the edge.

"Put it in you. I want to see it," Bastien gritted out. Working himself up and down like he was about to lose control.

I did as he asked and slipped the tip of the horn inside me. It was almost too much.

"Now fuck yourself."

The command rippled through me, and I obeyed without question. Our eyes locked. Our chests rising up and down in tandem. It was only a moment before the heat of my building magick crested.

"I-I'm going to come," I whispered, voice broken. Sweat dripping down the side of my face.

Bastien ripped the horn out of my hand. In one quick motion, he turned me around, lifted my skirt, and bent me over the table. Rough, hard thrusts brought me to my climax, the table shaking beneath my palms while stars burst behind my eyes. A curse and a moan left his lips, followed by the warmth I was craving. It spilled inside me, and a smile rounded my lips.

This was the only thing I ever wanted. Him. Completely feral.

He kissed my hair. My neck. The tops of my shoulders. "If you weren't pregnant before, you will be," he whispered. His fingers gliding through my wetness, playing with the mess he'd made. "If another man is going to touch you, he's going to know who you belong to." He swirled his fingers against my sensitive spot. I sucked in a shuddering breath. "Because you are mine."

CHAPTER 32
L'INÉVITABLE
CLAIRE

After discussing our boundaries for proceeding with this spell, Bastien and I walked hand in hand toward the door. We were about to step over a line together. And when it was done, I'd be free of Mama's curse *and* immortal. An illicit thrill I didn't bother pretending away raced down my spine. Not for the demon, but for the new life I'd have. Mama would never be able to hurt me again, and I'd be with Bastien forever.

Bastien pulled the door open, but the corridor was empty. No demon waiting for our answer. No Chastity standing guard. It was just us.

"Where—?"

Bastien's question was cut off by the blast of a horn. The sound echoed so loudly I had to cover my ears.

Footfalls came next. Three of Chastity's witches tore past us, their red hair and black skirts flowing behind them. They didn't stop to acknowledge us. In the distance, metal groaned, and a great booming sound filled the corridor. Another puff of dust rained down from the ceiling.

Bastien's hand fit around my waist, and he pulled me against him. When our eyes met, I didn't need to read his emotions to know what he was feeling. We thought we were safe inside Chastity's hidden underground fortress. But now, it was clear her defenses were being breached.

Bastien didn't tell me to go hide in our room. He caught my chin and forced me to focus on him. "Save your magick until it's absolutely necessary," he reminded me. "You cannot draw them to you. You wait."

I nodded shakily. Now that I'd seen how battles worked, I knew I couldn't expect to use my power and save us all. Because the other side had magick too.

Metal groaned again, and the walls rumbled. Bastien took my face between his hands and kissed me as if he might never get the chance to again. It was a desperate kiss. One that brought tears to my eyes, because this was the very last thing either of us had expected. When we broke apart, I rested my head against his chest, trying to will the tears away. We hadn't just brought warriors. We'd brought Tansy. And those children. If anything happened...

Bastien kissed the top of my head and held me against his chest. "Take my dagger."

I went very still. I knew why he wanted me to take a weapon, but the words caused a rush of memories. Rabbits splayed open on wooden tables. Women screaming in birthing beds. I was too useless to cast spells, so I was expected to help. But there was always so much blood. I couldn't. I'd faint, or nearly faint, then I'd be ridiculed and beaten for my reaction.

My family never tried to understand why blood bothered me so much. They didn't care. I was a burden, and that was all that mattered. Until the day Mama put a cursed necklace around my throat and sent me to become the sanguine partner of a fearsome vampire or die. Knowing either way, I'd be forced to face my biggest fear.

Why did everything always come back to blood?

"Take it!" Bastien said more urgently this time.

I fumbled for his chest rig and found the smooth leather grip of his dagger. The same one he'd held against my throat in an attempt to save me on that balcony. When I pulled it free, the polished metal reflected a woman I did not recognize. She didn't look like the girl who had once fainted at the sight of a cut finger. She was stronger.

"Stab the neck of anyone who comes near you," he whispered against my ear. "If you can't reach their neck, slash an artery."

I nodded.

He took my hand, and together, we ran through the dark and twisting corridors of Chastity's Stronghold. I'd been unconscious when they brought me in and hadn't had the opportunity to see just how elaborate the underground fortress was. But now it was my duty to defend it against the Witches of the Light.

A strange, creeping sensation sat in my stomach as we rounded the next corner. A dread I couldn't name settled in my stomach. I wrote it off as battle nerves. The last time we'd fought, we'd lost Devlinn and other brave soldiers.

Shouts filled the air, along with the sweet aroma of dark magick mixed with the tang of sweat. Hundreds were packed inside an entrance hall with cathedral ceilings. Bastien's warriors and Chastity's witches working together to brace the massive metal doors with wood beams and magick spells.

Natalia was giving an impassioned speech to a group of soldiers standing at the front with long pikes. Grunts and cheers went up in bursts.

The guilt was back, choking me until I could barely stand it. Somehow, this all felt like it was my fault.

"Claire!" I turned and found Tansy, sword in hand. She rushed over to me and threw her arms around my neck. I hugged her back fiercely.

"What are you doing here?" I asked over the noise of the crowd, pulling back to see her bloodshot eyes and hollowed cheeks.

"I'm here for Devlinn. He-he'd told me to find peace. And there's only one way to do that." Her voice grew stronger with every word. "I have to live."

There was a boom, and the metal doors groaned. I touched her cheek, memorizing her face. "Watch your back, okay? You're the big sister I never had. I can't lose you."

A weak imitation of her usual grin tugged at her lips. "I was raised to fight. Wand *and* blade. I'll be fine." She covered my hand with hers. "You take care of yourself. Do you hear me?"

I nodded once. Bastien set his hand on my shoulder. "Come, Claire. This way."

I looked at Tansy one last time before Bastien, and I melted into the sea of bodies. The disorientation of being lost in the crowd escalated my anxiety. All the bodies pressing in around me. I held tight to Bastien's hand until we found Chastity's tall, hourglass figure standing beside Gorrath. They were shouting orders at a gathering of red-haired witches. When they saw us, they dismissed the group.

I narrowed my eyes at Gorrath. Why hadn't he knocked on the door and told us there was an invasion? At least the demon had the good sense to look remorseful.

"What's going on?" Bastien asked.

Chastity glowered at him. "Somehow, the moon witches have found the hidden entrance to my stronghold. My scouts say a white-haired witch leads an army of weres!"

I didn't know if it was the anxiety or the choker, but my throat nearly squeezed shut once again.

"And," Chastity continued, eyes narrowing at me, "they tell me two *werewolves* snuck in with your force. When they tried to arrest them, they were stopped by your nephew, who said they came in with your host and were under his protection."

My wolves. She'd seen my wolves and thought they were werewolves. And Tyson had stood up for them. "Are you suggesting I planned this?" Bastien asked with a dangerous edge in his voice.

Chastity crossed her arms. "You tell me? I extend my hospitality, and you bring werewolves into my home!"

I went to say they weren't werewolves, but when I caught Gorrath's eye, I remembered what he'd said. He'd told me to put the moonstones on my wolves and ask for their names.

My stomach churned again, mixing with the throat-thickening anxiety.

"I tried to tell you," the demon said.

Bastien cut in. "Where is my nephew and the wolves?"

"They are my prisoners."

The door groaned again. More dust rained down. Bastien shielded me with his hands, trying to keep it out of my eyes. "You imprison allies when the enemy is at your door?" Bastien raged while debris continued to shake loose from the ceiling.

"He stood against my witches," Chastity fired back.

"He is my heir!"

"He's a fool!" Chastity shouted. "If he were my heir, I'd slit his throat and be done with it."

I'd heard Bastien call Tyson names. I knew that he hadn't wanted him as his heir. I knew he'd wanted to rip Tyson's head off when he caught him inside my room, drinking and playing Dépouiller. However, Bastien's high expectations for his successor seemed at odds with his duty to his family.

Mon sang, he called them. My blood.

He glanced around at the chaos. At the doors. Then back to Chastity. "If I am your enemy, then I will recall my warriors." Chastity's hard exterior showed signs of cracking. "You have your demon. And besides, you've said you don't need my protection."

Chastity let out a huff. "You think those creatures will spare you and your men?"

"No. Of course not. I will pull them back, and we will leave."

Gorrath was silent. A shocking turn of events, considering he almost always had something to say.

Bastien leaned in. "This is why peace is better than alliances with demons. He can't fight your battles for you. He can't even kill a single witch without terms."

"He's been spreading disease to them. I paid him for a plague."

Bastien sneered. "And what did that cost you?"

Fear flickered across Chastity's face, and for the first time, she seemed to understand that she'd erred. Bastien was the ally she needed.

And by the look on the demon's face, he knew it too.

"If you hadn't spent an hour discussing the repercussions," Gorrath said, unable to help himself. "We could've already been on the way to eliminate Shayla."

Spells were fired from the other side of the door, making it glow white like the moon and casting the entrance hall in an eerie light.

"If you want my help, release my nephew and the wolves," Bastien explained. He gave Chastity an honest look. "I don't know how Shayla found your stronghold, but it wasn't the fault of anyone in my host. I swear it."

For everyone's sake, I hoped he was right.

With a huff, Chastity snapped her fingers. "Release the prisoners." She seized a fistful of Bastien's shirt and hauled him down until they were eye to eye. "If you fuck me over, I will haunt your castle for the rest of your afterlife. You will know no peace."

Something close to a grin tugged at his mouth. "Understood."

The doors creaked open a fraction, iron dragging against stone, and a wave of nerves rolled through me. This was it. Bastien took my hand, the one that was holding tight to his dagger, and kissed the inside of my wrist. His breath cool against my raging pulse.

"Remember what I said."

His gaze shifted to the dagger still clutched in my grip. I swallowed and nodded. "I will."

Lovingly, he set his hand on my cheek. "You are fire."

I turned into his palm and kissed it. "You are mine."

He lingered for a moment longer, our eyes holding, before his attention shifted to Gorrath. "Take care of her for me."

A stunned breath left me. He was going to leave me with the demon?

Gorrath smirked. "I'll take care of her *for me*."

"That dagger works just as well on demons as it does on werewolves." Then Bastien raced off through the crowd. Chastity bristled and followed after him. Once he was gone, Gorrath offered me his hand. I stared at it, unsure what to think. Ten minutes ago, everything was different. Now I wasn't sure if he was my ally or my enemy.

"Let me show you that you're *more* than just fire." He tipped his chin toward a narrow stone balcony overlooking the entrance hall. "Come on. It's time to learn how your magick *really* works."

Gorrath wasn't proposing to protect me. He was offering to

teach me. Which was something I wanted. If I could help at all, and not distract Bastien, then that's what I was going to do.

Bastien had his teeth and his strength and his sword. And I had this.

Gingerly, I set my hand in his. And as soon as our skin touched, power flared inside of me.

CHAPTER 33
INTERLUDE
GORRATH

Werewolves and white-haired witches poured through the doors. By Damien's hairy dick, there were more of them than I anticipated.

Claire looks over the balcony ledge, watching with her hands wrapped around that dagger.

"So how do I help them?" she asks. "How do I use this power?"

I place my hands on her shoulders. Her spine stiffens.

"Close your eyes," I whisper. "And imagine you're the damp in the walls. The slow creep of mildew no one notices until it's in their lungs. The fever that ends with mourners in black."

Her breathing deepens. "You want me to imagine I'm death?"

I smile at the word. Death. Such a tidy little concept for something so expansive.

"You're more than death," I tell her. "You're the consequence they pretended wouldn't come for all the hate in their hearts."

"I am the consequence," she repeats.

"But you need to want it. More than anything. Can you do that for me?"

She hesitates. But she needs to understand this. "How do I do that?"

The perfect question. The most important question.

"I know exactly how your family treated you." She shifts her attention toward me. A flicker of fear passes over her. "They treated you like a disease they couldn't rid themselves of fast enough. They hated you for being a good apple in a bucket full of rotten cores."

Tears prick in her eyes. Good. She's getting it. "If they thought you were a disease, then be the disease."

I take her wrists and lift them into the air.

"Don't I need a wand?" she asks.

"You *are* the wand. Now focus. Feel your connection to the disease."

I drop her hands and leave her there to reach into the bodies below. Standing just far enough back to watch. The calm that settles over her face is not innocent. She's the fighter. She's the justice. The sword. The ghost she had to become to survive.

I watch as she begins to sow devastation. One by one, the werewolves begin to fall. The black pustules I planted in them earlier begin to erupt into fountains of rot.

Her eyes open slowly as she takes in her handiwork. "Is this me?" she asks. "Or you?"

"That's all you, love," I say, and I mean it. "I opened the door. You walked through it."

I don't tell her it's taking an incredible amount of my power to hold the door open. She might be a living relic, but the want in her is *endless*. It draws from her well of power too fast.

She lifts her hands higher. A werewolf howls in pain. I smile. "That's my girl."

"Bastien and I were going to say yes. Before this."

I lean against the balcony beside her. A half smile on my face. As much as I want that deal to happen, there is something I want even more. It has nothing to do with sex or disease. Maybe I've been inside her head for so long. Maybe it was the way she called me disgusting. But right now, the thing I want most of all is for her to be free. Free in the way I never would be.

"Let's talk about that later," I reassure her. "I want you sowing rot, not sowing a good time."

She laughs. And damn her, it makes me laugh, too.

"Why sex and disease? I don't get how those things go together."

"Really?" I say. "Disease is the most intimate thing in the world. Next to sex."

She doesn't say anything. She just keeps feeling into her power. Spreading more rot. I try to temper her as well as I can, but I have to pull from my own reserves just to keep her going. But I don't really mind. Not when she's got this smile on her face.

"I think I'm getting the hang of it."

She's becoming the consequence. She wants to make them suffer. And I love seeing it. "You're damn right you are. I knew there was a good reason why my power went to you."

She glances my way. "Didn't you choose me?"

I shake my head. "Once I spilled my seed inside that Kemp witch and gave her line the gift of my power, the magick took on a life of its own."

"So you didn't pick me for your revenge?"

Chuckling, I shake my head again. "It believed you were worthy to hold it. All on its own."

A beat of silence passes between us. Metal clangs and werewolves howl in pain.

"You're different from what I thought you'd be."

I bare my teeth in a grin. "Don't ruin my reputation."

Her lips twitch.

I rest my hand on her shoulder to stop her. We'd gone through more power than I'd realized. "Enough," I tell her. "You'll burn yourself out."

Reluctantly, she lowers her hands. The air is choked with the stench of rot.

When she glances back at me, I am part of her. I can see myself through her eyes. And I see the witch I used to be. The one who was so demonized by his coven, he started to believe he should become one. Who wanted to bring back the goddesses just to find a little joy in his life.

Who looked across the fire at Bastien and recognized something in him.

Just like she had.

We are not so different, she and I.

My attention settles on her throat. On the cursed choker. And even though my vision is blurring around the edges, I know she still needs a spell to be free of it. Because while my mother is dead and buried, hers is still after her.

And she's much closer than she realizes.

CHAPTER 34
ADIEU
CLAIRE

Gorrath suddenly shoved me behind him.

Weak from channeling so much power, I nearly lost my footing on the uneven stones. "What are you doing?"

"Protecting you."

Footsteps raced up the stairs, and that familiar sense of dread sat in my stomach. The one that I couldn't seem to release. After staring into Mellie's eyes, into Devlinn's eyes, there was nothing left that could break me. I'd seen the worst—smelled death—and I was not going to crumble now.

"I protect myself," I told the demon.

He smirked. "Of course you do."

A face appeared in the doorway that I'd known as well as my own, but I couldn't believe it. She shouldn't be here. She couldn't. But... she was. Mama looked exactly as I remembered. Except *everything* had changed.

Her long white hair was braided tightly against her scalp, woven with thin leather cords. Runes were painted in ash across her forehead and down the bridge of her nose. The symbols I recognized. They were protection symbols. Against demonic influence. Against disease.

Against... *me*.

"You—" The word broke apart in my mouth. I was five years old again, huddled on the kitchen floor with my back pressed against the cupboard, cradling my right eye while spilled potion ate through the hem of my only skirt. The air had smelled like fresh lemongrass and thyme and the salty tang of my tears.

By the age of five, I knew I was wrong. Not just for making mistakes, but because I wasn't the daughter she'd been promised.

Gorrath moved before I understood what was happening. One moment, he stood at my shoulder; the next, his arm was around her throat and his fist was buried in her braids, wrenching her head back so hard I heard the leather cords strain. His body pressed against her spine, all heat and fury.

I had spent years hoping to see warmth in her eyes. A shred of softness. A glimmer of something that might have meant *love*. But there was no warmth then, and there certainly wasn't any now. It was just unyielding hate. Now that I'd opened my heart to love, I could see what it had done to her. The way it had twisted her.

I hated—*hated*—that a small part of me wanted to save her. Even now. Even after everything that had happened. But I was experienced enough now to know Mama couldn't be saved. I remembered the look in Mellie's eyes, the one that felt so familiar to me, just before she killed Devlinn. Where her eyes held fear, Mama's held only disdain.

"Now is the time for Bastien's dagger," Gorrath growled over her shoulder. "End her."

The dagger? He wanted me to cut my own mother's throat? To coat my hands in her blood? It was one thing to know she was guilty of more than cruelty toward me, and another thing to carry out her punishment.

Everything I couldn't say stuck in my throat and hardened there. My body refused to move. I was five again. Ten. Fifteen. My whole childhood replaying at once. Standing in doorways like a ghost, hoping to be invited into the living world.

"Go on," Mama taunted. "Do as your demon master says. You filthy, evil little girl."

The world narrowed to the space between us. My fingers twitched around the dagger. And a voice pushed back against her accusations. I wasn't stupid. I wasn't evil. And I wasn't a girl. I was a woman wed with magick of my own. I knew things she'd never know.

If I didn't end this now, she would keep infecting the world with her evil. My heart pounded so hard I thought it might split my ribs. I tried to step forward, but my feet would not obey. Some invisible tether wrapped around my spine and yanked me back into place.

"Do it," Gorrath urged.

But I couldn't. *I couldn't.*

The truth bloomed in my chest like its own kind of rot. Not because I loved her. Not because she deserved mercy. But because she'd ensured I wouldn't be able to hurt her. The barbs on my choker pierced my skin, and blinding pain turned everything around me white.

The only thing I could hear was Mama's cackle as I crumpled to my knees. Drops of blood leaked between my fingers. My fingers slid through the mess until I found the thin chain at my throat—the only proof I could offer. I couldn't tell Bastien the truth about Mama, but at least now he could see it for himself. He might disown our child or me once he found out the depths of my betrayal, but there was no one else I wanted at this moment but him.

"Bastien," I said meekly, calling him to me.

Soon, he'd realize I was no orphan from the Nightfall Convent. I was not a Donadieu, but a Prideaux. I sat in my shame, wondering if it might kill me before the choker did.

"Claire!" Gorrath's voice drew my attention back up. "If you want me to kill her, I need a sacrifice. Demon law."

Gorrath was offering me another way. Where I couldn't strike against her, not with the choker's curse still activated, he could. But he needed a sacrifice, and I had nothing left to give. Bastien had told me Gorrath loved blood. So I lifted my husband's blood-covered dagger weakly.

Gorrath's mouth curved into a grim smile. He winked once. "That'll do nicely."

But before he could take it, Mama's eyes shone with the light of the moon. She seized the dagger from my shaking hand and, with a scream of triumph, drove it into Gorrath's belly.

The wet sound it made was sickening.

He staggered, looking more confused than hurt, as if pain was not something he was accustomed to. Then he fell to the ground beside me like a marionette whose strings had been cut. His demon blood mixed with mine on the stone floor.

His fingers searched blindly until they found mine. "Ah," he breathed, a weak huff of laughter slipping past his teeth. "That... was not the plan."

Tears leaked down my cheeks. Demons couldn't die. Could they? No, it was impossible. They were immortal. A bubble of blood formed at the corner of his mouth, proving otherwise.

With trembling hands, I took his horn out of my pocket and pressed it against his chest. The barbs made the pain nearly unbearable, but I couldn't let him die. Not like this. But nothing was happening.

"When it moves to you," he said weakly, "don't fight it."

I didn't understand what he meant. *Until I felt the heat.* It cascaded through my body in hot pulses, just like it had when I'd been unconscious, and he'd recharged my power.

The dagger, now coated in my blood and his, flared red. And so did his horn. And so did the air between us.

Fire licked up my ribs, down my spine, into my palms.

"I want," Gorrath rasped, "I want to talk to the girl who called me disgusting. Is she here now?"

Tears flooded my eyes. "Yes. She's here."

"Good."

The red light dimmed, then extinguished, and his fingers went slack. Gorrath, a demon and my friend, was gone.

CHAPTER 35
LE DÉVOILEMENT
CLAIRE

The barbs retracted, and I didn't know whether it was Gorrath's power or Mama's. The uncertainty made me furious.

"Why are you here?" I asked, smoothing back Gorrath's dark hair, unable to look at her.

Pain ripped through my scalp when Mama grabbed me by the root of my hair and hauled me upright. My knees scraped stone slick with Gorrath's blood, the warmth of it saturating my skirt.

"I sent you on a mission to locate demonic relics so we could destroy them. Not to make friends with demons."

She kicked Gorrath's horn off the balcony, where it clattered to the floor below. Then, with a violent jerk, she wrenched Bastien's dagger from his chest and wiped the flat end of the dagger across my cheek, smearing Gorrath's blood across my face.

"Come, Claire," Mama hissed in my ear. "We're going home."

Home.

For a heartbeat, I was back in the attic at Prideaux Hill, counting the cracks in the ceiling, trying not to cry loudly enough for her to hear. Back in that narrow bed, convincing myself that if I behaved well enough, if I prayed hard enough, if I proved myself useful enough, she would look at me and see something worth loving.

But that was not my life anymore.

My home was Château Rose. No. *My home was Bastien.* The thought of him gave me strength. "Prideaux Hill was never my home," I said, finally finding my voice. "It was a prison."

She yanked my head back so hard stars burst across my vision. "Was it now? This time, you'll be in a cage instead of a bedroom."

I clawed uselessly at her wrist as she dragged me down the stairs and through the tunnels of Chastity's Stronghold. I tried to fight her at every turn, but her magick compelled me forward. I tried to become the consequence, to spread rot into her body, but my power wasn't responding. I knew it was because I'd used too much of it during the battle. That's why Gorrath had stopped me. He hadn't wanted me to pass out.

We made it to another large door, where a group of half-transformed werewolves was waiting. Ropes were tied around my wrists, and a blindfold was tied around my eyes. Then I was shoved outside, into the cold wind, and tossed into a dark room. A door slammed shut. Suddenly, I was jolted forward, thrown sideways onto a hard bench. A silent scream built in my throat as the floor shifted again, and I fell forward onto hands and knees, feeling like I might be sick. There was something inside me that needed to come out.

"Be the fighter," a gruff voice said. *"Be the consequence."* Tears streamed from my eyes, soaking into the blindfold. How could I fight when I was alone? *"You're not alone,"* Gorrath insisted. *"You have me. And Bastien. And friends. Now fight!"*

I drew in a few calming breaths to slow my thoughts. When I quieted my mind, the answers came. Bastien had told me not all magick required a specific spell. My intuition was more powerful than someone else's words. When Gorrath taught me to spread disease, he hadn't given me a spell. He'd told me to become the thing that silently crept inside bodies. Turning the hate and bad intentions into rot.

And then Imogen's words. The ones I'd been so afraid of. She'd told me I needed to die to break the curse.

I held all of this inside me, sitting with it while the carriage swayed. Suddenly, I knew what I needed to do. It was a wild, reckless plan, but it was the only thing I could think to do. I swallowed hard, fighting back tears, and forced myself to stand. Each bump caused the carriage to rock, and I nearly toppled over more than once. With my hands bound and eyes covered, I searched for the lever that would open the carriage door with my fingertips. With the jolts and bumps, I nearly gave up hope that I'd ever find it, when my fingers found something smooth and cold.

The handle.

I closed my eyes and called to the fire inside me. To the magick that had chosen me. And to the spark of life that lived inside me. The baby that would be born a vampire.

Heat dripped through me like sweat. Like tears. Like a reckoning.

Gorrath thought we needed to come together to make a spell. But I already had all three of us inside me. I already had the answer. All I had to do was be brave enough to jump.

I pressed down on the lever, and the latch gave way. The door flew open. A rush of frigid wind whipped across my cheeks and through my hair. Of course, Mama didn't think to lock it. She only knew the broken girl I'd been when I left

Prideaux Hill. She didn't know the woman I had become. Or the witch I'd learned to be.

I had rebuilt myself from the wreckage she left behind. And now, I was the consequence.

The carriage thundered forward. I could hear the horses straining, the wheels grinding over frozen earth. Somewhere ahead, water roared.

"I've already died," I whispered into the wind. To the goddess. To the god. "I've already drowned in my own hate. And I was reborn in love. In his arms."

For a heartbeat, I felt the old voice of fear. The little girl who knew running away wouldn't do anything except make things worse. I comforted her and reassured her. "We are never going back. Never."

This curse only had as much control over me as I allowed. And I was no longer consenting to be controlled.

"Won't it hurt when we fall?" the little voice inside me asked.

"We're not going to fall," I said. "We're going to *fly*."

A spark of heat and the scent of smoke filled my nostrils. The fire inside me surged outward, devouring the ropes around my wrists in a hiss of flame until they fell away.

With a sigh of relief, I removed the blindfold. The world came roaring to life around me. The moon was nothing but a sliver in the sky. I smiled up at her as my fingers traced the lace that had choked me for so long. It was a symbol of obedience. Of silence. Of shame.

I twisted it around my fingers. "The woman who bore this curse is dead."

I gave the lace a sharp yank, but it remained locked around my throat. I didn't understand. It should've ended. I'd followed my intuition. I'd listened. I had all three powers inside me.

"You still need her blood." Gorrath's voice. *"Blood is owed."*

I set my teeth. I couldn't just fly back to Bastien. Not if I wanted to end this for good. Which meant I still had work to do.

With my face in the wind, I remembered the way Cora mounted a broom and took off into the night. Bastien had said it was a power held by very few Witches of the Darkness.

I spread my arms, imagining being weightless and free. Bending my knees, I leapt into the air.

The wind answered.

CHAPTER 36
L'ÉCHIQUIER
CLAIRE

All I needed was a drop of blood. One single drop of Mama's blood and I could complete the spell. It seemed simple enough. So when I launched myself from the carriage like a raven taking flight, I headed straight for the driver.

Only... it wasn't Mama at the reins. It was one of those half-transformed wolves with a wolfish snout and big hairy arms. He snarled at me and pulled on the reins to stop the horses. "You! How did you escape?"

Anger pulsed under my skin, and my magick begged to be let out. Mama wasn't here. Frustrated, I focused my energy on the carriage, and I sent a spell directly at it, knocking it over and trapping the wolf beneath the wreckage. The sound it made when it fell was oddly satisfying. A crash and a bang and a yelp of pain. The werewolf was trapped under the carriage, which was a good place for him to be. I needed answers.

I landed softly beside him and took in the black pox covering his skin and the growing pool of blood behind his head. Then I saw the fear in his eyes, which were the most human thing left about him. The stench of death filled my nostrils.

I'd done that. When he died, it would be my doing.

I swallowed the empathy rising in my throat because if I hadn't toppled this carriage, he would've carried out his mission.

"Where is Angelina Prideaux?" I asked, putting a purposeful edge of violence into my voice.

It was the voice of a woman who preferred warm weather and nights alone with her husband but would settle for the blood of her enemies when provoked. It wasn't tainted with Gorrath's anger, nor was it laced with the fear and hate I'd grown up on.

It was completely my own.

The wolf quivered. A long tongue licking his jowls. I crouched down, letting the blood caked on my face and my red eyes do the hard work of intimidating him. Then I asked my question again. "Where is Angelina Prideaux?"

"How did you escape? We bound your hands. We blindfolded you."

I pressed my finger to his forehead and allowed the magick to flow through me. Just a taste of the anger and heat contained within. It left a red burn on his forehead. He tried to shift the carriage off him, but it was too heavy, and he was already marked for death.

"You can either die swiftly and mercifully, or I can let you bleed out slowly. Your choice."

His big eyes shifted back and forth. "Miss Prideaux rode ahead."

I pressed my finger harder into his forehead, heat spreading deeper. He yelped. "And where was she headed?"

"She-she was going to meet her army. The wolves Shayla promised her."

I abruptly removed my finger and stood, not wanting the wolf to see the surprised look on my face. My mother was headed to collect an army. Her army. Of wolves? I paced back and forth, trying not to let my emotions get the best of me so I could think clearly.

After Bastien had taken me into his service, Mama had attacked the Kemps, killing their matriarch, and tried to destroy their relics. It had seemed so senseless to me at the time. In my naïveté, I even considered that she had come north to check on me. But what if it had only been a stop on her way to the Lawless Lands?

What if that's what Alec had left Château Rose to tell me? He'd worked as a pillow whisperer at the Veraleese Inn in Nightfall. People said all kinds of things in the throes of pleasure. What if he'd heard something he wasn't meant to hear?

He'd claimed he'd been scratched by a woman with white hair who transformed into a werewolf. Could it have been Mama?

I stopped pacing. Not wanting to believe it. Mama was a prideful and arrogant woman. But it was hard to imagine her with a pillow whisperer. I set that fact aside for now and kept thinking.

After she'd put a knife through Gorrath's chest inside Chastity's Stronghold, she'd told me we were going home. But the only way Mama could go back home now was with an army. She knew our coven didn't have the numbers or the support inside the Unified Territories to make the kind of impact she really wanted, but if she had the right leverage, she would become a legitimate option. If she showed up with an army of Diana's wolves, she might be able to draw those with a desire for freedom from the vampires to her.

I bit my lip, considering all of this while the wolf whimpered about the burn on his forehead. There was something I was missing. A piece that didn't quite fit. After meeting Gorrath, I'd come to learn a thing or two about bargains, especially magickal bargains.

What could Mama have possibly promised Shayla in return for an army of wolves? Certainly not coin. No, she had to have some kind of bargaining chip.

I thought of Sera, and I wondered where she was. I could only hope she wasn't convinced Mama's plot was a good idea, but a sick feeling sat in my gut. What power did she have to say no to our mother when Mama had raised us with little agency over our own thoughts?

I turned back to the werewolf, considering him once again.

Mama needed to be stopped, and I needed her blood, but I could only hold so much power inside me at once without depleting my magick. It was one or the other. But how could I get to Mama if she was standing beside Shayla and all these wolves?

I slid my hand into my pocket, and my fingers closed around something hard and soft. I removed the little seashell Gorrath had given me. The one he'd said was for a coven who needed it.

A terrible thought took root in my mind. "Where is this army?"

CHAPTER 37
CORROMPRE
CLAIRE

I'd never killed anyone before. Not like that. I knew the image of the light leaving his eyes would haunt me for the rest of my life. I wondered if this was how Mellie felt when she killed Devlinn. There was no one to clamp me in irons. I was left to punish myself.

On the back of a horse far too big for me, and completely unsure of what I was doing, I followed the wolf's directions, staying on the beaten path. It led me past a small gathering of brick homes and log cabins. Smoke rose in ribbons from cook-fires. I wondered if this was where the army was amassing.

Pulling on the horse's reins as I'd seen Bastien do, I came to a hasty stop, then dismounted, nearly stumbling on the way down. I left the horse tethered in the trees and continued on foot, keeping low along the tree line as I surveyed the village.

No one wandered the streets. The wagons sat abandoned on the road. It would have looked vacant if not for the long line forming behind a coach bearing Diana's moon.

Women stood shoulder to shoulder in the frost-covered grass. Children were clutched against their hips or clinging to their hands. One by one, they took their turn approaching the two white-haired women handing out bread. A third witch with elaborate braids and a thick fur stole moved down the line, pressing folded pieces of parchment into waiting hands. The women tucked them into aprons without looking down, as though they already knew what they said.

It looked innocent enough, Witches of the Light sharing Diana's harvest with the poor, but my suspicions rose when I saw the moonstones around their necks.

A gust of wind blew through my hair, and one of the witches stilled. Slowly, she turned her head toward where I was standing. I flattened myself against the tree trunk, pressing bark into my spine and willing my pulse to quiet. This wasn't the army I was looking for. It was something else entirely.

Chancing a look around the tree, I noticed the witch with the pamphlets was gone. In her place stood a black-furred wolf. Not the half-human kind that had attacked us in the tunnels or at Chastity's. This was a real wolf.

The same size and shape as my own pair.

She sniffed the air, and I stilled. If I wanted to keep moving unseen, that old draft horse wasn't going to help me. The only time I'd flown was when I leapt from the carriage, and I had no clue how it worked. I told myself I would learn quickly or be torn apart in the underbrush.

The wolf took one step into the tree line, then another. I dropped to my knees and scanned the forest floor until I spotted a broken branch thick as my palm. It would have to do. I swung one leg over the branch and straddled it.

I closed my eyes and thought of the freedom I'd felt when I'd jumped from the carriage. Of the way I felt like a raven taking flight. The wolves' shining yellow eyes appeared through the brush, and I knew I was out of time.

Freedom. Freedom. I repeated the word. Along with *hurry up.*

The air caught beneath me in a sudden rush and lifted me off the ground. Pine needles and bare branches scratched at my arms and legs, catching and tearing the fabric as I soared higher into the air.

A howl pierced through the quiet, as if the black wolf was calling to its pack mates. Alerting them to my presence.

Once I was clear of the trees, high above the forest floor, I could see everything for miles. It was freeing and terrifying, especially when I realized just how far up I was. I wrapped my arms around the branch, clinging to it when I spied a clearing about a mile past the village.

Pointed logs formed a wall around it, but inside, I saw movement.

That's where Mama was, waiting for me to arrive in a coach, bound and blindfolded, just in time to see her claim an army of wolves. I knew what unspeakable things she'd do with them when she crossed into the Unified Territories. She'd start with cutting off the source of dark magick by destroying every demonic relic she could.

I sucked in a shuddering breath. That's what I'd been sent to do. This is where I fit into her story. It would be a calculated strike if she already knew their location. Unlike the Lawless Lands, the people of the Unified Territories didn't expect war. Yes, there were thieves, and Mama did provoke retaliatory behavior with her raids on Witches of the Darkness, but no one was ready for this.

Urging the branch forward, I flew through the air, black skirts waving in the wind like a banner. Somehow, I managed to convince my tree branch to stop beside a thick pine tree that overlooked the fort. Perched on one of the highest branches, I saw hundreds of weres. Red fur. Black fur. Silver grays and snowy whites. All with the same human bodies and elongated snouts.

None of them had moonstones. And I didn't know how many were Witches of the Light who volunteered for this, and how many were villagers, like the ones I'd seen. Trading an empty belly for *this*.

This was what happened when powerful leaders fed their people nothing but fear. It turned good witches, *good people*, into monsters. Drones. An army of wolves ready to attack whoever. Whenever. And for little more than a hot meal and the promise of security.

I wouldn't have believed it if I hadn't seen it with my own eyes.

And there, parading through the lines was Mama. She was walking beside a witch with short-cropped white hair and big gold eyes. She was swaddled in a thick fur cloak. Around her neck sat a moonstone the size of a goose egg.

Where was my sister? Sera had to be here if Mama was.

"Your army is ready," the woman with short hair said. "The only thing left is my payment."

My stomach hollowed. I realized this must be Shayla. The witch who'd killed Bastien's friend, Hector, and sent his severed head to him in a box. Why was Mama with Shayla?

Shayla tossed a dead rabbit onto the ground, and the wolves lunged at the carcass. Fighting and clawing to be the one to gobble it up. I covered my mouth with a hand, while tears pricked in my eyes.

Was this what life looked like for the wolf I'd killed? Locked in a fort, awaiting orders? Ready to do whatever it took to survive?

Carefully, minding my balance, I removed the small shell from my pocket and held it between my fingers. The energy Gorrath had imbued it with thrummed against my skin.

Before I'd seen them, before I'd seen the village and the children, I'd intended on spreading my rot to all of them. But now, knowing everything I knew, it felt less like justice and more like murder. How could I kill all of them for the lies of people like Shayla and Mama, the only people who benefited from a system that kept people outraged and afraid. Who were desperate enough to become these *things*.

I couldn't do it, not even for a drop of Mama's blood, because that could be me, standing down there. Easily.

Sadness sat heavy in my heart. My chest. It lived behind my eyes. I wanted to cry for them, for me, and for all the people who were just trying to do the right thing.

Slowly, I went to put the shell back in my pocket, unable to do what I'd come to do, but a gust of wind slammed against me, and the shell slipped between my fingers and tumbled downward.

"No!" I silently screamed. Watching as it hit branches and bounced off tree trunks, gaining momentum as it fell. Until it ricocheted toward the army of werewolves and landed in the mud between two snarling bodies.

My breath was caged in my chest. I hoped and prayed that no one would notice it. Shayla and Mama were laughing as they watched another group of wolves fight over a dead rabbit. Shayla froze, like a predator who'd caught scent of their prey.

CHAPTER 38

LE CHOIX

BASTIEN

They took her.

My wife. My mate. *My Claire.*

It was my worst nightmare come to life. I'd been made to protect her. To shield her from pain. If I'd possessed a scrap of humility, I would have taken her back to Château Corbin when news of werewolves first reached me. I should've swallowed my pride. I should've chosen caution over conquest. But no. I hadn't.

And now my pride had led me here. To this.

Gorrath, dead.

Devlinn, dead.

Warriors—good citizens of Roselyn—dead.

Her heartbeat was the only reassurance I had that she was still alive.

I surveyed the devastation and made a decision. I wouldn't ask anyone else to follow me. Not again. Not anymore. Blood ran warm down the side of my face, and I wiped it away.

Stepping over bodies I had known by name, men who had

toasted at my table and laughed in my halls, I made for the twisting corridors that led toward the stables. "I need a horse."

Natalia planted herself in front of me and pressed her hand flat against my chest. As if she could physically restrain what I was about to do. "I know what you're planning," she said. "And you *can't.*"

I shoved her hand away and kept walking. "Collect the dead. Take everyone else home."

"No." She circled in front of me again, forcing me to stop. "I'm coming with you."

I snarled. "I thought you hated Claire."

"I do." Her throat worked. "I don't." She shook her head, almost angry at the confession. "Where you go, I follow. How else will I clean up your mess?"

I wanted to smile, but there was nothing left inside of me. Nothing but Claire. "You have your orders. Take care of the army. Lead them." I unsheathed my blade. "I'm going to get my wife."

We stared at one another. Then Natalia stepped back and dipped into a shallow curtsy. "Very well. I will assume command of the army."

I saw nothing as I walked. Heard nothing. Felt nothing save for the bond between Claire and me. It was the only thing I could focus on.

That was, until my nephew fell into step beside me as I climbed the long set of stairs that led to ground level, Claire's wolves trailing. At least Chastity had released them. Some small mercy in a field of ruin.

"You have Château Rose," I told him, not sparing him a glance. "Natalia will be your commander. Don't fuck it up."

"An honor. Truly, Uncle. Thank you," Tyson said. But he didn't leave.

I shoved open an exterior door at the top of the staircase, and he went to follow after me. "Go. Lead your people."

My nephew laughed tensely. "I know you're going to get Claire. I want to introduce you to someone who can help you. Well, *two* someones."

I spared a glance at the empty stairwell, then back at him. "You are not coming."

He went to pat the head of Claire's white wolf, but it dodged his touch. She climbed the last few steps and came to stand in front of me. I batted her away with my sword. I needed to get moving.

But the wolf growled before her fur began receding like morning mist. Her limbs thickened and lengthened. Her snout shortened. Where there had been four paws now stood a woman.

A woman whom I recognized. "You're Claire's sister."

Except she had moon-white hair. Not lilac. And she was a werewolf?

"Wolves can sense each other when they're wearing the moonstones," Tyson said, gesturing to the stone around her neck. "It's how Shayla knew where to attack us."

I ignored him, holding the woman's gaze. She had the same color eyes as Claire. There was a story here, but I didn't have time to hear it. The only thing I cared about was finding Claire.

"Seraphina?" I asked.

She nodded once.

"That's your name?" Tyson said.

She rolled her eyes. "I know where she is."

I grabbed my bloodstone and held it up for her to see. "So do I. All I have to do is follow this."

"But you don't know who has her."

I leaned in. "Who has her?"

She lifted her chin in a way that reminded me of her sister. "Our mother. Angelina Prideaux."

The breath left my lungs. I knew there was more to Claire's story, but I hadn't expected *this*. Then all the disparate pieces I knew about Claire began to slide into place. And I finally understood that this was the thing she hadn't been able to tell me. That it hadn't been convent sisters who had filled her head with hate, but the most venomous witch in the Unified Territories.

"Your mother, she's the one who put that choker on Claire. Isn't she?"

Sera nodded. "Yes. She convinced her, convinced me, that it was the only thing left to do. But I know she loves you. I've never seen my sister so happy."

I stared into her eyes, eyes that reminded me of my wife's, and hated that this life, this vicious life that I was giving her, was the happiest she'd been.

"If you want to save her, you'll need me. Us," Seraphina said, pointing to a man who had appeared at her side. One I also recognized. *Alec.*

Anger flared in my chest. He'd been the brown wolf? This whole time? I snatched his shirt and lifted my sword, ready to kill him where he stood for deceiving Claire and me.

Tyson grabbed my blade with his bare hand, stopping me from completing the kill. Blood ran between his fingers, a fierce look in his eyes. "He is here to help. Just like me. And her. You'll need all of us if you're going to get Claire back."

I stared at him, bewildered by his behavior. I'd just given him everything he'd wanted. My castle. My title. Why was he still here? I snarled, and he snarled back. "Let him go, Uncle. He is not your enemy, and we are wasting time."

Reluctantly, I released my hold on Alec. Tyson was right. This was taking up too much time. I needed to find Claire. "If you want to come, come. But if you interfere, I will not hesitate to kill you. *Any of you.*"

I made for the stables, but Sera grabbed my shoulder, stopping me. "My mother has made a deal with Shayla."

"What kind of deal?"

Sera swallowed hard. "I don't know. Mama didn't share every detail with me. All I know is that she wants the Blood Treaty destroyed. And she knows you are the key."

I tapped my sword against the ground. "The only thing I heard you say was that she has my wife. Everything else is just details."

I didn't care if they followed me or stayed. I had one focus. One need.

As soon as I mounted a horse, I closed my eyes and reached out through our bond. The world narrowed to a single point of heat inside my chest. "Hold on, my love. I'm coming."

I rode hard through the dark, navigating by my heart alone. For the first time in five hundred years, I was my own man. And the only person I wanted to answer to was my wife.

An overturned carriage appeared on the road ahead of us, lying on its side. Claire's scent was everywhere. I did not wait for anyone else to dismount. I threw myself from the saddle and tore the crooked door open with my bare hands.

Empty.

The brown wolf padded forward and dropped something at my feet. A length of rope, half-burned through. The white wolf had a strip of fabric in her jaws.

I took them in my hands, knowing my wife had been blindfolded and bound. And yet... she had still escaped.

"You heard what Sera said, Uncle. This is all a trap designed to destabilize the Blood Treaty. If she catches you, she knows you'll do anything for Claire."

I let out a hoarse laugh that held no humor. "I'm already on my knees. One day, when you have a mate, you'll understand."

The wind carried a sound to me. A voice. I did not remember walking away from Tyson or leaving the carriage. I only knew I was running. Branches tore at my coat as I plunged between the pines and vaulted over streams. Tyson shouted something behind me, but his words meant nothing. I raced faster, legs and arms pumping. Nothing mattered. Nothing else mattered. Except her.

CHAPTER 39

SOUMISSION

CLAIRE

From my perch in the trees, I held very still. Wind stirred loose straw near the fence posts. A pair of wolves shoved at each other over a scrap of meat. Shayla glanced once around the training yard, eyes skimming the wolves circling the perimeter, then she turned back to Mama.

I blew out a long breath of relief. The shell lay unnoticed in the soft mud. One of the younger wolves who was sniffing around for scraps got closer and closer.

No. No. Keep moving.

He sniffed it, then scrambled back. "Dark magick!" he shouted. "Right there!"

My heart skipped a beat. He couldn't have been more than ten or eleven. His voice hadn't even dropped. But his fear of that little shell was evident.

Mama and Shayla exchanged a loaded glance, and I knew, I knew, what was coming in the way prey always sensed the hawk before it struck. The wolves parted without being told as

Mama approached. She crouched down and plucked it from the dirt with two fingers, sneering like it was something vile.

I leaned forward, unable to look away. That shell was supposed to go to Shreesa and her family, to replace the ones Mama had already destroyed.

"Dark magick isn't just out there, in Chastity's disgusting underground lair. Where she devours children and tortures innocents for fun. It is everywhere," she said. "Damien and his demons threaten us at every turn. Even here, on Diana's sacred ground."

A few of the weres began to draw back, hackles raised, nostrils flaring.

"And if vampires have their way, they'd have you doing the same."

From the branches above, I could see the shell in Mama's hand. I needed to get it back. Without it, Shreesa's family wouldn't be able to defend themselves.

My mind raced through possibilities, each more desperate than the last. But I knew I needed to act fast. Mama wasn't going to keep the shell around. She would smash it under her boot, just like she smashed everything else.

"How do I know this?" she asked, head bowed. "My own daughter was seduced by it." The wolves howled. And I realized, she was talking about me. "That's right. I led a party of valiant warriors, just like yourselves. Fighters for Diana's love and light. And I watched as she sided with a demon. Helping him spread disease among your brothers and sisters."

More yelping. More howling. Shayla thrust her fist into the air and added a rallying cry.

Mama continued. "I told her to repent. To make amends. To come back into the light. But she didn't want to listen."

I dug my fingernails into the wood, feeling angrier by the

second. This was just another one of her stories, and she was leaving out the part where she was the villain.

"She allowed darkness into her heart, and now we must guide her back to Diana."

I had come here to break the curse at my throat. To take her blood and end this. Instead, I was watching her build an army on my back.

The thunder of paws came from outside the fort, and I carefully glanced over my shoulder to find the black-furred wolf and two pack mates weaving between the trees. My stomach dropped. In seconds, Mama was going to know the truth. *That I'd escaped.*

My pulse hammered so loudly I was certain they could hear it. The branch beneath my boots felt narrower than it had a moment ago. The wind tugged at my skirts. I could leave. But I wouldn't be safe. I'd never be safe so long as I had this choker around my neck.

At any time, she could activate the spell and take my life. Or I could do something to activate it myself. No. Leaving was not an option. I had to get a drop of her blood. But staying— staying meant near-certain death.

Unless... unless...

I swallowed hard, not wanting to choose this path but knowing I had no other choice. I was going to have to fall on my knees and ask for forgiveness. Bile rose in my throat at the thought of it. At the humiliation of kneeling in front of Shayla and these wolves and my mother. But if I was close enough to kneel, then I was close enough to grab the shell and slit her hand open.

Daring to let go of the branch, I set one hand on my stomach and made a silent vow. "I protect you. I protect us."

Then I looked at the crowd, at Mama whipping them into a

frenzy. If they wanted a spectacle, I would give them a show they'd never forget.

Head bowed, I stood at the entrance to the fort. Hands shaking. Thick copper-red hair, loose and blowing around my head like flames. The stench of refuse and decaying carcasses filled the air.

"I'm so sorry, Mama," I said, sucking in a gulping breath. "For everything."

When I lifted my chin and met my mother's colorless eyes, I could see she was more than surprised. She wanted to know where the coach was. She wanted to know how I escaped the ropes. She wanted to grab me by the root of my hair and drag me through the mud. I could feel it.

But right now, she wasn't able to show her true evil. She'd told all these wolves that I was the problem. That I was bad. Yet here I was, ready to come back home.

I took one step, then another, drawing closer to where she stood beside Shayla at the center of the fort. Bastien's dagger tucked into the leather belt tied around her waist. She still had protection runes drawn on her face to guard against demonic influence.

But I was no demon. No. I was consequence.

"I just wanted to make you proud. But I was deceived." I wiped away a tear and then the snot from my nose.

The weres didn't seem to know how to react. Here I was, the daughter of their leader, a Dark Witch, who was seeking forgiveness. When I reached the center of the fort, I fell to my knees. "I know I wasn't the daughter you prayed for. And I'm sorry for that."

Mama was rarely at a loss for words, but when I glanced up at her through wet lashes, I knew I had her right where I wanted her.

She set her hand on my head. The same hand that had struck me time and time again and called it my fault. The same one that had secured the choker around my throat. I held my breath, every muscle clenched tight. It was hard not to grab her wrist, reach for my husband's blade, and end this now. But I knew I had to wait for just the right time.

"I forgive you, child. For bringing darkness into your heart."

The assembled weres grunted and scratched at the ground. The putrid scent of death hung all around me. I kept my head bowed. Let the tears sting. Let them believe I was breaking.

I hoped that when this was all over, we could find a way to cure them of the disease Shayla had inflicted upon them.

"But," Mama continued. "Your fate will be decided by Diana. The moon goddess will choose if you should live or die."

I swore the cold mud had just swallowed me whole. Dread churned in my gut. But I forced myself to breathe. Closing my eyes, I let my magick creep out of me and into her. Hate was as good as rot inside the body, and now, I encouraged that rot to spread. To multiply.

Voices rang out. They wanted my blood. They wanted to see me pay. I waited. A moment longer. Another moment longer. I let the heat inside me build, spreading the sickness to Shayla next. The hate inside her was just as thick and familiar as Mama's.

Mama lifted her hands into the air and called to her goddess. "What say you, Great Mother? Should she live, or pay for her crimes with her life?"

The next thing I knew, the barbs of the choker were back. Pain lanced through me, and warmth began trickling down my neck. I had anticipated this. I knew I was nothing more than a prop in her story. But I'd experienced this pain. I'd known what it was like to smell my own blood and feel it drain from my body. It didn't cause the blinding panic that it had that night on the balcony.

The blisters broke out across her brow first. Angry pustules that popped and leaked black blood. Mama reached to touch one, and a sneer formed on her face.

She grabbed my arm and yanked me to my feet, determined to make a show of my death. I faced the crowd of weres with tears in my eyes. "The goddess has spoken! This is what happens to those who disobey!"

But it wasn't just me they were watching. No. They saw the way the rot was eating their leaders from the inside out.

Dizziness from the blood loss set in, but I battled through it, reaching for every drop of dark magick inside my body to push back against the barbs. It came in a rush of heat and power that made me feel alive.

Mama's grip on my arm slackened, and when it did, I reached behind me and snatched my husband's dagger from her belt and slashed it upward in a vicious line, hoping to slice through her arm. My cut met resistance, and Mama screamed. Her grip on me slackened.

Justice.

There was only one thing left to do. I lifted the blade to my lips, but Shayla grabbed my wrist before I could collect what I needed. Her golden eyes flashed with light, and she bared her teeth at me. A trail of liquid black rot dribbled between her lips and down her chin. "Stop this, and I'll let you live."

I narrowed my eyes. The pain in my throat made it difficult to speak, but somehow I found the words. "The God of the Underworld has spoken. And he says you will pay for your crimes with your life."

CHAPTER 40
ARRACHER
BASTIEN

What I had wasn't bloodlust. It was blood *rage*. The scent of my wife's blood unleashed the monster inside of me. The indiscriminate reaper. We'd cut down every guard outside the fort with little resistance. Now it was time to break through the gate.

"Uncle?" Tyson asked. "Is there a plan?"

I wiped a spray of blood from my face. "The plan is to kill anyone who gets in our way."

"So we're ignoring what Sera said and walking straight into a trap?"

I shook my head. "I already told you. The only thing I came for was my wife. And if you're too scared to stand behind me, then go. I don't need you."

Tyson narrowed his eyes in a way that mimicked his cousin, Natalia. "I am a man of Roselyn." He banged his fist against his chest. "And I will not leave one of my own to die."

I clapped a hand on his shoulder and squeezed.

"Let's get this door down," Tyson said. "You get Claire. The wolves will take care of the rest."

Together, we dropped our shoulders and slammed into the wooden gate, expecting it to buckle beneath our combined strength. I was angry enough to knock down a castle wall. Wood was child's play. But the gate had been properly reinforced, as if they'd been expecting us.

A fine strategy. However, I'd been tearing into forts long before anyone here had been born. The weakest points of these gates were the hinges. I drove my hand into the narrow seam beside the hinge post and wrenched it to the side, trying to rip them from the wood. Tyson saw what I was doing and joined me. With one more shove, the door snapped free.

We tossed it toward the woods. I drew my blade as an army of weres barreled toward us. Behind their half-transformed limbs, I saw my wife in a crumpled heap on the ground, lying in a puddle of her own blood. Her heart was still faintly beating, and that was all the hope I needed.

I set my teeth. Let them come. There was no army that could keep me from her.

Sword raised, I tore through the yard at a sprint. Claws tore at my sleeves, teeth snapped at my neck, but I did not slow. They were only obstacles. Only distance. Only the last cruel seconds between my wife and me.

But when I cleared the mob, and I saw the true horror before me, I collapsed onto my knees. "No," I breathed, though the word had no power here. Pain lanced through my heart, like I'd been struck by an arrow. It was so sharp, so horrible, I thought I might die from the agony. Unable to stand, I crawled to her on hands and knees, through the thick mud and blood that surrounded her lifeless body.

I touched her neck, which was slick with blood, knowing I couldn't even apply pressure to her wounds, because it would make the barbs sink in harder. There was nothing to do but watch the life drain from her, while magick I could not break stole her from me. And all I could think was how this was my fault. I should have made the deal with Gorrath as soon as he offered it. I should have fallen to my knees and agreed to anything. Anything.

Had it not been for my jealousy, my possessiveness of her, she could be immortal and alive. I had failed her.

Tears fell down my face as I wept for her, and for the child we were supposed to have. The one I promised to protect. The one I barely dared to believe I was strong enough to have. It was all slipping away from me.

Without anything left to do, I pulled her into my arms and cradled her limp body. But as soon as I lifted her, my dagger slipped from her hand. A choking sound tore free from my throat when I saw it tumble into a puddle of her blood. She'd tried. She'd tried to save herself.

"Claire, I'm here," I said, smoothing back her hair with my bloodied hands. "I'm here."

Beside her, a woman with long white braids, covered in black pustules, began to laugh. She was weak. Near death herself. I hadn't paid her any attention until now.

I knew Shayla's face, and this wasn't Shayla. Which could only mean *this* was Angelina Prideaux.

Beat.

Beat.

Beat.

There was too much space between Claire's heartbeats. But before me was a gift. If I killed her mother, the originator of the curse on her necklace, then perhaps I could save her life.

"You," I snarled at the witch. "You have tortured her for the last time."

Carefully, I eased my wife off my lap, but the motion was

too much for her injured body, and the beating *stopped*. I leaned down and pressed my forehead to hers, my body shaking. "No," I whispered. "You can't leave. You can't go."

She was gone. And I was... *nothing*. Not a prince. Not a warrior. Not a general. Not even a vengeful reaper. The only thing left of me... was nothing at all.

CHAPTER 41

REQUIEM

CLAIRE

The moment I opened my eyes, I knew something was wrong. I wasn't inside the fort, watching Shayla guzzle a potion given to her by one of her witches before transforming into a werewolf. I wasn't even lying in the cold mud. Face up. I wasn't even holding Bastien's dagger.

I was lying on something soft, and the air was thick with incense smoke. I drew in a deep breath, inhaling the biting scent of *frankincense*. Above my head, the vaulted ceiling stretched on and on.

Sitting up too fast, I groaned against the sudden dizziness. What had happened? The last thing I remembered was collapsing onto the ground. Blood was everywhere.

I lifted trembling fingers to my throat, and I realized the choker was *gone*. The only thing left behind were the ridges of scars. I was still wearing my bloodstone. I wrapped my hands around it and closed my eyes, hoping to call Bastien to me.

Maybe I had survived. Maybe Mama's blood had worked, and I'd been put here to recover. Yes, maybe Bastien was simply in another room.

263

"She's awake," came a gruff, annoyingly familiar voice.

Even though I didn't want to, I turned toward the sound, clutching the bloodstone in my palm like it could protect me when Bastien couldn't. I found myself in an elegant private dining room, lit by red-tapered candles dripping wax from iron candelabras.

"We were just talking about you, love."

Sitting at a polished obsidian dining table, set with plates of food and goblets filled with deep red wine, were two men. The first, I recognized instantly. Black curls and a single horn framed a face that looked far too pleased with himself. He still wore no shirt or cravat beneath his black jacket.

Gorrath.

But I thought he'd died. Mama had killed him. If that were true, then that meant I was in... the Underworld.

No. No. No. No. No.

I couldn't have died. I clutched my stomach, tears swimming in my eyes. I'd lost everything. Everything. The sounds that came out of my mouth were inhuman. Screeches. Wails. I felt nothing and everything all at once. A loss so profound I could hardly breathe. I went on for what felt like hours. Crying and sobbing and screaming until there was nothing left inside of me. Until, finally, I covered my face with my hands and closed my eyes.

A chair scraped loudly against the floor. Footsteps. Then I sensed the demon hovering over me.

"You're not going to let a little thing like death stop you? Are you?" I pulled my hands away from my face to glare at him. He was clearly amused by my reaction. "Come sit down at the table. I want to introduce you to an ol' friend of mine."

I peered around Gorrath's frame to see who this friend was. He was a collection of hard edges and sharp lines, including the two black horns that spiraled from his brow.

"Sit," he said, gesturing to the empty seat across from him with his wine glass. "Eat. Death has a way of making one hungry. Or, at least, that's what I hear."

Gorrath offered me his hand. "That's the God of the Underworld. Damien himself. Best not to keep him waiting."

My mouth fell open in shock. I couldn't believe *that* was Damien. He hardly looked like a god at all. With mousy brown hair and dark gray eyes, he looked very ordinary, save for the horns. In all of Mama's stories about the God of the Underworld, he was a monster. With burning pits for eyes. And he ate only the blood of children.

But here he sat, sipping wine.

Hesitantly, I let Gorrath help me to my feet and shuffled over to the table. I took the seat directly across from Damien. I sat stiffly, barely touching the edge of the chair, every muscle in my body coiled. The food in front of me smelled delicious, but I had no appetite.

I was sitting across from a god. One I had only ever prayed to once before, *when I asked him to make me unbreakable.*

"What do you want with me?" I asked. Bowing my head. Folding my hands in my lap.

He considered me for a moment, then said, "You have performed an immortality spell. Have you not?"

Confused, I glanced at Gorrath, who had taken a seat in the chair beside Damien. He grabbed a knife and a fork and immediately began carving into a piece of rare beef. The way blood oozed from the center made my stomach flip.

"Yes," I answered. "But it must not have worked."

Damien's mouth curled into a slow and knowing smile like he had been waiting for this moment. "Every immortal must sacrifice their life. Your husband did. Gorrath did. And so did every demon in my court and every star in Diana's. It is how immortality begins."

A slow, hopeful smile spread across my face. "Are you saying that it worked? That I broke the curse and became immortal?"

Damien nodded. "That's what I'm saying."

I nearly leapt out of my chair. I was going to go back home. To Bastien. To my life.

Damien watched me with a quiet, patient amusement as the excitement warmed every place that had gone numb and cold inside me. He propped one arm on the back of Gorrath's chair. "I can see why she won you over. The want inside of her is endless."

Gorrath nodded. "She is a true Dark Witch. Not one of those pretenders. Dressing in black and waving around relics like they know what darkness means." He lifted his wine glass in appreciation. "She's got a shard of darkness inside her."

The way the two of them beamed back at me stoked the growing pride in my chest. After everything I'd been through... after all of it... I was finally going to keep him. I was going to spend eternity with Bastien.

"There is one thing you should know," Damien said. "Immortality comes with a price."

I stilled, the excitement slipping out of me. "What kind of price?"

"First of all," Damien began, "you would no longer be a Witch of the Darkness."

Absently, I twirled a few strands of hair around my fingers. I didn't know what to say. I'd only just gotten my magick. I'd only just started figuring out my powers. The idea that they would just be gone left me feeling hollow all over again. "What would I be then?"

Silence settled around the table, and dread crept in. "Well, that's the thing you could choose," Damien continued. "You could become a demon of my court. You'd be more than welcome here. However, you'd no longer carry Gorrath's power. We'd select something new for you."

I knew I was sitting across from a god, so I tried to retain a bit of respect, but a demon? He was telling me that I'd done all this—collected Mama's blood and jumped out of that carriage—just to become a demon?

"Is there another choice?" I asked.

Damien expelled a sigh, as if disappointed that I didn't want to join him in the Underworld for eternity. "Your only other option would be to go back as a vampire. However, all the rules of vampirism would apply to you. Including drinking blood."

I let out a breath of relief. There was another way.

"And you'd be subject to the matebond."

"I already have a mate," I said. "Bastien. You know this."

He gave the barest shake of his head. "I'm afraid two vampires cannot be mated to one another. You see, they cannot bear children."

I glowered at Gorrath, who was shoving a piece of raw meat in his mouth. "Did you know this would happen when you sold me the idea of becoming immortal? Did you know what I would have to give up?"

My baby? My magick? Bastien? Everything?

Gorrath shook his head. Hands raised in the air. Mouth full, he said, "I didn't. I swear, I didn't." Desperate, he turned to Damien. "Tell her I didn't know."

"He didn't know," Damien affirmed. "These are my rules for immortality."

Gorrath swallowed down his large chunk of meat, eyes locked with mine. "There's gotta be another way." Then he snapped his fingers. "Could she trade immortality for her mortal life back?"

My breath was caged in my chest. Yes. I would trade

anything, anything to have my life back. Immortality was nothing if I couldn't have him.

Damien tapped his lip in thought. "That is a possibility," he finally said. "Yes, I think I could make that work. A trade then. Her gift of immortality in exchange for her mortal life."

I rose and extended my hand. "Agreed. Take my immortality and give me my life back."

Damien arched a dark brow. "So quick to give up forever just for some magick and a mate? If you went back as a vampire, you'd feel just as passionately about someone else."

He might be a god, but he knew nothing about love. "Respectfully, no I wouldn't."

Damien stood as well and shook my hand. "Then we have a deal."

A sense of relief washed over me once again. I wouldn't be immortal. But I would have one life with Bastien. One good life. Until, of course, I was reborn, and we'd be able to find each other again. This time, Bastien wouldn't hesitate to search for me once his bloodstone indicated I'd been born.

"Should we drink, then?" Damien asked, nodding to the goblet placed before me. "To your good health."

I lifted my glass to theirs and then took a sip. It was the most delicious wine I'd ever tasted. I savored the flavor, then set the glass back down. Anxious excitement to return to Bastien was collecting in my chest.

"There's someone who asked to see you before you leave," Gorrath said. He waved, and a set of doors opened. For a moment I didn't understand what I was looking at. Then all at once, I did.

Devlinn.

He was whole and well. Not a speck of rot to be seen. I opened my mouth to scream, to sob, to say his name, but nothing came out. My body moved before my mind could catch up. I crossed the black marble floor in a blur and collided with him, my arms locking around his shoulders as if he might disappear.

"It's good to see you too, Claire," he said with his familiar dry humor.

"I'm sorry," I choked. "I'm so sorry."

He pulled back just enough to look at me. "Sorry for what?"

"For everything," I said. "For Mellie. For pushing her. For not stopping it. For not being fast enough—"

"Claire." His hand came up to cup my cheek, steadying me. "Don't you dare be sorry. We all die." He smiled, and I tried to smile back at him. "Listen, I don't have much time. But can you tell Tansy something for me?" I nodded. "Tell her that I love her laugh. It's the thing that made me fall in love with her. And that I don't want this to be the reason why she stops laughing."

Tears flooded my eyes. "Of course I'll tell her that."

"And don't butcher my funeral." A grin pulled on his lips. "I want all the honors. Hero of heroes."

A broken laugh tore out of me. "I already miss you."

Carefully, he kissed the top of my head. "Me too. But we'll see each other again."

Then he was just gone. One second, I was holding on to him, the next he vanished. The doors closed and I was left with the emotions his absence left behind.

"You should be going too," Damien said. "If you open that door just over there, I think you'll find your way back."

I glanced in the direction he was pointing, and found a golden door was being etched onto the black walls.

"You better hurry before I convince you to stay," Gorrath quipped. "I know how much you like me." I pursed my lips and the demon snorted out a laugh, but the humor quickly evaporated. "If you ever need me, you know how to reach me."

I offered him a real smile. Then I headed for the gold door. Just before I seized the handle, I stopped. There was one thing I wanted to ask Damien. Something that I needed to know. "Whatever happened to your daughters? Where did they go?"

Damien studied me for a long moment. Then bowed his head. "I don't know. But, perhaps, one day, you'll be able to tell me where they went." He forced a tight smile. "I do miss them very much. Especially my Rosa. She was such a firestorm."

It wasn't the answer I wanted, not by a long shot, but it was the only answer I was going to get. "I hope you do find them. The world could use more joy. The fighting, the hate, it feels endless."

He nodded. "I know."

Whispering started just beyond the door. Words I couldn't quite understand called to me. I was reminded of the time when I opened the ballroom door and found Bastien standing shirtless in the greenhouse. His hands covered in dirt.

I knew, just as I had then, that I had the power to see him again. I could walk through the veil of death and return to him. All I had to do was say his name, and it would draw him to me. Touching the bloodstone, I whispered his name and opened the door.

When I awoke, it was not to incense smoke and the smell of frankincense. I was on the ground, covered in my own blood, the metallic scent filling my nostrils.

When my vision cleared, I realized Bastien was right here. And he had the woman I once called Mama in his grip. I tried to force myself off the ground, but my sluggish body struggled to bear my weight. He wasn't going to kill her. Not before I had the chance to do it myself.

My throat throbbed with pain, torn from whatever death had done to me, but I forced the word through my lips, a broken rasp of defiance.

"No."

Bastien immediately turned toward the sound of my voice.

And when our eyes met, for the briefest, most agonizing moment, he just stared at me, like he couldn't believe it. Then his sword hit the ground with a clang. Mama collapsed to the ground, weakened by the rot I'd spread inside her, and Bastien Allard, a vampire prince of the Unified Territories, fell to his knees and crawled toward me. Reached for me with bloodied fingers.

"Claire," he rasped.

He was everything. All at once. All-consuming. And just seeing him again made me feel like I was back in his gentle tide, floating down his river. At ease and safe despite the horror all around me.

I swallowed hard around the pain in my throat. "You know the truth. That she sent me. Angelina. She was the one. And I'm sorry. I know this is a betrayal of your trust."

He cupped my face. His thumbs traced the curve of my cheekbones. "Do you remember what I said I'd do to the convent sisters?"

I blinked. Confused. "There were no convent sisters. I'm a Prideaux."

He continued as if I had said nothing. "I told you I'd have them excommunicated from the faith. Didn't I?" I nodded. "I explained, quite clearly, that I'd tear down the Nightfall Convent stone by stone. That I'd make them pay for daring to put ideas in your head."

"You'd said those things before you knew the truth."

He drew me an inch closer. "Do you remember when I made love to you on the bed of our enemies? And told you I loved you with every shred of my being and nothing could change that?"

He leaned in, his breath skimming across my lips. The space between us shrank until I could taste his fury.

"But," I tried to say.

"My wife belongs to no one but me. Not some coven. Not some family. But to me. And only me. And no one," he said, "*no one*, harms my wife and lives."

He leaned into me and pressed his mouth against mine. It was a *claim*. A *resurrection* of my spirit. I fisted his jacket, dragging him closer, wanting to drown in him, in the way he kissed me like he could *pull* me back to life. I tasted blood. Mine, his, ours. It didn't matter. All that mattered was *this*.

He eased back far enough to look at me. I stared into the depths of his eyes, seeing him as if it were the first time. Like I had that night we met in the ballroom of Château Corbin. Except this time, I wasn't meeting the polished vampire prince who was being asked to put on a polite smile for the courtiers. I saw him, every dark, desperate, and unhinged part of him.

"I thought I lost you," he whispered, his voice raw, barely more than a breath. "I thought—" His hands slid down my neck, his fingers pressing against my pulse as if he needed to *feel* it, to make sure I was really here. His voice cracked. "You came back to me."

I covered his hands with my own, pressing them tighter against my skin. "Damien himself couldn't keep me from you."

Bastien kissed me again. Slower this time, in a way that truly brought me back to life. I'd choose him, again and again, over and over. It would always, only ever be him.

CHAPTER 42
CHÂTIMENT
CLAIRE

"Angelina Prideaux." Natalia's voice cut through the yard. "I should've known."

Bastien and I broke apart and found her standing at the entrance of the ruined training yard, blade drawn, the end of her braid dripping red. Behind her stood Bastien's entire force. Sir Gavin. Destinee Gris. Men and women whose names I didn't know but whose black and gold doublets marked them as ours.

These were my people. I was their duchess—mate to their lord—and yet I stood here unable to explain why my mother was at the center of this horror.

"I see that we arrived just in time for a prisoner execution." I couldn't tell if she meant Mama or me. Bastien stepped in front of me, and I knew we shared the same thought.

Natalia had distrusted me from the beginning. And now she had the proof.

Bastien snapped something at her in Sanguisi. I knew it wasn't friendly, despite how beautiful it sounded. I silently committed to learning this language that meant so much to his family.

"With all due respect, Uncle," Natalia replied, switching deliberately into the Common Tongue so every soldier in the yard could hear her, "you left me in charge. And as their commander, I led the army to ensure the Duke and his wife were brought home safely."

I stilled. She... *what?*

Natalia's attention drifted to where my mother lay on the ground. "I know what it's like to draw the disdain of your parents. I know what it's like to be called a disgrace."

The soldiers at her back banged their swords against their shields in support of her. I had expected suspicion. Judgment. Perhaps even an accusation. Instead, what I found in her expression was something far softer. Understanding.

She strode forward, but Bastien didn't move until she sheathed her blade. Natalia stopped an arm's length away and stared at me. Then, the woman who had never trusted me held out her hand. "I've always said your mother was a buffoon. Now I see she's far more malicious than that."

Heat rose behind my eyes before I could stop it. I had spent so long fearing this moment that I had never prepared for the possibility of being seen. I put my hand in hers, and we shook like equals.

"Don't even think about embracing me," she said.

For the benefit of her pride, I tried to hide my smile. "I wouldn't dare."

Natalia let go of my hand and glanced back at Bastien. "Where is Shayla?" She asked. All business once again. "Have you captured her?"

"Tyson and the wolves went after her," Bastien said.

"Ah." Natalia reached for her belt, unfastened a leather waterskin, and handed it to me. "You look half dead. Drink."

I accepted it and drank deeply. The water burned as it slid down my throat. My neck felt as though it had been scraped from the inside out, but I forced myself to drink as much as I could stand.

The sound of hoofbeats broke the hush as Lady Okeri rode in with Tansy behind her on the same horse. The moment Tansy saw me, the color drained from her face.

"We need a healer!" she shouted over her shoulder. Not waiting for the horse to stop, she half-slid, half-fell from the saddle, boots sinking into the mud as she ran for me. "If you weren't on your feet, I'd swear you were dead." She wrapped her arms around me, holding me gently.

I didn't tell her that I had died. That I'd seen the God of the Underworld. I didn't tell her that Devlinn had given me a message for her. Not yet.

She stepped aside and made space for the healer to tend to the wounds around my neck. I winced when she peeled off the black lace, which was caked with blood. "I'm sorry, my lady, but the lace is ruined." She dropped what was left of the necklace into my hands. It seemed so benign, so harmless. I stuffed it in my pocket, unable to leave it here.

The healer blotted an herbal tincture onto my torn skin, and I hissed in pain. Bastien knelt beside the healer and took the tincture from her. "I'll handle this." He bid me to lean back against his chest as he dripped the liquid onto my wounds, allowing it to wash the dirt and blood away. I couldn't look away from his face as he let the liquid run over my neck, washing away dirt and blood.

"What have you discovered about these weres?" Natalia asked while Bastien worked.

"Angelina purchased them from Shayla," I replied tightly. "She'd made some deal with Shayla."

Natalia cursed, then barked, "Buffoon!" at my mother.

Across the yard, the surrendered weres were huddled together. Bastien's soldiers were binding their hands with ropes, but I didn't see enemies. I saw a group of lost people.

"Turn and face me," Bastien said gently. I wanted to tell him that he didn't need to do this. The healer who was holding the bandages was perfectly capable of assisting me. Or Tansy, who was worriedly hovering. But I knew he wouldn't agree.

I shifted so that I was kneeling in front of him, and he accepted a small glass jar from the healer.

"They are villagers," I explained, as Bastien began dabbing the thick, sticky salve over my wounds. It smelled of honey and lavender. "People who were lured in by Shayla's promises. We need to help them."

Bastien glanced at them. "I don't know if there's a way to help them." Once he'd finished applying a thick layer of salve, he carefully wrapped silk bandages around my neck, while Tansy held my hair out of the way.

"Your mother is guilty of crimes against the Blood Treaty, and in Marius's name, the sentence must be carried out."

I shifted just enough to see her. The woman who had bound me. Betrayed me. Killed me. She thought she was going to get rid of me for good, but she hadn't. She'd only made me stronger.

"Claire should be the one to do it," Natalia insisted.

Bastien fixed his frost blue eyes on me. "As the Duchess of Roselyn, you may be the one to carry out her sentence."

If we waited long enough, Angelina would die from the rot I'd sown inside her. She was already writhing in pain on the ground. But she'd killed me. It was only fitting that I returned the favor. After all she'd done. To these people. To me. I staggered to my feet, and when I nearly stumbled, Bastien offered me his hand. Even though my dress was heavy with blood and mud, I had never stood taller. I had never felt more powerful.

"I am the consequence," I muttered. Words that Gorrath had taught me. Bastien placed his dagger in my palm and curled my fingers around it.

Natalia forced her to her feet while Bastien passed judgment. The black rot had turned her once haughty face to a ruin of pustules. Finally, the exterior reflected the hate within.

"Angelina Prideaux, you conspired to start a war. You cast spells that turned innocents into weres. You inflicted unspeakable harm on every member of your family, including the Duchess of Roselyn. For this, you are sentenced to death."

Angelina's lips parted, her throat bobbing like she might try to speak. "Don't," I warned. "You don't get to say a damn thing. No one asked for your last words."

Natalia forced her to her knees.

"I was your daughter," I reminded her. "All you had to do was love me." Angelina's nostrils flared. Her chest rose and fell in quick breaths. I took a slow step forward. "You enjoyed watching me suffer."

"You don't—"

I struck before she could finish. A flick of my hand, a crackle of dark magick, and suddenly she was gasping, choking on the weight of my power as it wrapped around her throat like an invisible collar. Her eyes widened, panic flashing as she clawed at her skin, trying to tear it away. I let her struggle like I had when she'd done the same to me. I crouched in front of her, my voice dropping to something dark.

"I will ensure you are not buried in our family cemetery. I will ensure no rites are given to you. Your soul will be cursed for all eternity."

"I always knew you were a demon," she gurgled. A bubble forming at the corner of her mouth. Black liquid staining her chin.

"No," I asserted. "I'm a witch."

For the first time in her wretched existence, she was not the one in control. And she *knew* it. "This is for every night I went to sleep, praying I was someone else." I pressed the dagger to her throat. "And for every lie you made me believe."

Just before I slit her throat, a voice said, "Claire! Wait!" I stilled. I would've recognized it anywhere. "Before you kill her, there's something I have to say."

CHAPTER 43
LIBÉRER
CLAIRE

I was one cut away from my justice, but the dagger in my hand faltered. Barely daring to believe it was her, I chanced a look over my shoulder to find my little sister standing a few yards away. Tears flooded my eyes. It was her. It was really her.

"Sera?"

"Claire."

Without thinking, I closed the distance between us, my arms finding their way around her, pulling her into a tight hug. At first, it was clumsy and awkward. Neither of us knew how to fit back together after everything that had happened. Her body was different, more rigid and wiry than I remembered. But it was her. My sister. I'd missed her terribly.

"Tell me you got my letter," I whispered into her hair. "Tell me you understand why I have to do this."

Sera tightened her hold on me. "No, I didn't get your letter."

"Oh, Sera." I choked on a sob, unable to let her go. "Did she bring you here? Did she hurt you? Tell me she didn't hurt you."

279

Sera cradled the back of my head. "Clairey." Her voice broke around the old nickname. "I've been with you the whole time." She dropped her voice. "As your wolf."

A pit opened beneath my feet, and my stomach dropped with it. Free-falling past every single memory I had of my wolves. The graveyard. The spark of magick in their fur. The human-like emotion in their eyes. And, finally, what Gorrath had said. *The moonstones.*

Finally, I pulled back and found that Sera was wearing the necklace she'd brought to me. She'd been trying to tell me the whole time, but I hadn't been able to understand. A thousand questions wormed their way into my mind. How did this happen? Did Mama do this to her? But they all died on my tongue when Mama opened her mouth.

"I never should've sent you to the capital with your sister! I knew you'd do something stupid! You could never follow the simplest of instructions."

She couldn't help herself. Even now. Even on her knees. The hate spewed out of her.

Defiant, Sera pulled a giant opalescent gem from her skirt pocket. It was the same goose egg-sized stone that Shayla had been wearing.

"Did you catch Shayla?" Bastien asked Tyson.

Tyson nodded. "We ran her down, alright." He tossed the severed head of a massive black wolf on the ground. It landed with a thud and a splatter of blood. Sera didn't even flinch at the sight of it. She kept her attention fixed on Mama. The moonstone clutched in her grip.

"I was headed back home, following every instruction you gave me. And on my way back home, when I stopped for the night at the Veraleese Inn, one of Shayla's werewolves attacked me. The ones *you* sent for!" she screamed, shaking the moonstone.

"Oh, Sera," I murmured, my hand covering my mouth. I felt like I knew where this was going. And it wasn't a place I was going to like.

"Without a moonstone, I couldn't control the shifting. I got stuck in my wolf skin." The rage was flowing through her now. And I found it was flowing through me as well.

"I followed them home. Listened to what you had planned. And made a decision." Her brown eyes found mine. "I went to find my sister."

"That was you in the woods, wasn't it? Outside the Kemps?"

"Yeah," she confirmed. "I tracked your scent."

"That's impressive," I managed, though the words tasted bitter. I wanted to praise her, to remind her that even now, she was extraordinary. But the truth of her situation made the compliment feel hollow. "Who were the other wolves? The ones who died?"

Sera gave me a sad smile. "Those were your familiars. Nice wolves."

I covered my mouth. The one who'd let me climb on his back? That was my familiar? And he'd died for me? "And what about the brown one?" I asked, looking around for his familiar shape. "Is he a werewolf too?"

Sera waved someone forward. And from the crowd, Alec appeared. Red-brown eyes. Charming smile. He was leaner and more wiry. My mouth dropped. I pulled him into a hug. "I thought you were dead."

"I never wanted you to worry about me."

Memories of my brown wolf drifted through my mind. Especially him watching me when I explored other uses for Gorrath's horn. Eyes narrowing, I pulled back and smacked his shoulder. "You were my brown wolf. The whole time? The *whole* time?"

He nodded sheepishly. "Yeah. I'm sorry about that. If you want to banish me, go ahead."

"I'm still considering it," Bastien remarked from over my shoulder.

"I'm not going to banish you." I smacked his shoulder once again for good measure. "But you're not allowed in my bedchamber anymore."

"I understand."

I hugged him again. And Sera. Pulling them both into a hug. I had never been alone. Never. These two had been with me, even when they couldn't say anything. They'd protected me. Fought with me. They'd been with me every step of the way.

We barely had a second to breathe before Mama ruined it. "Your sister has *poisoned* your mind."

Her lips were stained black, and I had no idea how she hadn't succumbed to the rot yet.

Sera took a step closer to where Mama was kneeling in the mud. "No, Mama," she declared. The anger and ache in her voice was like a wound being torn open. "The only one who poisoned me was *you*."

Mama looked at Sera, not with love, not with sorrow, but like she was something *ruined*. I knew that look. I had spent my entire life drowning beneath it. I just never imagined Sera would have to endure it, too. She spent her life being groomed to become the perfect weapon. And now, she had magick that she'd never asked for.

"What did I ever do to deserve a daughter so reckless?" Mama spat. "Fornicating with beasts. Drinking herself senseless? If you were attacked, it was because of your own foolishness. Not mine."

Sera took another careful step closer, her hands trembling at her sides, but the movement only made Mama's lip curl.

"After everything I've given you," Mama said. "Everything I sacrificed. And for what? For you to do the same stupid thing over and over again."

I met Sera's gaze, and a silent understanding passed between us. It was time to end this. Sera transformed back into the white wolf. As soon as her paws hit the ground, she tackled Mama to the ground. Growling in her face. Natalia had moved out of the way just in time. She gave me a nod of approval as I dropped to my knees beside my mother and stared into her cold, emotionless eyes.

"Choke on your hate." I slid the dagger across her throat and opened it. Putrid black liquid and warm red blood spilled out. There was a moment when she looked stunned. As if she hadn't truly believed I would do it. As if she had convinced herself, even now, that she was still in control.

I watched the light leave her eyes. I watched her take her last breath. And I felt nothing. No remorse. No grief. Nothing except relief that it was done.

I hugged Sera's furry neck, breathing in her scent. For the first time in our lives, we were truly free.

CHAPTER 44
AVÈNEMENT
BASTIEN

Claire didn't need to swing a sword to be brave. She didn't need to master spells or command her powers completely. Her courage wasn't for battlefield glory or for the welcome waiting at home.

She was courageous for me, for us, for everyone we cared for. Her quiet strength ignited courage in others. Because of Claire, the Prideaux coven escaped a fanatic's rule. The Unified Territories found peace. And her sister was finally able to live the life she wanted.

"Bastien, look," Natalia said, nudging me with the butt of her sword.

A horde of villagers was standing just outside the fort. Women and children. Elderly men. Young ladies and lads. None of them bore blades or crossbows. Just a look of bewilderment.

Natalia glanced at me. "Well?"

I tossed the question back to her. "What do you think we should do?"

She grunted. "Ask them what they want."

"A fine idea." She waited for me, but I nudged her with the butt of my blade. "Go on, Commander. Go make your inquiries."

Natalia gave me a wary look, sheathing her weapon before striding over to the growing crowd of villagers. Meanwhile, I paced along the fort's ramparts, scanning for threats and thinking about the weres. Tyson jogged over, his hands braced on his hips as he caught his breath. "Well, this went way better than I anticipated it would."

I managed a reluctant smile. "You? A pessimist?"

"Not at all!" Tyson protested. His grin faded. "But after Claire was taken and you went all dead-eyed, I worried I'd carry both your bodies home."

I didn't get a chance to thank Tyson for everything he'd done because at that moment, the mass of villagers gathered outside the fort began moving inside under escort. Natalia, signaling to the holding area, gestured toward where the half-transformed weres were kept, and the villagers rushed over, hugging and kissing them despite the ropes on their wrists. I realized then these weres must be relatives.

Natalia joined Tyson and me. "Apparently, Shayla didn't allow them to see each other after she changed them. It was part of her recruiting tactic. You didn't know what was really happening."

Some were kneeling over dead bodies, sobbing over them. Claire and those who had gravitated toward her—Okeri, Alec, Sera, and Tansy—wandered over to us wearing horrified looks.

"The extent of this..." Claire choked out, tears brimming but refusing to fall, heartbreak vivid on her face.

"When Mama talked about a world where Witches of the Light were safe," Sera added, "I never thought it would look like this."

Natalia, who had a great dislike of Claire's sister after she'd slapped her, gave an appreciative nod. "Shayla and your mother were kindred spirits. Unfortunately for them."

"When this is done," Lady Okeri said. "We're all going to need a stiff drink."

Tansy and Sera both said, "Cheers to that."

Tyson agreed. "When we get back to Château Rose..." he stopped, realizing I was glaring at him, and reconsidered, "you are free to do as you wish."

Beyond where we stood, a woman dropped to her knees in the mud and gathered a body into her lap—one of the fallen weres—rocking back and forth, her howl of grief tore through the yard.

As her cries echoed, the wind moved through the broken beams of the fort. Smoke from cook fires hung in the air. Somewhere in the crowd, a child was crying.

I saw how Claire absorbed the horror of war, realizing that surviving wasn't the hardest part—it was living with what followed. She lifted her chin, refusing to let her tears fall, and held her sister's hand, then Tansy's. Witches of Light and Darkness stood together before these weary souls.

One by one, the villagers began to notice them. Conversations trailed off mid-sentence. Even the half-shifted weres lifted their heads.

Their eyes weren't on me, or Natalia, or Tyson. They watched these women.

This was her moment. Her moment to spread her bravery. I wanted to reach for her, to hold her, but I wasn't going to dim her light. Not now.

"Blood has been shed on both sides of this conflict," Claire said. The entire fort went quiet. Even the wind seemed to hush to listen. "I know how devastating it is to bury family because of it."

She looked at her sister. Meanwhile, each eye was fixed on

her. Hope was spreading faster than the rot ever could, but it was almost too delicate for them to hold.

"I know what it's like to hate dark witches," Claire continued. The words were pulled from some wounded place inside her. A place I knew just as well. I'd been raised with the same hate. "My mother," she said, pointing to the woman who lay dead. "She told me they all had razor-sharp teeth and ate children."

A few nodded. Others muttered their agreement.

"But look at what Shayla did to *you*." Her voice wobbled, but she did not back down. "To your brothers and sisters. Husbands and wives. Mothers and fathers. She convinced you that in order to fight the darkness, you had to grow teeth too."

Chills ran down my spine. She wasn't wrong.

"I know what it's like to let hate take up so much space inside your body it feels like a living, breathing part of you." She thumped her chest. "A part that takes over your thoughts. Your actions. Even the prayers you pray at night."

More grunts and shouts came. But it wasn't all support, and I shared a look with Natalia and Tyson. Ready for the tide to turn, I prepared to defend my wife if needed.

"How can we trust vampires?" someone shouted.

A woman with a dirty apron and a baby in her arms stood. "They're bloodsuckers!"

I wouldn't ask Claire to defend my people and me. That was my job. "We live by rules," I explained. "A code of honor forged in the blood of twelve witches. Six from each faction. I was one of those witches." The next part stuck in my throat, but I forced it out. "The rules of the Blood Treaty establish trust between us. We do not rule over you. We are peace-keepers."

"And what happens if one of you breaks a rule?"

I swallowed hard. Claire's eyes found mine. But I kept my

attention trained on the one who asked the question. "There are severe consequences for the vampire who acts outside of the Blood Treaty."

"What kind of consequences?" he shouted back at me.

I lifted my chin, still carefully avoiding Claire's gaze. "Forfeiture of lands and titles. Banishment. Death."

A buzz of disbelief ran through the crowd. Faces twisted with worry, some inching toward hope, others back into fear. I held my breath, praying Shayla's horrors had finally exhausted their thirst for vengeance.

Tansy stepped forward, slinging her arms around Claire's shoulders and holding her tightly. The two stood side by side: Tansy, petite but muscled with brown skin and white braids, and Claire, curvy and pale with red hair cascading down her back. One refused to charge her powers, another struggled to define her magick.

Their show of unity meant more to me than I could put into words. "You can curse vampires as bloodsuckers," Tansy said, "but let me ask you this. Will there ever be enough blood to satisfy your hate?" A beat of silence. "Or is today the day you finally say enough!"

The crowd went silent again. My hands tensed, ready to grab my blade if need be. Not to hurt them, but to deter. No one would harm my wife.

Unbelievably, hope whispered through the crowd, smothering the flames of the fury that had been burning inside them.

Claire picked up where Tansy left off. "Life can be so much more than just surviving. There are beautiful, wonderful things that you can experience when you stop letting hate rule your life. Like love. And hope. I've seen it. I've felt it."

I waited. This was either the moment things changed or the start of another five hundred years of negotiations. One woman stepped forward. She was wrapped in furs and had dirt caked beneath her nails. She wore a look of exhaustion. "I can't speak for all the witches here, but as for my family and me, I'm ready to join you."

I could hardly believe it. Then another stepped forward. An older male. Human. His family was kneeling around one of the slain weres. "My only son joined with Shayla. And I encouraged him. I-I'd told him it was honorable." Tears fell down his face. "I thought this was what I wanted."

A younger woman, a shawl clutched around her shoulders, came to stand beside him. "What my father is trying to say," she began, "is that we've sacrificed enough for this war. Maybe it's time to sacrifice our old ways for the sake of peace."

More stepped forward. Witches and weres and humans. Until I had pledges from not one leader, but a hundred single voices. This was how the Blood Treaty was born. In the weary hearts and the fragile hope of people who were done with fighting. It reminded me of those first talks. When covens would meet and discuss what it would take to stop the fighting.

And I knew, as surely as I knew the weight of the sword at my side, that this was not my doing. It was hers.

Tansy appeared at my side, a fierce look in her dark eyes. "This was what Devlinn wanted, Your Grace." She wiped away an errant tear with the heel of her hand. "I can feel him here. I know he's with us."

I hadn't known Devlinn well. But I could almost see him leaning against the fence posts, arms crossed, smile crooked.

"I'm sure he is. And when we return to Chastity's, we're going to give him a hero's funeral."

The offer felt insufficient for his sacrifice, but it was all I had to offer. That, and the reassurance that Tansy wouldn't have to live a consort's life again. I would make her a lady.

"Thank you, Your Grace."

"No," I replied, meeting her gaze. Hand on her shoulder. "Thank you."

As more villagers shouted their willingness for peace, I stepped forward and raised my voice, knowing I needed to seize the momentum in the moment.

"Commander," I said. Natalia turned to me, a look of overwhelming surprise on her face. "Collect the family names of all those who wish to join the Blood Treaty. Answer their questions. Make certain they understand what it requires."

She dipped into a curtsy. "Of course, Uncle."

Claire met my eyes, and for a moment, the noise of the fort fell away entirely. I couldn't understand how anyone would look at a woman like that with anything short of wonder. How her own mother could've convinced her that she was unintelligent.

I wanted to tell her to sit down and rest. She'd been through enough today. But something told me that would only infuriate her, and I didn't want to spoil the moment. That was my fear. I needed to trust that she would take a break if she needed one. However, there was more I needed to say.

I found Tyson, Alec, and Sera clustered around the wolf's head. Alec and Tyson bowed. Sera simply crossed her arms. Her opinions about vampires had changed, but I clearly hadn't impressed her. Although she'd been in the room when I'd fucked her sister, so perhaps it was that.

I cleared my throat. "I don't have the words to express my gratitude to the three of you. Had you not followed me, had you not chased down Shayla, none of this would be possible."

Tyson tried to restrain a grin. "Does this mean I've proven to be more than just a royal pain in your neck?"

"Something like that." I scrubbed a hand over my chin. "Sera, Alec, could you excuse us for a moment?" Alec bowed, Sera sneered, then they marched off toward where Claire and

Tansy were speaking to the people. I gestured to a more secluded area of the fort where there were fewer people milling about. "I have a request to make of you."

Tyson shifted his weight. "Don't tell me you've rethought your decision to leave Château Rose to me?"

I shook my head. "I have broken the Blood Treaty, and I know it could mean banishment. Or death." Tyson tried to cut in, but I spoke over him. "If he takes my head, I want your word that you will take care of Claire. Offer her a place in your court. And treat my child as a son." Tyson went to say something else, and I could tell it was some long-winded speech. "Just say that you will do as I ask, and nothing more."

He set his hand on my shoulder and said, "I swear it."

I expelled a tight breath, trying to keep my emotions from showing on my face. Now was not the time to come apart. Not when so much good was unfolding around me.

Glancing past the fort and to the mountains in the distance, I forced a smile. "I think," I said slowly, "it's time to go back home."

For the first time in a long time, I didn't mean Château Rose. I meant Amara. The place I wished to return to with Claire. If Marius lets me live, I hoped to return to the banks of the Starfall River. I wanted to raise my son on the same trails I once ran. I wanted to fish, hunt, and grow vegetables beside a small cottage.

After five hundred years, I was ready to rest.

CHAPTER 45
DEUIL

CLAIRE

The next two days were a blur. We tended the injured and forged friendships with the local witches and humans. We broke bread with them and listened to their stories. One Witch of the Light who accepted Bastien's peace even performed a healing spell on my wounds, stopping the bleeding. She urged me to use the salve to lessen scarring, but I refused. I wanted the scars. They were proof I survived.

We returned to Chastity's Stronghold yesterday, and since then, I couldn't stop touching my neck. Only a thin gold chain, marking me as Bastien's mate, remained. No lace. Just the scars pulling when I turned or swallowed. Freedom from Mama's curse still felt unreal.

Today, Tansy and I volunteered to help Chastity's witches prepare the bodies of the fallen for death rites. They had fought against Tansy's help, but I'd insisted. Inside the cold, dark cellar, with the stench of death and dried blood saturating the room, we bathed them and applied ceremonial oils. Any who followed Damien, whether witch or human, were being prepared for burial.

Devlinn, who was being given the highest honor of a hero, would be burned in a pyre, alongside the body of the demon Gorrath. Thankfully, I wouldn't need to clean Gorrath or see his body before the ceremony. He was being personally tended to by Chastity. In the end, he had lived up to his bargain with her. He had protected her from Shayla. And he'd done the same for me, too.

When Tansy pulled back the black sheet that had been covering Devlinn, she sucked in a sharp breath. Tears immediately flowed down her cheeks.

"Could you give us some privacy?" I asked the other witches. Still clearly angry, they left the room in a huff without providing us further instructions on how to prepare a hero's body.

I wrapped my arms around Tansy as she sobbed into my shoulder. Pain clenched my chest, but I forced my own tears back. I had to deliver his message. I had decided against telling her I'd seen him. That I'd hugged him one last time. That I had the chance to apologize. None of it would ease the raw ache she carried. Stroking her trembling back, I whispered, "He loved your laugh. Did you know that?"

She sniffed. "What?"

I forced a smile. "Yes, he loved your laugh. He said it made him fall in love with you."

She shed more tears. "Who falls in love with someone because of their laugh?" she sputtered, managing a laugh herself. Even here, I understood what he meant, it was musical. "He wouldn't want his death to stop you from laughing again. I know it."

She wiped her face with a clean strip of silk, then looked back down at his body. "I know. It's just hard right now."

I nodded, unable to imagine her grief.

A soft knock fell against the cellar door. "Come in," I said, imagining it was one of Chastity's witches. But it wasn't. A younger witch appeared in the doorway. Her hair had been brushed and braided. Her face had been cleaned. She had been given a fresh set of clothes. But I recognized the hollowness in her eyes.

Mellie said nothing as she peered at us around the door. Her gaze fell to Devlinn's body.

"What do you want?" Tansy snapped. "Aren't you supposed to be with a guard?"

The girl lifted her chin and stepped inside. "She's right behind me." Mellie opened the door enough for me to see a female soldier standing in the corridor. "I wanted to offer my help preparing the bodies for death rites."

"Why?" Tansy asked.

A bit of the girl's confidence wavered. Her clenched hands trembled. "I trained with the priestesses who delivered death rites before..." Her voice broke, raw with memory. She shook her head. "I heard those witches snickering, saying you'll muck up his honors because you don't know the right prayers." Mellie let out a derisive snort that would've put Natalia to shame. "Bunch o' pompous jerks, they are."

"That's bold, coming from the witch who killed him!"

Silence filled the cellar. I held my tongue, knowing it wasn't my place to intervene. I'd already vouched for Mellie once.

"Fine." She stayed, arms crossed, as Tansy dipped a cloth in clean water, holding it over his body but unable to start. Fresh tears fell.

"Why?" she choked out. "Why?"

I pressed my lips together to keep my own tears at bay. Unsure how long I should let this go on. I didn't want something bad to happen again, but Tansy did deserve an answer.

Mellie bit her lip, fighting tears. "I'm sorry. I don't know

why I said that spell. I was angry. I'd watched those weres do
—" She shook her head. Fists clenched, she tried again: "I
didn't mean to kill him. I'll go."

She pushed her way past the door and then the guard, her
footsteps echoing as she ran. Tansy blew out a breath, dropped
the rag, then went after her. Worried she was going to strangle
her, I followed after.

"Mellie!" she shouted, drawing the attention of the witches
who were, in fact, snickering in the corridor. "Come back
here!"

The guard dragged her back to us by the arm. Tansy and
Mellie were both breathing heavily. Both angry, just for very
different reasons. Finally, Tansy dropped her hands to her
sides. The anger that had been raging in her quieted. "Teach
me how to say the prayers."

Mellie stopped struggling against the guard. "I'm not going
to do it if this is just your way to berate me some more."

Tansy shook her head. "I won't." She stepped aside, letting
Mellie pass. Her guard glanced at me for approval.

I nodded weakly. "She's not going to cause any trouble."
* * *

Once Devlinn's body was prepared for the pyre, we left
Tansy alone with him to say her final goodbyes. Mellie shuffled
beside me. Both of our sleeves were wet and rolled up to the
elbow. Both of us stinking of ritual oil and fresh herbs.

"What are you going to do now?" I asked.

She shrugged. "Find my guard."

I stopped. So did she. "No. I mean, after we leave. Chastity
won't let you stay."

She shrugged. "I'll find work. Maybe open a mortuary.
People will still need help with the dead, even with peace."

It was hard to imagine her, alone, cleaning bodies. Without
a coven, she'd be vulnerable. "Why not come with us?"

She waved her hands in the air. "No. You just take care of my siblings. Get them out of these parts. I don't care if there's a peace accord or not. Trouble will be back. Mark my words."

I wanted to reach for her, to set a hand on her shoulder, but I knew it would be too much. "We have room for you, too."

She scoffed. "And be treated like a criminal the whole time? Followed around by a guard? I'll take my chances on the road."

Devlinn's death was just as much on my hands as it was on hers. I had pushed her before she was ready. If I'd had magick when Shreesa was pushing me, I might've killed her too.

"I won't pressure you to come with us," I said, trying to push calm into my voice. "But you're welcome to join us. As long as you understand that you'll encounter Witches of the Light and people different from you in the Unified Territories. And if you hurt anyone or threaten them, you will face punishment. There won't be second chances."

She gave me a look, I thought she might agree, but then her eyes dimmed, and she left. I wanted to go after her, but knew it wouldn't change her mind.

A cold wind clawed at my face as I stood beside Bastien in the clearing outside Chastity's Stronghold. Tiny snowflakes swirled in spirals around the large funeral pyre.

Chastity's witches stood behind her. Each dressed in ceremonial black robes that were embroidered with crimson thread at the hems. The thing that surprised me the most was the horns they wore. Different sizes and shapes. Even Mellie was wearing a short, stubby pair that she must've smuggled with her.

There was so much I didn't know about the ways of Dark Witches.

There was one thing I knew that they didn't: what the God of the Underworld's horns looked like. The way they twisted from his brow. I also knew what his grace felt like. Even though my mother had insisted he was evil incarnate, Damien hadn't demanded I become one of his demons. He'd let me come back to Bastien. I touched the mottled scars at my neck, thankful for the life that he'd allowed me to come back to.

I glanced at my husband, carved from cold stone like his Château. I knew his lack of a smile didn't mean he wasn't happy. In fact, quite the contrary. He was about to secure a peace he'd long sought. The wind tugged at his cloak, revealing the bloodstone that pulsed at his chest. He wasn't hiding our matebond anymore. He was displaying it. Loud and proud for everyone to see. And it made me love him even more.

I wanted to reach for him, but I didn't. I stood beside him as his duchess. As his wife. Chin held high.

Chastity's crimson lips curled into a smile. "So, it's agreed," she said, extending her hand.

"It's agreed," he answered.

Her smile deepened. "Then, by the old magicks, let this accord be struck."

She extended her hand, and Bastien clasped it. A warm light formed between their palms, just as it had when he'd shaken the hands of all those people inside the fort.

"Now, I am under your protection."

"Now, I am your guardian. And I will protect this peace."

The cold wind howled around us, and Bastien turned to those gathered around us.

"Let this land be lawless no more. Let its people find peace. Let this moment signify the beginning of a long and lasting truce that serves the people and forges a new era of prosperity.

Cheers went up. Then a witch brought Chastity a torch. I reached for Tansy's hand as Chastity ignited the pyre. She passed the torch to Bastien, and he lit another side. On it went. We all took turns sending them off with prayers on our lips. Finally, Tansy took the torch and tossed it on top, and it landed right on Devlinn's chest.

I held her as it burned. Bastien stood at my side, one hand on my shoulder, silently supporting me. I don't know how long we stood there, watching it burn down. Long enough that my legs ached and my eyes were raw from tears. Until there was nothing left to see.

Bastien left me long enough to bring our horse around. Tansy rode with Lady Okeri. Sera with Alec.

Bastien helped me climb onto Lucien's back. The horse's hot breath puffed white in the icy air. He mounted behind me with the ease of a vampire. One hand resting protectively on my stomach. I still hadn't told him about meeting Damien, or the trade I'd made. Not because I wanted to keep more secrets, but because parts of my journey were meant to be private.

The choice I made to give up immortality wasn't something I needed to retell. It was deeply personal. And I didn't want to see guilt in his eyes every time I fell ill, or when I struggled. Or, when I eventually died. I wanted him to feel nothing but gratitude for the life we had together and for the ones to come. For the children that will stay with him when I'm gone and who will be waiting for me to be reborn. For the grandchildren and great-grandchildren who will get to know me as a young woman and who will teach me things.

My husband pressed a kiss against my temple. "Let's go home."

I nodded, leaning against his broad chest. Clicking his tongue, then giving a command in Sanguisi, Lucien began trotting away. The smell of the pyre lingered on my clothes and in my hair.

Chastity's voice chased us into the distance. "Don't forget! If you fuck me over, I will haunt you forever!"

Bastien and I shared a smile. "A truly horrifying prospect," he said. Then shouted back, "I couldn't possibly forget."

My friends joined us on the road, riding beside us. Natalia. Tyson. Everyone. We'd all come so far together. I took a moment to really look at all of them. To memorize their faces. Even the soldiers we'd brought with us.

The wind picked up as we rode out, carrying with it the scent of frost, distant pines, and old magick. For what felt like hours, we saw nothing but snow and ice. Bastien and I rode in silence. And soon, my tired eyes closed, and I drifted off to sleep.

CHAPTER 46
APAISER
CLAIRE

We made camp one last time as the sun dipped below the horizon. Bastien explained it was tradition to rest for a night before the trek up the mountains. One night to prepare the soldiers to see their families and mourn the dead privately. The sky was painted in golds and pinks and soft purples.

Our tent was small, but I didn't mind. The deer hide kept out the worst of the cold. As I ducked inside, the weight of the day settled over me until I couldn't hold back the tears. They dripped down my cheeks like hot streams, and I wiped them away as I collapsed on a pile of furs.

For a while, I was too tired and heartsick to do anything but lie there and stare at the flicker of the campfire beyond the tent's opening. Muffled voices nearby reminded me I wasn't alone.

We'd won. We'd negotiated the peace that Bastien had been chasing for centuries. Mama was gone. The choker was nothing but a scrap of lace. I had my sister back. But the cost was high. We'd lost Devlinn. And many families had been torn apart. Like the children that we'd found in the tunnels.

If I let myself think about it for too long, I would collapse. So I let myself imagine the future—a quiet life, far from battles. A life where Bastien and I could be at peace. Where the orphans we were bringing back with us to Château Rose could start a new life. I couldn't give them their parents back, but we could offer them a safe place to heal. Where they didn't need to worry about food or about someone stealing them in the night.

The flap of the tent stirred, and Bastien stepped inside. I sat up, wiping the moisture from my face. His pale blue eyes met mine, and for a moment, the storm in my chest calmed.

Whether it was our bond or just the sight of him, I wasn't sure. But when he sank onto his knees beside me and took my face in his hands, I closed my eyes and kissed him, fingers tangling in his hair, tears still falling.

With my lips pressed against his, I said, "We did it."

He didn't say anything. Instead, he kissed me again. Hungrier this time. Like it was the only thing he needed. Not my blood. Not my body. Just the heat of my mouth. Just... me. His hands slid from my face, trailing down my neck to my shoulders, his cool touch soothing and familiar. I clung to him, my fingers tangling in his hair, the silky strands a sharp contrast to the rough calluses of his hands.

His breath was uneven when he finally pulled back, his forehead resting against mine. "When we return home, we'll send out invitations for Tyson's Investiture. And we'll make preparations to leave."

The tears spilled freely now. I loved Château Rose. It was my home. But I was relieved to find a quieter life. Bastien wiped my tears away with the rough pad of his thumb.

"I'm sorry," I whispered. "I don't know why I'm crying."

His hand cupped my cheek, tilting my face so I couldn't

avoid his gaze. "Don't," he said, his voice firm. "You have nothing to be sorry for. Not with me."

The bond between us threaded through the spaces where words weren't enough. He tilted my chin, his lips brushing against mine again, this time softer, slower. The grief that had been sitting on my chest eased, one breath at a time, as his hands moved to my dress, fisting sections of the heavy fabric and pulling it up. Cursing under his breath when he found the soft stockings I wore underneath.

"Must everything about you tease me?"

He ran his hands up the smooth fabric and unhooked my stockings. His fingers on my bare thighs sent sparks down my spine.

"I need you," he breathed against my mouth.

I pulled him closer and unfastened his cloak. Its weight fell away, leaving only him.

There was nothing restrained about the way his hands roamed over my body, claiming every inch as though he could rewrite the hurt written into my skin. His lips followed, leaving a trail of gentle kisses along my neck, my collarbone, each touch lighting a fire that chased away the cold.

I didn't think of the war, the witches, or the wolves. For now, there was only the sound of our breaths and the slide of skin against skin as he pulled himself free and guided me onto his lap. I gripped his shoulders and sank down on him. Letting myself drown in the moment, in him.

With our foreheads pressed together, I didn't care who was listening or what they thought about it. I moaned for him. I twisted my fingers into his hair. Riding him up and down. Over and over. It felt good, but I was distracted. Too much had happened, and I felt disconnected from my own pleasure.

When our eyes met, his were burning with an intensity

that left me breathless. He knew I wasn't close. He could tell this was different for me. "Do you want to stop?"

I shook my head. "No. No. I need this too."

"Do you want me to open our bond? I can help you forget, just for right now."

Tears pricked in my eyes. "Please."

Just as he had the first night I met him, and many times since then, he opened the connection between us. I'd become accustomed to the feeling I had when it was open, but this time, the dominance of it was hypnotic.

"I have something for you. Something that might help."

He leaned back, fumbling with a piece of cloth, and pulled out my horn. The relic I thought I lost when Mama kicked it off the balcony.

"Where did you get this?"

"Natalia found it. She had it cleaned and blessed by Chastity's witches."

After everything that had happened with Gorrath, I thought seeing it again would bring up other emotions. But it didn't. The horn was separate from him. And having it back in my hands felt right. I gave Bastien a wary glance. "We don't have to use it."

"If it will help, I want to use it."

The horn's power switched on, vibrating insistently, as if it knew what I needed. He slid it between us, pressing it to the most sensitive part of me. My head tipped back. The force of the vibrations and our open bond pushed every thought from my mind. While he held the horn against me, I found a slow, steady rhythm. He kissed my neck. My breasts. Watching me intently as I chased the release only he could give.

His breath matched mine, jagged as the pleasure built inside me. Each whispered word sent me spiraling closer to release.

"Bastien," I moaned, not bothering to use our bond. What-ever came next, I would carry this with me. The way his name felt on my lips, the way my heart beat in time with the blood-stone around his neck.

And for the first time in what felt like forever, I let go of everything I was carrying and came hard around his thick length, moaning his name as stars burst behind my eyes.

He lowered me onto the furs as waves of pleasure crested over me, picking up his pace. I could tell by the strangled look in his eyes that he was close. So very close to coming all the way undone.

Then I saw the change. The blackness that crept into his eyes as his fangs lengthened. Unafraid, I tilted my head to the side, bearing my neck for him. He was everything, all at once. And I only wanted more.

Bastien pressed his delicious lips to my heated skin, drinking me in body and soul as he continued to fuck me like the world was on fire.

Like he was a god. My god. The only one worthy of worship.

I dug my nails into his skin as his bite stretched out my pleasure. Deepening it. Transforming it into something I could taste.

He groaned, the sound vibrating against my skin as my name escaped him. "This is for you," he said. My blood traced the line of his mouth as he came. Hard. The warmth filling me.

Our eyes met, and the blackness receded. Sweat dotted his brow. Blood stained his lips. But he didn't look any less beautiful.

"I love you," I whispered, taking his face between my hands. "I love you more than the sky could ever hold."

He licked his lips. Cleaning what he could of the stain

away. Then he offered me a smile. A genuine one I didn't see very often, but when I did, it was just for me. "I love you, too."

CHAPTER 47
VEILLÉE
CLAIRE

Two weeks later

Today was the day of Tyson's Investiture. The castle had been a flurry of planning and decorating. We'd hoped the short notice would have deterred The High Prince from attending, as a host of guards and coaches moved much more slowly through the hills. But Marius, along with Tyson's mother and father, had arrived just this afternoon.

We were both nervous about what Marius's arrival would bring, but neither of us was talking about it. Pushing thoughts of what could happen aside, I smiled at the adorable little girl who was sitting cross-legged on my bed, playing with my jewelry box. She was one of Mellie's little sisters, who couldn't have been older than five.

Tansy lay beside her, giggling along.

Her tiny fingers rifled through the collection of necklaces and rings Bastien had given me. Every so often, she'd pick something up, inspect it, then either hand it to Tansy or slip it on her small fingers. Part of me wondered if she even understood what had happened. Or why she was here now.

I watched her with tears prickling in the corners of my eyes. I knew better than most that children weren't immune to trauma. They weren't more resilient. If this was what she needed to feel safe and normal, then she could play with my jewelry for as long as she wanted.

Absently, I twisted the scrap of lace around my fingers. The only piece of jewelry I owned that didn't belong in a box. I didn't know what to do with it now that it was off.

Sera caught my attention in the reflection of my vanity mirror, and I immediately stopped playing with the broken choker. The silver gown she was wearing for tonight's festivities made her look almost untouchable, ethereal even, but I knew better. I let my gaze linger on Shayla's moonstone, which she was now wearing.

Sera arched a brow. "You're staring."

"I'm thinking," I corrected.

"That's even worse."

I huffed out a breath and turned back toward the mirror, adjusting the drape of my gown. The gold embroidery stark against the black fabric. In truth, this gown was the most decadent thing I'd ever worn.

"Are you almost ready?" Sera asked, tucking a strand of pale hair behind her ear. As she did, I noticed a mottled red mark on her neck.

Turning in my seat, I glanced between her and the little girl, then asked in a hushed voice, "What happened?"

She smoothed her hair back in place and looked away. "It's nothing."

I stood, brows pushing together. "It's not nothing. What happened?"

After looking uncomfortably around, she said, "It's *the bite*."

"What *bite*?"

"The one I got when I was turned," she said through her teeth.

"But that was so long ago. Shouldn't it be healed by now?"

She shook her head. "It's not going to heal. It's..." she dropped her voice. "It's a *mating* bite."

For a long second, I just stared at her. "From *who*?" I said.

"The man who bit me. Apparently, *he was my mate.*"

"How is that possible?"

She rolled her eyes like she hadn't just told me she'd been mated to a werewolf. "I don't know! I thought he was being romantic when he called me his mate. I was really into him, so I went along with it. I didn't realize he meant I was his *actual* mate because he was a *werewolf.*"

"Oh," I said, not quite understanding. Then I remembered the flash of memory I'd seen when I touched her fur. Of a woman and man abed. And realized what she meant. "Oh!"

She let out a bitter laugh, smoothing a hand down the front of her gown. "You're not making this any better."

I winced. "I'm just trying to understand."

She crossed her arms again. "You and me both."

I hesitated, then asked, "So what does that mean?"

"I don't know. There aren't exactly books on werewolf matebonds in Bastien's library," she said, keeping her voice low so the little girl wouldn't hear. "But I did find something about vampire matebonds that could apply."

My eyes widened, wondering what she could've found. "It said that if you reject your mate and, if after being claimed, kill him, you are cursed by the gods for going against their will."

I stared at her, waiting for the punchline that didn't come.

She let out a frustrated breath. "It explains why I can't use my magick. Diana cursed me for killing him."

"You've lost your magick?" I asked a little too loudly, and both Tansy and the little girl looked at me. I gave them a reassuring smile before pulling Sera further away from them. "You didn't tell me you lost your magick."

"I haven't wanted to believe it. But I have nothing. Nothing except the ability to shift."

I thought about this for a moment, trying to process everything she'd just told me. "What if you just ran out of magick? The full moon is on the way, and you can try then."

She bit her lower lip and shook her head. "It feels different than when I need to recharge."

We were quiet for a long time, just watching Tansy and the little girl as they continued to play with the jewelry. Something the two of us never did as children. If we wanted to play, we did it outside, away from everyone else. Staring up at the stars and making up our own stories about the witches in the sky.

"Is this the real reason why you're staying behind?" I asked. "Because you think you're cursed?"

Sera inhaled through her nose, then exhaled slowly, like she'd been bracing for this moment. "Here, the moonstone and the shifting don't raise as many questions. Besides," she said, glancing at the bed where Tansy and the little girl sat, "you've got friends coming with you. You don't need me."

I heard the bitterness in her tone, and it made me incredibly sad to see her in my shoes. For her to feel like an outcast now. It was not what I wanted. I swallowed, forcing the words past the knot in my throat. "I will always need you, Sera. You're my sister."

"I think..." She hesitated, her eyes flicking to the floor. "I think I need to find answers. Maybe the witches over the mountains will know more about werewolves. I'm going to start there."

I studied her, my chest aching, even though I understood. More than I wanted to. I remembered the nights we spent beneath the stars as children, dreaming of different lives, desperate for answers. Now, the need to figure out who we were throbbed in both of us. I tucked her hair behind her ear once again, revealing her scar, and gave her a small, trembling smile.

"Well, if you ever change your mind, you are always welcome to come with us. Curse or not."

She said nothing, and silence settled between us. We both watched the little girl as she held up a gold locket from the jewelry box, twisting it between her fingers. She smiled brightly and slipped it over her head. Tansy showed her how to open it, and her eyes lit up with excitement.

Sera shifted, giving me a weak smile as her hands fell to her sides. "Did I tell you that Tyson offered me a position on his council? Ambassador to the Lawless Lands." She let out a small laugh. "I'll come with him to oversee construction on the new castle and ensure the witches' opinions are made known."

I raised a brow. Knowing exactly the kind of vampire Tyson Allard was. "Oh, he did, did he?"

A burst of heat colored her cheeks. "I'm not *that* reckless. Don't worry."

I smirked. "Right."

She narrowed her eyes. "Claire."

I reached for her hand, threading my fingers through hers, squeezing once.

"You're not reckless." I squeezed again, softer this time. "You're just Sera. You have a wild heart, and you follow it without apology."

Something shifted in her expression.

"I love you," I said. "No matter what."

She swallowed.

Then, after a long moment, she squeezed my hand back. "I love you, too."

The little girl, now wearing at least three rings that didn't fit and a tangled mess of necklaces, giggled softly with Tansy, their feet swinging off the edge of the bed.

I set my hand on my stomach, and warmth spread through me, quiet and whole. I decided this must be what it was like to have a real family. I turned toward the door, knowing Bastien was about to enter even before I heard him softly knocking. "Is everyone decent?"

I giggled. "Yes, we're all decent. Come in."

The door opened, and my husband appeared. I didn't know why he despised finery so much because when he wore it, he was absolutely breathtaking. A black velvet coat framed his broad, muscled shoulders. Gold thread embroidered the cuffs and collar in an intricate pattern. Beneath the coat, he wore a high-collared waistcoat of gold silk with a line of polished jet buttons marching down the center. Finally, a black cravat was tied around the pale column of his throat, fastened with a slender gold pin. The only thing that wasn't black or gold was his bloodstone, which sat visibly against his chest, pulsing frantically with my heart.

"Ladies," he said in greeting. "You all look lovely."

As he took a step inside, a few strands of his golden hair fell forward, brushing the angles of his face. His pale blue eyes flicked down the deep neckline of the dress in a slow, indulgent perusal. He swallowed hard, then, through our bond, said, *"I keep believing I've grown accustomed to your beauty. I never do."*

I exhaled, steadying myself. *"Bastien—"*

He quickly closed the space between us and captured my hands in his, kissing both of my knuckles. *"How am I supposed to leave your side tonight when you look like this?"* His eyes locked onto mine, and the smirk faded, something *raw* taking its place.

"You can and you will," I told him, knowing sometimes he needed direction.

He nodded. *"If you insist."* His confidence faltered, just for a breath—a flicker of uncertainty I would have missed if I weren't already tangled in his emotions. Through our bond, I caught the sharp edge of his doubt, the fear he tried so hard to bury. It stung, that sudden distance as he closed the bond, walling me off from the storm inside him.

His attention shifted to the window, to the sprawling landscape he had watched over for centuries. The mountains and the pines. When he looked at me again, the vulnerability was gone, buried beneath a gentlemanly mask.

"You're sad," I said, unable to hold it in.

He touched the side of my face. *"I feel many things, my moonflower. But mostly, just love for you and the quiet life we're going to make. Together."*

Sera very loudly cleared her throat. "Can you two *get a room?"*

"We are in *my* room," I said, grinning as I turned to look at my sister.

She glanced from me to him. "I know how the two of you operate." She pointed to the little girl and mouthed, "And there is a child present."

He huffed something like a laugh. "You know, I think I liked it better when you were a wolf."

Sera's mouth fell open. "Did you just make a joke? On purpose?"

"Enough, you two," I said, intervening.

I set my hand on Bastien's chest, and he responded with a low, throaty growl that made my heart flutter. His hand drifted to my low back, pulling me closer to him. "As my wife commands."

A warmth spread from the tips of my ears to my toes as he looked into my eyes.

Sera let out a breath. "Alright, we should get moving before we miss the ceremony." She picked up the little girl and set her on her hip. "And you need to return to the nanny." The little girl frowned. "No! I want to go to the party!"

"I hear Nanny has tarts for you," Sera said, walking with her out the door. Tansy followed after, listing all the tarts the little girl would get to try. Her effervescent laughter drew my thoughts to the thing neither one of us was talking about. Our baby.

Once they were gone, Bastien didn't let go right away. Neither did I. I still hadn't received my moon cycle, but that wasn't unusual for me. I'd never bled like other women did, which at the time I'd been grateful for. Because when it did come, it was horribly painful, and I struggled to leave my bed. But this time, I hoped it meant something else.

"Are you ready?" I asked.

He leaned down and kissed me softly. A bit of red lipstick came off on his lips, and I wiped it off with my thumb.

"Tonight, there will be a new Duke of Roselyn. Which means, from now on, I will only have one job."

"And what job is that?" I asked.

He buried his face in the hollow of my neck. "To please my wife."

CHAPTER 48
LA TRANSMISSION
BASTIEN

The Grand Ballroom of Château Rose had never looked more regal. Candlelight flickered in every crystal sconce, casting a golden glow across the marble floors and gilded cornices. Servants in livery glided silently between guests, bearing silver trays laden with sugared fruits and delicate confections. Gold banners draped from the vaulted ceiling while black velvet hung behind the dais, and artfully arranged bouquets of winter lilies and hothouse orchids adorned the periphery.

It was more than I would've done, but Tyson was the new Duke of Roselyn, and I supposed if he wanted to indulge a little more than I did, it wouldn't be the end of the world.

Or at least that's what Claire had told me.

I adjusted my cravat, ignoring the way the fabric pulled at my throat, and surveyed the attendees. My brothers, Piers and Aurélien, who lived in neighboring lands, were sitting in the front row, beside Claude, Tyson's father. And then there was his lady mother. A horrible court gossip if the rumors were true. And seated in the place of honor was the High Prince himself, Marius.

He looked the same as always. With black curls tied loosely at the nape and a glass of champagne in his hand. He was whispering to Claire, who was seated beside him. I didn't like him sitting so close to her, but I had no choice in the matter. This might be my castle for the next few minutes, but he was the High Prince. And I'd done enough to draw his ire.

My wife was wearing a gown of black and gold. Her lips were painted. Her red hair was curled. Gems draped her wrists and fingers. She was a portrait of beauty. A goddess. My obsession. My *everything*. And if the gods were good, carrying my whole world inside her.

There was no heartbeat yet, but when there was, all the vampires would know.

As a string quartet played a lively minuet from the musicians' balcony, the rest of the guests found their seats. The air was alive with the flutter of fans and the murmur of speculation over who might secure a dance with the High Prince.

Each chair was filled with men and women whom I'd come to know over the years, their jewels catching fire in the candlelight. Each had trusted me to protect them. Now they were here to witness me pass my title to Tyson.

While part of me was sad to leave, I was less concerned with Marius's dance card and more worried about whatever punishment he had planned for my crimes. I had my reasons for taking my mate as a sanguine partner, but I understood that those rules were the foundation of trust between us and those we protected.

Tyson beamed at me from the bottom of the stairs that led up to where I stood on the dais. He was dressed in the black and gold of Roselyn, which suited him well. And for the first time since he set foot in my castle, his attire was actually appropriate for the circumstance.

I might've had my doubts when Marius had named him my heir, and in many moments since, but since our trip to the Lawless Lands, he'd begun to walk like a man of Roselyn and had proved his loyalty.

Now, he seemed eager to begin the ceremony. With his hands clasped behind his back, he glanced around the room. First acknowledging his sanguine partner, Lady Okeri, who was dressed in a lovely gold gown detailed with black beads. But his attention quickly shifted past her. I traced the line of his focus and found who he was watching. *Claire's sister.*

She was being escorted to her seat, in human form, by Alec. Her silver gown reminded me of her wolf coat. But it was the egg-sized moonstone around her throat that caught my eye. It was the same stone Shayla had worn. I don't know why, but I found it unsettling.

Natalia, who was standing beside me on the dais, dressed in the regalia of a military commander, nudged me with her elbow. I slipped inside her thoughts, knowing instinctively that she had something to say. *"She's trouble waiting to happen, that one."*

I hummed. *"Good thing you'll be here to keep a watchful eye on her."*

"So you agree there is something to watch?"

The music ceased as the ceremony was about to begin. Laurent, my Grand Advisor, anointed Tyson's forehead with water from the three rivers that ran through Roselyn. Then he prayed, calling on both Damien and Diana to give him strength and guidance.

"I believe you should follow your instincts in this matter," I told Natalia as we watched on. *"But do not allow your anger to cloud*

your judgment. Nothing is black and white. And not everyone is an enemy."

Once Laurent had finished his prayer, I waited to receive my nephew on the dais. With my fingers curled around my cane, I tried to relax the tension that had settled in my shoulders, but it was impossible. The room fell into a deeper silence as Tyson began the climb, step by step. A thousand thoughts raced through my head.

I chanced a look at Claire, who was smiling at me and sending encouraging energy. I needed every bit of it when Tyson reached the final step. He bowed to Natalia, then me. We bowed back. There was nothing left to do except say my part. The crowd waited attentively.

They needed reassurance that this change wouldn't disrupt their lives. That they were safe with Tyson in charge. I had to be confident and poised, no matter what.

"Kneel, Lord Tyson."

He did so without hesitation. His head bowed.

He was ready for this. Or at least more ready than I'd been at his age. And while I still wished Natalia were the one kneeling before me, I intended to renew my efforts to reinstate her claim to her father's duchy. *As long as Marius didn't order my execution.* There would always be a place for her here. But she was the rightful heir to Nightfall.

I lifted my cane, as duty required, and touched the tip of it to one of Tyson's broad shoulders. "Do you swear to defend the city of Roselyn and the outlying lands? Do you swear to protect the innocent and serve the High Prince with honor?"

"I swear."

I tapped his other shoulder. "Do you promise to uphold the traditions of Château Rose? To rule with wisdom, to lead with strength, and to fight with valor?"

"I promise."

I met Claire's eyes and saw she was wiping away a tear, but there was a fierce smile on her face. It gave me the strength I needed to say the last part.

"Then rise, Tyson of the House Allard, Viscount of Aurenne and Duke of Roselyn."

Once the words were out of my mouth, the ballroom erupted into applause. I held out my hand for him. He clasped it and pulled me into an embrace. More cheers came.

Emotion was thick in his voice when he said, "Thank you, Uncle."

"Address your people," I whispered, patting his back.

It was done. I was relieved of my duties. A peaceful transition of power from one vampire to another. Tyson had inherited a peaceful border and would oversee the construction of a new château. It was time for a new ruler, one who cared about pageantry and appearances.

Tyson faced my people—*his people*. He gave a short speech that I barely heard over the ringing in my ears.

I didn't like being on the dais. And now that I'd done my duty, I wanted to leave. Glancing at Claire, I said, *"I need you,"* through our bond.

She gave me a cheeky grin. *"It would hardly be proper for you to take me in front of all these people."*

I forced myself to smile back at her, letting her believe that's what I meant. Or maybe she knew and was just trying to lift my spirits. *"Then I suppose I'll have to torture myself a while longer."*

After his speech, we descended the dais and marched down the center aisle. Tyson and Natalia led the way, while I followed after. My household staff moved swiftly around the room, refreshing goblets with sparkling wine, and filling the tables lining the back with pyramids of sugared fruits, delicate pastries, and glistening meats under silver domes.

The orchestra launched into a sprightly waltz, and the polished parquet was soon alive with laughter and dancing. I dodged conversations and found my way back to my wife, who was nibbling on a pastry. The pink flush in her cheeks was a welcome sight. Now that everyone knew she was my wife, there was no need to hide the truth anymore.

I took her hand and pressed a kiss against her knuckles. "I am not worthy of such beauty." She flushed a deeper shade of red, then took my arm. "Shall we?" I asked.

I introduced her to a few important guests, but I was mostly trying to avoid Marius, who was chatting animatedly with Tyson and our brothers. When Tansy approached, wearing a black dress, and asked if Claire would dance with her, I was more than happy to oblige. "Have fun."

The two of them twirled around the dance floor, giggling. Tansy had agreed to come with us to the capital. Not as a consort, but as one of Claire's ladies-in-waiting.

Natalia materialized at my side. "Do you care to dance?" I asked.

My niece let out a disgusted grunt in response. We both chuckled, content to watch the revelers from a distance like two unfriendly birds. Tyson waved Sera and Alec over to introduce them to my brothers. The pair seemed just as uncomfortable with attention as I was.

"*Do you really believe their story?*" Natalia asked, her arms crossed.

"*About what?*"

"*That they killed Shayla.*"

"*Shayla didn't just give them her moonstone. Of course, I believe them.*"

I had to believe them. Otherwise, I wouldn't be able to leave. Knowing the border was safe was my greatest accomplishment.

Natalia's lips pressed into a thin line. *"She's still a Prideaux. And he's still an idiot."*

"Claire is also a Prideaux," I reminded her.

Natalia scoffed. *"She's different."*

I raised my brows.

"She's an Allard."

That she was.

It was good to have Natalia back on my side. I was going to miss her fiercely when I left. But we were at the end of an era. She and I had spent many nights in this castle, sharing laughs and exchanging barbs. But now, I was moving on.

I noticed the way Tyson's shoulders straightened when Sera whispered in his ear. *"Can we speak? Privately?"* He placed his hand on Sera's lower back and guided her toward a receiving room just off the ballroom, Alec trailing behind them.

Natalia scoffed again. She was full of venom tonight. *"Like we can't hear them. We're vampires."*

I let out a reluctant chuckle that died quickly. *"I have bigger problems than Tyson."* I gestured to the High Prince, who was cutting a path directly toward us. It would seem I was unable to dodge my brother any longer.

Natalia lifted her wine glass to her lips. *"He's not going to decapitate you. After your success in the Lawless Lands, you are a hero."*

My niece was wise, but she was still too young to realize there were worse fates than death as an immortal.

"Mon sang!" Marius said in greeting. A jovial light danced in his dark eyes as we clasped hands. "It is good to be back at Château Rose again. How long has it been since my last visit to these snowy mountains?"

I forced a tight smile. "A hundred years, Your Grace. Give or take."

Natalia choked on her sip of wine.

Marius let out a bawdy laugh. "Surely it hasn't been that long!"

"I believe your exact words were, 'I'd rather cut off my left testicle than be forced to endure the carriage ride again." I smiled weakly. "Which is why you've insisted that my last hundred Sanguination Balls be held at the capital."

Natalia gave me a look from over the top of her wine glass. I added a smile that likely came off as a sneer. I was already weary of the political maneuverings of the capital, and I hadn't even left Roselyn. But I knew he hadn't come to talk about old times.

While Natalia and Marius exchanged pleasantries, I cast a look at Claire, who was still dancing with Tansy. I'd been trying so hard to protect her from my nervousness, but by the way she immediately stopped dancing to cut a path toward me, I knew I wasn't doing a very good job.

Claire dipped into a graceful curtsy as she approached. "Your Grace. Are you enjoying yourself?"

"Poppet!" Marius exclaimed. "There you are!"

Of all the names he could have for my wife. The urge to rip his arm from his body and beat him bloody became all-consuming. I had to fight the change with everything inside me. "You know she is Lady Claire now."

Marius's smile lingered on her for a moment too long. "I do. And what a lovely lady she makes." He plucked a goblet of wine from the tray, swirling the dark liquid. "Let's retire to your study, brother. We have much to discuss."

And so the time had finally come to hear my sentence for breaking the law and taking Claire as my sanguine partner. I bowed to my wife. "If you'll excuse us, my dear."

Marius shook his head. "No, no, no! She comes too. The more the merrier, after all."

I took a slow breath, my jaw tightening. I wanted to argue

with him, but it was useless. This was what he wanted. And so long as he didn't hurt my wife or say anything inappropriate, I would have to endure it. I offered Claire my hand, and she accepted it.

She was trying to pierce through the wall I'd erected around our connection to read my emotions, but I wouldn't let her in. If she knew how worried I was, it wouldn't be good for her.

CHAPTER 49
LE TRÔNE
BASTIEN

I fell back on the pleasantries Marius expected. After all, I was still one of the twelve vampire princes, and I was obligated to uphold a code of honor. With one hand behind my back, I escorted my wife and my brother to my private study. Well, I suppose it was Tyson's study now.

Two attendants opened the double doors, bowing low as we passed through. This room had always been a place of quiet, a space where I could think clearly. But now, the air was tense.

Marius made his way to the oversized armchair near the fireplace and settled into it, crossing one leg over the other, his goblet resting on his knee. He was dressed in a tailored black tailcoat and blood-red brocade waistcoat. The cuffs of his white shirt were fastened with onyx studs, and a signet ring with the Allard crest sat on his finger.

He pointed to the empty chairs across from him. A command disguised as an invitation. Reluctantly, I guided Claire to a chair and took the seat beside her. Once we were all comfortable, Marius let out a long sigh. "It's so good to see you two."

I knew I was meant to be agreeable if I hoped to earn his favor, but I was a man of war. I had only a small tolerance for pretty words and pretenses. "Your Grace, I think we all know why you asked for this meeting."

Marius chuckled. "I have missed your humor, brother. It's as dry as the wine Yves always brings back from Château du Mer." His gaze slid past me to Claire. "Speaking of wine. Poppet —hand me that bottle over there. My glass has run dry."

Claire made to move, but I held out my hand, stopping her. I tried to keep the anger out of my voice as I gave him one last warning. "Do *not* call her that again."

The humor drained from Marius's face. "Careful, Bastien. You're on thin ice as it is."

My rage was too close to the surface for caution. "If you think for one second that I'll let you come into *my* castle and speak to *my* wife—"

"*Your* wife? Is *that* what she is? Because last I checked, she was your *sanguine partner*. The fact that she was your mate must've slipped your mind."

I clenched my jaw. "Yes. I broke the law. I took my mate as my sanguine partner. The Council of Elders believed doing so would drive a vampire mad, and yet somehow I have managed to keep my wits about me."

Marius didn't like that answer. Not at all. "But you weren't content to keep her on as just a sanguine partner. You married her. Sealing your bond. Behind my back. Without my permission."

"You're right. I failed to ask your permission. I was a little busy running your army."

"See, this is exactly the problem," Marius asserted. "You think you're above every law our people created for us."

We were both out of our chairs now. All pretense of civility gone. I shoved him hard enough to send him slamming into the back wall. The force of it cracked the stone behind him, and several pictures fell off the walls.

His eyes widened, just for a second, before narrowing into slits. "You don't want to fight me, Bastien. I've always been stronger than you."

What was left of my control snapped. I closed the distance between us and had him by the throat before he could blink. My fingers dug into his flesh, his muscles tightening against my palm. "No, Marius. I've always let you win."

Marius pulled his dagger from his chest rig and lifted the blade to my throat. "You might be stronger, brother, but not smarter."

"Enough!" The word ripped through the room. My wife put her hand between us, her eyes already glowing crimson. "If you lay one finger on my husband, I'll find out if vampires burn as fast as witches do."

Marius relaxed his grip, easing the dagger away from my throat. I did the same, my fingers loosening from his neck but not letting him go. Not yet.

"I didn't come here to lay fingers on your husband," Marius said. "I came to hold him accountable for what he's done."

Claire lifted her chin in defiance. "Who cares if he lied about our matebond? Who cares if he took blood from me?" she demanded. "He did it *for you*. To fight *your war*. To be *your general*. Which he did *without question* and *won*. You should be offering us your thanks."

For whatever reason, my wife's anger seemed to pave the way for cooler heads. Marius put his dagger away, and I let go of him. We both straightened and tried to appear gentlemanly once again.

"You might've won the war for the border, but the capital is locked in its own battle." Marius dusted off his jacket, continuing. "The nobles argue about the cost of this peace. As well as the gold required for the new castle and the soldiers needed to protect it." He canted his head to the side. "And with your stunt at the Sanguination Ball, followed by your roguish behavior, you have caused me unnecessary problems."

I held out my arms, knowing he came to do more than just exchange angry words. Marius had made excuses for me at the Sanguination Ball when it appeared that I'd bitten Claire without contract. But now, he was done covering for me. "Enough. Tell me my punishment."

Marius looked from my wife to me and back to her again. "There is only one thing I could do to truly punish you, Bastien."

"Which is?" Claire demanded. "You claim not to want to hurt him."

Marius's smile widened. "Bastien, your punishment is to handle the mess you created. You will return to the capital at once, and you will become the new High Prince of the Unified Territories."

I froze. That was not what I was expecting.

My brother took a step closer. "You'll be in charge of answering all the courtiers' questions. Placating the lords and ladies. Holding court. And your wife will help coordinate sanguination balls and name day parties and the like."

High Prince. He was going to trap me in that wretched castle, surrounded by liars and schemers, until it suffocated me. Until it drove me mad.

"No," I said flatly.

Marius's eyes gleamed. "Just think of all the parties and dances you'll be hosting to win the nobles back over to your side. And all the financial documents you'll review to levy the coin needed for that new château."

"I don't do parties," I said, running a frustrated hand through my hair. "And I don't fret over coins. I'm a commander. Not a politician."

"You are now," Marius replied. "This is your punishment. The position is yours. As is the burden."

I set my hand on the desk I'd sat at countless times, pouring over maps and strategies, trying to quiet my thoughts. This wasn't a death sentence. This wasn't banishment. However...

"Marius, I promised my wife..." I began, trying to find the right words. "I promised her we'd live a quiet life. She has sacrificed more for our people than any lord or lady who dares judge us." I rubbed at the bridge of my nose, then turned to face him. "This is the last thing she deserves. Don't punish her on account of my behavior."

Claire, who had gone rather pale after hearing this news, came to stand by my side. Neither one of us quite able to process the gravity of the situation. Of the enormity of this demand.

"Your life won't be quiet," Marius said more gently. "But your wife will want for nothing. Your children will have the best tutors. You'll have your pick of blood nannies so your wife can rest." Claire and I exchanged a look. "It's either this or I have your head. Banishment is not an option."

My heart broke when I saw the tears shining in her eyes. "We'll do it," she answered.

"No. I promised you—"

She took my face in her hands. "If it's the capital or death, then I'll take the capital."

I closed my eyes, the fight leaving my body. "Fine. We'll do it."

Marius's smile was smug. "I *knew* you would."

Once again, Natalia had been right. Marius hadn't come to

chop off my head. I was too valuable to him now. Instead, he had sentenced me to a throne.

Claire and I did not return to the party. We returned to our bedchamber, which was a smaller room inside the Duke of Roselyn's private residence. We didn't talk much. We sat on the floor by the fire and watched the flames as they danced in the hearth. She cried for a while. I held her, saying nothing.

Later, when we finally crawled into bed, she couldn't sleep. So I told her a story I remembered from my youth. One that my granny used to tell. I just kept talking until she finally fell asleep. As soon as her breathing changed, I lay beside her, wishing for the relief of sleep but knowing this was the cost of immortality. The curse of it. To never die, to never rest.

My thoughts turned to whom I would ask to accompany me to the capital and whom I should leave behind to help Tyson. For whatever reason, Imogen's face appeared in my mind.

What was I going to do about the old Witch of the Tide? Should I tell Tyson, and risk exposing her further? Or should I allow her to live undisturbed under the castle?

I closed my eyes and drew in a deep breath, remembering what Natalia had said about not trusting Tyson's story. I decided that my nephew didn't need to know about the seer that lived below the castle. The fewer who knew, the better.

Claire stirred, and I set my hand on her waist and pressed a kiss into her hair. Savoring these last few moments inside the castle that made me into the man I was today.

CHAPTER 50
QUIÉTUDE
CLAIRE

Tiny snowflakes swirled in the crisp evening air, catching on tree branches and blanketing the world in a powdery white. It was quiet. And still. Just how I liked it. I didn't know how many more moments like this we would have. Not where we were headed.

I leaned my head against Bastien's shoulder, sighing contentedly as we made our way up the hill. Normally, he would be riding with the guard. But today, he decided to ride in the carriage with me. One arm wrapped around my shoulders, the other splayed protectively over my stomach. I didn't know how to tell him what it meant to me. To have this. To have him.

The coach lurched to a stop, and I pulled back the curtains, excited to see a familiar sod roof and little chimney puffing smoke. When the door was opened, the scent of pine and burning wood drifted in. I took a deep breath, letting the familiar smell wrap around me, the memory of our last visit filling my chest with a bittersweet ache.

Bastien's fingers stretched into my hair, and he pulled me into a kiss. "Are you ready?" he asked against my mouth.

I nodded excitedly. This was the reunion I'd been waiting a long time for. Bastien exited the coach first, then held out a hand for me, ready to help me down the stairs.

A gust of wind lashed at my face as I slid my gloved hand into his. Snowflakes were already tangling in his hair, his pale blue eyes bright against the winter landscape. Months ago, I would've shivered. But now, lit from within by my own fire, I barely felt the chill. That didn't stop Bastien from settling a thick cloak around my shoulders and pulling me against him.

A sign that read, "*Tooth* and *Hare*" greeted us. Along with a short witch. Her apron was dirty, and her red hair was pinned in a messy bun atop her head. I was sure she made plenty of jokes about the girl who threatened her with a fire poker. But that was fine by me. Her kindness had confronted my worldview and was one of the sparks that changed my life.

"Rabbit stew for your companions, and thick red wine for you, Your Grace!" Shreesa held the door while we stomped our snowy boots on the mat. "I heard a rumor that they're making you the High Prince?" she exclaimed, patting the side of Bastien's face like he was just a little boy.

He offered her a smile even though I knew he was not happy about his new role and likely wished she hadn't brought it up. "I want to know where you heard this horrible rumor."

She laughed and closed the door behind us like we were old friends. The heat from the fire and the aroma of hearty stew were inviting.

"Stay as long as you like, Your Grace." Shreesa glanced at me and offered me a friendly smile. "And who is this lovely young woman? Your new wife?"

My throat closed, and speech became too much. Bastien spoke for me. "Yes. This is the Lady Claire Allard."

"Well, isn't that wonderful?" She admired my red hair. "And a Witch of the Darkness no less. What an honor to have you here, m'lady. Please, take a seat. I'll get your supper."

She gestured to the long trestle tables while she disappeared into the kitchen, and I took a seat on the bench, feeling empty. After working this moment up in my head, I'd expected more. I swore she'd at least remember my face.

The door opened, and our traveling companions streamed inside. Tansy. Sir Gavin. Mellie. The sixteen-year-old girl we'd found in the caverns. We were taking her to the capital as our ward after a long conversation with Tansy. I hoped coming to Shreesa's was a good first step on her journey to expand her understanding of the world. She, however, wanted nothing to do with Bastien or me. She purposefully chose a seat at the other end of the tavern.

"Destinee is on Mellie watch," Bastien explained as the former commander of Bastien's cavalry took the seat across from the girl. "She won't be getting into any trouble while we're here."

The rest of our riders followed after them. Our guard and the loyal attendants Bastien had asked to accompany him to the capital.

A trencher of steaming hot stew was placed in front of me, and I drew in a giant breath of it. "This is exactly what I've been craving," I told Bastien, picking up my fork and spearing a carrot. "No one makes stew like Shreesa." He watched me eat with mild amusement. "What?"

"It's just good to see you eating again. For a while, I was worried."

For the last two weeks, food had not agreed with me. And because of my weakened state, Bastien had gone on his own hunger strike. But now, I couldn't seem to stop eating. Something in him had shifted as well.

"Later?" he asked. Brows inclined. One word and I was nearly ready to set down my fork.

My body still rode on the edge of desire, especially when he looked at me like that, but it no longer controlled me. Now that I'd become the rightful carrier of this generational power, the magick that I'd inherited flourished under his attention. Every once in a while, I still heard Gorrath's gruff voice in my head, but thankfully, he held his tongue more often than not.

"Later," I replied, shoving another carrot in my mouth.

The smile on his face faded. "What is it?" I asked.

He brushed back one of the curls Tansy had put in my hair and tucked it behind my ear. "I'm just trying to memorize this moment. Exactly as it is. I never want to forget how beautiful you look right now."

It was the kind of declaration that warmed me from the inside out better than magick ever could. The only thing absent was his emotions. Ever since Marius doled out Bastien's punishment, he'd been keeping a guard around his feelings.

I finished my meal in relative peace. It was good to be out of the carriage. But every time Shreesa bustled by, I couldn't help but feel the tiniest bit disappointed. As time passed, Bastien and I entertained members of his guard. Soon, the crowd began to thin.

"I'm ready for bed," I admitted, stifling a yawn. Full. Warm. And ready to spend a night with my husband in a real bed.

"Should we give Shreesa our gift now? Or wait until the morning?" Bastien asked.

I stuck my hand in my pocket and fished out the shell Gorrath had given me. Shreesa might not remember who I am, but I didn't want to make her wait a night to receive this relic just because I was disappointed.

"I think I'd like to give it to her now."

Bastien lifted my hand to his cold lips and pressed a kiss against my knuckles. "As my lady wishes."

He waved down the elderly witch, and she took the seat across from us. "How was the meal?"

"Wonderful," I offered. "Truly delicious."

She beamed. "And the wine?"

Bastien eyed his tin cup, which was just as full as when she poured it. "Excellent, as always, Shreesa."

"Then what can I do for you?"

Bastien deferred to me. I drew in a breath and stuck out my hand, offering her the shell. "We brought this back for you. A gift."

Her watery eyes widened as she graciously took the little shell in her hands. Stroking it as if relishing the power. "Your Grace. You remembered us?"

"Actually," Bastien said, "It was my wife who procured this relic for you. From Gorrath himself."

Shreesa's attention shifted back to me. "You got this from Gorrath?"

I nodded, a dim smile forming. "Yes. I remember that you had lost your last relic in an attack by the Witches of the Light."

Shreesa leaned forward, as if seeing me for the first time. Her eyes bounced from mine to the thick scars around my neck, then to my hair. "Wait a moment. You-you're not the girl with the cursed choker, are you? The one who came as His Grace's sanguine partner, are you?"

I nodded, so relieved and grateful that she did remember me. "Yes. That was me."

"Well, I'll be," Shreesa said. "Look at you now. I didn't recognize you."

Heat collected in my cheeks. "My hair is different."

She shook her head. Her bun lolling from side to side as she did. "No. Not just the hair. It's everything. Your aura. Your voice, even. You're a completely different person."

I knew by the way she smiled at me that she believed the change was for the better. A sense of relief washed over me, knowing that I had been memorable to her.

"I understand now," I told her. "What you were trying to tell me. What I was too afraid to see." I set my hand on my chest. "It's the heart of the witch that matters, not the source of her magick." A lesson I learned the hard way. "I'm very sorry for the way I behaved last time I was here. For threatening you with—"

Shreesa's face softened. "There's nothing to forgive. I'm very, very proud of you."

A tear slipped down my cheek, and I quickly swiped it away. These stupid hormones were to blame.

Bastien was watching us, a small smile playing on his lips. "So am I."

"You shouldn't have any more problems from the Prideaux witches," I said, trying to stop myself from crying. "No one will be coming for your magick any time soon."

"All the same, I'll keep this one safe." She tucked it inside her apron. "Now, you've been on the road for days. You and His Grace should head to the bathhouse. I'll have the temperature adjusted so you don't overheat your blood." She wagged a finger at me. "Women in your condition shouldn't sit too long in hot water."

I eyed her suspiciously.

"Don't look at me like that. I can always tell when a woman is with child."

Bastien and I exchanged looks. "On my honor, I'll ensure she doesn't get too overheated."

She handed Bastien the key to the bathhouse. "See that you do."

We said our goodnights, and she promised to bring me scones in the morning. Bastien guided me out the back door and across the cold grass. Everything was exactly as I remembered it. The black lake. The little homes. The witch sitting on her porch. When I'd first come here, I'd assumed everything and everyone was here to hurt me, including the man escorting me.

Now, with kinder eyes, I saw this place for what it truly was. A warm, family home, where generations lived together and provided a safe place for travelers.

Bastien unlocked the wooden door, and I was overcome with a sense of deja vu. The black stone, the gentle candlelight flickering above the steaming pool, the scent of herbs and pine lingering in the air.

I could feel Bastien's eyes on me as I entered. This was the place where he'd saved my life. Where I'd been reborn in the water. My husband came behind me and set his hands on my collarbone. I leaned into his touch. Enjoying it. Finally, we were truly alone. Caught somewhere between responsibilities. Not quite the High Prince and Princess. Not quite parents. Not quite anything, except who we were to each other.

Slowly, silently, he pulled the strings of my cloak, releasing the knot until it fell to the floor. Next came the buttons on the back of my dress. The fabric spread apart inch by inch until he could slide the sleeves down my arms, and the material puddled at my feet.

"Claire..." He said my name like a prayer.

I stepped out of the dress and eased my back against his chest. He dragged his hands up my bare stomach until he reached my breasts. Goosebumps dotted my skin despite the warmth of the room. He gently cupped them, and I found they were sensitive to the touch.

"You're trembling," he whispered against my neck. "Are you alright?"

I hadn't realized I was shaking until he drew attention to it. I shook my head. "It's the good kind of trembling. It's just... you. Your touch."

"Well, in that case..." Gently, he removed the pins Tansy had placed in my hair and let my hair fall. Then he smoothed it over one shoulder, his lips following, ghosting over my neck. Over the scars I'd bear for the rest of my life.

"You're perfect," he said. The reverence in his voice nearly undid me. "Exactly as you are." He spun me in his arms so I was facing him, then, with his eyes fixed on me, he lowered onto his knees.

Just when I thought he was getting ready to unclasp my garters, he pressed a kiss against my belly, his arms wrapping around my waist, holding me close.

Tears filled my eyes, and my fingers tangled in his hair. "You can hear him, can't you?"

He looked up at me. "Just now. Yes. I can."

Something raw caught in my throat. The love. The deep, unadulterated love that he had for me, for us. It was as present as the steam hanging in the air or the scent of herbs.

It was everywhere. All around me.

He grinned against my thigh, his teeth scraping over the thin material of my stockings, and I gasped. I knew what he wanted. And I wanted it too. It had been weeks since he fed properly. Getting by on nothing more than finger picks.

His fingers curled around the straps attached to my nylons. He looked up at me, his eyes dark, his jaw tight. "May I?" I nodded, barely able to speak. "Tell me to stop if it's too much," he whispered, his voice rough. "Tell me to stop, and I will."

"Don't you dare stop."

The ink bled into his eyes, and his fangs lengthened. At one point, I'd been unable to watch him drink, but now, I reveled in it. Loved the dark thing that he became for me. I wanted to unleash him.

His tongue traced up my skin, just beneath the apex of my thighs, then he sank his teeth into me, his mouth sealing over my skin as he drank. A cry tore from my throat, pleasure and pain blurring into one as my body arched into his, my fingers tightening in his hair.

I felt his hunger, his need, and it mirrored my own, the bond between us open and thrumming once more. I hadn't realized how much I'd missed until right now. The ache for him.

He growled with pleasure, and the sound vibrated through me. I shuddered, my knees giving way. He wrapped his arm around my waist, holding me against him as he continued to drink, his mouth so cold that it burned. But this wasn't a feeding. No. It was just a taste. A tease. As much for me as it was for him.

He lifted his head, his lips stained red, his eyes wild, feral. "Mine," he growled. "You are mine."

I brushed my thumb over his lips, wiping away what was left.

"I'm yours," I whispered. "Just like you are mine."

Satisfied, he hooked his fingers into my garters and slowly, deliberately removed them, one by one, his mouth following the path of his hands. Lazy strokes of tongue tasting my skin. The feeling of being worshiped and cared for rolled through me. Desire and heat pooled low in my core, making me wet.

He rolled the stockings down my legs, his lips trailing over my ankles before unlacing my boots and removing both completely. When he finished, he looked up at me, and I swore he was the only god I would ever worship. The only name I'd ever cry out.

As he stood, his hands slid up my body, trailing a path until he reached my face. Then, and only then, did his mouth claim mine. Between kisses, he stripped off his shirt, trousers, and boots. Until he was just Bastien, and I was just Claire. Nothing more. Nothing less.

His gaze roved over my body, over my breasts, and paused at my belly. I did the same, my attention snagging on every part of him that I loved so much. His hard, muscled lines, the thick, jagged scars, and his hardness.

He took my hand, eyes locked with mine, as he guided me toward the pool. "Knowing that you are with my child. That you're carrying a piece of me. It makes you irresistible."

I couldn't stop the smile that rounded my lips. Bastien checked the water temperature to make sure it wasn't too hot, then helped me in. The water was perfectly warm as I sank down into it. Once Bastien was fully submerged, he took me in his arms again. I tangled my wet fingers in his hair, my legs wrapped around his waist, pulling him closer against me.

"I crave you," he rasped, just as his hardness sank into me, filling me up and giving me the delicious feeling of satisfaction that only he could. My breath turned shallow as he began a tortuously slow rhythm, designed to make me come apart in his hands. Easing out and in. Again and again. Tasting me. Touching me. Owning me.

As the water lapped around us, the steam curling through the air, he whispered my name again. "Claire... my moon-flower. My princess."

I gasped when he found that one spot that always made me weak.

Slow and steady, he kept up his pace. The water splashing against my neck. Desire reflected in the pools of his eyes. Each thrust driving me closer to some edge I would never come back from. An edge I never wanted to leave.

Our foreheads pressed together. Eyes locked. Our blood-stones connected. Every piece of us intertwined. This was how it was always meant to be. He was the mate, the man, the monster, who understood the darkness in me.

"My prince," I whispered back. "My love."

There was nothing more powerful than this man and the love we bore for each other. He was my greatest source of magick. My light in the darkness. The moon to my sun. Just Mine.

ALSO BY AINSLEY JAMES

The Vampire Prince Duology

Bastien + Claire's Story

Book 1: Fated to the Vampire Prince

Book 2: Sworn to the Vampire Prince

The High Prince Duology

Yves + Cora's Story

Book 1: Coming October 16th 2026

About the Author

Ainsley James writes darkly romantic fantasies steeped in forbidden love, magic, and heroines who discover their power. She loves Halloween and struggles to resist a graveyard tour. She lives in coastal Virginia with her incredibly patient husband, four children, dog, and two cats.

In addition to her books, Ainsley offers private coaching for authors, helping writers break through blocks, develop stories, and cultivate authentic, unforgettable voices. You can learn more about individual coaching programs on her website or by sending her an email. She also runs a Discord for writers called Hype Girl Besties, where she hosts writing sprints and lively bookish conversations.